THE MIDNIGHT MAN

Recent Titles by Simon Clark

BLOOD CRAZY
HOTEL MIDNIGHT
THE NIGHT OF THE TRIFFIDS
VAMPYRRHIC
VAMPYRRHIC RITES

LONDON UNDER MIDNIGHT *
LUCIFER'S ARK *

available from Severn House

THE MIDNIGHT MAN

Simon Clark

This first world edition published 2008
in Great Britain and the USA by
SEVERN HOUSE PUBLISHERS LTD of
9–15 High Street, Sutton, Surrey SM1 1DF.

British Library Cataloguing in Publication Data

Clark, Simon, 1958-
  The midnight man
  1. Horror tales
  I. Title
  823.9'14[F]

  ISBN-13: 978-0-7278-6637-0   (cased)
  ISBN-13: 978-1-84751-061-7   (trade paper)

*"Angels in Moon Street" was inspired by the visionary essays of
Richard Middleton (1882–1911).*

All Severn House titles are printed on acid-free paper.

Typeset by Palimpsest Book Production Ltd.,
Grangemouth, Stirlingshire, Scotland.
Printed and bound in Great Britain by
MPG Books Ltd., Bodmin, Cornwall.

Prologue

I

{La Rochelle, France. Date unknown}

When did I first see you? When did I know our lives would collide? What quality did you possess that had the power to transform my world? What was this day?

I shall tell it as I remember. Picture a February sun so low and so bright it dazzles. You walked across the square with the sun in your back. To me, you were a silhouette as I hid from humanity. My eyes were drawn to you. You were, it seemed, a silhouette of impossible dimensions.

Then, as you passed, you turned to gaze up at the church tower. You can't have noticed me, a young woman in torn red skirts, kneeling by the cart that dripped blood on to cobblestones. That was the moment I saw your face in the full light of the sun. All the world froze. You were dressed in the blue blouson of a working man. Yet strapped across your shoulders like a musket was an easel. You carried cases in your hands, a leather satchel across your back, all speckled with paint. Beneath one arm, a canvas stretched tight across its frame. It was the portrait of a man with huge, blazing stars about his head. He did not yet possess a face. Only a featureless yellow disk like a low moon. On your head was a straw hat. Your beard was red; your eyes inflamed. They burned, as if you'd beheld an object that shone so brightly it was meant for no mortal eyes to see.

I froze because revelation pierced my heart. My life would be transformed. I knew it. Just as I knew that you would be the force for that change.

II

{PC Morrow's filed statement, London, 1st January, 1888}

Sir, I found the woman in Camomile Street at five o'clock in the morning. It had recently stopped snowing. The ground was white all over with no footprints or signs of struggle. The figure sat hunched on a step of the Seers' Chapel. Her head hung down so the chin touched her chest. Her hair was unpinned; she wore no coat or shawl. Snow covered the back of her head, neck and shoulders, meaning she had not moved in the last half hour. Even though it is a thoroughfare between Bishopsgate and Aldgate, there was no horse or foot traffic on account of the heavy snowfall.

I recognized her as Violet Goodwin, the mother of two young children. Goodwin's skin held bluish tints. The tip of her tongue had blackened and protruded between her teeth. When I bent down to examine her for discernible injuries her eyes suddenly opened. Her scream that accompanied the action was most shocking. I daresay I have never heard anything like it before. Although she'd been unconscious for at least half an hour, she screamed with a great ferocity. When I asked if she could walk she looked up. I think she recognized me because she became calm. All the agitation passed. I said I would help her to stand. She agreed and appeared easy with herself. Certainly in no pain. As she stood, however, she cried out again with such force it set dogs barking in their yards. With both hands she lifted her tunic jacket. All of a sudden a great deal of blood spilled out on to the snow. Then she called out in a very shrill way before falling backwards. By the time I'd reached Goodwin what remained of her life had taken its leave.

III

{Eugène Delacroix, 1849}

'A portrait, or painted landscape, is a bond that marries the mind of the artist to the mind of the spectator.'

IV

{Deposition of the Lambeth Board of Guardians}

A young woman known as Mitre Rose was found bludgeoned to death in Lambeth, 30th July, 1888. Described as a 'deaf-mute', she slept in cheap lodging houses when she had money. Mitre Rose kept her belongings in pockets sewn beneath her skirts. Listed, hereafter, are her possessions: a blue cotton handkerchief, a pair of men's woollen socks, three squares of coarse, white linen, one cotton cap, one red hair ribbon, a small calico bag containing assorted scraps of cloth, darning thread, soap, and a triangle of clean, white silk that parcelled a lock of baby hair.

V

{Doctor Anders, The Hague, 1882}

Yesterday, I saw Vincent van Gogh's poignant sketch of the streetwalker called Sien, with whom he lives. Entitled 'Sorrow', the portrait bears the words 'How can there be lonely, deserted women in the world?'

Nidabi's Journal

15th July. If I speak my name to a stranger they will repeat it correctly. When it is written down they frown and say it wrong. My name is Nidabi. For a stranger to pronounce it properly I think it should look like this on the page: Nid-ah-bee. Not that anyone showed an interest in my name until I began my new life six days ago.

Last week I was riding in the Colonel's brougham. That is an enclosed carriage drawn by two horses. I sat alongside the Colonel. His two protégés sat opposite us. When we travel in darkness I like to look out of the window. Reverend Pryke told me that at night London becomes a town of a magic dream. He must have meant this is because the lights in the houses glitter all golden in the dark. So, as the carriage ran along quiet woodland ways near the river I enjoyed gazing across the water at the big mansions that blazed with dozens of lamps. But the Colonel and his protégés had plans for me. They were disappointed by the ladies' fight at the boatyard. One of the ladies hadn't appeared. The two that had fought each other were very tired from their other work.

Men had taunted, 'Call this sport! Bring us two cats that can fight!' They drank brandy so their swearing became very violent. When one of the women fell she hurt her back so badly she couldn't stand again. Straight away, the Colonel marched from the boatyard. As he is the plumpest man I've ever seen his face shook strangely. The skin around his side-whiskers was as purple as a plum. Thereafter, we rode in the carriage, but because progress back to the city was slow it made the Colonel angrier rather than cooling his nerve. As soon as he pinched me through my skirts I knew that would encourage his protégés to torment me. These were military men that the Colonel has taken into his service. Though he dressed them in the knee breeches and velvet cutaway coats of footmen, he devotes his days to training them to be champions at sport – one day boxing, another day gymnastics, and so on. Tonight, the sport would be me. I knew the course it would take, for it had happened often in the years I've been at the Colonel's house. No tears, I told myself. No tears whatsoever, Nidabi. Why waste them? The process would go through its customary stages. Rest assured. I would have no influence over its progress. Nor believe for a moment I could even moderate it.

The Colonel pinched my chin, pulling as he did so, to draw my head forward.

'You look pretty tonight,' he announced grandly. 'I should say you've been one of my finer investments.' Then to the men sitting opposite us, 'What do you say to that, gentlemen? An accurate observation?'

'Yes, Colonel,' they replied in their obedient, soldierly way. 'Indeed.'

'Oh? You can't find fault with her? Not one!' He didn't let

go of my chin, but pushed my head back so it thumped against the buttoned plush.

'Well . . .' began one.

'Yes, Middleton?'

'Her nose isn't as straight as it ought to be.'

'Hah! Yes, of course.' The Colonel's eyes bulged. 'Nose isn't straight! I see that now! Wrenshaw? Tell me what y'see. What's wrong with the girl?'

'Her skin is coloured too darkly.'

'Agreed. And, moreover, she has such dark eyes. Did you ever see a woman with eyes that are black?'

'Black as coal they are, sir.' Middleton spoke, eager to please the Colonel. 'What's more, she has too much brain for a girl of twenty years.'

'Too much brain? Wha' the devil . . . too much brain? Ah ha! Too clever, y' mean?'

'Yessir.'

'Yes, too clever for her station. Indeed, for her profession – hah! Women like Niddy here don't need big brains to settle a man's needs.' His lips, I remember, were all loose. Not only did they quiver, they made a clicking sound the way an old dog will click its jowls when it shakes its head. 'Don't be shy. Tell us what you learned to make a man groan with pleasure. C'mon, Niddy, speak up! How do you hold him?'

'My name is not Niddy, sir. It is Nidabi.'

'Nidabi.' Middleton repeated my name like it tasted dirty in his mouth. 'Nidabi? What kind of name is that?'

'Not the name for a Christian woman, is it?' added his comrade.

'By Jove it isn't, sir!' The Colonel spoke as if my name angered him. 'The man I bought her off told me it was the name of a pagan devil.'

'Then this creature isn't a God-fearing woman, then?'

'Oh, she'll be pagan, mark my words.' The Colonel reached inside my jacket. 'This is pagan flesh. Every dev'lish ounce!' He pinched my breast.

'You're a strong man, sir,' Middleton observed, 'but that didn't hurt her.'

'They don't feel pain, Middleton. Nor can they think like us.'

'I bet she don't know nothing about our Lord Jesus, sir.'

'Ignorant as a cow at pasture, Middleton. Ignorant as a cow at pasture.'

I'd squeezed my fists to stop myself crying when the Colonel pinched my breast, but I had to speak. They shouldn't say things about me that weren't true.

So, I spoke out. 'I know this is 1888. That means it is one thousand eight hundred and eighty-eight years since the birth of Jesus Christ.'

'Colonel, did you hear the way she spoke the name of our Saviour?'

The other joined in. 'The bitch made it sound dirty, like a swear word.'

'Bloody pagan.'

'Dirty mouthed whore.'

'You filthy little bitch!'

I got so breathless I thought I'd be ill. But instead of being sick all these words came shooting out of my mouth. 'I can read. I know what Jesus Christ did. And—'

'Shut your dirty mouth.'

'And because you've done evil to women he won't care when you're laid in your beds dying. And your insides hurt so much that you're crying for your mothers.'

'Shut up!'

'Your souls have rotted!' These were fiery words. They would get me punished. 'He won't listen to you! Try it if you don't believe me – go on, just you try!' My outburst shocked the three men so much it made them pause.

At last the Colonel roared. There were no words. Just anger, pouring like a dam burst through his mouth. He didn't hit. He pushed. Like a bundle of rags I flew off the seat straight at the carriage door. I remember being surprised that suddenly I was out in the open. I was flying in the air. For a moment, I found myself thinking I'd never come down; that somehow I'd soar into the night sky, where the moon was shining bright and there I'd find happiness.

The ground, however, wasn't going to be robbed of me. There's a man called Newton who proved with his apple that objects will for ever fall to earth. I don't remember hurting any part of my body. The moment, however, I realized that above me were tree branches, lit vivid green by a streetlight, was the same moment that I knew I lay in the road. Even as I stood up to dust my skirts, the Colonel's brougham had turned. It bore down at me, so that I had to put up my hands to stop the horses trampling me into the mud. Moments later, the Colonel and his protégés emerged from the carriage. They moved with quick steps that were full of purpose. I knew what that particular purpose would be. I looked round. *If there are passers-by . . .* This road, however, ran through a heath. There were cottages, yet they were derelict places, just grim skeletons of buildings. Unloved, untenanted; abandoned to slow decay. Windows had the same dull gleam as dead eyes. Dark pathways ran off across a desolate wasteland that could have been the haunt of lonely spirits. In this forlorn place there would not be another single living person to witness what happened next.

The Colonel cast this menacing sentence at his driver. 'She'll make some noise – be ready to keep the horses steady.'

Despite his girth he walked quickly. In his right hand he carried his swagger stick, a yard-long shaft of black ebony that ended in a clenched fist of pure silver. Extra weight had been added somehow. He boasted often as we walked in the garden, 'Kill a man with this, Niddy. Break his head like an eggshell.' Then he'd slash rose heads, making the blooms burst in a flash of red. Now, as I stood beneath the gaslight, he smiled while tapping the silver fist against his chin. Yes, he was enjoying this.

'Niddy, oh, Niddy,' he breathed. 'A creature like you speaking about our Saviour, Jesus Christ, is not only offensive to our Christian ears, it is a blasphemy that demands severe punishment. What if every pagan Jezebel spoke thus of our Lord? Your words are a cancer. We must cut them out.' His eyes blazed with such ferocity. The men at his side grinned. They knew what was coming. There'd be pleasure in watching before they, themselves, joined in. For my part, I tried not to move at all. If there was any act of defiance remaining inside of me, it beheld me to stand there. To look him in the eye. Not to beg. Not to flinch. The Colonel despised the way I met his gaze. He pushed me back against the street lamp so violently it made me gasp.

'Ah ha . . . felt that, didn't you?' He pressed the ebony staff across my throat. 'Or were you just pretending? Hmm? This is the moment, Niddy, we find out once and for all.' He raised the stick, ready to inflict the first blow.

'*Please!*'

The voice came from none of the three men, nor the coach driver.

The Colonel grunted with surprise. 'Who the devil said that?'

'Please reconsider. It is wrong to strike a lady.'

'A lady. Pah!' The Colonel scowled into the shadows. 'This is nothing but a whore.'

'She is a woman, sir.'

'Blast it. Where the devil are you? Come out where I can see you.'

From the shadows stepped a slight figure. Clearly from his frockcoat and top hat he was a gentleman.

The Colonel groaned as he recognized a type he held in utter contempt. 'Ah . . . a *young* gentleman. Probably full of poetry, no doubt. Go home. This is none of your business.'

'It is my business, sir. You threw this woman from a carriage. I've just watched you assault her. Any gentleman would make it his business.'

Middleton spoke. 'Then you'd be 'appier walking round with your 'ands over your eyes, then you wouldn't go seeing matters that offend.'

'Absolutely.' The Colonel was impatient now. 'Now, *sir*, be on your way.'

'I will not walk away from this.'

'Oh, good heavens, man. Don't you see what this is? She's a concubine – a whore.' He turned my face to the light. 'What's more, look at the colour of her skin!'

'Then if she means nothing to you, leave her alone.'

'Before I forget my manners, good sir, on your way.'

'No.' The gent stepped forward. I couldn't see his face. He seemed an assembly of shadows beneath a top hat. Even though he spoke firmly his voice was soft. Perhaps the softest I've heard from a man. 'Listen, I will pay ten shillings.'

The Colonel blinked. 'What? You want to buy her from me?'

The protégés grinned at each other. They'd found entertainment at long last.

The Colonel was enjoying himself, too. 'My, my. Ten shillings will buy you plenty of female company, young man. But why not find your own tart?'

'I will give you ten . . . no, fifteen shillings. That's all the money I have with me.' The stranger pulled coins from his pocket.

'By Jove, your sap must be rising tonight.'

'I'll pay you, then you will permit her to leave.'

The Colonel stroked his face as he considered the offer. 'Fifteen shillings? Very well, we have a deal. Wrenshaw?'

'Sir?'

'Collect the gentleman's money for me.'

'Yessir.'

Wrenshaw walked briskly toward the stranger then held out his hand.

'Mind it's all there, Wrenshaw. Fifteen shillings. Not a penny less.'

The stranger began to count florins into Wrenshaw's hand. The Colonel gave one of his little coughs to attract Middleton's attention, then made a slight gesture with his finger as if the digit was falling down. Silently, without the gentleman seeing, Middleton crouched behind the man's legs. Wrenshaw gave the man a push in his chest. Back went the stranger over Middleton's hunched form. Coins clattered across the road. All three men roared with laughter. This was their entertainment at long last.

The stranger gathered himself, then quickly stood. 'Sir, we had a deal.'

'I don't make deals with cretins.'

'Fifteen shillings—'

'Fifteen shillings! Do you know how much money I've invested in this girl? Dresses, hair ribbon, soap, perfume – why I even paid for her tuition in the arts.' He laughed. 'The art of pleasing a man. That comes to more than any fifteen blasted bob.'

'I can bring more—'

'More of the allowance your doting father gives you? Learn the ways of the world, you idiot. I own fifty thousand acres of arable. Every year I plough in hundreds of tons of pig muck and lime. Now each acre is worth treble what I paid for it. And I've ploughed money into this . . .' He shoved me against the lamp column. 'She was a grubby little street girl. Now she is fragrant; she *resembles* a lady. More importantly, her talent is to bring pleasure. You follow?'

The stranger said nothing. His eyes, which had been hidden

by shadow, now revealed themselves in a silvery glint. For a moment I wondered about that glint, then I realized its cause. His tears reflected the illumination cast by the lamp.

The Colonel spoke with contempt, 'Oh . . . go home, little boy.'

'I've failed.'

The confession surprised the Colonel as much as it amused his two protégés.

'Yes, absolutely,' the Colonel agreed. 'You have failed. Now pick up your pennies. Go home to your mother.'

The man's head hung oddly, as if his neck could no longer support it fully. Then he walked from the light into the darkness beyond.

'Well . . .' The Colonel faced me. 'So much for your chivalrous young hero.' He struck me on the breastbone with the swagger stick. His anger at the interruption strengthened his arm. The pain caught me by surprise, so I cried out. 'Will you shout for Christ now, you witch?' He laughed as he ripped away my bonnet, so as to expose my face for the next blow.

Against the arc of stars the shaft formed a black line. I saw the Colonel's plump hand grip it, ready to deliver the beating. Then something astonishing. Another hand folded about the staff. My eyes followed the next movement in wonder. The hand drew the stick from the Colonel's grasp in a way that was all so stately, as if engaging in some strange, nocturnal dance. Then the Colonel pushed me. I fell on to the grass at the edge of the common; I'd have gone all the way on to my back but a fence stopped me, so that I was held in a sitting position. Now, it came. A sudden fury of movement and sound.

I heard the Colonel thunder, 'Get a hold of the fool. Beat the blasted daylights out of him!'

Dazed, I sat there, my back to the wire fence, the stars and moon burning bright. I wasn't certain if I were awake or dreaming. The stranger had returned. The hat had gone from his head. He still held the Colonel's stick. This he swung at Middleton. It did nothing more than make a clicking sound, yet all of a sudden Middleton turned away like the fight no longer interested him. Then I saw dark liquid run over his face.

Wrenshaw is a fearsome boxer. He punched at the stranger. He landed blows, I know he did. Only the stranger didn't notice them any more than if they were moonbeams touching his face. As the stranger lashed out with the Colonel's stick I recalled the silver fist, and how my master boasted he could kill a man with it. I saw how the formidable staff fell on Wrenshaw's shoulders. All of a sudden the prizefighter turned his back on the stranger. He used his arms to protect his head. But that weapon has the weight of a blacksmith's hammer. Blow after blow – the stranger beat the pugilist's head. Even though Wrenshaw tried to stay on his feet his knees gave way. When he fell the stranger didn't stop.

'Enough . . . *Enough!*' This was the coachman crying out in horror. When the stranger turned his cold eyes in the direction of the coach, its driver didn't hesitate. He lashed the horses into a start that sent the Colonel's brougham racing away along the street. During this, the Colonel had been standing there as if the life had been robbed from him. Now he started running after the coach. In utter fright he cried for it to stop. Then, when he realized the coachman was stopping for no force on earth, the Colonel ran by me. In his haste to flee he hadn't noticed the wire fence at the edge of the green. It must have winded him as he struck it. Even so, he began to scramble over in order to escape.

The stranger didn't have it in his heart to allow the Colonel to be free. He had a passion on him. I don't think he could have stopped himself if he tried. In a moment he grasped the Colonel as he tried to climb over the fence, just inches from me. The stranger pushed the Colonel's face down so the wire ran across it. Now that face was little more than a foot from my own. The pressure of the steel line formed a valley in the Colonel's flesh from his forehead to his lips. I found myself looking up into those two grey eyes I knew so well. For the first time I saw fear there. Absolute fear.

Slowly, with a purposeful action, as if some other being dictated this is how it was meant to be – and I to witness it – the stranger gripped the back of the Colonel's head. Then, not only did he force the head down against the fence wire, he moved it back and forth along the steel strand in a sawing motion. The Colonel's eyes flared with agony. He grimaced as a cry burst from those loose, wet lips. Meanwhile, his nose parted into two halves. Blood fell in a dark rain.

Despite the agony he cried, 'Take her. Take her, you blasted devil! She's yours!' *His injuries distorted the words until they were almost unintelligible.*

Then the man stopped the disfigurement, yet he didn't release the pressure. He just held the Colonel there for a long time. It was as if the stranger's mind had travelled to some faraway place. Perhaps to a fabulous realm where he enjoyed the society of mysterious companions – ones that did not possess a human face. This uncanny departure left the body behind to resemble a stone carving, empty of a thinking mind.

'Didn't you hear me?' The Colonel howled in panic as much as pain. 'You've won. She's yours . . . please don't hurt me again! For the love of God—'

'God.' This was the word that brought the stranger's spirit winging back. With the streetlamp burning behind him, so etching his body in silhouette, his arms rose. It was as if a soul had re-entered a dead husk. He inhaled deeply then stepped back. The Colonel rolled off the wire with a grunt to thump down into the grass. He was so terrified he lay there without uttering another word. The stranger reacted with surprise. His actions were of a man stumbling across a terrible crime. Everything about him suggested horror at what he saw, coupled with a deep sympathy for the victims. He went first to the unconscious thug. When he saw there was nothing to be done there he went to Middleton who sat on the pavement, nursing his shattered face in the palm of his hand. Blood dripped on to the cobbles.

The stranger flicked a handkerchief from his pocket. 'Please . . .' When he tried to offer help Middleton flinched away with a sob of fear.

When the man realized Middleton would continue to refuse assistance he took my arm to help me to my feet. I looked up into a softly featured face. The eyes were brown; they lacked the harsh glare of the Colonel's. In a voice you might use to address a frightened child he said, 'You're free.'

'I don't know where I should go. I lived with . . .' I nodded at my wretched master, shuddering at our feet.

'Nowhere at all? You've no other home?'

'No.'

'Then you're quite alone?'

'Yes, sir.'

'I see . . .' He looked searchingly at my face. I believe there was something in my features that he needed to see. At that moment he found it. 'I can give you shelter. That is, if you don't mind coming with me?'

'I shan't mind at all, sir.'

He walked along the street, which was still in the grip of night. I waited. Then, when he was thirty paces away, I followed. Only once did I glance back at the Colonel and his two protégés. Only once. One protégé still lay flat. The other had managed to stand, but he had no fight left in him. The Colonel sat rocking back and forth as blood poured from his face. As I turned away I promised myself, you will never see them again – not ever. A moment later the stranger stopped. So I stopped. There were still thirty paces between us.

He looked back. 'Why walk so far behind?'

'I've been instructed that whenever I go with a gentleman I keep a distance, so people don't realize I'm with him.'

'Walk with me.' He waited without moving until I caught up. Then he walked again. I stayed at his side. And that was the start of my new life; the full moon shining down.

Ty's Book

16th July. I queued at the street pump with my water jug. An afternoon hot enough to make the walls of the old Roman amphitheatre appear to wave with the suppleness of corn in the heat. Everyone in Arles was thirsty. Those with money bought wine at the cafés; those who had none drank water. The line at the pump, however, was a long one. A child, who had broken his jug, knelt to wail over the shards of brown clay. Some women fussed to help him. At the head of the line an old matron with thick arms pumped the iron handle so hard it squealed louder than the child's cries. All of a sudden, a transformation took place in the queue. A moment's silence. Then, although they took care not to lose their place, they all leaned outward to study something that interested them. The silence broke as the women started speaking.

'Oh, see who it is?'

'He's come back. I thought he'd left for good.'

'Who is it?'

'You've not seen him before? Good heavens, you must be the only one who hasn't.'

'It's the madman. The one who thinks he's a painter.'

'Is he really mad?'

'Just look at the expression on his face. Good grief! See those eyes!'

One woman held a protective hand over her throat. 'When he looks at you he stares right through your body.'

Voices rose as the women became angry. 'They should get rid of him before he kills somebody.'

A teenager with big, frightened eyes hugged a water pail to her chest. 'My father says no woman is safe while he's around.'

'Look at the lunatic's hands. See how big the fingers are!' The woman nodded. 'Just imagine if you woke up in bed with those around your throat.'

Gasps of fear ran along the line.

'Stand back,' warned an old woman. 'Here he comes.'

They pressed their backs against the stones of the wall. Pedestrians parted before the man as he walked along the centre of the street, carrying bundles and his easel strapped across his back.

'My God, he *is* mad. I've never seen eyes like that in a human face before. Who is he?'

A woman spat the words as if it was bad luck to even utter the name aloud: 'Vincent van Gogh.'

I'd first seen the man in February. I learnt that he'd not lived in Arles for long, that he was from the north, a Dutchman. On that winter's day, six months ago, his appearance had been a shock to me. But it wasn't his unusual features, the fiery red beard, or the way his eyes burned. It was my conviction that I would know him one day. Ever since then, whenever I could, I followed at a discreet distance, so I could watch him paint without being noticed. In all that time I'd not spoken to him. He never even knew of my existence. Today, in burning July, he moved along the street with his artist's tools: the bags, the satchel, the easel, the canvases under his arm. Paint of all

colours streaked his belongings. Prussian blue covered his
face in a dash of elfin freckles. On his feet were heavy
workman's boots. One broken lace had been carelessly
replaced by a scrap of green ribbon. To protect his pale skin
from the sun he wore a straw hat, stained with at least a
hundred different colours.

From a grocer's shop boys called out. 'Sir, you appear to
have stepped in some dung . . . *your own!*' They laughed. Even
the women in the queue stopped pretending moral outrage.
The insults amused them. Another boy taunted, 'Monsieur
Van Gogh. Your hat is on fire!' He flicked a cigarette butt at
him.

The cigarette missed the artist. He continued walking
without acknowledging the cruel jokes.

With their wit depleted, they resorted to name calling.
'Imbecile . . . pervert.'

'You maniac!'

'How many times have you shook hands with the one-eyed
snake today?'

'Where do you hide your mother's drawers?'

Even the women sniggered at this one.

The artist stopped dead. Then turned to the boys. I'd heard
the way he looked at you described as a 'thousand league
stare'. A description intended to stress lunacy, but despite its
intention to insult the man it was apt. Monsieur Van Gogh's
eyes seemed to burn through people. Come to that, the stare
burned through walls, through forests, through mountains, or
so it seemed to me. When he glared at the gang they all stopped
their taunting. They even retreated into the shop where they
felt safer. Without a word, Monsieur Van Gogh walked away.
A boy, however, from one of the cafés, who'd been goaded by
his friends, ran at the artist. The boy swung out his arm. It
sickened me that the man would be attacked in the street by
these ignorant people. I anticipated a violent fight, with a mob
of Arlesians attacking the artist. Instead of striking the man,
however, the boy tried to drag the satchel from his shoulder.

Monsieur Van Gogh's strong hand caught the satchel. The
boy could not match the man's strength. He jerked at the strap
then let go. Content with the prank he ran laughing to his
friends. Although the man still had his satchel it spilt its
innards. A silvery cascade of what appeared to be little fish

fell on to the road. Patiently, he crouched down to retrieve them. I saw the fish were, in fact, tubes of paint. Everyone laughed as he collected up his materials. It was an awkward task because he still held on to the rest of his possessions, no doubt wary of another boy deciding to snatch a bag or a canvas.

I found myself so hot with anger that I had to speak. 'It's not fair.'

The women in the line turned to me, surprised by my choice of words.

'Don't waste your pity on him, dear. He's mad.'

'Monsieur Van Gogh is an artist. He hasn't harmed anyone.'

'Mark my words, girl, he will soon enough.'

A big woman in black skirts stared hard at me. With a knowing nod she turned to the others. 'This is Ty. One of the cats from the brothel.' Her expression turned to one of disgust. 'Don't pay any attention to her.'

The women ignored the artist in favour of me now. They scowled as one spat, 'You know you're not supposed to use this pump. Use the well in the yard of the whore house.'

'The water's bad there. It makes us sick.'

'Believe me, dear, it isn't the well that makes you sick, it's what the soldiers put inside of you.'

'Hmph . . .' The old widow pulled her skirts back so even my shadow wouldn't touch them. 'Shouldn't you be earning your money?'

'I need water.'

A woman in a red bonnet called to another further up the line, 'Marie . . . Marie? Show this creature the newspaper.'

'I'll lose my place for the pump.'

'Don't worry, Claudette will keep it for you. I want you to show this *lady* something.'

Marie set down her pot, then hurried along the line of women that clutched their jugs. They glanced from the artist picking up his fallen paints to me. They were enjoying both dramas.

'Here.' The one in the red bonnet held out her hand for the newspaper, which Marie handed to her. 'Look,' she told me, 'but don't touch. You won't be able to read, but see the picture? The woman lying dead in the gutter? That is in a place called London. The citizens of London have woken up with good sense. They have decided there's a way to deal with women like you, little brothel cat. It says here that London has been killing your sort, like we destroy vermin.' She jabbed her finger at the drawing. It depicted a woman in torn skirts lying dead on the ground with her arms flung above her head, then she jabbed the finger at me – close but not touching, never touching. 'Listen to me, Ty. This is a warning to your kind. The government isn't going to tolerate you any longer. They're going to send legionnaires to your homes, then you'll be sorry.'

The women were all so tall. It was like standing in a forest. They stared down at me with such cold lights in their eyes. A brutal stare that strove to crush my spirit. Although I had no water I ran from the line. For a moment nothing else mattered but to dash away, clutching my empty jug. Then all of a sudden I stopped. I glanced back at Monsieur Van Gogh. He still picked paints out of the filth. A slow, difficult job as he was wise enough not to set down his possessions, because a group of boys hung around, ready to kick a dirty boot through one of his paintings. Fury blazing inside of me made me act. I sped at the gang. The nearest I pushed hard enough to make him grunt. With the warning made that I would tolerate no mischief from them, I strode along the road to the artist. There I set the jar down, pulled my skirts a little higher so I could kneel, and helped him gather up the paints. They were heavier than I imagined. Some of the glittering foil tubes were full; most, however, were crushed flat in order to extract every blob of expensive colour. For a while we worked together. His large, square fingers gently plucked a tube from the dirt then placed it into the satchel. I copied him. All the time he never appeared to notice I was there. He said nothing. He never even glanced at me. I risked shooting a glimpse at him. The man's eyes were rimmed with crimson. The heat, and staring for so long at the landscape he painted, had taken its toll. His face was thin, too. Cheekbones pushed at the skin, as if attempting to break through. When he attempted to reach a tube of brilliant scarlet that was just beyond his grasp I passed it to him. He took it, then lightly rubbed the tip of his thumb through paint oozing so vividly on to the foil. Once he'd placed the last tube in the satchel, he gathered his belongings around him so they were evenly distributed, and rose to his feet. For a while, he stood gazing up at the eaves of the buildings as they drew thick, black boundary lines between houses and blue sky. The sun blazed, yet he glared back into it, as if testing its power against his own. A moment later he snapped his head down to look at me. His eyes were a brilliant blue. But then, as he tilted his head slightly as if to assess the distribution of my features, the eyes subtly shifted their colour. The intense blue became a clear green; a shining green – like the green of a rare crystal.

'How old are you?'

I replied, 'Twenty.'

'What is your name?'

'Ty.'

He blinked. The eyes were blue again. 'Ty,' he said, repeating my name. His voice, though gentle, appeared to conceal a formidable, hidden power. There was barely a trace of his home country accent. 'Thank you, Ty.' With that he walked along the street without looking back.

For a time, I watched him dwindle into the distance. He carried bags, the canvases that hung on twine from his shoulders, the easel, all those paints. *They are a burden that goes beyond mere weight. They weigh heavy on his soul, too.* One of the boys kicked my water jug where it sat on the ground. Its shards flew across the road to land in the gutter. The women laughed loud enough to make sure I heard their pleasure at the death of my pot. The gang fled into the square, perhaps hoping I'd chase them. Weeping wouldn't mend the jug. Neither would chasing the boys. As I smoothed down my skirts I noticed a smear of yellow paint from one of the artist's tubes against the dark skin of my hand. For a moment I intended to wipe away that dash of brilliant sunflower yellow, but then I decided it was fitting it should dry there, bright as a star that would guide me to my destiny.

17th July. Place d'Sucre means the place of sugar. It is a square in the back streets of Arles. Its northern flank is blocked by the forbidding mass of the slaughterhouse. The other buildings, forming the remaining flanks, are a coffin maker, a tanner, a cobbler, a soap factory and a clutch of grim dwellings. The slaughterhouse feeds materials to manufacturers in the neighbourhood. There are carts full of crimson gore that could have rumbled from some forbidding empire of the damned.

Bloated flies darken the sky. Ravens, drawn by mounds of raw flesh, sit menacingly on rooftops to scream their threats. The soap factory is cursed with the strongest smell of all. Even hardened soldiers screw their eyes shut when the odours strike. Yet every so often, from some unknown source in the Place d'Sucre drifts the sweetest incense imaginable. The breath of angels.

I have lived here since the death of my father. Sharing a room with me in the lodging house are my brother and sister. George, aged seven years, and Brionne, five. Across the street, a huge white bull bellowed as the slaughter man approached to perform his dawn ritual. He sharpened a razor against the strop, whistling as he honed the blade. Consumptives formed a line by the abattoir gate – a gathering of living skeletons. Their eyes held such a haunting quality. They carried tin cups, which would be filled with blood from an incision in the bull's throat. In a second the cup would be full, a crimson head foaming over the rim. After the cups of the sick were filled, and they'd handed coins to the slaughter man, one of the apprentice boys would force a cold smoothing iron against the bull's wound to stop the flow. In this way the beast could be 'milked' again tomorrow morning. Meanwhile, the consumptives desperately swallowed the hot blood as fast as they could, to capture the bull's vitality before it evaporated into the summer air.

When I returned home from work that morning I found my belongings in the street. Madame Vires stood framed by the front doorway. Her black skirts and black shawl always make me think of the fierce ravens that loomed over the square. She rested her hands on her hips as she glared at me.

'You've had plenty of warnings, Ty. Now you've strained my patience to breaking point.'

'But I will have this week's rent by tonight.'

'And last week's rent?'

'I paid. I gave it to Paul on Sunday.'

Paul, a squat youth, pushed his face from the shadows behind his mother to shout, 'Liar!'

'Paul took my money, Madame Vires. He promised to give it to you when you returned from church.'

'A place you've never been,' Madame Vires responded coldly.

'I will have the rent tonight. I promise.'

'I've heard enough of your promises to last a lifetime. Now . . . all your belongings are here.'

'I can pay more if you—'

'No. I've been polite. Don't make me lose my temper.'

'Please, Madame—'

'Don't you understand, girl. Go away from here. Go – go.' She made shooing gestures as if chasing a cat out of her larder.

'But I have to wait for George and Brionne. The Night Woman hasn't brought them back yet.'

Paul lunged his head forward by his mother's elbow. 'She brought your brats back an hour ago.'

I looked up at my room window. My heart fell when I couldn't see their faces.

Paul grinned. 'I took the brats to the abattoir. I fed them to the slaughter man's dogs.'

Madame Vires hissed, 'Paul, have you swept the yard yet?' She didn't wait for him to invent an excuse. 'Do it now.' Then she turned back to me. 'So, girl, you've had two weeks' free lodgings from a poor widow who has sons to feed. Count yourself lucky I don't have you thrown in jail.' She slammed the door.

'I don't have any place to go. Where will the children sleep? Madame Vires?' You look a fool asking a locked door questions, I told myself. But all I could do was stand there beside my bundled possessions.

An upstairs shutter banged open. Paul shouted down, 'I saw you at the pump yesterday. Ask the crazy painter for a bed! He'll gobble you up for breakfast!'

He closed the shutter with a crash. Across the street the consumptives watched all this. But there wasn't a flicker of interest in their sunken eyes. They drank what remained of the bull's blood from their cups. Then they moved slowly away, touching the wall for reassurance, in case they should need its support.

At that moment the Night Woman approached with George and Brionne. I shivered at the prospect of having no home. *What do I say to my brother and sister? Where would we sleep tonight?*

Nidabi's Journal

17th July. In this house I no longer shudder when I hear the call 'Nidabi?' The voice that speaks my name is not harsh, nor as loud as a drill sergeant's. No sounds of fury. No violent movement. I have lived here for eight days. I'm accustomed to its scents, sounds and appearance. At this table in my room, the sunlight flooding in, I can enjoy the luxury of making my writing a playful thing. Already, I believe I have improved my use of words.

Descriptions: A swallow flies up to its nest in the eaves above my open window. Far in the distance is that Father of Rivers that gives London its life. The whistles of river boats are so far away the sounds are softened, subtly transfigured into the voices of cattle lowing to one another in summer meadows. It is as if I've not only moved from one house to another, but that I have ascended to a magic realm. My days are spent in dream-like serenity. Colours are now brighter, the perfume of flowers richer; birdsong is more than random whistles; it is a symphony of beautiful piping that celebrates all creation. Now, for Lamplands – this house that throws its protective arms of stone around us – how best can I describe its imposing form? The swooping bird inspires me: if I were granted the ability to see through the swallow's eyes I would see this. A window framed in white-painted wood. Inside the room: a girl of twenty years, by the name of Nidabi. She sits in her green skirts and white blouse to guide a pencil across the page. When the bird sweeps in its high curve through the sky it sees the liquorice black roof tile, the red chimney pots. To soar higher reveals new vistas. The big house stands alone in a full acre of land. Trees have been allowed to grow unhampered, so it appears that Lamplands peeps mysteriously from a forest wilderness. Beyond its high walls are more mansions, only these have yielded up their lawns to new redbrick villas that front busy streets. Further away, the silver vastness of the river stretches to the Palace of Westminster with its clock tower that rings the hours across the city. Picture Mister Swallow flitting through the open bedroom window, then with fluid agility gliding along the landing. A smart right turn would allow the bird to swoop down the grand staircase. A moment later, the nimble creature would wing on a level plane across the entrance hall that is adorned with a vast Byzantine lamp that, when it shines through the front doors, can light half the drive. A feather might brush a portrait, or stone bust, as our avian visitor flies along the passageway to find the master's study. There, the eye of the bird would observe a man in black. Height: five feet three inches. Aged about thirty-five, he holds a book in one hand as he reads. He is thin. There is no heavy muscle to weigh his bones. His hair is blond, while his eyes are brown, an unusual combination that is most striking. This is Pastor Hux. A gentleman of refinement as well as learning. Here, in the crucible of my imagination, Pastor Hux will see the swallow fly through the open door. He will smile with quiet amusement at this novel sight: a bird passing through his house with such grace; a feathered spirit of untamed places. Our visitor sweeps by him, briefly fanning his brow with cooling air, then it sails through open windows, to soar up across the face of Lamplands to glimpse the woman, Nidabi, writing her journal, before soaring away above the earth.

I have decided I will go downstairs to speak to Pastor Hux. He has shown me a great kindness. Nevertheless, I can't stop asking myself what he intends for his new servant. Surely he has plans for me, doesn't he? Even so, I sense I shouldn't question him outright. There's an emotion working inside of him that troubles me, despite his gentle manner. Long ago, I read an old book called *The Grand Saint Graal.* Some of it came to mind the night Pastor Hux struck down the Colonel and his protégés in torrents of blood. As unwelcome as a ghost, a line from that volume revisited me with such cold power that it made my heart pound: *here begin terrors.*

Later. This afternoon Pastor Hux said, 'Nidabi. Please sit down. No, not across there. Sit here, next to me. Now . . . I must ask you some questions. They might make you feel ashamed, but

I require you to speak truthfully. Do you understand what I'm asking of you?'

'Yes, master.'

'Remember, what I asked you to do?'

'Yes, master.'

'And that is?'

'Don't call you master. Call you Pastor Hux.'

He smiled. 'Then I am Pastor Hux. Not master.'

'But m— Pastor Hux. Every man who has ever owned me . . . I've always called him master.'

'Nidabi.' He touched the back of my hand; a gesture of affection. 'I make no claim to possess you. Not in any shape or form. You are your own property – *you own yourself*. You do understand?'

'Yes, sir.'

'Now, for those questions. They are not frivolous. It's important I know about your life.' He smiled again. 'So I can help you.'

'Thank you, Pastor Hux.'

For a while, he gazed out on to the sunlit lawn. Its grass was like rough pasture, while the trees presented a formidable green barrier between Lamplands and the city beyond. When he spoke it was in gentle tones. 'Nidabi, it was necessary that you spent the last few days enjoying a respite from the outside world. You suffered terribly in your previous life. Nevertheless, I wish to introduce you to society, and then make plans for your future.'

'Whatever you decide, Pastor. I will do as you ask.'

'My plan, Nidabi, is that *you* will decide your own future as a free human being.'

'Sir?'

'Never mind that for now. You say you are twenty years old?'

'Thereabouts, sir.'

'But you don't know your date of birth?'

'No one's ever asked.'

'Then today is your birthday . . . Nidabi, don't look so perplexed. You are twenty-one years old today. It's an arbitrary date, but from now on the 17th July is the anniversary of your birth. Your special day.'

A strange fluttering began in my stomach. 'Thank you, sir.'

'Now, don't cry.' He grasped my hand. 'Do you know where you were born?'

'Yes, Pastor. The Colonel told me I was born in the jungle.'

Pastor Hux shook his head. 'This Colonel . . .' His skin flushed. 'The man's a bastard.' For a moment I feared he would fly into such a rage that my heart pounded.

Pastor Hux walked to the French windows where he gazed out, hands clasped behind his back. I noticed the left hand crushed the right, so the fingers became bloodless. When he spoke again, he made his voice calm. 'The elm is full of white doves. There are rabbits in the garden, too. If you look out at dawn you see them . . . dozens upon dozens . . . My neighbours set snares for them. That is something I cannot abide.'

'Where am I from, sir?'

'I can't begin to guess, Nidabi.'

'My skin is so dark people say I must be heathen.'

'Your colouring is perfectly charming. No, more than that. Infinitely preferable to the bleached faces of my neighbours who pose as ladies, and pretend that God has placed them in positions of supremacy.'

Again, I sensed a fire burning in this man. He conceals it within an exterior of calm, but how it roars. Like a furnace!

'My first master told me he bought me from an Egyptian merchant.'

'You recall arriving in England?'

'I only remember Dover, sir. I worked there until the Colonel bought me. One of the reasons he chose me was because I'd been taught to read. Then I came to London to work.'

'This *work* . . .' He gazed through the window. 'You say you *worked* for the Colonel?'

'Yes, sir.'

'And that would be . . . domestic service? Cleaning his house? Cooking?'

'Oh, no, sir. My work was to please the Colonel and his acquaintances. He would say: "Niddy, I'm going to send my friends to your room. Make sure you send them back with smiles on their faces. Smiles, Niddy. I want to see them smile." '

'I see. Then they used you?'

'My first master told me that I would always work as a whore.' I found myself talking quickly. It was nerves. Talking stopped me feeling frightened by the way he stood so stiffly, with his hands behind his back, one crushing the other. 'The Colonel lived in a big house. There were no lawns, only a quadrangle of crushed limestone, which he called the Parade Ground. He would drill his protégés morning, noon and night. There were also running tracks, boxing rings, a pit for dog fighting. He declared that sleeping indoors thickens the blood. Mostly he would sleep outside on a canvas bed. And he would have his manservant pile fur rugs over him . . . so high.' My words tumbled out. *The way the Pastor's hands torture one another!* One thumb pressed the other so hard I feared a bone would snap. 'He said that because I was a heathen I must live in a room above the stable. Although when he was away I would climb through a window into his library. There were hundreds of books that he never even touched. I could take them without him ever knowing. Once I started reading I couldn't stop. I like de Quincey, Mrs Gaskell's *Life*, and a book of Hebrew grammar took my fancy – I love the shape of the words. And I found great pleasure in astronomy books. There were lots of those, but they'd never been read. I learned that stars are really vast bodies of fire like the sun. And the moon, sir! There are mountains on the moon. Did you know that, sir? Huge mountains.'

The Pastor continued to stare through the window, his head tilted back a little so he could watch doves in a tree. His body quivered, as an emotional pressure rose with a force that was nothing less than volcanic. 'Nidabi. This Colonel . . . what did he look like?'

'You saw the Colonel the night you rescued me, sir. A big man with a jutting stomach. He carried a cane tipped with a silver fist.'

'I saw him?' He turned round, a frown narrowing his eyes. 'I actually saw him?'

'Sir, you fought him and his two men. You remember? There was a wire fence . . . you held the Colonel's face to it. It cut him here.' I touched my nose.

'My God,' he whispered. 'Oh my God.'

In those brown eyes I saw he was remembering events that appalled him. The protégé with the broken face. The other one that he beat so furiously with the cane until the man lay still as a corpse. For a moment I anticipated Pastor Hux would collapse in a faint. How can he have forgotten such a fight?

Taking a deep breath he said all of a sudden, 'We'll dine out!'

'Sir?'

'You enjoy dining out?'

'I've never been to an eating house in London, sir.'

'Never dined out in London? It's your birthday, Nidabi. Of course we must celebrate. Go change your clothes. We leave at six.'

'I've never ridden through London in the daylight. At least not with the carriage blinds open.' I must have appeared foolish because I repeated the statement so often during that journey by hansom cab.

Pastor Hux wore a black suit. His glossy top hat rested on his lap. 'This is the Strand,' he told me. 'It must be the busiest place on earth. All that human flesh . . . it's a wonder the pavement can support its weight. Surely one day it must give way . . . all those people will tumble into blackness. Blackness everlasting.' A sombre spirit threatened to steal over him. I tried to deflect him on to some other topic.

'I'm envious of you, Pastor.'

'Why's that?'

'Any time you wish, you can ride here to see London.'

'Nidabi, no man has ever seen London.' He noticed my puzzled expression. 'Fifteen years ago I became a close friend of a young Dutchman who'd come to work in an art gallery. At night we walked for miles. We explored every street, every alleyway; we marvelled at it all. One night he turned to me and said, 'I have only just understood this truth. No man has ever seen London.' He meant the *theoria* of London. To be granted a vision of its myriad of components that create its soul. And he longed to do just that.

'Was he granted his wish?'

'He's still searching for the ability to see the essence – the quiddity – that he believes runs like a spirit bloodstream through all things – all buildings, landscapes, trees, people – everything.'

'I would very much like to meet him.'

'I would like to meet him again, too. Alas for me, he lives in France now. And there he labours so hard to become an artist.'

'Then I might see his paintings? What's his name?'

Outside the cry of a newspaper vendor sounded over the rumble of carriage wheels. In a rising wail he called out, 'Murder . . . Murder in Brixton!'

'Driver, driver.' Pastor Hux rapped on the carriage roof with his knuckles. 'Driver, stop here!' He flung open the door before the hansom cab had time to stop. 'Today is your birthday. You shall have chocolate.' His mood seemed to have switched again. It was quick, excitable, even spreeish. 'We must hurry or the crowds will have the tables!'

I'm not used to crowded places, the clatter of horses by the score, or even the appearance of men and women beyond those that the Colonel employed, or had me entertain. The scent of perfume streamed from passers-by to mingle with the odour of meals being served in restaurants. A whirl of faces, colourful bonnets and tall black hats danced around me. I almost fell I was so dizzy, but Pastor Hux guided me into a building with marble walls that were veined in pink. Despite the Pastor's fear that the shop would be busy most of the tables were empty. Near the counter a dozen women sat on a long bench. Several were knitting as they drank from china cups. Pastor Hux chose a small table against the wall; he held out the chair so I could sit. Then he sat opposite me.

'Your dress looks very well on you. Is the jacket comfortable?'

'Yes, thank you. I am grateful for the clothes.' My dress and jacket of iridescent green were so vivid they appeared to be striving to compensate for the Pastor's mournfully black coat from which peeped shiny white cuffs and a stiff shirt collar. I sensed Pastor Hux chose to speak of inconsequential matters, as if, perhaps, there were subjects he did need to discuss, only this wasn't the time.

He nodded at our surroundings. 'Here they serve chocolate in the Spanish manner.'

I didn't know what that meant.

'You do like chocolate, Nidabi?'

'Oh, yes, thank you.'

'Then you shall have chocolate as in Spain.' He beckoned a waiter, who placed an oval tray in front of us. Painted on it was a dancing woman in crimson skirts. Within moments the waiter brought pink cups full of a steaming liquor. This was the chocolate – very strong and thick. With these were glasses of iced water.

'The custom, Nidabi,' he told me, 'is to take a draught of water after every sip of chocolate. The water cleanses the palate so each sip of chocolate is as pleasurable as the first.'

I did as he suggested. The chocolate blended sweet with bitter in a marvellous way. As I drank I noticed he glanced at the women at the bench. They shot glances in our direction. Clearly they were discussing us. I surmised the beat of their subject matter: *Why is the distinguished gentleman with her?* The women were not naive. Knowing smiles revealed they understood *exactly* why a gentleman chose the company of a woman like me. Some of the ladies shot dagger glances at me. At that moment I realized that not only did they reveal their disgust, there was a dash of envy, too. As if they wondered what I possessed that they did not. They didn't expect I'd meet their stares, but I did meet them eye for eye. Presently, the women's faces flushed, then they looked away from me. A victory, I decided, then spoke in a louder voice so they'd overhear. 'Recently I've been reading about the constitution of the universe. Although I knew that all objects, including our bodies, are built from atoms, I hadn't anticipated that atoms obey strict physical laws.'

The Pastor's eyes met mine. An understanding passed between us. He realized I was saying this for the benefit of the chattering women who wore their prejudices as blatantly as their garish bonnets. They glanced at each other with baffled expressions as I spoke.

'For example,' I continued, 'the hydrogen atom on earth bears the same spectral signature as one on the moon. There is also a belief that the atom is not only indivisible but endowed with enormous energy.'

'A poet might agree, Nidabi, and I quote: "in a grain of wheat beats the heart of a star." '

Unable to understand our talk of atoms the women at the bench were flustered in defeat. They returned to their chocolate, one spilt a large drop of the liquor on to her starched white blouse, which led to nothing less than a tintinnabulation of her woes in general. Pastor Hux clasped his hands together on the table as he smiled fondly at me.

That evening I felt as if I'd been crowned queen of the whole wide world. A strength blossomed within me. I grew confident. Whatever life could bring I could meet and conquer. The sun hung low in the sky. Gas lights – oh, hundreds of gas lights – began to twinkle on the Strand as we strolled along the pavement. This quarter of London sang with music from the street players. Once more, the sensation flooded through me that I'd been transported to a celestial paradise. Lamps became stars. Minstrels sang with the sweetness of angels. Overhead, lines of cirrus flamed red as if touched by the breath of dragons.

The Pastor took me to a building that proclaimed itself the Opera Comique. After he purchased tickets we moved into its cavernous interior. Here there were rows of chairs, plush with crimson fabric.

'This is the Royal Circle,' he told me. 'This is where we sit.'

Although the seats were filling rapidly with cheerful crowds of men and women, none stared at me. There were no glances that spat: 'You don't belong here.' Instead, ladies smiled a thank you at me, while gentlemen graciously nodded when they found their seats along the row. This process necessitated the Pastor and I to rise each time. This wasn't a source of irritation to me – no, it was more like a dance that everyone enjoyed – sitting, standing, hello, thank you, pardon me, enjoy the show. Above me, on a pale blue ceiling, were painted jolly faces – a heaven of merry laughter. Gods of joy. Lovely scents filled the air – cigars, perfume, oranges.

'Are all theatres like this?' I asked.

He raised an eyebrow in surprise. 'You mean to say you've never been to the theatre before?'

'No, sir.'

'Not even a music hall?'

'They always told me my skin was too dark for polite society.'

'Well, enjoy the play, Nidabi. And once again a very happy birthday to you.'

'But what shall I do, sir?'

'Do?'

'How do I make entertainment of a play?'

Often his expression was lost to one of brooding remoteness;

this time he smiled warmly. 'You do nothing, Nidabi, other than wait for that curtain there in front of you to part. Then you sit here comfortably, and look at the performance on stage.'

'I shall, sir. And I won't make a sound, trust me.'

He chuckled. 'This is the Opera Comique. Laughing and applauding is not only tolerated, it's positively encouraged. Don't wear such a worried frown, Nidabi. Follow my lead.'

My eyes roved across the audience to apertures in the walls where parties of three or four were ensconced that were so finely dressed they must have been lords and ladies. As I gazed in wonder, Pastor Hux clicked his tongue. 'Oh, by the way, in the carriage earlier you had a question about my artist friend. It had slipped my mind, but you'd asked me his name. He is called Vincent van Gogh. Vincent wrote to me earlier in the year to say that he was moving from Paris to the south. What struck me was his passion for the sunlight there. Its brilliance, he told me, has the power to transfigure mundane objects into something glorious. Imagine if sunlight of such miraculous power could fall on to the darkest quarters of London, Nidabi. Just picture the transformation of so many wounded lives.' His eyes dulled as they turned inward again. For all the world, he appeared to gaze on a particularly grim vista. Yet at that moment the audience stirred. A burst of light flared against the curtain as it glided apart. Pastor Hux blinked. 'Ah, Nidabi, it's just about to begin . . .'

Now, it's long past midnight as I write. This is Lamplands. A tranquil oasis of birds and rabbits and trees. Long ago the clock downstairs chimed twelve. I can still taste the pleasant mingling of beef with red wine that we ate in the restaurant. Close your eyes, Nidabi. You still see the theatre stage. It presents a sunlit place in another country as a row of girls sing their love song. Ah . . . here it is. A gentle knock on my bedroom door. A sound I've anticipated ever since I arrived at the Pastor's home. Adieu.

18th July. This is what happened when I heard the knocking on my bedroom door. On hearing the light tap on its panel I rose from the table. A candle burned in its holder. There wasn't a breath of air on that balmy summer's night as I stood there in my nightdress. At any moment I expected the door to swing ajar. Pastor Hux had to be my night visitor as there were no domestic staff resident. So . . . now this gentle tapping on the door.

Why doesn't he enter? This is his house. He can walk into any room he pleases. But he is a gentleman. To walk in uninvited would be unthinkable to him.

'Pastor Hux. The door is unlocked.' There . . . said it. Invitation made. I was not afraid. Not after the terrors of the Colonel's *hospitality.* However, I'd hardly drawn breath after speaking when the light tapping sounded on the door again. *This is strange.* Then the Pastor is not like any other man I've met. He's kindly. He considers what effect his words might have on others before he utters them. When there was no further knocking I went to the door and put my ear to it, my palm resting lightly on the panel beside my face. *Perhaps he decided his appearance at my room was improper. So might he have returned to his own bed?*

I closed my eyes in order to listen as hard as I could. I fancied I heard an unsteady breathing, as if the Pastor was nervous of how I'd respond to this night-time call on me. *Does he fear rejection? Or is he afraid of his own intentions?*

I must be the one to speak. 'Pastor Hux . . . don't be hesitant. If you wish to come into my room I shan't mind at all.' I listened again, yet could hear nothing.

Until the scream. A scream of such loudness that the door vibrated against my hand. I recoiled in shock. The scream continued. A woman's scream that combined pain, terror, despair. Its explosive power drove me back, covering my ears. Then the cry became guttural. In my mind's eye I saw hands around the woman's throat, squeezing, crushing. I flew at the door. Gripping the handle, I twisted – pulled. The door opened a fraction. Then it was seized from the other side to be yanked shut. I tugged at the handle but it stayed firm. The scream tore through the house again. A howl of torment. *Murder.* It could be nothing else.

I beat the door with my fists. 'Leave her! Do you hear me? *Leave her alone!*'

Then the Pastor's voice came urgently through the timbers. 'Nidabi. Stay in your room. Lock your door. And for the love of God keep it locked!'

The scream rose in pitch. Then stopped. Absolute silence

rushed into the vacuum. I stood at the door for several moments. I did not try to open it. I wouldn't disobey the Pastor. Eventually I returned to bed to watch the candle slowly burn out. One by one, the shadows in the room grew into a clutch of sinister phantoms as the night's darkness conquered all.

Ty's Book

18th July. This café is where I come after I've finished work at around three o'clock in the morning. This is a place for darkness prowlers, or people too drunk to find their way home, or those who find themselves without lodgings. I must count myself among the latter now. My brother and sister are safe at the Night Woman's house. She will give them a bed and food for ten francs a week. Her husband insists there is no room for me. Make of that what you will. At this time of night the café is peaceful. Most of the clientele sleep with their arms as their pillows on the tables.

A huge counter of oak that's a tarry black runs along the far wall. The proprietress tells her customers that the counter is built from the timber of a Spanish pirate galleon that foundered after a battle a hundred years ago. To prove the story she will point out shards of cannon ball embedded in its carvings. Behind the counter, tiers of shelves bear dozens of green bottles along with jars of brandied peaches. The wine is drawn from a reservoir of gleaming white stone in what they call the Greek Style. My father believed the oblong reservoir once served as a sarcophagus in the Classical age.

Gas lamps are turned down low. Even so, it's light enough to write in my book as I sit in one of the booths. My pencil scrapes against the paper loud enough to occasionally rouse the old coachman at a table nearby. He raises his head. His face bears the ribbed imprint of the straw table mat where he's rested the side of his face.

'Who's that breathing?' he asks, three quarters asleep. 'I say, who's that breathing?' It's the scratching of my pencil against the page that mimics respiration. 'I can't sleep with people breathing in my ear.'

This stirs a thin man with grey hair that sticks out like gull wings at either side of his balding head.

Befuddled, the coachman repeats, 'I said, who's that breathing?'

The thin man grunts, 'We're all still breathing, thank God. Go back to sleep.'

The coachman appears satisfied with the answer. He lowers his head on to the ribbed mat. At the bar the proprietress drinks brandy to keep awake. She gazes into thin air. Her mind isn't here in the café with its sad, lost regiment of drowsy men and women. We, like the wrecked galleon, whose timber bones form the counter, have been washed up here by bad fortune. No doubt in her imagination she escapes to a brighter, happier world. I'm keen to write because of what happened here last night, but I don't want to rouse the coachman again, so I wait until he falls into a deep sleep before I take up my pencil. Scrape . . . scrape . . . how the words sail across the page . . . they are vessels that carry the cargo of memory.

Twenty-four hours ago I sat in this very booth. The outrage of being thrown out of my room at the Place d'Sucre had faded. I'd worked well. Now there was enough money for George and Brionne's lodgings at least. Two hours after midnight the Madame insisted I finish work; she is adamant I keep my features as fresh as possible. So I retired to the night café to write in my book. As always, it grew silent as drinkers either went home or drowsed at the tables. Even the proprietress lays her head on the bar. Her silver-flecked hair had begun to escape its pins, so some strands dipped into spilt wine.

All of a sudden there was noise bundled together with motion. As I had an urgent need to write I didn't look up. Instead, I heard the new arrival's voice. It boomed in deep bass notes that vibrated the table under my palm. In the voice there was an infusion of melancholy that sent shivers through me.

'Madame Reive. Don't be angry with me. Please, look . . . I brought you a gift because you are always so kind.'

The proprietress groaned. 'Oh . . . it's you. Didn't I tell you, Vincent?'

'I am here to make amends. I shall be good from now on.'

'Oh, you better be. I won't have you shouting at my customers.'

'The farmer swore that all artists should be put to work on the treadmill.'

'I don't care, Vincent. Don't berate idiots. Ignore them.'

I glanced up to see Vincent van Gogh advancing toward the woman. He wore the blue labourer's suit of old. 'Look,' he boomed, 'I've been out to pick you wild strawberries.'

'At this time of night?'

'They are very small – the sweetest you'll taste.'

'Vincent, they are in your hat.'

He placed his straw hat on the counter. 'They are for you. When the dairy opens I will buy fresh cream.'

'You'll do no such thing, you madman.' The woman's sudden smile made her tired face ten years younger. 'I'll put the strawberries in a bowl then you can have your hat back. But, I warn you, it'll be sticky.'

'I don't mind, because I've made you smile.'

'Idiot.' Her smile widened. 'Brandy?'

'I'm already intoxicated on the night air.'

'Does that mean yes to brandy or no to brandy?'

'Wine, please. I must be clear-headed enough to work tomorrow.'

She worked a brass pump that forced red wine from the reservoir into a glass. The force of its passage through a cherub's mouth set in the stone formed a pink froth at the top of the glass.

'Ah, Madame Reive . . .' The red-haired man smacked his lips with relish. 'That wine is perfectly terrible.'

'And you are perfectly mad, Vincent. Now go away. I need to sleep.' Although dead tired the smile remained to recapture some of her youth. After she waved him away, she lay her head back down on the counter that she claimed was made from a pirate ship.

Vincent van Gogh. I'm drawn to his eyes, which constantly shift from blue to green, then back again. Children call him Goblin Eyes, then fork their fingers at him. Adults dismiss him as insane. I know he's prone to explosive outbursts, but these often stem from him passionately striving to express himself in words, yet finding those words won't free themselves from his lips. Then it's like witnessing a cauldron boil over. Speech isn't Vincent's medium. His passion for the world is expressed in painting. Without him knowing I was there, I've followed him along country lanes to watch him paint trees like they were the portraits of people. When he renders them on canvas, those olive trees become like living beings that writhe before their own searing emotion. He works as if carving the paint on canvas. He does this for hours beneath the hot sun until he falls to his knees exhausted. As he works he grimaces. His head dips, twists; he mouths words; sighs, curses, snarls. A schoolteacher saw him at work once and commented that Vincent van Gogh doesn't so much paint as fight with all his heart. That he forces himself to match on canvas what he sees inside his head. The schoolteacher admired Vincent's struggle, yet added, 'This art of his – it's a battle to the death.'

On the night Vincent brought Madame Reive the strawberries he turned around so he could survey us, the denizens of the night café. His expression was fathomless. Briefly his gaze settled on men dozing at a round table in the centre. One was an old sailor whose legs had been cut away at the knees. The other, a man blinded by working at the limekiln, muttered in his sleep as his fingers tapped an unconscious rhythm on the table top. Both wore coats that had collars frayed to wisps.

Dare I invite the artist to join me? The thought came with a shocking suddenness. *Go on, Ty. Do it!* I coughed to attract his attention. He came forward. Then chose the booth beside mine, and disappeared from sight.

Now I've made a complete idiot of myself. My cheeks burned with shame. *He either thinks I'm silly, or plan to work some money from him.* With my teeth fiercely nipping my bottom lip I returned to writing. This time I dug my pencil hard into the paper. Its point snapped with a click. I stared at the pencil, annoyed at breaking it before I had chance to finish my page. As I could no longer write I lifted my head. At the end of the booth's wooden panel a face appeared; a pair of eyes met mine. Again the colour shift in the eyes – from green to blue, then back again. Where the man's skin was free of the red beard it had been charred by the sun. My breath caught in my throat because he held out his hand to me palm up. *Does he want money? Or my book?* I stared back, unable to say a word – not one – even though my inner voice berated: *Ty, speak to him, damn you!* His expression was so stern I began to feel uneasy. Then he raised his red eyebrows before directing his eyes toward my pencil. He flexed the fingers of the open hand a little. A 'give me' gesture. Hypnotized, I handed him the pencil. He sat back, hidden by the panel of the booth. A moment after that he leaned from his booth again. In one hand he held a razor. The blade caught the light with a silvery flash. In the other hand he held my pencil pinched between finger and thumb. Its point now sharp again. Muttering a thank you that sounded boorish to my ears, I took the pencil from him. He nodded, withdrew to his sanctum. A cloud of blue tobacco smoke rose from it as he continued with his pipe. For a while I sat feeling like I'd been crowned queen of fools. *I should speak to him . . .*

We were destined to sit like that for the next hour – Vincent in his booth, me in mine, a girl with a knot in her tongue. One so suddenly shy she couldn't utter even a syllable. However, the blind man moved in his chair and instantly a cascade of coins fell from his trouser pocket to roll across the floor with the sound of a hundred tiny bells. The blind man roused himself from his sleep. 'Who's doing that? Please, we're trying to rest.'

His companion, the sturdy old sailor without legs, assessed the situation after scowling under the table. 'Gone and lost all your bloody money, Bernard.'

Blind Bernard squeezed his pockets with huge, grasping hands. 'Thief! Who's robbing me? Who is it?'

'No one's thieved it. Fell out of ya pocket, ya daft bugger.' The sailor whistled. 'S'wonder ya could walk wi' all that metal in ya trousers.'

Bernard became agitated. 'That's all I have, Captain. All I own in the world is in my pockets.'

'Well, my friend, it's all over the bloody floor now. The cleaning woman's going to be living the good life when she sweeps them buggers up in the morning.'

Such an expression of woe possessed the blind man's face that immediately I went to him.

As I picked up the coins he asked, 'Captain, what's happening now? I can hear someone close by.'

'You've just bought yourself a very pretty whore.'

'I don't need a woman.'

'Bernard, you don't know how beautiful she is. Twenty years of age, I'd say. A dash of Zouave blood. Her skin is pure gold. And she has the blackest, glossiest hair you've ever seen.'

Blind Bernard panted. It struck me he was afraid to protest.

'Don't worry, sir,' I told him. 'I'm gathering up your money for you.'

The rest of the clientele slept or pretended to sleep. Even Madame Reive dozed soundly; she had been drinking brandy all night. One individual, however, was wide awake. A youth skulked toward me from the shadows; his skin a waxy yellow, his eyes glittering when he saw the coins. I tried to gather the money faster because I knew what the youth intended.

The Captain chuckled. 'What delicate fingers. She has such clean fingernails, Bernard. Are you sure you don't want to spend some money on her?'

Bernard shook his head, trembling. 'It's all I have in the world, Captain.'

The approaching youth wore a hungry expression as he stared at the cash. Before he reached the first coin a square figure blocked his way as surely as a fortress gate. 'We've done this work before,' Vincent said to me as he crouched down to help retrieve the coins. The youth decided the forces stacked against him were superior to his. He shuffled back to the corner with a bitter shrug. Vincent added, 'You helped me with my paints a while ago, when the boy tried to steal my satchel in the street.'

I nodded.

'Your name is Ty?'

Again, I nodded.

'You were brave to help me. You know they say I'm a crazy painter?'

'Yes. But you're not mad.'

'I'm sure I'm part mad.' He smiled.

The Captain snorted. 'You two can murmur sweet nothings when you've picked up my friend's money. Didn't you hear him say that's all he has in the world? Do you want him to starve?'

'Don't worry, sir.' Vincent's deep voice was gentle. 'We'll find every last sou.'

'See that you do.'

'What's happening now, Captain?' Blind Bernard turned his head as he tried to interpret our movements by sound alone.

'They are finding your money, Bernard. But the buggers aren't doing a very good job. There's a man now . . . the crazy foreigner that lives in Place Lamartine . . . he's pretending to help . . . really he's wanting to *romance* the girl. Hah! Bernard, make sure he doesn't use your money to rent her charms.'

Bernard's milky eyes bulged. He was so nervous he licked his lips. Emotion robbed him of speech.

The Captain leaned sideways so he could watch us. 'You have to check the cracks between the bloody slabs. Coins roll into 'em.'

'We will, sir,' I said as patiently as I could.

The Captain sniffed in contempt. 'And under the other tables. Coins roll some way, you know. I've seen the little buggers roll right across this floor to the counter.'

'We will.'

'And don't go stuffing any of that cash into your own pockets.'

Bernard was so frightened about losing his money he gasped, 'Heaven help me. What's happening, Captain?'

'Just making sure the strumpet and the mad bugger don't thieve your cash.'

'Oh . . .' This was too much for Bernard. His head sagged as if he'd faint.

'See what you're doing to my friend? Keep one sou of that and I'll have the law down here.' He jiggled his leg stumps. The man was enjoying the drama of this, with himself centre stage as the great protecting hero of his blind friend. 'Of course, a sensible person would have brought a candle from the counter to make sure they found it all . . . then you like it to be a puddle of shadows down there, don't you?'

'Sir,' Vincent said calmly, 'we will return every single coin to your friend.'

'Well . . . you know you can do what you bloody want. Bernard's eyes are like two boiled eggs and my legs don't go

further than me blasted knees. You could rob us both to Hades
and back, and we couldn't do beggar-all about it.'

In a very small voice Bernard added, 'I do need that money,
please. If you would be so good, please.'

'Here you are.' Vincent extended cupped palms. Mounds
of coins glinted there. 'Hold out your hands and you'll find
mine with the money. Put it into your pockets. There . . . carefully now.'

Slowly the blind man transferred the coins to his coat pocket.
The Captain watched with total fascination. I passed the coins
I'd picked up to Vincent; the process was repeated until the
old man had back every last one.

'Well, Bernard.' The captain clicked his tongue. 'You should
have most of it back. I kept a very close eye on the two
buggers.'

'Thank you.' Bernard's eyes glistened.

'Watch your step in future, Dutchman. You too, little doll.'
The Captain's eyes squinted with ferocity. 'In London, they've
taken a cull of working girls like you. They're slaughtering
'em by the dozen. Everyone's talking about it. Londoners are
all bloody barbarians, but they've got the right idea this time.
Take the hussies off the streets and stick 'em in the bone
yards. Mark my words, little doll, what they do in London
today, we'll be doing in France tomorrow.'

The blind man was troubled. 'Don't talk to the girl like
that, Captain. She helped get me my money back. Please,
Captain . . .'

The Captain leaned forward to pat Bernard's hand. 'Now,
how about a drink, old friend?'

'Yes. Thank you. Thank you very much.'

'Don't you worry yourself. Let old Captain take care of
you. I'll order the drinks. You can pay the waiter when he
brings them across.'

Vincent caught my eye. 'I'm going for some fresh air,' he
said. 'Would you care to walk with me?'

I retrieved my book as the Captain called out, 'Waiter . . .
waiter! Your best brandy for me and my old friend here.'

We left the café to meet the sun rising over Arles. The dawn
chorus swelled from the trees that lined the boulevard. In
the café, the eyes of Vincent van Gogh had been blue, now

the light played its tricks. They became emerald as he paused to gaze at the mist that flowed between the roof tops and deep blue sky.

'You will be good to old Vincent today,' he told the rising sun. 'Vincent needs to work without you burning his hands again.' He blew on sunburnt knuckles. 'I'll cut reeds from the river bank then draw in the fields. Wild flowers by the thousand rendered in ink. The reeds are very good . . . better than pens if you cut them properly . . . that is, if the sun doesn't blind me today. Then, I should not complain . . . I moved from Paris for the sun. Now I get more light than I could have believed. You will walk with me? Yes? Sometimes I walk too fast for people. Pull my sleeve if I rush . . . pull it hard, OK?'

'OK.'

'I came to Arles because I thought living here wouldn't be so expensive. But I need five francs a day so it isn't any cheaper. Yesterday I paid forty francs for twenty metres of canvas. Paints cost the earth. Then you helped me save my paints from those boys, didn't you?'

'They made me so angry. I wanted to beat their stupid faces.'

'Ty is a tigress.'

'People shouldn't be so cruel.'

'Like the Captain in the café?'

'He's stealing the blind man's money, isn't he?'

'And he wanted to frighten you about the London murders.'

'They've tried that before. Sometimes they even pin newspaper stories on to the brothel door. Slaughtered women? They think it's a big joke.'

'Do the stories frighten you?'

'No. What's more, I don't believe the English are barbarians.'

'You are intelligent. You use your brains better than most. Better than me!' Vincent smiled warmly. 'I lived in London once. There are plenty of kind people there. Beautiful buildings, too. The Palace of Westminster at sunrise; the dome of St Paul's Cathedral floating on the mist. Wonderful! Though there are fearsome slums that are hell on earth. There were stories in those places. As if each street was a book full of dramas . . . I know I don't make myself clear. But . . . ah, London! London is a big, *big* beast. If you don't learn how to live in it from the start it can devour you . . . I left because London became too ferocious. Even though I loved it I had to go home to Holland. If not, Vincent would have become its prey. Here, Ty . . . what did I tell you? Pull my sleeve if I walk too fast. You're having to run to keep up. Pull!'

I pulled the blue sleeve of his jacket.

'That's the way . . . whenever I rush. You tug at the old red bear's sleeve.'

I laughed as I saw his face surrender to an even friendlier smile.

By now the day had brightened. The sun's touch became warmer by the second. Workmen hurried out of their homes for the day ahead. Most called at the bakery to buy fresh bread, half of which they devoured for breakfast as they headed to their workplaces; the other half they'd save for lunch. A cart drawn by a black mule with long, drooping ears rattled by. The cart's driver dozed in his seat with a cigar hanging from his lips. A girl sang in a nearby house as she opened its shutters. As soon as the sun laid its hand on the town its heat drew scents from the boulevards. The perfume of vine blossom clinging to old stone walls; a faint hint of cedar from roof timbers; all soon to be chased away by cooking aromas.

'Back there in the café, monsieur—'

'Vincent. That's my name, Ty. Monsieur makes me think of bossy men in black suits that believe God created them to rule over us. So, call me Vincent . . . or old lunatic. Either, I don't mind. Ah, you're tugging my sleeve. Good. That's the way.'

I managed to catch my breath. 'Back there in the café?'

'Yes, so you were saying. Café. Go on.'

'The poor blind man. You didn't give him back the money he dropped.'

Vincent stopped dead. He expected me to accuse him of theft. Then berate him for being the mad foreigner. He knew the rhythm of those insults by heart. *Mad painter. Crazy Dutchman. Lunatic!* He'd heard it all before. Sorrow burned in his eyes, yet as he turned away I grabbed his sleeve.

'No! You didn't give him back what fell on the floor. *You gave him more!* I saw you take coins from your own pocket, then put them in his hand.'

'Then we are still friends?'

'Why did you give the blind man your money?'

'Because I'm crazy. See those people over at the barber's shop? The way they look at me? Those gestures with their hands? They know I'm crazy.'

'You are *not* crazy. Don't be cruel to yourself. You gave a stranger money. That is love.'

He put his fingers to his lips. 'I'd prefer not to talk about money, Ty.'

'Whatever you want.'

'What I always *want* is art. Talking about it. Doing it. Drawing. Painting . . . squeeze colour directly on to the canvas from its tube. Work it with a knife! You know, Ty, that is my passion.' He smiled. 'That passion makes me the biggest bore in Arles, if not its greatest lunatic.'

'No, I love to hear you talk about art. And I've seen your paintings.'

'Where?' He was genuinely surprised.

'As you carry them back from the fields.'

'Hah, I've become my own gallery.' He laughed. 'Hang portraits on my head and back – see? There's room for a land-scape on my chest.' A warm sense of humour bubbled up inside of him. 'There's the church. Isn't she beautiful? A thousand years old. Built from the bones of martyrs.'

I stared hard at the walls. I could see only stones.

'That's how I would paint it. The bones of martyrs cemented by the blood of Christ into a towering house of God.'

'The church will be your next painting?'

'Not yet. As soon as I can afford more oils this old red bear is going into the hills to paint cypress trees. I've painted their portraits every day this week.'

'Why? I mean, are they special trees?'

'Cypress trees are hairs that grow out of this animal's back.' He paused to stamp on the ground. 'Out of animal earth. Out of its flesh.' The huge hands raked the air as he became animated. 'The cypress is the symbol of death. Lovely green extrusions that whisper the song of the dead.'

'Then your work communicates through symbols?'

'Symbols are everywhere.' He glanced toward the church. 'The sign of the cross. And see the stained glass? The image of the man with feathers on his trousers? Feathery trousers – what ho! – that's all I thought until I learnt it is medieval code. The code for an angel. In painting, a juniper bush represents chastity. Ivy is a symbol of fidelity. Colours likewise. Red is murder. Yellow is friendship. I love yellow paint: all shades – yellow that's as pale as butter, or great big burning yellows that shine like the sun. And over there? There's a symbol on that wall that speaks to me now.'

I'd become dazed by this rush through Arles with the artist. He talked with such fiery passion. 'Symbol?' I asked, searching for some mysterious rune.

He pointed with his hat. 'A baker's shovel. That means breakfast. Fresh bread hot from the oven. And coffee. Lots of good strong coffee. Is Ty hungry?'

Smiling, I nodded.

'Then what are we waiting for? If I walk too fast tug my arm!'

As I picked up my skirts, so I could match his pace, sunlight turned the Rhone into a river of gold. That same light transformed Arles into the town of a magic dream. And, at that moment, it seemed I walked in the presence of a god.

{London, 18th July, 1888}

TO THE COMMITTEE CHAIRMAN, CHAPEL OF ST JUDE, BLACKHEATH

We, the senior members of the congregation, wish to advise the Chairman of our concern regarding the activities of one of our members. Be it known that Mr Posthumous Hux has for some months bestowed upon himself the title of Pastor. We are at a loss to understand why he should adopt the title as he has no qualification granted to him by any ecclesiastical body. We salute Mr Hux's charitable work in the poor areas of London. He tirelessly visits the sick, the elderly, and those less fortunate than ourselves. However, of late, his compassionate zeal has become excessive. We fear this will reflect badly on our chapel. Of even greater concern, Mr Hux has tended to devote his charity to women of an undesirable class. We speak of women so debased that they accept money for the most unhygienic practices imaginable.

We request that the Chairman raise our concerns with the committee, and the said committee remind Mr Hux that he

*must not assume the title of Pastor without proper creden-
tials, and, furthermore, he should desist from squandering
acts of Christian charity on women that are bereft of civilized
morals.*

Nidabi's Journal

18th July. Evening. Rain all day. Pastor Hux left Lamplands
before I went to breakfast. One of the servants had set aside
oatmeal and eggs. All cold. I daren't ring the bell for more,
because the staff that Pastor Hux employs don't wait on him
as in other households. Meals are delivered from the kitchen
downstairs to the dining room in a cabinet hoisted by cables
through a shaft in the wall.

It seemed calm after last night's commotion in the corridor
outside my room. A woman screaming. It had been murder I
reasoned. My thoughts were of a woman being strangled by
an intruder. After all that frenzy I couldn't sleep for hours.
Now the Pastor is gone. Where? I don't know. Yet as I stood
at the window watching the rain I realized I was alone in the
house, the staff having left after their day's work. What's more,
I was alone with a body of facts that chilled me like the touch
of death. Last night there'd been the sounds of murder being
done. Disturbingly, I'd heard the Pastor's voice, too. I found
myself asking myself whether the intruder had been a woman
who the Pastor had tackled? Several times I went to the corridor
to examine its bare boards. A dark, penny-sized disk suggested
that blood had been spilt.

Lamplands stands with three floors above a cellar. I searched
room after room, half-expecting to see a person lying dead,
their eyes bulging so dreadfully I'd scream in horror. Most
of the dwelling was empty of furniture. The rugs had gone,
too. The cellar door was locked. As was a corridor on the upper
floor – the one that runs into the north wing of the house.
Every now and again I stopped to listen. Often I ventured a

tremulous, 'Hello? Can anyone hear me?' I listened, antici-
pating a moan of pain by way of answer – an irrational thought,
I know. However, by then a cold dread like a clinging London
fog had attached itself to my nerves. That dread haunted me
as I opened every door as if it were a portal to a tomb. Yet I
discovered nothing more. By the end of the search I was
convinced the only living soul in Lamplands that afternoon
was myself. Also, I calculated that out of perhaps thirty rooms
only half a dozen were fully furnished. On the study desk I
saw pages of the Pastor's handwriting. He'd been copying
verses from the Bible. 'I shall not want' and: 'The world
passeth away and the lust thereof'. Books pertaining to theo-
logical matters, such as *Incendium Amoris* by Richard Rolle,
a mystic of the medieval age. Newspaper cuttings about children who had died of neglect. An essay in the Pastor's hand
entitled, 'Deeds, Not Words'.

Driven by unease, I passed through the gloom-filled house
again. In my state of mind, doors began to resemble dark tomb-
stones, the groan of ancient floorboards under the weight of
my feet could have been the ominous stirring of demons. Even
the click of rain on windows became the tap of skeletal fingers
to warn me of horrors to come. The locked way to the upper
corridor began to play on a nerve. *What's beyond the door?*
The answer to what happened last night, of course.

Whatever needed to be revealed about the enigma of
Lamplands lay the other side of that forbidding timber barrier.
This thought worked at me, like the bite of a fly. An itch that
could not be soothed: a fury of maddening irritation that made
my skin crawl beneath my clothes. At that moment sheer
insanity stole over me. I knew that this was no way to repay
the Pastor's kindness. But I must satisfy myself that those
rooms were as peacefully, and *bloodlessly*, empty, as those in
the rest of the house. I could not rest until I'd seen for myself.
That's the only way to stop the woman's terrified scream that
still resonated inside my head. One question dogged me: how
do I penetrate those secret quarters? I'd found no keys. The
windows had their curtains drawn, so I couldn't simply see
inside if I elected to climb a nearby tree. There was, however,
a stone ledge that ran in a continuous band beneath the
windows – those oh-so-forbidden windows of Lamplands. All
it required was for me to climb out of one of the upper rooms,

to which I had access, then inch my way along the ledge to the windows of the north wing, where I might find one of them ajar. True, the ledge was thirty feet above the ground, but it did appear to be fairly broad. I could make that short journey, then put an end to that banshee screech inside my head for good.

Rain. Wind. A narrow ledge. Height greater than I expected. This is insane. I'm going to fall. Those words beat inside my head as I climbed out of the landing window to stand on the ledge. A ledge that wasn't as level as it appeared from a distance. Its surface sloped downward to aid the shedding of rainwater. Moss had made its home there, too. My feet slipped on it as I shuffled sideways, my back to the wall of the house. Look to your right, not down, I told myself. Never *ever* look down. All this, for what? To check the status of those locked rooms? Yet I felt compelled. I recalled the sounds of murder last night. I had to satisfy myself that those quarters didn't contain a guilty secret. Ideas swam madly like too many fish in a tiny bowl. I could run away. Pastor Hux didn't force me to stay. But where would I go? No friends, no relatives. I, Nidabi, am alone in the world save for Pastor Hux, the kind man who rescued me from the Colonel. But is he a gentleman? What did he do to the woman last night that made her scream so? *Go back to your bedroom, Nidabi. Go forward to peer into that secret chamber. Leave here . . . go into the city.* All these thoughts that clamoured; that contradicted; that made my blood run hot. Then a near miss. My foot skittered off the ledge. Now I did look down. Thirty feet below the rose garden writhed before the blast of air: thorn-covered limbs raked the air. Raindrops struck my face. Panting, I regained my balance. Even so, my entire body trembled so much my teeth chattered. *Nidabi, you idiot. Go back inside.* But a superior force drove me on. If I could satisfy myself the sealed north wing was harmless then I could return to the house, content to stay here until Pastor Hux determined my future.

I continued along the lip of stone that projected a mere ten inches – ten slippery, moss-shrouded inches from the face of the house. If I fell? I foresaw a screaming plunge; those monster thorns on the rose bushes! They'd flay my skin and rip my eyes before I shattered my skull on the ground. Madness to continue, yet I'd go mad with mental torment if I did not. The first window of the north wing was perhaps eight paces away. I moved crabwise. Sliding my right foot six inches, then sliding my left foot to rejoin its partner, and so on. All the time I kept the cold wall pressed firmly against my spine. My back began to ache with a ferocity I've never known before. I wanted desperately to relax that stiff, upright posture, but I knew I had to keep my centre of gravity slightly backward, otherwise I'd simply topple forward into the unforgiving arms of the earth thirty feet below. As I shuffled sideways, I found my eyes range forward to where the wind tossed the trees. Now I could appreciate that despite our urban location, it appeared we inhabited a tract of wild forest. Garden overgrown, lawn knee-deep; a statue of a child drowning in poisonous hemlock; monstrous elms furiously shaking their limbs in great tides of cold air. A deep gloom engulfed the garden as if the lid of a tomb descended on the world.

A hard edge against my hip told me that I'd reached the first window. It was locked. What's more, this one was heavily draped on the inside, so that required me to venture further along this narrow lip of stone. With my back aching, I continued my sideways shuffle. Beneath me, I saw a fox pad toward the house. In the centre of the drive it paused, then looked up. Its amber eyes met mine. The points of its ears rose as it witnessed something that aroused its curiosity. I daresay it had never seen a human climb across the face of the building in flapping skirts, with long hair trailing down. The animal found my progress fascinating.

'You think I'm mad, too, don't you?' I must be mad, talking to a fox as I inched toward the next window. This would end with me toppling forward to break my lunatic neck. I winced as the next ledge thudded against my hip. The second window. I twisted my head to look back over my shoulder as, of course, it would be suicidal to actually attempt to turn round on my dangerous perch. I found myself telling the fox, 'Would you believe it? The curtains are closed.' A swirling tide of madness rushed to engulf me. I haven't drunk brandy since my arrival. Yet I wanted brandy now. I wanted its burn. The bruising grip of a man, too. A soldier with scars on his flesh, or a blacksmith with hands as hard as granite. Wild, fierce thoughts. An antidote to the terror of standing here with nothing to grip on

to. 'I've lost my wits,' I confessed to the fox that regarded
me with laughing, amber eyes. 'I don't belong here.' Vertigo
pulled hard. 'Brandy and lust – that's what I need.'

The fox yelped its bark. Rain stung my eyes. The rush of
air beneath my skirts chilled my bones. 'Here I am at the
window, Mr Fox. After coming all this way I can't look in.
Poor Nidabi. Poor heathen Nidabi . . .'

Then, two things. First: I saw that the curtain had caught
on a washstand, so it created an aperture perhaps five inches
wide. Second: a shocking, *monstrous* second: Pastor Hux
arrived home. Two hundred yards away, his black gallower
drew the open-topped carriage through the gates. The gallower
is a huge, fearsome horse, visibly mismatched with the small,
two-wheel carriage. Nevertheless, it effortlessly drew the
vehicle for mile after mile without tiring. Pastor Hux sat on
the driver's seat. An ebony figure in a top hat and long coat.
And here I stood, like some great raven, with flapping skirts
for wings. I was in the middle of the house, in clear view of
anyone approaching along the drive.

I'd never anticipated the Pastor's return so soon. The shock
had the same effect as a slap in the face. I woke from the
strange fancies that possessed me as I tottered there upon the
rain-sodden ledge. Below my feet, the fox darted away into
the bushes. Of course, every nerve howled at me to scurry
along the ledge then scramble in through the window I'd
emerged from. If the Pastor saw me here, clearly trying to
break into part of the house he wished to remain private, he
would immediately force me to leave . . . worse, he may call
the police. Either way, it would be the workhouse or jail. So,
the only answer was to scramble inside because he couldn't
fail to see me hanging on to the naked masonry, thirty feet
above the front door. And yet . . . and yet . . .

This window! The curtain! How it caught would afford me
a glimpse into the forbidden room. I need only take three
sliding steps to my right, then I could see inside. I glanced
forward. The Pastor's carriage clipped along the track to the
house. He'd pass right below me before following the driveway
to the back where the stable lay. Without doubt he'd see me
as the carriage was an open one. Common sense dictated the
dash to safety. And yet I was only ten seconds from my goal.
At this distance, and with the veiling power of the rain, I was

confident the Pastor wouldn't notice me yet. In a moment his carriage would disappear under the overhanging elms, then Lamplands would be completely obscured to him until he emerged again just fifty yards from the house. Even though the gallower moved briskly I calculated I would have thirty seconds to look into the room, then hurry back to my open window. A second's delay and the Pastor would emerge from the tree cover and see me. I moved with reckless speed. Three sliding steps, one of which shot my foot over the edge; fight for balance; then with the glass at my back I twisted so awkwardly it hurt my spine, yet I ducked down to peer through a pane where the curtain had snagged. Growing louder, the sound of approaching hoof beats. Water beaded the glass. A gloom-filled interior. I wiped the pane. Hoof beats became an ominous rumble. I pressed my eye to the window to witness absolute horror.

Inside. A bare room. Devoid of rugs. Stark walls. Then – in the centre – a chair. But what an extraordinary chair! A chair like a throne. Stoutly built from dark timber. Gigantic iron bolts secured the chair's feet to the boards. Dangling from the ends of the arms were stout leather belts with evilly glittering buckles. Similar belts were fixed to the chair legs. Yes, a throne of sorts. Just to see the terrible thing made my blood run cold. Its black woodwork oozed menace; those leather straps spoke blatantly of restraint, of torture, of pain so unendurable the chair's occupant would fling themselves from the seat if they could escape its clutches. Dear God in heaven. Who is secured there? What cruelty is inflicted upon them?

Hoof beats, louder, *louder* . . . I hadn't counted the seconds. Any moment now the Pastor would drive his carriage into plain view. Gasping with pain from my ungainly crouch, I straightened. Trees heaved like the waves of a dark green ocean. Any moment the man – the owner of the terrible chair – would burst from beneath the branches. Now I couldn't afford the time to shuffle with my back to the wall. If I was seen or fell the outcome would be all the same to me. I turned, so I moved like a tightrope performer. Holding my breath, forcing my balance to remain true, I walked forward with my left hip brushing the wall. The nature of the hoof beats changed as the muffled thump gave way to a sharper clip-clop as the carriage emerged from beneath leafy boughs. The open window appeared in front of me. My walk became a run on the treacherous ledge. Then the open window devoured me as I dived through its frame and into the enveloping curtain.

19th July. Morning. Last night the rain didn't stop. Pastor Hux served supper at nine o' clock. He explained he'd trained as a ship's surgeon, although his weak stomach denied him a career at sea. He added in a jocular way that his experience with the surgeon's scalpel came in useful when carving cold mutton. With that, a jar of curried pickle, which was a bright dandelion yellow. The condiment tingled my tongue so much it made my eyes stream. The Pastor quickly handed me a glass of cold water to quench its fire.

All in all I was composed. Yet, just an hour before, I'd tumbled back through the landing window as the Pastor's carriage emerged from the trees. I held my breath when he greeted me twenty minutes later. I was convinced he'd noticed me. But he made no mention of it, so, to my relief, I believe he did not see my ungainly entry into the house after all. My back still ached. A bruise the size of a hand bloomed on my shoulder where it struck the frame. Somewhere along the way I'd scraped the side of my hand, too. However, I'd changed my clothes, dried my hair, and now we made small talk about the weather.

'I've never known a summer like it, Nidabi. We've had more rain than sun.'

'This house is big enough to be a world in itself. I hardly notice the rain.'

'Only much too big for just one man. I wish I could fill it with children.'

'Perhaps you will one day.'

'My life is God's, Nidabi. For me to devote it to one family would be wrong. More bread?'

'Yes, please.'

'Take what you need. Don't wait to be asked. My . . . what have you done to your hand?'

My mind whirled as I scrambled for an answer.

'It's been bleeding, Nidabi.'

'My dressing table drawer was jammed. I caught it against the chair when I pulled it free.' Why did I have to use the word 'chair'? I'm sure I gave an unusual weight to the word. It's because the moment I invented the story about hurting my hand I pictured the chair in the north wing. That great timber throne. Its monstrous proportions. Its threat of torture. Those ugly leather straps. I visualized a possible occupant of the chair. In the same moment I saw myself a prisoner of its forbidding timber structure. I imagined agony; the implements of pain ripping my flesh.

'Are you all right?'

'Pardon?' My mind had flown to the locked room.

'If you wish, I can replace the chair?'

He knows I've seen the torture chamber. My eyes fixed on him. 'The chair?'

'Yes, the one you hurt your hand on.'

Relief came in a gush. 'It's fine, thank you, Pastor. I was merely clumsy.'

'How've you spent your day?'

'Reading.'

'Oh?'

He doesn't believe me! I plucked a name at random. 'Laing.'

'Ah, *A Modern Zoroastrian.*'

'Yes. I was fascinated by his explanations of the mind. That it is something like a complex engine that runs on the fuel of experiences in our formative years, rather than breeding.'

'Indeed,' he said, 'take an infant child from deepest Sumatra, teach him English, educate him at Eton: he will be the intellectual match for any London barrister.'

The chair . . . I endeavoured to expunge all memory of the grim chair in its forbidden chamber. Instead, my tongue ran faster in the hope he wouldn't notice my nervousness. 'I wish to read more about atomic theory, too,' I told him. 'Every object in the world is composed of tiny particles that are bound together. This plate. The jug. Our table. Your . . .' I found myself wanting – *needing* – to say chair. Oh, the constitution of the mind, indeed. Whatever you wish to remain secret you find yourself blurting clues. *Chair, chair!* Perversely, I wanted to shout the word. With an effort I continued speaking, 'Your pocket watch. Even your body. All atoms. Individual specks of matter held together by an invisible power.'

'That's why I found your company unique. Your passions

lie beyond dresses and procreation. You desire to unravel the secrets of the universe. The way you have educated yourself is nothing less than miraculous. A formidable intelligence is at your fingertips, Nidabi. Use it wisely.'

'Do people think that it is wrong for a woman to be intelligent?'

'Wrong?' He smiled, yet his eyes held a sadness I knew so well. 'No, not wrong. Your intelligence will be an inspiration to others. By the way, today I had some business affairs to attend to. As I drove back through the gates . . .'

My stomach muscles clutched. *He's seen me. Clinging like a moth to the wall.*

'. . . I suddenly remembered where I'd heard your name before. Or at least a variation of it. Nidaba.' He poured a glass of water. 'Nidaba was the Sumerian goddess of wisdom. Nidaba? Nidabi? They couldn't be much closer, could they?'

'I don't know who named me, Pastor.'

'You never knew your parents?'

'No.'

'Or birthplace?'

I shook my head.

He gripped the glass so hard his fingers turned white. 'You know . . . Nidabi . . . lately my mind races forward . . . it draws astonishing conclusions from seemingly random facts. As if events, chance meetings, or an unexpected letter are really the components of a single mechanism – one that turns its wheel toward a climactic event. Today I received a letter from my friend the artist, Vincent van Gogh. You could almost smell the French countryside in it, Nidabi. Sunlight on wildflowers. The vineyards.' His eyes were points of light, shining at me. 'He mentioned meeting a dark-skinned girl. For a moment I thought he was describing you. Dark eyes, dark hair. Unalloyed beauty. Vincent and I haven't corresponded for months. Then out of the blue a letter?' He tried to unravel the mystery. 'Perhaps there is some other hand in all this.' His eyes no longer looked outward, but instead roved over some inner landscape of the heart, searching for signs of a miracle. At last he blinked as if waking. 'I'll bid you goodnight, Nidabi. I'm going to work for some time yet. Don't be alarmed if you hear any noise.'

{'To sacrifice every personal desire.' Pastor Hux, 1888}

On meeting a stranger there are, it has always seemed to me, two distinct reactions revealed by the individual's facial expression. One, you perceive cool diffidence, or, two, the warming smile of potential friendship. My first encounter with Nidabi produced a unique third reaction. Nidabi beamed at me with a warmth that also mingled astonishment. As if when she gazed on my face she recognized some quality that rendered her amazed. A quality, moreover, that instilled within her soul an ineffable delight. I confess there are times I invent reasons to attract her attention, just so I can reassure myself that I haven't imagined that smiling astonishment, which so lifts my spirit. It is an expression of total faith in my power to perform wondrous acts. Soon I will begin that work. Together we will transform the world.

Ty's Book

23rd July. How can I do this? How can I keep this pencil moving? How do I stop my arms trembling? How do I shut out the sound of thunder? Or ignore the pain in my body? What can I do to quell this fear?

Today. A poisonous day. Until this morning my life had turned for the better. The Night Woman agreed to keep my brother and sister for twenty francs a week. As from Monday I have a room in the house where I work. The brothel-keeper is a kind man. He insists I must not sleep in the Night Café when there is a spare bed now Louise has left Arles to be married. He also has me eat supper with his family before I start work in the evening.

Only today . . . *today!* Hell burned on earth. It made us demons. It drove us to commit evil. From this monstrous day no action will be restrained by morality.

In the past week I've spoken to Vincent, the artist, several times. Once he was sitting inside the doorway of his house on Place Lamartine. The sunlight made his red hair shine like polished copper.

'Good morning, Ty,' he said. 'I'm writing to my brother. I'm writing about you.' He smiled. 'Don't worry. I am writing about how beautiful you are. Skin with coffee tints. Black hair that shines. Chestnut eyes. Let me note what you're wearing.' Glancing from me to the notepad, which he rested on his lap, he made swift strokes with a pencil. 'Good Arlesian dress to the ankles. Blue material with orange spots. Blouse with blue and orange vertical stripes. Red ribbon in your hair.'

'You've drawn me?'

'A sketch . . . it deserves to be better. Until it is worthy of you I shall refer to you in my letter as Mousme.'

When I had the opportunity, I followed this man to the fields as he carried his easel, paints and tools of his art. I moved furtively so he wouldn't see me. There, I'd secretly watch him as he painted the land. The canvases blazed yellow. Yellow corn, yellow sky, yellow sun. Yet in the midst of beautiful Provence countryside in that searing light there were dark secrets. I'd read about ancient times when the Romans put out the eyes of rebels then forced the blind men to harvest the grapes by touch alone. Even fissures in sun-baked earth appeared to mimic the hieroglyphs of a secret code that warned of horrors to come. 'Beware, Ty. Grave dangers are coming your way . . .'

Today, I took candied fruit to George and Brionne at the Night Woman's house. They are reasonably content there but want to live with me again. There is a tenement that has vacant rooms with pleasant views over the river. I am saving eight francs a day for the rent, which will be payable in advance. After visiting the children I intended to come back here to sleep as it would be a busy night. The barracks had won additional leave for their part in a musketry competition. However, I saw Vincent stride out of town on the road to Tarascon. I tried to talk myself out of following him. He'd be embarrassed if he knew I watched him paint, but I found the temptation overwhelming. Part of me wondered if I had become like the alcoholics who go straight from their beds to drink brandy until they're confident they can face the world. Nevertheless, I yielded to my compulsion. I mirrored his pace as he left the houses behind to follow a lane through the cornfields, yet I kept under cover. Whenever he paused to light his pipe I ducked down behind a bush. See? That's how a thief behaves. There I was, perfidious spirit, to rob Vincent van Gogh of his privacy.

The straw hat shaded his face from a sun that beat down with an indefatigable strength. Often he walked with his head to one side as if he listened to sounds from the earth. As if something buried long ago murmured secret things. Rocks thrust out of the cornfields like grey fists. In deep gullies thorn bushes grew in wild profusion. Their millions of tangled limbs could have concealed a whole army of demons. It was as if we had passed through a portal into a supernatural realm. Here, there were no houses. Behind me, Arles rested blurrily beneath a haze of blue from countless cooking fires – suddenly it had become so remote. When Vincent reached a break in a hedge he stepped through it to set up his easel. I could see his subject would be the tall domes of haystacks that stood in the field. The nearest stack played host to a pair of noisy crows. After setting up the easel, then laying out the paints on a small folding table, he hurried back to the hedge where he dropped to his knees. He reached down into the vegetation. I watched as he returned with his straw hat gushing with water. He flipped the hat round on to his head so the water poured down his face, cooling it, a respite from the heat of summer. That heat drew from the soil a rich aroma that made me think of it as a living beast, hot after a night of rutting.

So, hidden by long grasses, I watched Vincent work another bare canvas up into a picture. He built layer on layer of pale yellow, then rendered the haystacks in shades of orange with flecks of gold. Even the cypress tree he painted in the background dripped with what appeared to be yellow stars. When he worked he moved like a musician playing a violin rather than a painter – as if he heard a primal melody. When the paint dried on the brush he moistened it with his tongue, so presently his lips turned golden. Feverishly, he layered more colour on to the canvas, much of it squeezed directly from those silver tubes. Movements that had been smoothly graceful became rapid – jerky – as if reacting to physical pain. Like the canvas had been transformed into a furnace that burnt him every time he got close. But like a moth to a flame he was drawn back again to sear his flesh. He muttered to himself –

threw down the brush. The next moment Vincent flung off the
hat so he could rake his fingers through his hair. Passion
surged inside of him. He turned on his heel as if to run away,
then dropped flat on to the ground. When he didn't move –
and it seemed never would again – I found myself flying from
where I'd hidden in the long grass. I was convinced he'd
suffered a fatal seizure. He lay on his back. His eyes were
open – staring into the blinding heart of the sun. For a moment
I tugged at his jacket while shouting at Vincent to wake. But
he lay there – so much like the corpse of my father when I
found him lying on the kitchen floor. Even so, there was a
conviction I shouldn't let him slip away. I vowed to fight for
him. It all became a blur but I recall snatching his hat from
the ground, running to the spring beneath the bushes, then
hurrying back with it, water jetting through the woven straw.
Hardly any liquid remained in the hat. Nevertheless, I poured
a trickle on his face. Then I did it all over again. Twice, three
times. Four? *Ten!* I don't know. When I lined the hat with my
handkerchief it held more. Now I could pour a torrent of cool
spring water across that broad, sunburnt forehead. This time
his body convulsed. A gasp erupted from his lips. Then he
sagged back, his eyes closed. Even though he was now
breathing I had to somehow get him out of the sun. I shouted
to wake him. When that failed I tugged his arm, then struggled to roll him over like a barrel toward the shade. Desperation
made my nerves jangle. For the next ten minutes I fought to
move him. However, despite the man being undernourished I
found it impossible to budge him more than a few centimetres.
Now the sun would be his murderer. What a wild, desperate
creature I must have looked, trying to roll him toward the
shade. And all the time the conviction grew that shortly Vincent
van Gogh would need an undertaker rather than a doctor.

'Bloody hell! What's going on here?'

I twisted to see a powerfully built man of around forty years
of age in a wicker cart. A brown pony grunted between its
shafts.

'He collapsed all of a sudden,' I blurted. 'I thought he was
dead.'

'Blow me. There doesn't seem much life in him now.' Then
a thought occurred to the man. 'Hey, you're not robbing him,
are you?'

'No! I'm trying to help him.'

'Hey, I know who it is. It's the mad foreigner.'

'He's my friend. Please help me move him out of the sun.'

'Ah? Friend?' He pulled a cigar from behind his ear, then sniffed it. 'You'll be one of the women from the brothel, then? I heard he mixes with your sort.'

'Listen to me. You've got to help him.'

'Help him? Not on your bloody life. What I will do is report this to the mayor. The pair of you deserve to be on a charge. Decent women use this road. Last thing they want is to come upon you two. A lunatic and a whore.'

'Please.' I softened my voice. 'My friend will die if he stays in this heat. Please help me move him.'

He gripped the cigar between yellow teeth. 'What's in it for me?'

'I have six francs. You can have that.'

'Ha! I've got more cash than that stuck in the filth in the back of my cart!' He clicked his tongue. 'No, I'll report this to the mayor.'

'Please. You can have anything you want!'

'How old are you?'

'Twenty years.'

'For a twenty-year-old brothel cat you've kept your looks – not many of your sort do. Too much brandy, too little sleep, too much of the other.' He gestured for me to approach. When I was ten paces from the cart I stopped. The stench from it was incredible. Through holes in the wicker sides I saw that the man sat on the body of a hefty sow. More dead swine covered the cart's boards, while piglets that were green with decay were heaped at the back. This man was the field monger. He collected beasts that died of disease from the farms. These he'd take home to boil for their fat, which he'd sell to the soap-makers. Now this conveyor of death appraised me.

'All right.' The field monger climbed off the dead sow, then jumped to the ground. 'We've got a deal.' He grinned. 'No, girl. Put your money away. That doesn't interest me.'

He stomped through the gap in the hedge. Grimacing, as if he'd got close to something foul, he glanced from the painting on the easel to Vincent lying unconscious on the ground. From his expression you could tell that he was afraid some contagion would leap on to his unprotected fingers if he touched

the artist's bare skin. Instead, the man picked up each leg
by the ankle then dragged him roughly to the bushes. Once
he was satisfied Vincent was fully in shadow he dropped the
legs.

'There he is,' the field monger announced. 'Like Sleeping
Beauty. Now.' He eyed my figure. 'We've got a deal.'

'Yes, sir.'

The man licked his lips. 'Lift your skirts.' He made a twirling
motion with his finger that meant turn round. 'That's the way.'
He chuckled. 'Time for an honest workman to collect his
wages.'

There's a brothel-keeper to make sure men don't treat the
women harshly. Here there was no kindly guardian. The field
monger, who ripped apart dead beasts for a living, had the
opportunity to hurt me. It was his pleasure to act in a way
that'd be forbidden in the house where I work.

When he'd finished he buttoned himself saying, 'Don't shed
any more tears, little blossom. Women of your sort heal
overnight.' Whistling, he returned to the cart to resume his
seat on the corpse of the sow. The pony shook its head, restless after its wait. 'Oh, by the way, little blossom. I'm going
to report you and the bloody madman. You're not fit to be
loose amongst decent folk.'

Though it hurt to move my legs I ran forward. 'Monsieur!
You promised!'

'You'll find a promise to a whore isn't contractually binding.'
He laughed. 'Get yourself home, y' bugger, before I kick your
backside.'

'You won't tell the mayor. He'll have us arrested.'

'Why the hell should I care about that? Now, get out of my
sight!'

'If you tell, be warned, you'll suffer the consequences.'

'Consequences? Ha!'

'If I'm arrested the officers will question me.'

'They won't believe a whore's ravings.'

'That's why I'll say nothing. I'll pretend to be terrified of
you. My words won't condemn you, but the fear in my eyes
will.'

His dull eyes narrowed as he began to understand. 'Just
you—'

'And the mayor has the biggest dairy herd for miles. He

won't sell his dead animals to you because he'll lose votes if he's seen trading with a woman-beater.'

The field monger flushed crimson. 'You're the one I've heard about. They say you've got more brains than half the town put together.'

'And I've outwitted you.' The words sped from my lips. 'That's why you won't have me arrested. If you do, you'll be ruined.'

'So you have got brains. But they won't do you any good. Intelligence is no better than witchcraft for your sort. It'll murder you in the end!'

Then a revelation. 'Monsieur, I know the truth.'

'Know what?' His stupid eyes darted like a trap was closing in on him.

'You're frightened.'

'I'm not!' he barked.

'You are. I've worked it all out. You're frightened of me.'

'*Never.*'

'You're scared that I'll devise a way to make everyone in Arles hate you.'

His expression of anger was replaced by one of horror. 'No. You can do nothing to me.'

'I can. I only have to use this.' I touched my temple. 'I can plant ideas in people's heads about you. A whisper here; a suggestion there.'

'You witch . . . you blasted witch!' Fear gripped him now. Even so, he wasn't done yet. 'You've got your way. I won't report *you*. No! I'm going to write a letter to the mayor about your mad friend there. I'll make something up about him harassing me. The authorities will run him out of town!'

An animal sound ripped from my throat. Before I knew it I was hurling stones at him.

'Hey, stop that, you bloody – ah!'

A dried lump of dirt I pitched burst against the cart to spatter grit into his eyes.

I howled like a demon. 'If you tell, you'll regret it!'

As he wiped his eyes he bellowed, 'All right. You've asked for it!'

The field monger's a big man. Once he'd clambered down from the cart he could kill me. No one was here in the fields. I glanced back at Vincent. He was still unconscious. There was no one to help me. I saw the man reach back into the cart, pull aside mouldering piglets, then return with a heavy length of chain. Once more in a white heat of unthinking – unplanned! – action I scooped up a flint the size of a hen's egg. This I hurled as hard as I could. It struck his head with a cracking sound. He roared a curse. From a gash in his forehead blood streamed down his face. Anger rather than pain motivated him now. He bellowed he'd smash my bones with the chain. By this time, however, he held the links in one hand while pressing the other to his wounded forehead. The reins had slipped to dangle on the ground. With ferocity bursting like lightning inside of me I struck the pony on its rump. Instantly, the animal lurched forward, letting out an enraged bray as it did so. Then it bolted.

The field monger flung aside the chain, so he could scramble to grab the fallen reins. He shouted for the pony to stop. Only the animal had become too enraged to hear its master's voice. Instead it dragged the cart, the field monger and the dead swine, at furious speed down the track toward Arles where it vanished in a pall of white dust.

I was convinced that the bully would return. But time passed without a sign of him. I couldn't even hear the rumble of the cart any more. All I could do now was tend to Vincent. At last he recovered enough to stand. His eyes were only part open. He couldn't lift his head properly; I'm sure he never even recognized me. Somehow, I gathered his belongings, strapped the canvas across my back, then, with him leaning against me, we walked back to his home.

Now the weather has broken. The sky is a sick-looking rust colour. Lightning flashes are an ominous, glaring brown. I've seen nothing like it before. It could be a thunderstorm raging at the bottom of a muddy river. The world as I've always known it has become hopelessly muddled. Today, it seemed as if the earth broke open to haemorrhage hell on to its surface. I fear the brute that I hurt hasn't finished with me yet. I wonder if Vincent is dying. And this thunder growls a promise that worse lies ahead.

{Lamplands, London, 23rd July, 1888}

My dear Vincent,
    I confess: your letter made me offer a cry of hallelujah! There's scarcely a day that passes when I

*don't wonder about how you fare in southern France
after the turbulent hell of Paris. Are you in good health?
Have the sunlit vistas of Provence engendered change
in your painting? But this geographical divide between
us? There's many a time I wish we could talk like we
did in the old days when you lived in London. Those
walks that lasted a whole night from the chapel to
Westminster Abbey! We were closer than brothers. We
were two men with but a single heart and mind. We
talked endlessly how we should perform good deeds
on earth. I tell you, our thoughts beat to the same
rhythm.*

*Now again: Our lives resonate as one. I wrote to you
about Nidabi, an unfortunate girl, who had been nothing
more than a slave. I described her dusky skin, her hair
with its cobalt lights, her dark eyes, her exotic genesis
in a land beneath a different sun. Although which land?
That I've yet to determine, possibly India or Persia. She
pronounces her name Nid-ah-be. It appears a variation
of Nidaba, the ancient Sumerian goddess of wisdom.
Now yet another miracle. You write to me about Ty, who
serves one of the brothels in Arles. Your description of
her, together with the pencil sketch, remind me so much
of Nidabi, whose shining intelligence is a constant source
of delight.*

*Write soon about Ty. She is so fortunate to fall under
the protection of my one true friend, Vincent van Gogh.
Tell me your plans for her. How you intend to rescue her
from the damnable pit of whoredom. I know you of old.
You will expend every ounce of strength in saving her.
And say you will come to London, too, my friend.*

*Now here's my handshake, know that its grip is one
of true comradeship. And as we proclaimed so often in
parting: 'Deeds, not words!'.*

Yours,
Hux

Ty's Book

28th July. Death? Not yet. Please not yet. The refrain continued as we walked through the maze of alleyways. The sun had dropped toward the roofs but still held a fierce sting if one stepped out of the shade. Vincent fiercely clutched a leather satchel that contained his inks and paper. I saw his lips were grey. Dark crescents cradled his eyes. His voice had turned hoarse. Every so often he'd pause to cough. His collapse earlier in the week had frightened me so much the girl I share the room with tells me I cry in my sleep.

Vincent appeared short of breath. 'The tenement by the river. You're going to have it?'

'I should know by the end of the month.'

'It's money, then?'

'The landlord wants a month's rent in advance.'

'It is hygienic enough for you and George and Brionne?'

'It's spotless. And there's a fenced yard where the children can play, too. My little brother is mischievous but he'll be safe there.'

Perspiration formed above Vincent's red eyebrows. 'My brother, Theo, sent me cash today . . . I need to buy paint. But I can give you money for the rent.'

'No, monsieur.'

'It's not charity, Ty. It's one friend helping another.'

'Please don't press me to take the money. I nearly had enough but I was foolish to buy a new jacket. My fault for allowing vanity to rule my head.'

'I will give thirty francs to the children for their birthday.' A gauntness was etched on his face.

'Vincent, you don't know their birthdays.'

'I can only be early or late.'

'No.'

'My thirty francs will migrate to the pockets of an innkeeper.'

Vincent continued up the narrow street that had begun to thicken with men and women in evening clothes as they strolled to cafés.

I said, 'Although I am grateful for your generosity, you need materials for your work, and I know you owe ten francs for a new canvas.'

'That can wait.'

'And you should use some money to see a doctor.'

'A doctor?' Confusion clouded his face.

'You were ill earlier in the week.'

'Something I ate, Ty. A piece of mouldy cheese.' He licked his grey lips. 'But you? You were there, weren't you?' He searched his memory. 'You must have been to bring me home.' His voice rose. 'You followed me. Why? What do you want?' Suspicion made him narrow his eyes.

'I was interested. I love to watch you paint.'

'Oh, no, Ty. Never watch me work. Promise you'll never follow me again.'

I started to speak but an expression of loathing rolled over his face like a darkening cloud. 'Even my own family told me I look like a madman when I paint. Tics. Grimaces. Talking nonsense. I won't let you turn me into a freak show!' Pedestrians gave him a wide berth. Their eyes said it all.

I longed to reach out to steady him. To say something kind. Only he flinched away when I approached.

At last he took a deep breath. 'You've your work, Ty. Don't be late on my account.' He'd stopped in the middle of the narrow street with its crushing press of houses that suddenly seemed so claustrophobic. Now he resembled one of those olive trees he painted so often. One of the ancient sun-blasted ones that thrust out cruelly twisted limbs. The muscles of his neck stood out in hard ridges. A vein pulsed in his forehead.

Death? Not yet. Please not yet. The words haunt me. Passers-by stared at him. Some were frightened, some angry. One of them was the field monger. A scab crusted his forehead where it had been struck by my stone. He muttered, so only I would hear: 'I know where you work, you bloody whore. When I pay you a visit, just you wait and see what happens.' The thug bustled away.

A moment later that unnatural tension passed from the artist's body. His shoulders sagged. Exhaustion swept the light from his eyes. Instead of continuing to where his model waited, he limped back the way we'd come.

The church clock chimed seven. I was late for work after all.

{Angels in Moon Street, R. Middleton}

Tonight I ventured to the moon. There, I saw grey angels haunting its great windy wastes. They stole from yards that back on to the slaughterhouse. Always there is screaming in this cold, bleak world. Mostly it is the scream of dying swine beneath the axe of the slaughter men, who labour through the hours of darkness. Sometimes the screams are from humans in their own sties. Here, the cry of 'Murder!' is as regular as the Imam calling the faithful to prayer. This is Moon Street, its angels more dead than alive. Hollow-eyed apparitions. Female, yet they reek of man at his most bestial. Poor, broken angels that ooze from alleyways to smooth down rucked skirts, or tidy strands of loosened hair. Then they haunt Moon Street once more until the next fleeting tenant of their charms appears. All this while Queen Victoria sleeps in her fragrant palace. All this while the Archbishop dreams of his own breed of angel: illuminated trifles that glide on the light breeze of his imagination.

Yet this is an altogether more pungent reality. Moon Street juts like a malodorous pier from the sucking pit that is Whitechapel. Its factories and carcass boilers insult the atmosphere with their fumes. Warehouses loom above us, mournful as gravestones. Blood from slaughterhouses casts a red stain on the river. The workhouse is overladen with a cargo of despair; its mortuary seldom vacant. Always in this street there is talk of violence. They believe Death will visit them as it has never visited before.

After my visit to the 'Moon', as its denizens term it, with its grey, shuffling, angels, I take my leave. On my walk home I ponder London's secret. How can this poverty-drenched quarter coexist with the lofty mansions of Belgravia? How can Moon Street share the same fabric as wealthy Park Lane? After all, these roads are more than a mere assemblage of houses, London, herself, is more than a tangled skein of streets, and overhead heaven is more than a meeting place of individual stars. What is this secret that makes words into a book, Moon Street into a pit of deepest hell, houses into cities, and restless and immeasurable stars into a coherent and constant universe?

Ty's Book

29th July. Voices caught my attention as I bathed. A deep, melancholy baritone. The rising 'No, no, no,' of the brothel-keeper. I scrambled out of the bath to dry myself. The voices continued, so I opened the door a little to hear the drift of conversation coming upstairs. For a moment the voices were drowned by a clatter of soldiers hurrying back in time for midnight curfew. Then the voice came clearly.

'No, Monsieur Van Gogh. No!'

'You won't let me talk to her for one moment?'

'We have been busy tonight. I've given her time to bathe.'

'Will you permit me to wait?' Vincent's speech was hesitant. Often he found it difficult to talk to people. 'I will be good.'

'You sure you're not here to cause a scene?'

'If Ty doesn't want to see me I will understand.'

The brothel-keeper was still reluctant. 'We have men waiting.'

'Of course, I will leave if you wish, monsieur.'

'Maybe in the morning would be wisest. Everyone will have slept by then.'

I dragged a nightshirt over my wet back. I heard the door to the street opening accompanied by the brothel-keeper's reassuring tones that the next day would be best for everyone. Down the wooden steps I went three at a time.

'No! Wait!' I raced into the hall. 'I want to see Monsieur Van Gogh.'

'All right, Ty.' The man nodded. 'I'll be in my office if you need me. Monsieur Van Gogh. I hope you are feeling better in the morning.'

Vincent was grateful to be able to speak to me, but as so often with him the words wouldn't come at first. The brothel-keeper discreetly closed the door after motioning to three girls to return to the kitchen where they'd been drinking coffee.

He thrust out a bouquet of wild roses tied with a clean strip of silk. I noticed he'd taken care to remove the thorns. 'For you. I am a clumsy beast . . . clumsy red beast.' He ruffled his own red hair. His attempt at a smile couldn't break his expression of sadness. 'You helped me out of the goodness of your heart. Then I was angry with you.' He shrugged in a way that expressed his desire to say more but found words inadequate. 'I ate something bad. I shouldn't have complained . . . you know . . . dark moods sometimes.' He tapped his temple. 'They call it the black dog. The malady of artists.'

I thanked him for the flowers as I stood there dripping on to flagstones in my nightshirt. Vincent glanced into the shadowy corners of the hall as if a creature would dart out at him. There was still a nervousness that unsettled me.

'So, my apologies are tied with silk in your hand.' Vincent's laugh sounded like a cough.

The brothel-keeper showed his face. 'We have customers, Ty?'

'Thank you for allowing me into your house, monsieur.' Vincent touched his eyebrow in salute. 'I'm glad we're still friends, Ty. Good night.' With that he appeared to almost shrink through the door like a departing spirit as a gaggle of herdsmen bustled in, flushed with drink.

Nidabi's Journal

30th July. That night, rain. Raindrops tapped madly at the pane. The fox barked in the rose garden beneath my window. I woke to these sounds. They were enough to unsettle me. Darkness became a tangible weight. I could sense its suffocating pressure. Furniture became phantom shapes in my bedroom. At one point

I clutched the covers against my face because I was sure the door was slowly swinging open to reveal a pair of glinting, demon eyes.

After a while, I lit the small oil lamp on my bedside table. It cast scant light, but sufficient to offer comfort. Because once more I realized I'd dreamt about the locked north wing of the house, and that barren room with the monstrous timber chair. I dreamed a man with glaring eyes fastened my wrists to the chair by its leather straps. Maybe now the little parcel of flame in its glass cylinder would chase the nightmare away. I rearranged my pillows then lay back. Rain rose and fell in that hiss which is so redolent of respiration. Downstairs, the clock struck midnight. That's all I remember until I awoke again. *This is what I saw.* An apparition hung in the centre of the bedroom. Stark white. Alabaster skull framed by something darker than the shadows that crept across the walls. Blazing from the revenant's face, two red eyes, each centred with a fierce black pupil. The phantom's attention fixed on me. Its glare swept through my flesh with a searing intensity that locked me rigid with fear. Suddenly, it strode forward; a jerky, unnatural gait of something that had only regained the power of locomotion after years of entombment. It approached the foot of the bed, then leaned forward. With one claw it seized the bedclothes then began to drag them downward from my body. I rubbed my eyes in disbelief. Surely, that would be enough to dispel this nightmare.

My heart lurched. The apparition was still there. Only now it advanced toward me with its hands held out. Its eyes fixed on *my* eyes. In the light of the lamp I saw it clearly now. A wild mass of hair sprang from the she-ghost's head. Above the red eyes were the black arches of her eyebrows. Above those the skin had been disfigured by scars. Two vivid wounds bisected each other to form the sign of the cross on her forehead. Her lips were full, almost swollen. Looking downward, I saw she wore a white cotton nightdress that was mottled with patches as if she'd lain in a grave. Closer she came, her breath hissing.

The scream that had been growing in my throat shrivelled at the sight of this creature. All I could manage was to whisper, 'Please don't hurt me.'

'Mow . . . Mowz-zur.' The voice was guttural. An inhuman sound. 'R-razz-uh sss . . . see mow-zur.'

'I don't understand.'

She darted forward. Gripped my wrist with one hand, yanked it down to force it against my breast. She flung forward her other hand to press her fingers against my lips. They were so cold. The chill of the tomb. One-handed, she pressed me back to the bed as she touched my lips with fingers tipped with ruinous fingernails.

'R-razz s-see yoh mowz-zur.' The effort to make me understand produced a ferocious scowl on her face. 'R-razz re-eed lay-dee mowzzur.'

Perspiration trickled down my face. What was this thing? Why would an intruder break into a house wearing nothing but a nightdress?

She made a guttural croak. 'Kkk-x. K-x.'

I shook my head. I'd never heard a foreign tongue spoken like this before.

She still held me down; however, she took her fingers away from my mouth so she could pat her chest. 'R-razz. Nem. You? Nem?' A thin finger pointed at me.

'Name?' I understood. 'You want to know my name?'

The woman gave an emphatic nod.

'Nidabi.'

'Uh?' She frowned. 'S-slow. Read . . . your . . . mowze.'

'Read my mouth?'

'Uh.' She nodded furiously. 'Talk z-slow-uh.'

I tugged my earlobe. 'Can you hear?'

She shook her head.

Despite her appearance my nerves began to calm somewhat. The stranger's air of violence was receding, so I mouthed. 'My . . . name . . . is . . . Nidabi.'

Again she looked puzzled. 'Nar-bee?'

'Nid-ah-bee.'

'Nid-ah-bee. Nidabi.' She nodded to the rhythm of the syllables. 'Nidabi.'

'Yes. You?'

'Row-zzuh.'

'Rose?'

The image of the monstrous chair in its locked room flashed through my mind. In it I saw this creature strapped – twisting, writhing, grimacing . . .

I asked, 'Do you live here?'

Again the guttural throat clearing. 'Ecks . . . ecks.'

'Are you saying Hux?'

A nod. 'Ecks m-make me stay.'

'He's forcing you?'

'Hmmm!' Rapid nods. 'Ss-see-yuh.' She released me so she could present her wrists. Across the bones the skin had rubbed away to reveal a raw, glistening pink. Yet again I pictured those brutal leather straps on the chair. Then she snatched my right hand, so she could use it to point at the window.

'N-Nidabi go home. Go 'for Ucks wake.'

'You're saying I should leave?'

A nod.

'Why?'

'Me Row-zuh.' She touched her eye. 'Looked out. I-yuh, see Ucks when he . . .' She made a clubbing action with her fist. 'When hit woman in thar s-snow. W-woman's dead. In grave. You under . . . stand?'

'Rose. You're saying that Pastor Hux killed a woman?'

'M-murd-duh.'

'I can't believe that Pastor Hux would hurt anyone. He's such a kind man.'

Rose showed me her bruises again before urgently stating, 'We clothe . . . Hmm! We from howz-uh. Go fast.'

'Rose. I can't just leave. What if you were mistaken about Pastor Hux? You said it was snowing. Maybe – ah, Rose . . . no . . . stop it, you're hurting me.'

Rose wrenched me bodily from the bed. Then she tried to drag the nightdress up over my shoulders. 'Nidabi . . . clothes on . . . boots.'

'No, stop it!'

'Pastor Ucks . . . murder us.'

'Rose! The Pastor won't harm us. He won't murder—' The collar of my nightdress twisted around my neck. I couldn't finish the sentence as Rose exerted her strength to tug the garment clear.

Then a voice cut across the room. 'Rose! Leave her!'

I could see nothing because of the material over my face. A moment later I was free and falling back on to the bed. Panting, I sat up to straighten my nightdress.

'Nidabi.' As the Pastor stood there in his dressing gown his face was ashen with shock. 'Please forgive me. I'm so sorry about this.'

Meanwhile, Rose stood with her head bowed down; her chin rested on her chest. Face sullen. Her arms hung limp by her sides.

Pastor Hux apologized again, then, 'Did she hurt you?'

'No, but she . . .'

'Yes?'

'Pastor, I couldn't understand what she said. But I could tell she was upset.'

Why did I lie? Why didn't I repeat Rose's accusation that the Pastor had committed murder?

'The poor child,' he murmured. 'She's quite deaf.'

I didn't intend to say anything more – certainly not repeat Rose's accusation – but one glance at those ghastly abrasions on her wrists made the words tumble out. 'She's been hurt. Who did that to her?'

'Poor Rose inflicted those injuries on herself. I have to restrain her.'

'What on earth for?'

'I was afraid she'd kill herself.'

'But you can't imprison her.'

'Nidabi, Rose isn't a prisoner.' He took a deep breath. 'I found her last year living in a derelict stable near the docks. She suffers a profound deafness and she's known only as Mitre Rose – the Mitre being the ale house where she drank. She earned money from the sailors in return for . . . well . . . She also consumed large quantities of opium. I brought her here to Lamplands to convalesce. Unfortunately, opiate possesses its victim like the very devil.'

'But she is free to go?'

'When she is well, Nidabi.'

'But you won't permit her to walk out now?'

'Nidabi. Her addiction is ferocious. Rose suffers from paralytic seizures. She's also in the grip of a fantasy that there are gentlemen wanting to kill her. When the craving for opium is at its strongest that's when I fear she will harm herself. I secure her in a chair for her own good. However, she's freed herself before in the past.'

'I see.' I gulped at the sight of the mournful figure known as Mitre Rose, her body corroded by narcotics. 'I'm sorry, Pastor. I didn't realize.'

'But it reveals you to be as kind as I've come to believe. It's only right that you should protect poor Rose. She has suffered dreadfully. See those scars? Here and here?' He mirrored the marks on his own forehead. 'After a mob of sailors had used her they cut the sign of the cross on her forehead.' He turned to her. 'Rose. Rose?' Gently, he waved to attract her attention. 'Rose. Time to sleep.'

She nodded. But instead of walking to the door she made straight for my bed.

'Ss-zleep here . . . Nidabi.'

'No, Rose. You must return to your own room.'

Violently, she shook her head. 'Here wi' Nidabi.' The voice was sullenly defiant. 'Here.' She tugged back the blankets.

'Rose, my dear. Come back to your room.'

'Ah – ah sleep here.'

She began to climb into bed. Pastor Hux reached out, putting a gentle hand on her shoulder. At his touch she let out a piercing cry, then turned on him. Ferocity transformed her face. Her red eyes bulged. One pupil shrank to a fierce black point; the other dilated hugely to fill the orbit of the eye. Her bare arms darted like striking snakes, first to scratch the Pastor's jaw, then grip his neck. He begged her to stop, to be calm, but a violent rage seized her. Rose pushed him back toward the wall. Her fingers turned bloodless white as she gripped his throat. He didn't strike back, but made gentle gestures with his splayed hands. However, I saw that the madness in her concentrated solely on ending his life. Rose's inhuman strength bore him effortlessly backward. His feet slid uselessly on the carpet as he tried to keep his balance. When his heels struck the raised hearth of the fireplace he tripped backward. There was no fire burning but it dashed the fire irons across the marble hearth. This clash of metal against stone roused me. I ran to try and pull Rose away from her benefactor. But it was like tugging at an enraged bull. I could feel her bones jutting through her tightly stretched skin, yet that demon strength forced the Pastor to the floor as she choked the life out of him.

You've got to do something. The words pulsed inside my skull. *Do something now or the man will die.* I was almost insane with panic. So, picking up the iron poker, I brought it down smartly across Rose's shoulder. For all the effect it had it might as well have been a feather. Beneath the woman I saw the Pastor's eyes roll up into his head; the tongue jutted between his teeth. *Do it, Nidabi! Hit her again!* The heavy iron poker clunked as it slammed against the woman's protruding bones. Although a grunt escaped her lips she didn't appear to notice the blow. Mitre Rose was locked inside the fatal fascination of crushing the man's windpipe. So I beat her back as if pounding a drum, perhaps dealing a dozen strokes with that sooty iron bar. She grunted at each fierce blow. But did she look up? No, her head remained down, her hair swishing in the Pastor's face as those red eyes of hers glared at the dying man.

If I strike the head? Aim a blow at her temple? The thought sickened me. I couldn't bring myself to bludgeon her skull. Instead, I screamed as I lashed at Rose's elbow. This time was different. Her head snapped so she stared up at the ceiling. Her wild hair fell back from her face as her mouth yawned an O of pure agony.

When she looked round for her attacker I could see every shred of sanity had vanished. Mad eyes rolled in their sockets. Nothing human remained in her expression. In an instant she'd forgotten the Pastor. Me now. That's who she wanted. The poker slid from my fingers as she advanced. A snarl rolled in her throat. I retreated until the bed struck the back of my legs. That's when she leapt at me. I turned, hoping somehow I could escape the room by scrambling across the bed then dashing for the door. Before I reached the other side of the mattress her hands found my hair. With a tug that must have separated fifty strands from my scalp she tried to drag me on to the floor. However, I managed to inch forward on my hands and knees. Her breath gusted into my neck. *Don't let her drag you back!* That was my only thought of self-preservation. I gripped the ironwork at the head of the bed, then held on. Even though I didn't look I knew she'd climbed on to the bed behind me so she could grip the collar of my nightdress. This she tugged with both hands. The front of the collar dug into my throat, choking me. All I could hear were her wild grunts of triumph. I managed to glance to my right where Pastor Hux still lay prone. With every ounce of strength I tried to call to him but the band of fabric dug so deep I could not breathe, never mind shout.

Then she shifted one hand from my collar to my hair, so she could rip at it, like a madman tearing grass from a field. This was too much. The pain in my head; the breaking sensation in my shoulders. In the face of such an onslaught I couldn't hold on any more, and let go. The sudden lack of resistance caused Rose to lose her balance. In the space of a second she'd released her grip on me, tumbled backward, then came a violent concussion that rocked the bed.

I closed my eyes tight expecting a murderous assault. The mattress, though, was still. The room, silent. Cautiously, I opened my eyes. There in the lamp light was Rose. She lay on her back with her arms straight out at either side of her. Straightaway, I saw that the back of her neck rested on the iron frame at the foot of the bed. Her throat was extended, the chin raised, eyes open.

I stared at her. So still, so very still. I couldn't believe it was the same ferocious, screaming, female whirlwind of just a few moments ago. After a while, I realized Pastor Hux had picked himself up from the floor. He moved toward the woman as she lay there.

'Oh, Rose,' he murmured. 'My poor Rose.' Lightly he stroked her face. Then something yielded inside of him. He dropped into a kneeling position at the foot of the bed. I can still hear the sound he made as he wept.

It took time to gather our composure. When we could speak our conversation went something like this:

He said: 'I'll run for a doctor.'

'Don't. Rose is dead.'

'Nidabi, understand this, there'll be an investigation.'

'You mean the police will come?'

'Yes.'

'But those bruises on her wrists and ankles?'

'I'll explain fully.'

'No, Pastor. They will claim we've murdered her.'

'You don't understand, Nidabi. The police will take my word.'

'No! *You* don't understand!'

'Nidabi—'

'The detectives will find her bruising. They'll see the injuries where I struck her.'

'You hit Rose?'

'Of course I hit her. She was trying to kill you!'

We stared at the corpse, bathed in a cold, grey light as dawn seeped through the pouring rain.

I spoke forcefully, 'No doctor. No police. We'll deal with this.'

'We can't. We have to inform the—'

'They will put us on a charge, Pastor. You're a gentleman so they won't hold you in jail. I shan't be so lucky.'

'Nidabi, I'll explain.' Defeat haunted his eyes.

'I'm a whore, remember. They won't spare me.'

'Oh, dear Lord, guide us.'

'Pastor, did anyone know that Mitre Rose was here at Lamplands?'

'No.'

'There. That's one of your prayers answered.'

'God, please bring me wisdom.'

'No power on earth can bring Rose back. We must tell no one about this.'

He directed that wounded gaze at me. 'What you're proposing is wrong.'

'Pastor, it is expedient. Listen. We will dispose of the body. We shan't put it in the river because that will appear as if her death is the result of a planned crime. We will dress her in day clothes and hide her in your carriage. Later, you'll drive to one of the slums. At the first opportunity we'll leave her body without us being seen.'

'Oh, Father, is there no dignity?'

'You did everything you could for Rose. Your duty is done.'

'If – if it really is for the best,' he stammered, 'we could drive in after midnight . . . when there is no one about.'

'No. A gentleman such as yourself at that time of night will attract attention. Make it dusk before the street lamps are lit. Illumination is at its poorest then.'

'Poor Rose.'

I saw he wavered, so I continued briskly. 'She'll be quickly found. Detectives will soon identify her as Mitre Rose, a prostitute and opium eater. They will conclude a man beat her to death because he was violent with drink.'

Hux pressed his hand to his mouth in grief. A cold clarity possessed me, however. While the Pastor mourned, I dressed

Rose in clothes she'd brought with her from the workhouse. Through an India rubber tube, which I inserted into her throat, I forced a mixture of brandy and morphia down her gullet. I carefully returned her meagre possessions to pockets hidden beneath her skirts – tea, soap, tobacco, strips of rag, and so on. As she'd recently bathed I mixed a little soot and garden dirt then rubbed the filth on to her knees and elbows. I worked more under her fingernails with a matchstick. Once the Pastor's domestics left at four we moved the body to the two-wheeler carriage. There, Rose could be hidden under the seat beneath a rug. At eight sharp we made the thirty-minute ride into the Eastern quarter of London. Rain fell in sheets that writhed across the rooftops. The river had become as black as tar. This could have been the outer fringes of Lucifer's underworld. A dark smear of hell invading England's green realm.

The Pastor no longer protested. He accepted the wisdom of my plan. Moreover, he did not demur when a narrow street between two windowless warehouses presented itself with a complete lack of people. A state of affairs that would last only a moment. Pastor Hux softly bid the horse to stop. We drew the dead body of Rose from beneath the seat. With the Pastor keeping watch, I took a moment to arrange the body on the ground. A pose that would match the aftermath of violent assault – legs bent awkwardly at the knees, arms flung out.

Finished, we returned to the carriage. I bade him to drive slowly away so as not to attract attention. I glanced back just a single time to see the forsaken figure forming a soft, dark mound on the pavement.

{London, 31st July, 1888}

TO THE COMMITTEE CHAIRMAN, CHAPEL OF ST JUDE, BLACKHEATH

Further to our recent letter we, the undersigned, wish to notify the committee of our growing concern over the activities of a member of our congregation, one Mr Posthumous Hux. We have learnt that Mr Hux, while having the appearance of a gentleman, is sharing his home with an undesirable. Clearly, it is a matter for Mr Hux that he feels compelled to live in such an unsanitary manner, but his dubious proclivity, together with his excessive zeal for charitable works, will, if they become public knowledge reflect badly on the brethren of St Jude's. We beg, therefore, that a deputation be despatched to Mr Hux's residence to inform him that he is no longer welcome as a member of our congregation.

Ty's Book

31st July. Vincent van Gogh strode across the bridge. Early morning mist still floated on the river. Everything he needed he carried. An easel strapped across his shoulders like a rifle. A folding stool. A leather satchel full of paints, brushes, turpentine. Fresh canvases stretched across frames. These were tied by strings which he looped over his neck. He wore the straw hat dashed with a hundred paint splashes. That 'thousand league stare' of his was fixed on the horizon. Just when I told myself he wouldn't notice me he smiled.

'Vincent salutes you, dear Ty.' He touched his red eyebrow in salute. 'You're up early.'

'I've been to see my George and Brionne.'

'They must have been pleased to see their sister. Have you told them about their new home?'

'I daren't yet, just in case I don't have the rent money by the end of the week.'

'You'll do it. I believe in you.'

'Thank you.'

Vincent cocked his eye at me. 'Is there something wrong?'

'My brother isn't feeling well.'

'I'm sorry. Is there anything I can do?'

'He's coming down with a cold. I'm going for some medicine for his throat.'

'I've been teaching a doctor to sketch so he owes me a favour. He will see George.'

'Thank you, but it's nothing but a chill. Half the children in town are sneezing.'

'If it gets worse, let me know. I'll have the doctor there.'

I smiled. 'I will.'

'And without delay. I might be a cracked pot of a man but I can still run like the wind to the doctor's house.'

'If anything, he's complaining he can't play in the pond today. He loves to catch newts. He plans to count every single creature there but I don't think he understands that he might be catching the same one two or three times.'

He gave a sharp nod. 'Then the pond will have the greatest newt population in the Republic. Good morning.' He raised his hat then continued walking.

For such a long time my life had a simple routine. Work. Look after my brother and sister. Now that rhythm had acquired complicated beats. I found I thought about Vincent most of the time. His poor state of health worried me more than I could say.

Already men in their blue workmen's clothes thronged the streets. Haze from the first kitchen fires of the day seeped into the sky above the town. With the scent of smoke drifted odours of freshly baked bread. At the apothecary I paused to count my money. In the window stood big glass jars full of coloured liquids – violet, blue, and yellow. Suspended in a bottle of brandy was a two-headed viper. When I went inside, the clerk was surprised that I didn't ask for my usual tonic. Instead, I bought a linctus that he assured me would soothe the rawest of throats. Of course, it was more expensive than the other brands but George could barely speak; it even hurt him to cough. Once I'd paid for the medicine I hurried back through the streets. As I weaved between two carts, a hand circled my wrist with crushing force.

'Bloody hell. It's the little brothel cat.'

I screwed my eyes against the glare of the sun as I looked up to see who'd seized me.

'You and me have got some outstanding business to settle. Have ya seen what you did to my bloody head?'

'Please. Let go of me.' I recognized the voice of the field monger.

'You can go when you compensate me for assault.' He was a rough man and shook me like a rag doll. 'What can you give me? Eh?'

Men nearby winked at the man. They weren't going to take my side in this.

'How much money have you got?'

'I've had to buy medicine for my brother. Please, monsieur. Don't hurt me.'

'Hell, you should have thought of that when you were chucking rocks.'

I kept a firm grip on the blue medicine bottle as I tried to wriggle from him. With his open hand he slapped the side of my head.

'I've had a belly full of you,' he snapped. 'Here, give me that.'

He tore the medicine bottle from my hand.

'Please. Give that back to me, monsieur. My brother needs it.'

'I'll tell you what he needs. He needs putting in a sack with you, then both of you want chucking in the river.'

'I really do need the medicine.'

'Oh.' His heavy face broke into a grin. 'So this stuff is important to you?'

'Yes, monsieur. It is.'

'Good. I wanted to hear that.' He smashed the bottle against the cart. 'Now clear off before I thrash the life out of you.'

There's no changing this. No repairing the bottle. No saving its splashed contents. Even though I knew this I still cried over its loss. Replacing it took a full hour. I ran to the brothel-keeper, who took care of my savings. Then I bought more medicine before hurrying to the Night Woman's house.

She answered the door at my second knock. The old woman stared at the blue bottle in my hand. 'You've wasted your money buying that,' she said with such a grim expression my blood turned cold. 'I'm so sorry, my dear. I'm never mistaken in these things.'

I stared at her.

'Come in, Ty. You must nurse George for as long as he needs you.'

In the yard children laughed as they played happily in the sunshine. All I could do was follow the woman into the dark interior of the house.

Nidabi's Journal

Sunday 1st August. Morning. Pastor Hux left early to visit the sick. Since the death of Mitre Rose he has become yet more melancholy. Sadness reaches over him like a dark shadow. I tell him that he isn't to blame for the way she died. However, he won't discuss it. What's more, I believe he's convinced himself that Rose's attack on him, and her tragic passing, never really happened. This denial of reality troubles me. If he puts it out of his mind now I'm sure the memory will revisit him one day soon in a devastating manner. So, with the Pastor refusing to even allude to Rose, he continues his work with the dispossessed in the slums. Meanwhile, the rings under his eyes grow darker.

This morning, gloom – all gloom; rain clouds lumber overhead. Church bells peal from neighbouring parishes. Those descending melodies of tolling bells are the saddest of songs. The churches appear to call out a question to one another, and each answers with its own dolorous tale. When the Colonel possessed me I was convinced that somehow the bells talked about me. For a time it filled me with despair. *Did you hear what Nidabi did? Did you hear what she did last night? She took the seed of twenty men. That's what Nidabi did . . .*

Today those strange fancies returned. I couldn't help but sit here in my bedroom alone, and summon to mind the phantom of Mitre Rose. How her red eyes burned out of the darkness. How, later, we flung her dead body into the filthy gutter. So how could I stop myself imagining that the bells, cleaving the morning gloom, were talking to each other again after all these years? *Did you hear what Nidabi did? She took the life of a poor, lost woman. She discarded her body in the rain. That's what cruel Nidabi did.*

* * *

Sunday: afternoon. Strange thoughts. Haunted by images of death. I found myself tied to them. For hours I morbidly stared at the iron bed frame that broke Rose's neck. The smell of death clung to the air; it seemed to stain my hands. When I went to the window I could have sworn an open coffin lay in the long grass. On looking again I recognized it as an old water trough. More than once I imagined I saw a dead face in the shadow beneath the bed, all stark and white, and staring at me with rage-filled eyes. Coffins, phantoms, skulls, lonely cemeteries, a demon hand reaching for my throat. I could fill a hundred pages with such macabre thoughts. But a pain darted through my stomach. My month was up. I'd not set aside anything in readiness so decided to go to the laundry room where I could prepare some rag in the usual manner. Quickly, I headed downstairs through the house. A grave silence pervaded that mausoleum of a building. A silence broken only by the ominous tick of the grandfather clock in the hall. With it being Sunday the domestic staff would be at their homes, so I was here alone; I, Nidabi, mistress of this desolate place.

A door behind the staircase descended to a stone-flagged passageway that led to the kitchen and so on. A musty smell lingered, as these back rooms hadn't been aired since yesterday. A newspaper had been left next to the coat stand. I told myself to walk straight by. But I couldn't ignore its headline: *DEAF-MUTE BRUTALLY MURDERED.* A drawing of Rose lying dead in the street. Beside that grim etching a black obelisk of newsprint. It seemed to stand vertical from the paper. Nothing less than a gravestone carved from monstrous words: *bones fractured, flesh bruised . . . defenceless woman slaughtered.* If I'd believed the death would go unreported I'd deluded myself as badly as Pastor Hux.

'Throw the paper away,' I told myself. 'Burn it.' Only I had to read it all, didn't I? Of the poor broken corpse being discovered by an errand boy. Pressmen described every stitch of her clothing. It said though she wasn't a respectable woman all of London had been gripped by terror, people declared they were afraid to go out alone at night. My blood ran scalding hot in my veins. In my mind's eye, I could see police constables in their dark uniforms pounding on the doors. After that, jail cells, stern magistrates, the gallows . . . Even as I clutched at the newspaper I heard a clatter from the kitchen. *Nidabi, they're here. The police will take you away!*

Despite an instinct to flee I found myself racing toward the kitchen, my skirts flying. If the police were there I'd tell them Rose's death was my doing, that Pastor Hux was innocent. At that moment the single thought shining like a brilliant star was to protect the man who had saved me. I shouldered the door open, so it crashed back against the cupboards.

Police. I expected police. A blue-black swarm of them, hungry for the arrest. Instead, there were two women. The taller of the women was young, very pretty, and with the most utterly beautiful tresses of blonde that tumbled to her waist. The other, a hollow-eyed creature of perhaps forty years, had wispy hair streaked with white. Both stopped dead. Both stared at me in surprise. Images of constables vanished when I saw what the women were doing. Each had a cotton pillowcase into which they'd been stuffing the Pastor's things. The tall girl froze in the act of slipping a pewter cup into the pillowcase.

'*Thieves!*' My voice came in a roar of fury. 'Put everything back!'

'We were here first,' snapped the gaunt woman. 'Find your own stuff.'

The tall, pretty one looked to her friend for reassurance.

The gaunt woman nodded at the pewter cup in the girl's hand. 'Take it.'

'No!' I advanced on them. 'Give me that.'

'Not on your life, girl.' The gaunt woman slipped a honey jar into her pillowcase. 'You keep a grip on that pewter, Dolly. There's money in that, girl.'

The one called Dolly obeyed. Ascribe it to the maelstrom of the last three days; ascribe it to the belly pain tangled up with the tumult of emotion it brings, but as furious a passion as I've ever known visited me. I lunged at the tall one to grab that beautiful long hair in both hands. She gave such a shriek. Oh, mercy. It hurt her so much her face turned as red as a beet.

'Thief! Thief!' I shouted, even though no one else could hear. 'Thief!'

'G'on, Dolly! You're bigger than the bitch. Push her down.'

With this command the gaunt woman swung her bag at me.
She was so weak, however, that its weight pulled her off
balance. She fell back across the table. Immediately she put
her hand on to her side, while her eyes scrunched tight.

'Lord sakes, Dolly,' she croaked. 'Knock her out before she
kills us all.'

Dolly managed to cuff my head. Only I had hold of her
hair, so I could pull her head forwards, then downward, until
it was almost level with my knees.

'Oh . . .' The girl was frightened now. 'Grace. Stop her,
please stop her!'

'I won't have you stealing,' I yelled. 'The Pastor's a good
man! He doesn't deserve to be robbed.'

The older woman straightened herself; although pain
distorted her worn features. 'Child, we're not stealing.'

'Why did you put those things into the bags, then?'

'Because he . . . oh, will you stop ripping out Dolly's hair?
You're murdering the poor girl!'

'Not yet. I'll not let go until the pair of you are out of the
house.'

'Listen to me, child.' The gaunt one put down her bag.
'Pastor Hux doesn't mind us girls helping ourselves to food
every now and again. Especially if we're too sick to work.'

'Too sick to work?'

'You know what I mean. You're one of us, I can tell. We
all have that special look, don't we? Oh, for pity's sake: stop
yanking poor Dolly's hair.'

This time I did let go. Torn strands of yellow clung to my
fingers as Dolly sat down on a chair to sob in a heartbroken
way.

'There, there, Dolly.' The woman spoke softly. 'Don't take
on so. We just gave the girl a fright, that's all. We're all friends
now.'

My glare was as *unfriendly* as I could possibly muster.

'You're one of his new girls, aren't you?'

'I am the guest of Pastor Hux.' There was frost in my voice.
'He is upstairs in his study.'

'No, he ain't.' This time it was Dolly who spoke between
sobs. 'That animal and trap are gone from the stable.'

'He's up our way, visiting the poor devils who've got it
bad.' The gaunt woman gave me an examining stare. 'You're

a dark beauty, aren't you? A regular Indian princess. What's your name?'

'Nidabi.'

'Nidabi? That's a new one on me.' She pulled out a stool to sit beside Dolly. 'Good Lord, I reckon we're both ripe for a mug of tea.' She glanced toward the kettle where it sat on the range blowing steam from its spout. 'This lady here is Dolly . . . Welsh Dolly.'

'I'm not Welsh. I'm Scottish.' Her voice, though soft, held no hint of Scotland.

'Well, wherever you're from, you're Dolly West. I'm Grace Tarant.'

Dolly appeared more herself now. With a terse, 'You really did hurt my head, you know,' she stood up with the announcement she'd mash the tea.

'So, my dear,' Grace said in a friendly fashion. 'You'll know by now what the Pastor expects from his girls?'

'He never laid a finger on me.'

'He never will, either.'

'Why?'

Dolly answered fast. 'He's an angel in human form, of course.'

'Yes, Dolly,' Grace agreed, a little too knowingly. 'Close as one of the Lord's angels as you'll ever find anyway.'

I asked, 'What do you mean exactly: expects from his girls?'

'For us to be saved from our old way of life.' Grace read the expression on my face. 'How long have you lived here, Nidabi?'

'Long enough to respect the Pastor's house.'

'You've not had chance to speak to one of us girls that come here?'

'You're the first I've seen.'

'Listen, I'll explain a few things.'

'You better not say anything bad about the Pastor.'

'Sit down, dear. That's better. I won't bite, trust me, child.'

I did sit. What's more, I realized I'd dropped the defensive pose. When I glanced at Dolly putting milk in the tea, I realized that she had a friendly face though her eyes were still teary from my hair-pulling. Grace wore the face of a consumptive that made it a bit forbidding, but her eyes weren't at all unfriendly.

'Listen. It's like this,' Grace began, 'for the past few years Pastor Hux has done his ministry in the poorest places of London. He doesn't ask us to sing hymns, because he always says: deeds, not words, are the road to God. When us working girls are sick he gives us our doss money when he can. If we're in a really poorly way, or can't get taken in by the infirmary he sometimes brings us here. He provides a bed. Feeds us up. There's many he gives his cure to. You know? The opium smokers that are in danger of losing their wits for good.'

I thought about Mitre Rose's passion for opium and that monstrous chair. I pictured writhing women restrained by its leather belts. How they'd howl for hard drink or the opium pipe.

'Last year, the Pastor found me living outdoors. I'd got an awful swelling here.' Grace touched her side. 'The flesh had fallen off of my bones. The Pastor brought me back to rest me up, and fed me on good broth, but you want to know something special? He sold the carpets off his very floors so he could buy me medicine. Now I'm as good as new . . .' She smiled, pleased she could tell the tale.

'But the Pastor is rich. Why should he sell the rugs?'

'Oh, he doesn't have any money, child.'

'There's the house.'

'Not his.' Dolly poured more tea. 'Lamplands belonged to his uncle. Even though Pastor Hux can live here all his life it will never be his to sell.'

'That's right.' Grace nodded. 'It's . . . oh, I forget . . . it's a legal paper that the lawyers've done. The Pastor's next of kin, whoever they are, will have it when he's gone to his reward, then it'll pass to their kin until the whole thing falls down in ruin.'

'It's held in trust?' From the pair's blank expressions I realized they weren't familiar with the term. 'I thought the Pastor must be rich.'

'*Rich?* Nidabi, where are his servants? Look at these broken pots.'

'He's a man of God. He'll be frugal.'

'Frugal, maybe. Poor as a church mouse, definitely.'

Dolly added, 'He has an allowance paid to him every week, but it's not much.'

'Rumour has it that he'd have been a wealthy man if he joined the family business – they cast them big guns for battle-ships. Pastor Hux was having none of that. He despises killing. So his grandfather cut him off without a penny. It's only his uncle that provided for him.'

'That's not going to stop his work, though.' Dolly sipped her tea in a surprisingly dainty way. 'Not tempest, nor war.'

Grace chuckled. 'He's going to keep saving us trollops until the day he dies.'

Dolly dropped her eyes as if imparting a truth that I might find painful. 'Only you've got to play it like he wants.'

'What do you mean?' A prickly note crept into my voice.

Grace sighed. 'The Pastor's a good soul. But he's got this idea – this *queer* idea about us that's glued tight inside his head. When we've been here, and he's made us well, he has this notion that we won't go back to working the streets. He convinces himself that we leave here to get respectable jobs. That we mend our ways – stop our drinking and stay out of opium dens.'

I became prim again. 'To lead a respectable life – that's commendable, isn't it?'

'Oh, yes, perfectly upstanding. Only most of our sort haven't the gumption for that kind of life, sweetheart. Working the streets is all we know. Some of us strive to get a position in domestic service. But the smell of sin isn't easily shifted. As soon as an employer gets a proper whiff of it, we're out of the door without a by your leave.'

'It's true,' Dolly said, 'I've tried for shop work, but as soon as they hear we've done whoring they turn us out.'

Grace sniffed. 'When you're without respectable wages you fall into old ways – it's either that or starve.'

Dolly squeezed my hand. A gesture of affection that made me guilt-sick. I wish I hadn't pulled her hair so hard. 'Once you leave here you pretend to the Pastor that you've found decent employment. You say "Yes, Pastor Hux. I work in a lovely shop in Pimlico." Something like that. Remember to send him notes telling him you're happy in your new life, that you're joyful your street-walking days are behind you.'

I shrugged. 'There's no obligation to tell him anything once you've left here. Why bother with the pretence?'

Dolly indicated the pillowcases stuffed with food. 'Because

we're never going to be rich. The Pastor will still help us when he can. And he doesn't mind us taking a bite to eat.'

'And the pewter cup?'

'It doesn't bother him. He's not one for possessions.'

'There's another reason we keep pretending he's saved us from the streets.' A blush touched Grace's thin face. 'For helping us . . . for believing we are good people, and for his tender heart, we can't do nothing but love him.' She smiled. 'Just like you've fallen in love with him, Nidabi. Just like all us poor wretches. You'll do anything for him. Anything at all. You'd rob a bishop for him. All he has to do is ask.'

Dolly added, 'Course, he never does ask.'

'It's not true,' I responded. 'I'm not in love with him.'

'Ha. So you can't bring yourself to admit it? Mark my words, Nidabi. You'd walk on hot coals for him. You'd do murder for him. Do murder ten times over if his life depended on it.'

I sat silent after that. Rain clicked against the kitchen window. For all the world it could have been the ghost of Mitre Rose, her dead fingers tapping the glass to remind me exactly what I had done for Pastor Hux. The way I had struck Rose with the iron poker; how I had tipped her dead body out on to the pavement. Shudders ran through me.

At last Grace rested a hand on my shoulder. 'You look like you could do with leaving alone. Just think on, though – Pastor Hux isn't like any man you've met before. Play along with his ways. Agree with whatever he suggests. When he tells you it's time to make your own way in the world again, agree graciously and move out.'

'When you leave you could join us. It's not altogether such a bad life,' Dolly said. 'I might even have a corner of my room that I can spare you. Just don't go pulling my hair again.' Her smile broadened. 'Right, I'll say good day to you.'

'Take care of yourself, child.' Grace kissed my cheek. 'Don't make him disappointed in you. Then you'll be all right.'

Soon they were out into the rain. They hurried along the tree-lined drive, their shoulders hunched, their shawls pulled over their heads.

Now here I am – writing in my room again. Lately, I'd come to believe my future lay here with the Pastor. As I end this page I realize I'm not so sure.

Ty's Book

8th August. 'It's morbid of me. I shouldn't do this.' I spoke
these words to Vincent van Gogh when he climbed the high
mound of earth that carried the rail track. He must have seen
me brooding up here and decided to join me.

He shielded his eyes against the setting sun. 'You're
watching over your brother's grave, Ty. There's no shame in
that.'

'I can't understand how it happened so quickly. I left
George at the Night Woman's house with nothing more than
a sore throat. When I got back with the medicine she told
me it was diphtheria. He was always so strong for a little
boy.' I had repeated these words to Vincent so many times
since George died last week. Now five days after the funeral
I'm perched up here like a sorrowing crow to watch over his
grave. The freshly turned soil is a raw wound in the earth.
My little brother lies at the bottom of a pit. A crushing mass
of dirt above him. I feel its weight, too. Mixed with that dirt
are fat cemetery worms, blood-red, gluttonous. There are
countless bones from ancient interments, the thousands of
people who lived their lives in Arles before entering that
dreadful field of death that sends waves of cold terror at me.
I'm crushed by fear for my sister. If I've failed our brother,
then what does the future hold for her? Added to that, memories of my dear father working all those extra hours so he
could pay for my education; the emotional pressure is suffocating. The times he'd say, 'You'll never work with your
hands, Ty. Learn from your books. Your intelligence will give
you control of your destiny.' There, I have tears all over the
paper again. The writing will be smudged. Not that I care. I
lean out of the window to curse all of creation. I don't care.
I curse everyone. George's face that was golden brown turned
grey, his eyes grew dull, he died in my arms. Listen! My

father was a sergeant. He left Algeria to be garrisoned here in Arles. My mother died bearing Brionne. My father worked his fingers to the bone to give his family a good life. His heart ruptured when he was fifty-three years old. I've tried to continue his good work and raise my brother and sister. And as so many townsfolk turn their back on my family because we are Mulatto, a mixed breed, so providence turns away from us, too. Now there is only Brionne and myself. Our family is degrading toward nought.

Later. So many tears on the paper. It's anger now rather than grief. I wish I could shatter Arles with my rage. I long to rip up cobblestones with my bare hands, then hurl them through every window. Only I am determined to cast my mind back to the words of the artist as he stood beside me in the dusk. We perched at the edge of the high mound where the railway runs into town. When I finished my own bitter words he took my hand in both his massive palms, then touched it to his bearded chin. The man's eyes shifted from green to blue in the setting sun.

'I vow I will paint George as he was alive,' Vincent told me. 'Then pray to God with all my heart he could step out of the portrait and return to you. Only this is a time when nobody can speak the words that will make everything right for you.' He squeezed my hand tighter. 'I'm worse than anyone in saying the right thing. All I can tell you is whenever you wish to talk, or even be angry and curse, then come to me. Find me at home, or in the fields.'

'I can't interrupt your work.'

'My work will be done another day.'

Although I couldn't speak, I managed to nod.

'This will be clumsy,' he murmured, 'but I can't phrase it in a gentler way. George's end was as bad for you as it was for him. He's not suffering any more. You are. One day you will be able to recall George again as a healthy, happy boy.'

A train huffed along the track behind us, its carriages full of faces. At that moment people no longer seemed real to me. Ever since George died the foreground had receded deep into the background. The universe had been leached of colour.

As the train rumbled toward its terminus I commented, 'George loved to watch the trains. He told me that one day he would drive a locomotive right around the world.' I chewed down on my lip. Tears pushed through again.

Vincent spoke carefully. 'When I paint at night I observe the heavens. For me, the stars are the same as the black dots on a map that represent towns. Those shining lights above us are our destinations. But whereas we can take the train to Marseilles or Paris, to reach those worlds above us we must surrender this life. Death is our locomotive to the stars.'

Vincent may have added more. When I came to my senses I was running down the embankment. My skirts caught on bushes. Branches snatched my hair ribbon away. I tore my blouse. A torrent of dust swept me along. I don't know if the artist followed, or whether he called to me to stop. I'd become this hurtling body, that's all; a speeding thing without thought or feeling. I scrambled over the fence, leaving strands of hair where they caught on a nail. As soon as I was free of the cemetery I plunged into the tangle of alleyways. Faces blurred. I beat aside clothes hanging on lines across the closes. Mattresses dangling out of windows to air had become the lolling tongues of corpses. Doorways were tombs. In that state of mind even the river became a fathomless abyss of shadow that carried lost souls into eternal night.

That evening I arrived at work with a flask of cognac three quarters gone. The rent money I'd saved was no more. George's funeral had taken it all. So, no home yet for me and Brionne, my five-year-old sister. Anger became a force that drove my work all through the night without pause. Men's pleasure over this writhing, frenzied devil often curdled into fear. They soon hurried away in silence. I finished the remaining cognac in greedy gulps. Though it burned my throat it did nothing to pacify the demon raging inside my head.

{PC Morrow's filed statement, London, 9th August, 1888}

Sir, I attended the post-mortem of the murdered woman known as Mitre Rose. Doctor Phillips stated the deceased had been an inveterate consumer of opium. Moreover, there was a full pint of brandy in the stomach. Despite her grimy appearance she bore a distinct scent of quality soap-stuffs. Hair: lice free. Abrasions encircled her wrists and ankles, indicative of restraint by cuffs. Fresh bruising striped her back, possibly

*the result of being beaten by a rod while in a crouching pos-
ition. No bruising to forearms to suggest protective stance.
Cause of death: a violent blow to the back of the neck that
severed the spinal chord.*

   *Addendum. I was one of the attending police officers the
night Mitre Rose was found on Old Conduit Street. It had
been raining. The pavement surface was thickly covered in a
noxious slime that accrues when workmen sluice detritus in
the adjacent slaughterhouse directly on to the road. I found
copious amounts of this dark, pungent liquid on the deceased's
clothes, hands and face. Indeed, myself and PC Barrett were
compelled to wash our footwear immediately thereafter. The
upshot of all this: although the liquid was smeared on many
parts of the deceased, it was entirely absent from the soles of
her shoes. I venture, therefore, that Mitre Rose did not die in
the street. My suspicions are that she was killed elsewhere,
then disposed of from a vehicle. This act was executed in a
most clever fashion in order to mislead the detective in charge
of the inquiry.*

Nidabi's Journal

14th August. The men stood silently. *Detectives.* The words
went ringing through my head. *The detectives know that Rose
was here at Lamplands. They have come to take the Pastor
away.* I hurried down to the hallway, ready to fight with every
last shred of strength to stop them arresting the Pastor. Yet,
these men in their long black coats and shiny top hats filed
out through the door. Their faces were dour; each gave Pastor
Hux a cold stare as they passed by him. He nodded a courteous farewell to each man. The last to leave turned back,
probably hearing my tread on the stair. His eyes roved over
my face; his disgust showed itself clearly – no, *blatantly*. Then
he joined his companions who were climbing into an assort-
ment of carriages. The horses were impatient to leave, as if

Lamplands frightened them. It didn't take much urging to send the beasts trotting along the drive, their hooves splashing puddles. Pastor Hux stood in the doorway, his hands behind his back, watching long after the last carriage had vanished from sight.

The effect of the visitors on him shocked me. 'Pastor Hux, who were those men?'

'Deeds, not words, Nidabi. Deeds, not words!' His voice rose. 'That's what I've lived by. That's what I told those men ... those guardians of a Christian chapel.'

'You know them?'

'Oh, yes, Mr McAndrew, Mr Gammly, Mr Brown, Mr Sutton, the entire parade of pompous, self-serving hypocrites.' He struggled to control his rage. 'They granted me some of their *valuable* time to offer insights into my work. Apparently, my charitable endeavour is overzealous. They consider my domestic arrangements unsanitary. They even ordered me not to use the title pastor.'

'But you are a pastor.'

'Not in their eyes. To them, I'm *Mr* Hux. To devote one's life to humanity in the name of God doesn't require a man to sit an approved examination paper.'

There was such a distillation of pain in his eyes that I felt moved to grip his hand. 'You are a good man, Pastor. One day your deeds will be celebrated.'

'If God wills it. In the meantime, they strip me of a title that they've not even awarded in the first place. They insist I stop my work with the poor. Moreover, I am no longer welcome at the chapel.'

'Come with me. You should sit for while.'

'Fifteen years I've worshipped there. That's where I met the artist who is the only man I can call a friend. Vincent van Gogh became my brother. We shared the same conviction that we were born to serve Man!' He seized the big front door to slam it against the jamb, then drove the bolts home; they made the sound of gunshots. 'There! See that, Nidabi! It's over. The entrance is locked. The world with all its pain and misery stays at the far side of those timbers, I remain at this.' His eyes stared in the fixed way of a dead man. 'I'm done with life, Nidabi.'

'Pastor, you should take some brandy.'

He didn't respond.

'Or, if you would prefer to retire to bed, I can take you there?'

Silence. Just that fixed stare as he leaned against the door. It was as if he prepared to hold it fast in case the outside world should assault it.

At last he whispered. 'Nidabi? I've failed, haven't I?'

'No.'

'All for nought. They said my acts of charity were frivolous.'

'They weren't.' I was close to tears.

'I wish I could believe you, Nidabi. I'm a man of straw. I'm all used up.'

'You aren't. Listen, you have not failed.' I pressed my argument home. 'Remember, Pastor. Deeds, not words.' I gripped his hand again. 'Deeds, not words!'

'I don't answer to that pompous cabal.'

'No, Pastor, you do not.'

'My work reflects the glory of God Almighty, not the squawking occupants of that mausoleum of a chapel.'

'What you say is the truth, Pastor. You are not their servant.'

He took a deep breath. Suddenly he appeared taller. 'Nidabi.'

'Yes, Pastor?'

'I need you to gather all the food, blankets and soap you can. Bring them here to this door!' Then, with an exalted spring in his step, he ran upstairs.

'I'm sorry. There's not a great deal,' I told him as he returned, carrying a large book bound in red leather. 'I have a box with a hundred bars of kitchen soap. There are jars of fruit. Cans of meat. Twenty blankets that don't require airing, but I can add another dozen if I hang them outside this afternoon.'

'Nidabi. Look at these.' Excited, he thrust the open book toward me. Pasted there were letters and postcards in different hands. 'They are the reason I do this work. Look! These are from the women I've helped in the past. See this one? "Dear Pastor Hux. May it please dear Jesus that these lines find you well. You will be heartened to learn that I have found respectable work as a governess here in Greenwich. I don't know how to thank you for saving me from my wretched ways." And this one! From a girl that had been prisoner in the most evil establishment you could imagine. "My dearest Pastor, my friend here at the bakery is writing this on my behalf. However, I have begun to learn reading so everything will be all right for my future happiness." Look! Dozens of letters from people who matter to me. They've left their squalid practices behind to find new lives.'

Though I remembered what Grace Tarant and Dolly West had told me about the letters being pure make-believe, I was happy for him. The pleasure they brought made you think he'd dance in the air when he read them aloud. Yet I fancied I caught the reek of gin from those scraps of paper with their chaotic, scribbled lines. Sheer passion fired him while he declaimed in vigorous tones: 'Deeds, not words, Nidabi. Today, we will show those hypocrites the meaning of charity!' He flung open the doors. Sunlight flooded in. 'They will hear about our act of Christian love. It will strike dismay into their hearts. But they'll be powerless to stay our hand!'

The sun had burnt away the cloud by the time we'd reached Limehouse, that hinterland which rides the back of the snaking River Thames. Within moments, however, smoke from domestic hearths and factories alike once more darkened the sky. Through congested streets the Pastor guided the big, black gallower that drew the open cart. Slow progress to be sure. Pavements thronged with sour-faced men. A group of women gathered outside a tanner's yard to smoke their clay pipes. There were girls from the match factory who wore cowls to hide faces ruined by phossey jaw. The girls were employed to dip matchsticks into volatile phosphorus; its chemical venom devoured jawbones; once pretty faces became as green as moss. After the sweet air of Lamplands this quarter extruded every vile smell imaginable from overburdened sewers beneath our carriage wheels, to the miasma of abattoirs and carcass boilers, to the million chimneys that gifted their own odour to the sky. Here, people who couldn't afford a room paid a penny to sleep in the coffin factory. Their bed for the night? A coffin, or 'narrow house' as their tenants grimly called them. The thud of hooves was drowned by the slum's own symphony – women singing, calls of beckoning, of warning, threats of violence, angry voices bawling; the screech of a fiddle played by a madman. The lunatic melody poured forth from a mean dwelling with cracked window panes.

Yet in the midst of this dark, stench-filled hell there came a miracle. The sun pierced the fumes to bathe us in a warm glow. All of a sudden the demented musician recaptured his gift; the music became beautiful. Then the strangest thing happened. Washed by sunlight, hearing the heart-melting violin, it seemed to me time melted away. I was ten years old again in some lovely garden that until now I'd completely forgotten. From a vine I picked grapes that were a huge, glossy purple. The taste was exquisite. That sweet flavour of the grape drenched my senses once more. It was at that moment I realized an important truth: Pastor Hux and I had crossed a significant threshold. We were no longer part of London, or indeed the world. When Mitre Rose died we kicked free of modern society. We no longer held allegiance to it, nor did its customs and laws rule us now. Even though I could reach out to touch these Londoners, or run my fingers across the grimy houses, we were not part of this world now. *We've crossed that mythical river of no return.*

Pastor Hux's face held the expression of a man eager to do good works. He could have been a doctor on a mission to cure the sick. All of a sudden my heart was filled with such warmth for him. We were comrades now. An army of just two souls on a God-given crusade. *Deeds, not words!* For my part, I glanced at the big wicker basket strapped to the back of our trap. Its swelling mound of contents had been covered with a blanket before we'd left the house. More than once a child darted alongside the basket to push its fingers under the fabric to explore what treasure might lie there. Each time I turned back to flick them away with my glove.

Pastor Hux's attention was fixed on what he intended to accomplish this afternoon. 'Nearly there,' he uttered. 'Nearly there now.' He reined the horse to allow an elaborately decorated brougham pulled by two horses to pass in front of us. It stopped to discharge a soldier with a flushed face. Another man in uniform stepped up to the carriage. Inside, a woman with a powdered face beckoned him in.

The Pastor sighed. 'Round and round the mulberry bush. Isn't that so, Nidabi?' He nodded at the brougham in its gaudy livery of gold and crimson. 'Here the devil inspires men to provide a house of sin on wheels.'

'Where are we going with these goods, Pastor?'

'To the poorest part of the slum. Then we demonstrate to the world what charity means.' When I said nothing he glanced at me. 'Are you frightened, Nidabi?'

'It will be a dangerous place, won't it?'

'It's daylight.'

'What do you plan to do with the provisions?'

'Wait and see, Nidabi. We're almost there.'

On my first night at the Pastor's house a sense of foreboding had crept over me. Words I once read in a book rose unbidden inside my head. Despite my elation of just moments ago, they did so again as he turned off into a squalid byway: *here begin terrors.*

We entered a dark quarter where the street grew so narrow I could reach out from the vehicle and brush the moss-covered brickwork with my fingertips. Drops of water fell on to us from sunken roofs. Shops here didn't display wares in their windows. Instead, a single narrow opening led to a cave-like aperture inside where strong-armed proprietors stood guard over their stock. When the Pastor reached a row of cottages he stopped the carriage, then rose to his feet. The brick face of one of the hovels had bowed out from the downward pressure of the roof. A balk of timber had been jammed against it to prevent it from collapsing into the yard. Children tugged at one another, a noisy, tumultuous group. Watching them were five bickering women. An old man sat on a crate smoking a pipe.

'Ladies.' At first the Pastor's voice was hesitant. 'Ladies. Please, can I, ah . . . ?'

No one looked our way. I sat in the open carriage with one hand clutching its wooden frame. Such a sense of unease ran through me. I longed to tell the Pastor to drive out of here as quickly as he could. Whereas a moment ago the windows had been as blank as dead eyes, now faces appeared at the panes. Pale faces with eyes that fixed on us, less with curiosity than with hunger.

When the Pastor clapped his hands I flinched. *Please. Let's get away. It's dangerous here.* My heart beat faster as windows filled with more gaunt faces. Some held a glint of malice in their eyes.

Pastor Hux called out, 'Ladies . . . ladies . . .' This time the women turned to stare at him. 'Ladies. In this basket are grocery provisions, soap and blankets. I invite you to step forward and chose an item of each.'

Their eyes narrowed in suspicion. The street became silent. The kind of silence that is chillingly ominous.

He appeared surprised that no one approached the carriage. 'The soap is carbolic. There is canned mutton. Very whole-some for children.'

An old woman with a crafty face laughed – a jagged screech of a sound. 'Take it all up to the palace, mebbe the queen'll take the bloody lot off your hands.'

'No, madam, you don't understand. I'm not selling these items.'

'Ah, like that, is it?' The woman sucked on her clay pipe. 'There's nothing under these skirts that'd interest you.'

The Pastor addressed the crowd again. 'No. I don't want payment of any kind in return for these goods. I bring you a simple gift in the name of Jesus Christ.'

A young woman with a baby in her arms lurched forward. 'You mean we can take this stuff for nothing?'

'Of course, my dear. Take what you need.' From where he stood in the carriage, he leaned back over the seat to pick a blanket from the basket. 'Here, this is new. Take a piece of soap as well . . . can you manage with the baby?'

Swiftly, she sat the baby in the dirt then darted forward. She took the gifts with a garbled, 'Obliged, sir.'

Good Lord. It was like a magic act. From there being a dozen people in the street suddenly it was crammed full of men and women. Also, emerging from the gloomy shops, were the proprietors. There was no doubting their anger.

As women helped themselves to the Pastor's goods he held out his hands to calm them. 'Please don't push. Choose one blanket, soap . . . no, madam, please take just one, then there'll be plenty to go round.' The horse whinnied as the crush of people pressed forward to reach the basket strapped to the back. Hands feverishly grabbed what they could. 'I'd prefer that women only collect the items, sir . . . sir, would you put the blankets back? I wish the women, only, to take them.'

A man in a filthy cap yelled, 'Go hang yourself, why don't

you?' Roughly, he shoved the mothers aside before he scooped up a dozen cans of meat.

'Sir!' Pastor Hux jumped down from the carriage. 'I insist. They are for the women.'

'Pastor!' I yelled. The vehicle lurched as more men forced their way through the crowd to help themselves. 'Pastor. Stay in the carriage. Don't leave it!'

A gang of thugs pushed everyone back. One used a dagger to slice through the basket straps. The men grinned at one another as they carried the basket into an alleyway. Women swore at them; the gang cursed back. When the thugs raised their fists against anyone who came close the tumult grew more frenzied. Dogs barked, children wailed. I stood up to call to the Pastor. I could see his top hat at the far side of the yard as he attempted to reason with the man who'd taken an armful of food. The gallower whinnied. It would have walked away there and then if it wasn't for the wheel brake. I'd called to the Pastor without success when I felt a hand roughly grasp my forearm. I looked down to see one of the shopkeepers. Angry red blotches inflamed his face.

'What the 'ell do ya think you're doing here?'

'It's charity, sir. We don't mean any harm.'

'Charity? Damn ya blasted charity. Ya giving away stuff for nothing. How am I supposed to sell my bloody stock if ya do that?'

'Please don't pull my arm, sir.'

'I'll do as *I* please seeing as ya plan on puttin' me out of business. Ya bloody heathen.'

Another shopkeeper called out, 'Go on, Frank! Put your belt across her back.'

This gallower was a bad-tempered beast. Noise agitated it. Screams grew louder as those who'd been late for the Pastor's charity tugged blankets out of the arms of those who'd been more fortunate. When a woman barged against our horse it sank its teeth into her shoulder. She howled. This prompted the beast to jerk the carriage. Now I lost my balance as the shopkeeper tugged my arm so fiercely I feared the limb would fly out of its joint. I fell out of the cart into the mud.

'On your feet,' bellowed the shopkeeper. However, he'd released his grip on me, so I scrambled under the shaft forks. I made sure I kept clear of the horse's tramping hooves, mindful that one stamp would snap my bones. Even so, the wheels skidded forward a foot at a time. If the brake failed the cart would run over me in an instant. All I could see now, apart from the mud-caked road, were the skirts of women and men's boots. We must escape before the rest of the mob turned on us. Dazed, panting, my legs so weak I couldn't stand, I crawled out from under the carriage. It would be safer to seek the protection of a wall where the crush of people wasn't so bad. As I reached it a figure leapt at me. Expecting a blow, I shielded my face with my arms.

'You should be sorry you came here. The pair of you have caused a riot.'

I knew the voice. The way the soft words had an unusual stress as if the speaker worked hard to conceal a stammer.

'Up to your feet, Nidabi. Otherwise they'll tramp all over you.'

'Dolly?' I looked up at the woman who tugged me upright. 'Dolly West?'

'At your service.' She hauled me through the milling crowd toward the carriage. The mob bayed at two women who boxed each other for the possession of a blanket. 'Now, back on to the seat and hold yourself tight.'

At the far side of the carriage I could see Pastor Hux. He was hurrying back as the horse whinnied.

'Thank you, Dolly.' I grabbed the rail in order to hoist myself in.

Instead of pushing me on to the seat, she suddenly pulled me back. 'For goodness sakes, don't tell the Pastor you saw me here. *Promise me you won't.*'

I was puzzled but nodded, 'If that's what you wish.'

'I don't want the Pastor to know I'm back on these streets. He thinks I'm nannying for a family in Richmond. Now get yourself up there.'

Then, as if she'd been a spirit, Dolly West dissolved back into the multitude. She'd vanished by the time Pastor Hux turned to survey the mob.

'They're animals!' I cried as I sat beside him.

'They're humanity,' he replied. 'Poverty does this. Poverty sends them mad.'

I saw a trickle of blood run from his mouth. A slap on the side of my face made me cry out. Mud by the fistful was being hurled. An instant later, a bottle narrowly missed the Pastor's head to smash against a house wall. That's the moment he knocked the brake free. Instantly, the horse lurched away at a gallop. Even so, the rain of muck still fell on us until we were clear of that sordid quarter.

As the shouts died away, the Pastor turned to me. 'Don't worry, Nidabi. We will win them over eventually.'

I stared at him. I couldn't believe what he was saying.

He gave a determined nod. 'Have faith. We will fare better at this tomorrow.'

20th August. The 'tomorrow' became yesterday. And more of those 'tomorrows' came and went. Pastor Hux sold yet more of Lamplands' meagre furniture. Monday, we ventured to Limehouse with tallow candles, lice combs, jars of honey. We returned covered in filth thrown by the denizens of that hinterland. Tuesday we went to Whitechapel with three hundred bars of carbolic soap. My jacket was torn in the ensuing fracas. The Pastor suffered kicks aplenty. On Wednesday we loaded the carriage with bacon. The shopkeepers lay in wait for us. They took everything, then threw stones. My ear bled from a graze. In the midst of the riot, the Pastor stood up and prayed until a bottle struck his temple and felled him. I managed to drive the carriage back home. Thursday, Friday, Saturday. Different slums. Results identical. On Sunday, as the Pastor drove along Aldgate with a consignment of flour, a pair of police officers stepped into the road in front of us. One raised a hand for us to stop.

The second constable approached the Pastor. 'Sir, I must instruct you to go home.'

Pastor Hux shook his head. 'Let me pass. I'm here to conduct missionary work.'

'Sir, we've had complaints from tradesmen. They say you're ruining them.'

The Pastor's face quivered with emotion. For a moment he couldn't speak.

'Please turn your carriage, sir, then go home.'

'Listen, I'm not harming anyone's trade. I'm merely distributing comforts to the poor.'

The constable was stone-faced. 'Whenever you appear in the East End you cause a riot. People have been hurt.'

'I will not turn back.'

'Then I am empowered to arrest you.'

'Stand aside, Constable. Stand aside!' Tears sprang from the Pastor's eyes. Whether it was rage, or sorrow, at being thwarted from performing his charitable act I don't know. One fact was transparent though: the way the police officers glanced at each other. They suspected he'd lost his wits. One drew his truncheon.

'You'll not be changing your mind then, sir?'

'Never. Those people need me.'

'Pastor.' I squeezed his arm. His taut muscles quivered beneath the sleeve. 'Don't confront them. The constables will get their way in the end.'

Through gritted teeth he hissed, 'I can't let them stop me. I cannot fail. While I've got breath in my body I must keep giving. Deeds, not words.'

Soothingly I said quietly, 'Not today, Pastor. We'll come back later.'

'People are dying of hunger.'

'We can't serve them if we're in prison.'

'Come, sir. Please step down from the carriage.' Both police officers had drawn their clubs now.

I whispered so the men wouldn't hear. 'We can return at night.'

This time Pastor Hux put his hand over his eyes as if he suffered a punishing headache. At that moment the ability to speak passed from him.

'Sir.' The constable adopted a menacing tone. 'You'll do as we ask.'

'Gentlemen,' I began, 'my master has taken ill. If you'll permit me, I'll drive him home.'

The most senior of the pair studied the man's ashen face then turned to me. 'If you do, we'll say the matter is settled. Do you understand what I'm telling you?'

'Yes, sir.'

'Very well.' He motioned for me to turn the cart round. 'Easy with the animal, miss. Tell your stable lad not to hitch a gallower of that temperament in future. It's too wild for town streets.' Then he nodded at the hunched form of the Pastor. 'Have a doctor call on your master. He looks in a poor way to me.'

'I will. Thank you, sir. Good day.'

After turning the carriage, I urged the horse to a brisk trot. The policemen watched us go, no doubt to ensure I didn't head for the slums through one of the side streets. Beside me, Pastor Hux kept his eyes closed all the way home. I'd humoured the policeman when he suggested I call a doctor, but the way the Pastor's face had set into an uncanny mask unsettled me. It added to the growing sense of foreboding that disaster inched ever closer.

Ty's Book

21st August. So the days pass. The women in the house where I'm employed are kind. They say I should take Brionne to the coast for a few days. If I do that, however, it will take what money I have managed to save for the rent. It's now my dearest wish to make a home for myself and my sister. These days I rarely see the artist. He tells me he is in a continual fever of work. One of the shepherds has told me that he sees Vincent van Gogh working at night in the fields outside Arles. Vincent hangs lanterns on olive tree branches all around him so he is bathed in light. Yesterday, I saw Joseph Roulin, the postman, bringing Vincent home in a handcart. The artist had suffered one of his seizures out in the fields again. The postman's blue uniform was smeared with dust from dragging the artist out of the dirt. When I saw Vincent lying prone in the cart, canvases piled across his chest, his lips were bright blue. When I asked the postman if he was dying, he replied, 'In the name of God I hope not. He's eaten paint. I don't know why, but I'm frightened it might be poisonous.' Monsieur Roulin looked at me. He is a big man of around fifty years, with a curling beard that comes halfway down his chest. 'You're Ty?' he asked.

'Yes.'

'Ah, Vincent talks about you. He calls you Mousme.'

'You won't send me away, then?'

He looked at me in surprise.

I added quickly, 'I want to help you move him into his house.'

'Why, of course, mademoiselle. I'd never send away a friend of his.' When we reached Place Lamartine Monsieur Roulin unlocked the door. Then, together, we carried Vincent's paints and canvases indoors.

'My friend would never have forgiven me if I'd left these in the field,' the big man explained. 'This stuff costs Vincent a fortune. It's only a pity I had to pile them over him like this. But no one else would help me bring him home. There . . . would you pass me the easel? And his hat? Ah, what a hat! See the paint splashes? A work of art in its own right. Thank you. There are folk in this town—' He glared at the surrounding houses. 'There are folk who call our friend crazy and shun him, but they'd steal the clothes off his back if they had the chance.' Monsieur Roulin took a deep breath. 'Now, stand back, Ty, while I carry my friend . . . no, I'll pick him up, you're such a tiny thing . . . all right, all right, if you insist.'

I helped support Vincent's head while Monsieur Roulin slipped his strong arms under the unconscious man's back. Then he carried Vincent indoors as if he were a sleeping child. When he laid him down on the bed Monsieur Roulin shook his head. 'It's like carrying a bag of straw. There's no flesh. He should eat more meat.'

The bedroom's pale blue walls were crowded with canvases. They blazed with vividly painted landscapes and portraits. There was even a portrait of the bearded postman who now used the cloth from the washstand to tenderly wipe dust from Vincent's face. I recognized an ink drawing of myself by the window. While on the wall above a straight-backed chair was a painting of the little bedroom where we now tended the stricken artist. Every detail was there – the red floor tiles, the nightstand with its basin of water and his razor, two chairs, the bed with its pillows. The painting of the bedroom only neglected to include its occupant.

That occupant now lay flat on the bed. The sunburnt face with paint-smeared mouth. A red beard offset by Prussian blue lips. His eyelids opened every so often, but only briefly, as if they were a tremendous weight that the artist could only bear for the briefest moment. Roulin wet the cloth from the bowl so he could clean away the paint that he feared might be poisonous.

'What a day,' Roulin groaned. 'I'm worrying myself into fits over this man. I love him, yet I despair. I'd take him home to convalesce but my wife has her hands full with the children.' He shrugged. 'Should I telegraph his brother in Paris?'

'I'll look after him.'

'You?' The words he uttered next didn't come easily: 'You have your work to go to.'

'Yes, the brothel; there's no need to be shy of saying the word. I'm not ashamed. My brother is dead, but my sister is only five years old. She needs the money I earn to keep her from starving.'

'Vincent's right. You do have fighting spirit. You have brains, too.'

'I'm going to look after him until he's well. If he dies, then I will stay here and die with him.'

This gave him a start. 'Don't say that, young lady.'

'Nevertheless.' I moved the chair so I could sit holding the artist's hand.

'I'm sure he'll recover.' I could see Roulin loved him as much as I did. 'Listen. I'll bring sour milk. It's not pleasant but if he empties his stomach . . . it's the paint you see . . . I'm worried about that.'

So the postman brought sour milk, then did what had to be done. Roulin and I remained with Vincent for most of the day, then after the postman had gone back to his family I stayed. By the evening Vincent managed to sit up in bed. He drank coffee, ate some bread, then asked for his tobacco. From his shy demeanour I realized he was embarrassed about the seizure.

When I asked what happened his response was, 'Oh, the heat. I'd forgotten to wear my hat.'

'It's not the heat alone.'

'Maybe the work. I paint in a continuous passion of excitement. You see, Ty, I have to make the most of this light. It's transforming how I work. Here, the sun is so different. Its rays flood through everything; it makes the olive trees live like people. It shines through the earth to illuminate its heart.'

'Vincent. Why did you eat the paint?'

He reacted as if I'd just uttered the most ridiculous thing

in the world. Then he ran his tongue over his lips with its traces of blue. His green eyes became troubled as if he was on the cusp of remembering.

Gently, I said, 'Monsieur Roulin was frightened that you'd tried to poison yourself.'

'I think about colour all the time. Everything possesses not just a colour but its *own* colour that distinguishes it from everything else. Listen, Ty. There are people in the world who claim a tree has its own spirit, as does a chair, or a stone. There are saints who tell us that sin wears a different colour to piety. Scarlet women. Black-hearted murderers. All revealed by colour. Poets have written about the *sound* of colour – that it has its own music. Therefore, do you think that it's possible that colour has its own taste? So that's maybe why I . . .' He wiped his lips then stared at blue speckles of paint that had transferred to his fingers. 'Ty, if I work with as much passion as I can muster . . . increase my efforts to such a pitch as if human lives hung in the balance . . . convince myself a bad picture results in the deaths of innocents, then that will spur me on. I'll produce paintings with the most powerful arrangement of colours that the human eye has ever experienced.'

'Vincent. Is that why you think my brother died?' My question made him flinch. 'Do you blame yourself for George's death because you painted a picture that was no good?' He screwed shut his eyes; tremors jolted his shoulders. I pressed on. 'If you digest colours inside your body, do you believe it will enable your soul to touch the soul of the paint?'

He whispered, 'To my ears, that sounds rotten with delusion. Do you think I'm insane?'

'You are working too hard, Vincent. You'll become ill.'

'I will risk my own life for my art. I accept the risk.'

There's no talking Vincent van Gogh out of his quest for the faultless picture. He sets his goal on an unreachable summit. Then work is a precious balm in its own right. I demand that the brothel-keeper give me more hours. He shakes his head, then intones the same reasons for not overworking as those I recite to Vincent. *But, listen to me.* Stand by little George's grave in the cemetery. Hear the cough that robbed the air from his lungs. Imagine him gasping: *why didn't you work harder, Ty? If you'd earned more we could have lived in the house by the river. There the air is cleaner.* My brother's dead face rises up through clods of soil, his blue eyelids drawn down over swollen mounds that are his eyes. The mouth yawns wide. Now, cross the bridge of his tongue to the diphtheria membrane that seals his throat like the wall of a tomb. *Sister, if we lived in the new house I wouldn't have fallen sick. I'd still be alive . . .* Then my brother's cough becomes louder. As if it's built for days in that grim chamber underground; its volume is so great it will burst from the grave to shatter my spirit. With an upward surge, as if to break free of the grave, George's head rises clear of the earth. Then invisible hands grip his limbs to drag him back down. His face sinks beneath the clay. I throw myself on to the burial plot to claw aside the dirt before the cemetery demons can trap him again.

Visitors to neighbouring graves have helped me to the shade where they urge me to refresh myself with water. They tell me the tricks that grief can play on the mind. So – it's work for Monsieur Van Gogh. It's work for me. That precious balm.

{PC Morrow's filed statement, London, 21st August, 1888}

Sir, further to my memorandum of the 9th August, which reported my attending the post-mortem of Mitre Rose, I have recently had occasion to speak with Jack Swain, a night watchman, employed by a wine merchant on Old Conduit Street, the same street where Mitre Rose was found. Although my interview was in connection with theft from another part of the premises, he showed me the thief's method of exit through a hatch that leads directly on to a warehouse roof in the said street. I asked if the hatch was habitually left open and he stated: 'My employer tells me to sit on the roof when I smoke my pipe as he fears another outbreak of fire would ruin him.' The upshot of this is that several times from dusk until dawn Swain takes to the rooftop. It occurred to me he might have witnessed events leading to the deposit of the deceased, Mitre Rose, on the evening in question. In response to my query he replied, 'Yes, I remember that particular evening I noticed an unusual occurrence. A lady sat with a gentleman in an open carriage.' I enquired why that should appear unusual. He responded: 'Because the carriage was drawn by one of them horses no one in their right mind would keep in a town. A big gallower that's been bred wrong. A monster of a beast.

They're sent by the devil. Fifty years ago a gallower like that kicked my brother to death. Smashed his bones – did it with spite in its eyes.' I asked if he'd seen the pair deposit anything on the pavement. He saw nothing to that effect as he was called away to a rear gate. Later, he witnessed a crowd assembling in the street. I conclude that gathering was as a result of finding the deceased. When I called upon Swain to recollect details of the pair in the carriage he said he could not, other than an impression that the woman had dark skin. I asked if he meant African. His reply: 'No, sir. I served in the Yorkshire Light Infantry in northern India. Her skin was the same as the natives there.'

Nidabi's Journal

22nd August. The day after the incident with the policemen I looked out of my bedroom window. Pastor Hux, dressed in a white shirt, black trousers, and quite hatless, busied himself loading canned foods into the two-wheeled carriage. The horse wandered about the drive untethered. How my heart slipped into the pit of my stomach.

'No,' I told myself, 'please don't let him be like this.' He moved between the carriage and a pile of groceries in his bare feet. Even from this distance I could see his flesh was grimed with dirt. As he worked, he talked constantly, even though there was no one there. Leaving the bedroom, I raced down to the front door. A light rain had begun to fall but the Pastor didn't notice. A greyness infused his face, while the brightness of his eyes unsettled me.

'Pastor,' I said in a deliberately casual manner, 'you should have called. I'd have helped you load the carriage.'

'Good morning, Nidabi. I couldn't sleep. Thought I'd make an early start.' He spoke as if it was usual to work outdoors in bare feet. 'I realized we can carry more food for the poor if I distribute it across the full dimensions of the carriage.

See? God-given inspiration!' He'd already filled the basket in the back. Now he built the meat cans in a silver wall that ran the length of the seat.

I agreed, 'The carriage will carry an enormous amount but, Pastor, where will we sit?'

'Oh, don't worry about trifles. I have created a plan that will feed a thousand people today. A thousand of the poorest, Nidabi.'

'Should I tether the horse?'

'No, there's fresh grass for him. He needs to be strong . . . strong as an ox!'

'But I'm afraid the horse will roam out of the—'

'Nidabi! Don't you see, we are embarking on charitable work at its most glorious!' He seized my arms in a crushing grip. A look of exultation inflamed his face. 'We will toil together and show all those hypocrites that I am not crippled by my zeal for charity, but that I'm transfigured!'

I glanced at the carriage with its load. The wheels splayed outwards under the gravity of hundreds of cans. Even the ferocious strength of the gallower would be defeated by that massive cargo.

'Shouldn't we go back inside,' I suggested. 'The rain's—'

'Pish-posh rain!'

'I'm also concerned about the roughness of the crowds, Pastor. They steal our gifts before they reach the people we're trying to help.'

'I've thought of that. See!' The man lunged at the carriage where he dragged a long object from beneath the seat. When he thrust it out for my inspection I flinched. Even in the rain the knife glittered. Its formidable blade chilled my blood. A blade that terminated in a murderous point.

'I abhor violence.' He brandished the weapon. 'But if I produce this it will maintain order.' The grin on his face was a wild one.

In the pouring rain the carriage sagged under the weight of its load. By now the gallower, which he intended would haul the vehicle, used its powerful jaws to violently rip down branches from the trees for no apparent purpose. *The beast is as mad as its master.* I hated the thought, but I couldn't prevent it as the horse attacked the trees with its great yellow teeth. Its eyeballs rolled, showing a blaze of white. Foam sprayed from its mouth as it grunted with maniacal pleasure.

'You know, Nidabi – science! That's it: *science*. In the future, science will provide a new way!' He pointed at the carriage with the dagger. 'Wheels! We won't need wheels any more! Science will transcend the wheel.'

'Pastor, please come indoors.'

'Last night I sat up drawing plans. It all came so clear. My mind has never been so *alive*. I will commission an engineer to build a balloon – a vast, *vast* balloon . . . one the size of St Paul's Cathedral. Then we can distribute food to not just London, but the entire world. Africa, Asia—' Abruptly, he paused, then looked from the dagger in his hand, surprised by its presence, to the carriage piled with canned meat, then to the horse attacking a tree. 'Nidabi . . .' He struggled to catch his breath. 'This isn't right, is it?' His voice dropped to a whisper. 'All this . . . it's wrong, isn't it? There's too much of this—' He pushed over the wall of cans that filled the seat. 'There's far too much to carry.' Pastor Hux rolled his eyes down to his feet as if afraid of what he'd see there. His muddied toes were submerged by a puddle. 'Oh, my dear Nidabi, am I really standing outside without footwear?'

'Yes, Pastor. You must have forgotten to—'

'Forgotten to dress? Yes. That's it.' Exhaustion shunted the wild elation from his face. 'You know there's too much of that – whatever it is – on the little cart. Yet just for a moment back there, I really did believe I had the answer. All those hungry people . . .'

'Don't worry, sir. I'll take care of everything.'

I supported him as he limped back indoors and helped him lie down on a settee where I covered him with a blanket. Should I summon a doctor? But if I did, would they take the Pastor from me? Wouldn't it be wiser to feed him wholesome meals? And if he can rest without any more nervous excitement then, perhaps, all will be well. Won't it?

{*Pastor Hux, London, 25th August, 1888*)

My dear Vincent,

    How are you, old fellow? Does your paintbrush create new wonders? Have the critics woken to the value of your work?

    Remember when we discussed the frailty of our

bodies? We both suffered with our nerves. I always maintained that our spirit was too powerful for the shell that contained it. Well, shamefaced, I confess that I suffered a breakdown of sorts. I am fortunate to have Nidabi, one of the kindest souls on earth, to care for me. Every two hours prompt she brings me warm milk and bread. Then she stands fiercely at my elbow to make sure I eat every sop. I tell you, Vincent, this woman is heaven sent; she is physician and guardian angel merged into one.

Nidabi's Journal

28th August. Pastor Hux tries so hard. Every day he tells me he is better. He eats everything I put before him. But he's not right yet. He shouts in his sleep. Indeed, there are states when he is neither awake nor sleeping. Then he cries he can see Mitre Rose in the room. That she carries her coffin on her back like the shell of a beetle. That she looms over his bed to glare down at him, her head and body framed by the long wooden box. Only her eyes are no longer eyes . . . but he cannot bring himself to name what's set there so repellently in her face. When the Pastor's fully awake he denies he's seen Rose. His refutation is in the form of: 'What made you think I saw a woman?' Even though the *woman* he cared for has been dead only a matter of weeks, he never mentions her by name. On the occasions I've spoken about Rose and the accident, his expression is one of puzzlement, as if I'm talking about an incident with which he is unfamiliar. It reminds me of his fight with the Colonel and his protégés. Pastor Hux appears to have no memory of the men.

Sometimes I wonder if a fear of death haunts him. I've learnt his Christian name is Posthumous. It's rare to call a child this now but in centuries gone by the name Posthumous would be given to a boy whose father died prior to the birth.

I know he dislikes the name. Posthumous would be a constant reminder that he'd never set eyes on his own father. I imagine him as a child, brooding by the grave of his dead parent; his eyes for ever drawn to the earth which contains that cold flesh.

The days drift by. This summer is a dark, rain-filled one. Often it thunders. The lightning isn't blue or silver but a dirty yellow at best, or even a lurid brown at its dullest. Brown lightning? I've not seen a storm like it. When it's clear at night I gaze at the heavens. There is a telescope in the study. With it, I have viewed the circular lakes on the moon and its mountains. I try to map a little of the lunar topography every day. Why do I do this? To distract myself from the Pastor's illness, because I see danger ahead. Dread smears the air like a grim mist.

Dolly West, the girl I believed I'd caught stealing from the kitchen, calls by every other day. The Pastor doesn't know of her visits but they are welcome to me. Dolly and I have become firm friends. She has told me about her happy child-hood in the countryside. However, fate proved unkind. In adult life her husband died soon after they married, so she tried to find respectable work in London. Poverty, however, soon forced her into whoredom. In truth, she is a beautiful, warm-hearted girl. I don't think there's a soul who can help taking to her charms. Pastor Hux saved Dolly from the work-house when confined there with a fever. Fortunately she is robust now. I've even teased her that her waist is verging on plump.

I told Dolly about the universe. But when I did so she laughed out loud, saying that astronomy is ridiculous and that stars are 'celestial light shining through a firmament', no more substantial than a gleam of light from a lamp. What's more, she refuses to believe that there are mountains on the moon. Often she asks me to read one of the sensational newspapers to her. She enjoys reports of murder, although her face becomes the very picture of horror as I reach the description of the actual death-stroke.

'Imagine the hands of a strangler on your throat, Nidabi!' she'd fluttered. 'Imagine his big, hairy hands gripping your neck. What would you do?'

'Kick him and shout,' I'd replied.

'They say that a murderer only has to look you in the eye

for you to fall in a dead faint.' Dolly shuddered. 'I think I'd
die of fright before he even touched me!'

When she asked me to read about the killing of Mitre Rose
I didn't read it all. I passed over the paragraph where police
said they wished to interview the occupants of a carriage seen
on Old Conduit Street the night the body was found. One, a
gentleman in a top hat; the other, a brown-skinned woman.

Ty's Book

30th August. I met Vincent this morning. He'd shaken his head
as a storm swept through the town. Gales brought red dirt
from the fields to paint buildings the colour of rust.

'It's the very demon, isn't it?' Vincent spoke these words
on the Rhone bridge. The river was tainted with the red dust,
lending the impression a vast animal had been butchered
upstream. 'When I paint out in the fields the storm howls in
my ears. I have to weigh the easel with rocks and lash the
canvas to the frame. Work is impossible!'

As he stood there angrily facing the torrent of air, I touched
his quivering arm. 'Vincent. Why don't you paint me?'

Later in the house. Shutters rattled as the gales struck them.
Spurts of red dust jetted through window frames to speckle
the table top. Vincent sat me on a chair. He didn't tell me
how to pose. Quickly, but gently, he moved my head, my
arms, then positioned the angle of my body. He finished by
brushing my hair with his fingertips until he was satisfied it
was in the right position. With lamps forward of me, so they
shone on my face, he began work at the easel. From what
I've seen of other artists I expected him to spend time mixing
paints on a palette. But often he ignored the palette entirely.
He chose to squeeze paints from the tube directly on to the
canvas. These he worked with a knife. His concentration was
phenomenal. Without the straw hat to hide his hair it blazed
in a halo against his head. His eyes were in a constant state

of flux – they shifted from subtle shades of green, to fiery blue, to ice grey, as he moved his head. His entire body was in ceaseless motion as if his flesh expanded then compressed to deliver the paint from his very veins, through his finger-tips, to the canvas. As I posed for him in that room, that was so strongly scented with paint and turpentine, I asked myself questions: I know Vincent makes use of the town's brothels, but why not mine? Why doesn't he come to the house and ask the brothel-keeper to direct him to my room? Does he not find me pretty?

A shutter broke free to slam with a crash. I must have flinched because Vincent fixed me with that thousand league stare of his. 'You've moved, Ty. Raise your chin . . . a little more. That's it.'

As if with a new lover, who demands more than my body can physically give, to maintain this pose is agony. Not to move for a full hour. My back felt as if it were on fire. When it seemed I couldn't hold myself still for another minute Vincent said: 'Relax.' He scraped the palette with a knife before rubbing away waste paint with the remains of a shirt.

'I'll show you it when it's finished,' he told me. 'Sit for another hour, then I'll have your face and body line. There's cold water in the jug if you're thirsty. Use the cup not the wine glass, I've got turpentine in that.'

'Will you finish today?'

'I'll have your portrait down. But to finish it. Ha! That is a new process. Your hair is black but I will dash it with blue – intense flame blues that are like lightning at midnight. Then comes the undulating, serpentine borderland that is your scarlet hair ribbon. That ribbon forms the boundary between you – the woman – and your background. That background will be as much an evocation of your personality as your face.'

I turned to the plain wall behind me.

Vincent shook his head. 'Forget the wall, Ty. When the storm has blown itself out I'll take the portrait into the fields. I'll find a good vigorous cypress full of greenery then paint that as your background. The cypress! A living furnace of the most *vivid* green I can make.'

I remember that Vincent van Gogh had once told me that the cypress tree is the symbol of death. *Why will he marry such a tree to the image of my face?* I wanted to ask the question, only he'd begun to work again. In a darting hand the brush whispered across the fabric as he transferred something of my soul to the canvas.

Outside, the winds sent a long, sorrowful cry across the rooftops. A haunting song that reminds us all of the skull beneath our skin.

Nidabi's Journal

30th August. A future less dark? A way to turn back the hands of the clock? The one that ticks as ponderous as a funeral drum. Tonight the house is silent, and dark and as still as the grave that contains Mitre Rose. You see, it's when I close my eyes, images flicker in my head. I see parcels made up of brown paper. They fly through the sky like dirty snowflakes. I see the laughing mouth. That gap in the front teeth. Blood running across the paving stones. A luscious, pulsating living crimson. And that sound her throat made? When I tried to sleep just now, the sound filled my ears; that hog-like grunt. Now the hallway clock – the one I've come to *hate!* – sends its chimes through the house. One, two, three . . . it summons midnight in a morbid voice.

To write down the incidents of your life is to regain control of them. It's either that or yield to a madness that tries with all the fury of Bedlam to break my soul. To yield is death, Nidabi. To yield is death.

Thursday evening, Limehouse. The cankered slum of East London. This hinterland of narrow streets, alleyways, secret back yards: all oppressed by nothing less than an infestation of squalid hovels, slaughterhouses, herring vendors, carcass boilers, brothels, gin palaces, opium dens. A raucous warren swarming with men, women and children that poverty has transformed into shambling beasts. Limehouse is a place that some believe God has *spurned* in His *horror* and *disgust.*

Though He may have *forsaken* this *foul* progeny of London's making, one man has not. Pastor Hux. He returned with our carriage laden with parcels of salvation wrapped in brown paper. For most of the day we'd worked together. He'd been calm. We'd chatted about my drawings of the moon I'd shown him earlier in the day. As we talked about all things lunar we made packages of food. In each was a measured quantity of cheese, bacon, salt and tea. Parson Hux had regained a completely realistic view of our work; there were no fancies about titanic balloons. No. We would distribute parcels at a time of night when the streets were quieter, so there'd be no repeat of the commotion we'd caused on our previous visits.

At ten o'clock on a chilly August evening we drove along Narrow Street close to the river. I wore a full riding coat of plum velvet over my skirts. The Pastor was, as usual, clad in a long coat and top hat. The same calmness that the Pastor enjoyed also soothed the gallower. The beast pulled the carriage without ill temper. Meanwhile, rain fell in short bursts. Street lamps sizzled as raindrops struck the hot glass that enclosed incandescent mantles. The inclement weather drove people into their homes or into taverns. I glimpsed many a saloon bar. They were brightly lit; full of laughing men and women, who raised foaming tankards to their mouths. Cigars filled the rooms with a mystic blue haze.

When Pastor Hux noticed I stared into each passing tavern he spoke to me with understated humour. 'Distance confers an air of romance, don't you think?' In another tavern the whole room sang together as a man played an accordion. A lament with a haunting melody, a siren's song that melted my heart. He glanced at me. 'Do you wish you were part of that life, Nidabi?'

'They're smiling because of the drink. I wouldn't like to share their society.' Though the way my heart tugged at the sight of those friendly people I wasn't so sure.

'You and I, Nidabi: we are outsiders. It can be lonely. That's our nature: outsiders to the core. We can never change.'

'I think you're right, Pastor.' I set my face lest it reveal my thoughts.

Houses appeared as nebulous forms in the misty rain. Damp forced chimney fumes downward into the street where they prowled like rapacious phantoms. When the Pastor turned into a road lined with mean little houses, the windows revealed themselves as gravestone shapes that gleamed a sickly yellow. At the entrance to an alleyway a woman stood sheltering best she could with a shawl over her head. As the Pastor braked the carriage, she pulled the shawl away and stepped out into the light of a street lamp. Damp ringlets of hair lay across her shoulders. She regarded the pair of us, wondering what service would be expected from her. Pastor Hux, however, reached behind to take a parcel from the basket; this he offered to her.

Suspicion tightened the woman's face. 'What's that?'

'Some food. Bacon, cheese—'

'Customary to give a lady money for her time – you know?'

I explained, 'We want nothing in return. It's an act of charity.'

'Charity? Oh, you'll want me to kneel and pray, then?'

'No.' The Pastor's voice was gentle. 'My motto is deeds, not words. Nothing is expected of you but to make the most of this gift.'

'Give it here, then.' When she took the parcel a thought occurred to her. 'Spare us sixpence, mister? I need me doss money.'

'I'm sorry, madam. We have food but no money.'

She shrugged then ducked back into the alleyway.

Best be moving on, I told myself. She's probably going to fetch some men to test his assertion that we don't have money. I glanced down at the Pastor's feet. In the footwell beside them was the stout dagger he'd carried before. Thankfully, the Pastor urged the horse to walk on. Even so, I expected burly men to charge from every passageway.

'One package delivered safely, Nidabi.' He smiled. 'It won't change a life, but if we can fill a stomach that's a start, hmm?'

'Though they might not thank you, I'm sure they are grateful. Just like I'm grateful for saving me.' A little voice inside my head said: don't ask the question, don't ask the question – and yet it was one I found myself blurting out. 'But why whores? Why do you feed the streetwalkers?'

He stared at me.

Nervous, I found myself stammering, 'There are poor children everywhere. See, there's one mite curled in the doorway. So, why prostitutes?'

His eyes fixed me. What thoughts swam in those depths I don't know. I'd witnessed the melancholia, the sudden exhilaration, the act of savagery on my former master. When he looked at me, dark-skinned, Nidabi, what did he see?

He sighed. 'Some years ago, when I became friends with the Dutchman, we eagerly attended services at the chapel. Our devotion to the minister's sermons was absolute. After chapel we'd walk for hours so we could discuss the Bible. Often deep into the night. One evening we found ourselves in Whitechapel. This was the first time I'd seen streetwalkers. Vincent explained the nature of their profession. Emotion burst over me as if it were a cloudburst. As I stood on that filthy street I was overcome by a feeling of love for these women. To most they're nothing more than walking corpses, yet I saw pain and loneliness.' He stopped the carriage to hand parcels to a pair of young women who stood beneath a lamp. We moved off again. 'I tried to forget about them,' he explained. 'I felt shame for wanting to help them. No one else I knew even pitied them. Whoredom is degeneracy in extremis – or so I was told by my betters. The single person I could confide in was Vincent van Gogh. Only by then he'd returned to his own country. I was left believing I was the only person in the world who longed to improve the lot of these *scarlet* women. For months the passion to do *something* grew so intense that it turned into desperate misery. Then I received a letter from Vincent that proved we shared the same soul. He wrote that he considered all whores to be his sisters. Like him, they were outcasts from society. As soon as I could I began my work with these poor women. Naturally, I wrote to Vincent. I told him I felt the same and I outlined plans to pay them money so they'd no longer be forced to sell their bodies. Vincent replied that he could do little to help me; he was so poor as he'd failed to sell any of his drawings. He had, however, fallen in love with a prostitute called Sien. He took Sien and her children into his home. He planned to marry her. Meanwhile, the hypocrites gathered like wolves. Even Vincent's own father, a priest would you believe? His own father threatened to lock my dearest friend in a lunatic asylum if he married Sien.' The Pastor's face became a mask of brooding anger. 'Mean, despicable . . . they forced Vincent to abandon the woman.' For a moment he said nothing, the only sound the echoing clip-clop of hoof beats in the deserted street. 'I won't be beaten . . . neither will Vincent van Gogh. I received a letter from him yesterday. He tells me he's met a woman who works in a brothel. He's too shy to reveal the depth of his friendship yet. But my intuition suggests that one day she'll become his wife.'

'Then his family will accuse him of insanity again.'

The Pastor smiled as he tapped the side of his nose. 'Vincent has learned his lesson. He's told no one else about his relationship with the woman but me. Not even his own brother. My guess is, he'll keep the relationship a secret until they are married. Fait accompli. It will be too late to throw him into the madhouse.'

Pastor Hux drove slowly through the slum. When the church clock struck midnight we still had at least half of the parcels. Most women accepted the gifts of food. A few were suspicious. One woman who appeared cracked in the head threw the parcel back at me. At one point a drunken soldier pursued the carriage. He blathered about the parcels. 'What's in 'em? Where are y' going? Who are ye?' When the soldier wasn't satisfied with our replies he walked alongside so he could reach into the basket. The Pastor twisted round in the seat and showed the man the knife in his hand.

'Blast you, I only asked.' Despite the belligerent tone the soldier stopped following.

The Pastor shook his head. 'Who'd have thought handing out free food would be so difficult? Another five minutes then we'll go home.'

I was so numb with cold I barely managed a nod. The Pastor was keen to do his duty so he walked the horse at an excruciatingly slow pace. He handed down more brown parcels to streetwalkers. Rain dashed our faces. For a second, lightning lit the street so brightly it hurt my eyes; thunder shouted over the rooftops.

'It's an evil night, Nidabi.'

Now I wonder if he'd glimpsed the future with those brooding eyes. Because no more than ten minutes later we turned our attention to a broad street that bore the name Viaduct Row. At this time of night it was a gloomy cavern of a place. Probably one of the most ill-lit streets of the borough. We'd both heard voices. A man's and woman's slurred with drink. Though they weren't raised in anger there was something fractious about them. I flinched as lightning seared the night sky. For a split second it lit Viaduct Row in a blaze of silver. A man in workman's clothes walked with his arm around a woman, who wore a dark bonnet of some sort. She wagged a finger in the man's face. The hand he draped over her shoulders moved down so he could squeeze her breast. Darkness swallowed them as the lightning died. Thunder shunted directly behind with a crash that shook my skull. The gallower twitched as the storm grew more violent. It stamped the ground; its eyes rolled – the image of a nightmare beast. One look at the Pastor's face in the gloom set off my worst fears.

'What's wrong?'

'That woman across there.' He pulled the brake lever.

'Leave her. She's with a man. There'll be trouble if you approach them now.'

'I know her.' His eyes burned like twin torches in the gloom.

'It doesn't matter. Drive on, Pastor, we'll find more people soon.'

He hissed, 'She shouldn't be here.'

Meanwhile, the voices from the pair still carried across the street. 'Here,' the woman snapped. 'Nuff of that. What about my money?'

The man grunted words I couldn't make out. The tone suggested he didn't want anything more to do with her.

The angry woman followed him into the dim light. 'For the nice thing I done for you I deserve double.'

The drunk waved her away.

Her voice rose. 'Oi! You give me my sixpence, or I'll follow you back to your missus!'

The man fumbled coins from his pocket, then flung them into the gutter. 'Take yer blasted money.'

As he walked away lightning burst over the street again in a searing splash of silver. It revealed the woman on her knees picking up the coins. She was bedraggled-looking, aged around forty, all her clothes were old apart from the black straw hat, which had been pushed askew on her head. Though she laboured to retain a dignified composure her features had lost cohesion due to alcohol.

The Pastor stiffened. 'I know that woman,' he said in tones that conveyed a sense of crushing defeat. 'It's Agnes Cutler.

I found her at the side of the canal; she almost died of pneumonia. I helped her find respectable work.'

'Pastor, if they return to their old ways it's not your fault.'

He tried to make sense of it all. 'But I received a card from her this week. She told me she'd been hired as a nurse.' A vicious blast of lightning exposed Agnes Cutler as she weaved back along the street.

Again I tried to soothe him. 'Don't blame yourself. You tried your best.'

'I don't understand.'

'It's hard for women like us. If they don't have education there's not much other work they can do. Pastor, stay in the carriage. Don't go to her.'

'Nidabi, remain with the horse.' He ran toward the woman. She didn't look back, so didn't see him. I stared into the black cavern that was Viaduct Row. A large building loomed in its centre; a monstrous presence that did nothing to ease my sense of alarm. Its tall Gothic chimneys were like menacing cobras, poised to attack.

Remember the women that this man had helped. They wrote to him, telling lies that they led respectable lives, though most must have slid back into their old whoring ways. They sent those letters to please him. It wasn't *their* fault that streetwalking was the only work open to them. It wasn't *his* fault that he couldn't guarantee that they'd enjoy respectable employment. Even as I sat there in the storm I feared my own future might consist of waiting in these byways for a man who'd give me a few pennies. Now unease worked its evil on me. Where's the Pastor? A thief might appear to steal the horse. What can I do to prevent it? The knife! I bent down to feel for it with my fingers. In vain I searched the footwell. Then understanding dawned. The Pastor must have taken the knife with him. To hell with the horse and the food parcels. I wasn't going to fight for them. I climbed down from the carriage, then hurried into the dark heart of Viaduct Row. My damp skirts clung to my legs and snagged at my boots, threatening to trip me. As I moved deeper into the dripping chasm of buildings I saw that the street narrowed all of a sudden into a path lined on one side by a row of tiny cottages. As far as I could tell the entire area was deserted. Not a soul to be seen. At this early hour all the dwellings were in darkness.

The storm dealt another lightning flash. This time it revealed Pastor Hux and Agnes Cutler. He talked as if beseeching, his gestures impassioned.

As I approached the pair I heard her say, 'Well, I can do nothing about that, can I? It's me nature.'

'Agnes, let me help you.'

'I'm not going back to your old ghost house . . . dull as a grave it is.'

'Agnes—'

'What you can do, sir, is give me a blasted shilling. Then I can get a glass of somethin'.'

He spoke kindly, 'I can't give you money, but I—'

'Well go 'ang yourself, then.'

'I can give you food for a decent meal.'

'Decent, ha!' She gave a drunken laugh. 'You know what decent is, Pastor Hux? Decent is boring. Decent is 'aving no fun.'

'Agnes, this isn't like you. You're a fine woman.'

'Decency is death. I'd rather wake up with a sore 'ead and a sore watchemacallit . . . and know I've had some fun, instead of sitting in bloody Lamplands watching you pray.'

'Come back to my carriage. I'll give you food.'

'No, give me a shillin'.'

I watched the pair revealed by lightning bursts. Vivid faces that appeared so unreal they made me think of grotesque masks, then all was plunged into darkness so I heard only voices; the Pastor's gentle tones pitted against Agnes's slurred anger.

'And tell me this, Pastor,' she was saying. 'Why didn't you take any of us women to your nice soft bed? Is it true that somethin's missing from your body? That your soldier never reported for duty? C'mon, dear. Have a go at this.' She pulled her skirts up over her hips. 'You've paid for it a hundred times over.'

'Agnes, cover yourself.'

'We lasses got to work to eat, y'know? And, y' want to know the truth? All them tarts you saved are back on the street. Oh, they all write you sweet lines to say they're doing nicely-nicely in respectable lives. But they're all here, infesting these backyards. In the filth. All working on their backs, sweating like devils. Or their skirts like this.' She hoisted the fabric up over her hips. In the lightning flashes her naked buttocks showed a luminous blue. For a moment I could fully believe this chuckling creature had risen from beneath the ground like a sprite. 'Pastor Hux, Pastor Hux,' she sang his name as she danced around to show him the naked portion of her body.

Somehow the Pastor underwent a transformation in the lightning flashes. I watched the change take place. It was all like a dream. While her back was turned to him he reached round her, seized her chin then pulled her head back. In that light the throat appeared like a raised curve of a limb, almost impossibly long, white as bone. Her eyes widened in surprise.

She's going to scream, I thought. She's going to scream 'Murder!' Only there was no scream because he drew the blade across that great expanse of naked throat. It opened a deep V-shaped gully in her flesh. Something between a piggish grunt and a crackle erupted from her throat with a loudness that was shocking.

For my part I watched in disbelief as the woman dropped down on to her back. The black straw hat fell from her head. Her bare legs moved as if she tried to push herself across the ground; the heels of her boots gouged at the muddy pavement . . . then they stopped dead. I expected the Parson to run back toward the carriage. No. That's when nightmare took over. He dropped to his knees, the knife in his hands. In a silent frenzy, his eyes wide open, unblinking, he repeatedly stabbed the woman. The blade made a strange popping noise when the point dug into the flesh. I flinched at the sound, as it burned itself into the atoms of my soul. Moments later, he raised himself. Still he fixed his eyes on Agnes as she lay staring up into the falling rain. Her mouth yawned wide. A gap showed in her front teeth. And that frozen look of surprise? I'll remember it until my dying day. No cries of murder. No running footsteps. No pandemonium. Only silence. Even the storm had passed.

The ride home. A dream; a nightmare; a fevered vision. As Pastor Hux and I left the slum an utter sense of horror filled me. An insane conviction for sure, but I expected to see the butchered woman chasing after us, her head lolling across her shoulders. The great gash in her throat oozing scarlet tides. She'd run faster, blood would surge from the vile wound to drench houses, besmear windows, violate the doors with that brutal, shouting crimson. Then the running corpse would leap on to the carriage to gouge our faces with its claws. Terrified to look back, lest my imagination chimed with the truth, I lashed the horse into a gallop. When a wheel struck a rut what remained of the parcels flew out into the night air like brown snowflakes. For some reason they spurned gravity – or so it seemed to me – they tumbled end over end. I never saw if any fell to the ground. After that, all I remember was urging the beast ever faster, until it sped like a black rocket in the direction of home.

1st September. Friday. Strange, dream-like. When we returned home I stripped away Pastor Hux's bloody clothes, then burnt them in the range before the arrival of the domestics. As I bathed him he said nothing. I could have been washing a cadaver for all the life in him. He slept all Friday. I thought I was going mad. I had no sense of time. My world had slipped out of focus. Walking from room to room. Wringing my hands. Picturing Agnes Cutler falling down dead. Asking myself aloud what I should do next. Then sitting to write like a demon in this journal. After that, I forced the lock on the Tantalus in the library. Once the decanter was free I emptied every last drop of brandy down my throat.

I woke on the sofa with the early morning sunlight streaming through the windows. With it being Saturday the domestics would only be present until noon. They didn't venture beyond the kitchen, unless invited above stairs by the Pastor. For a time, I did creep on to the staircase that led down to their workplace. Although I couldn't hear the entire conversation I could make out they talked in an excited way about a killing in Limehouse. The word that constantly reverberated along the passageway was: *blood.* It was a word they returned to constantly. Blood . . . blood . . . blood . . . It smeared the very air. *Blood.* Heaven save me, it held a promise of more evil to come.

When the domestics returned to their homes I went to the Pastor's room. He lay in his nightclothes in the four-poster bed. He stared at the canopy above him. For a moment his stillness horrified me. *He's taken his own life.* The conviction gripped me so hard I trembled. *He's killed himself rather than live with the terrible thing he's done.* However, a red butterfly alighted on the curtain along one side of the bed. His eyes tracked the insect to where it had alighted and flexed its blood-red wings.

Pastor Hux watched it without moving a muscle of his body. 'Don't kill the butterfly, Nidabi.'

I stepped closer to the bed. 'Pastor, what shall we do?'

He shook his head as if my words mystified him.

'The woman died,' I said. 'This morning the domestic staff couldn't stop themselves talking about the murder.'

As if a sudden pain struck him he grimaced. 'I hurt Agnes, didn't I?'

'She goaded you. Many a sane man would have struck her.'

'But would any sane man butcher her like that?'

'You were exhausted. You've been working so hard, you could—'

'But I hacked open her throat.' He ran his hands through his hair. 'It was all those letters from the women. I was so proud – sinfully proud of what I'd done. But they lied to me. It was all a joke. I – I'd never saved anybody. I got them well again just so they could go back to whoring their wretched lives away!'

'Easy, sir. I'll fetch you a drink.'

His gripped my forearm so hard I cried out. 'Do I deserve drink? What do I deserve, Nidabi? What's my final reward?'

'Sir, please—'

'I'll tell you, shall I? A noose! That's my reward, Nidabi. Death!'

'No, sir! I shan't let them hang you.'

'You can't stop the police, Nidabi. They're going to string me up like a pig. Then bury me in quicklime. I'm going to burn, Nidabi. I'm going to burn for ever.' His eyes rolled. 'I've murdered my own future.'

'It's been a sickness with you, sir. You've been ill. What happened to the woman was just a symptom of the malady.'

'I killed her.'

'It won't happen again. You've worked too hard to let it all go for nothing.'

'My charitable work has failed, that's the truth of it. Now I must be punished.'

'You've not failed. Here! *Look at me.* Have you failed with me? Have you?' I ripped my arm free of his grip then slammed both fists down on to his chest as he lay there. 'You rescued me. If you did that you can save other women, too. You won't preserve everyone. But there'll be some who have a better life because of you.'

'That doesn't alter the fact—'

'Damn the facts. You saved me. So I'll save you!'

'You can't.'

'I can.' Again I crashed both my fists down on to his chest.

'You can't, Nidabi. Because I'm going to kill again. You see, I *want* to.' His eyes gleamed. 'I can feel the need. When I cut that woman's throat . . .' He licked his lips. 'Such power.'

'It's the sickness making you talk like this. Just like a drunkard says things they don't mean.'

'I'll write a full confession. Take it to the police.'

'No!' I pointed my finger at him. 'Never . . . *never!*'

A silence fell after this. Sunlight streamed through the glass. The red butterfly remained on the curtain.

At last he stirred. Raising himself from the bed on one elbow, he fixed me with a solemn gaze. 'Nidabi, you think there is a chance I might get better?'

'There is, sir. Believe me.'

'I need time to recover.'

'Lamplands is just the place. It's very quiet.'

'So be it. But you must put me in the north wing . . . no, hear me out, Nidabi. I must be locked in the sanatorium there, so if I experience that seizure again I won't be a threat to anyone.' His gaze became penetrating. 'That includes you, Nidabi.'

'I can't, sir. A prisoner in your own home? It's unnatural.'

'Regardless. That's the way it's got to be.'

I followed him along the corridor. Instead of putting on day clothes he wore his dressing gown, a richly decorated garment in green. At the twin doors that led to the north wing he stopped, produced keys from his pocket, selected one then unlocked the door. After that, he gave me the keys. Then he slipped the velvet cord from its loops on the dressing gown and handed it to me with the words, 'Sometimes the women who were addicted to opiates would do everything in their power to harm themselves. Even though I'm no addict you must take similar precautions with me.'

'I'm not happy about this, sir.'

'Needs must.' His face had a waxy appearance as he struggled to contain an emotion that mounted inside of him. 'You can permit me books and paper. If I write letters, read them first before posting in case I describe anything I shouldn't. Give me only a spoon to eat with – absolutely no knives.'

'I don't think that's necessary. You're very much master of yourself.'

Taking a deep breath he said, 'I wish that was the case. It's difficult to . . .' He cleared his throat. 'Difficult to make the words lucid. You understand?'

'Yes, sir.'

Perspiration gleamed on his lip. 'No razor. It won't be safe. You will shave me.'

'I don't know if—'

'I'll prepare a . . . safe procedure.' A tremor affected his cheek. 'Now please hurry.' He swept along the corridor to a stout door that had been reinforced with massive hinges. Three large bolts sealed it shut. 'This . . . keep me here.' He slammed back the bolts. 'Nidabi, remember! Don't let me out. Even if I beg to be released. Even if I rage at you. Don't unlock the door. Never open it!' He pushed open the door, then surged through as if propelled by some invisible force. Inside the room, that monstrous timber chair. Leather straps dangled from the arm rests. The dark wood, its titanic proportions, it might have housed some malignant spirit that revelled in the torture of anyone who occupied its seat. A throne for the damned, indeed. This was the room I'd seen through the gap in the curtains. It wasn't as empty as I first believed. Against one wall stood a narrow bed. All in all, a grim, forbidding chamber.

Pastor Hux nodded toward a door. An urgency quickened his words. 'That leads to the bathroom. There's no exit but the one we entered by. There are no glass bottles or sharp instruments. Nidabi. See the chair?' His brown eyes gleamed as he stared at the cruel thing that appeared more like an instrument of pain than an item of furniture. 'Later, that will become important.'

'I'm sure it won't come to that.'

'The chair will be vital to preserve your safety. Now, please, don't question me when I tell you what you must do now. Return to the passageway. Shut the door behind you. Draw the bolts to lock me in. Remember, if I demand you free me, don't! Keep me here until I'm myself once more.'

'But how will I know if you're well?'

'Use the best of your abilities to assess me. Now lock me in.'

I hesitated.

'Do it!'

As I moved back, trembling, he suddenly hissed, 'Wait!'

If he asks me to release him now, how can I refuse him?

Fear gleamed in his eye. 'Nidabi? When we walked here from my bedroom . . . were we alone?'

'Of course, sir.'

'You didn't see two women following us?'

I gave an emphatic shake of my head.

'You're quite sure?' He grasped one hand in the other. 'One of the women . . . there was something *wrong* with her face.' He stared at me expectantly, perhaps trying to gauge from my reaction whether I had, in fact, seen anyone.

I grew so tense I thought for a moment I'd cry out. Nevertheless, I waited for him to add more. Perhaps to reveal that one of the women was Mitre Rose with her coffin on her back, as he'd described her before. I didn't doubt he saw the slaughtered body of Agnes Cutler stalking him in his own house, her throat all bloody, her eyes fixed on him. What now? Would he lunge at me? Would he run out through the door? If so, how could I force him back here? It wouldn't be long before the commotion brought the police. I'd witnessed murder. I did nothing to prevent it. Already I could feel the constriction of the noose around my neck. *He hangs. I hang.* A stark truth, but truth nonetheless.

For a moment he battled with whatever impulses urged him to madness. The tremor in his face got worse. His breath became laboured. Perspiration gleamed on his forehead. Then: 'Go on, go on, please . . .' He motioned gently with his hand. A signal that I should leave. 'Go on, please . . .' Raving, shouting, curses, threats, fury. I'd have found an uproar easier to take. This muted, 'Go on, please.' Those expressive eyes. He was beseeching me to leave while he exerted whatever resources he could to master his self-control. That did it: a flood burst inside my heart. Though my vision was streaked with tears I rushed at the sanatorium door. Somehow I found a way through it, before pulling it behind me. Then I dragged shut the first bolt.

Since I deprived Pastor Hux of his freedom I check him on the hour. I've found a hole in the door, drilled for the purpose of viewing the chamber's occupant without being seen. For a long time yesterday he stood exactly where I left him. He still moved his hand: that heartbreaking gesture to leave. 'Go on, please.' The pattern had fixed in his head. Everything is to learn myself. However, I found that at the bottom of the door there is a hinged flap some twelve inches long by four high: through this I slid a paper plate bearing cheese, bread and cold beef. When I returned an hour ago I decided to remove the uneaten food. The evening was warm enough for it to spoil quickly. Quickly, I looked in through the spy-hole. Pastor Hux stood with his back to me. He stared at the massive chair bolted to the centre of the room as if appraising it in some way. Crouching down, I lifted the hinged flap so I could reach in to retrieve the untouched meal. My fingertips hadn't even reached the plate when a blow struck my arm. The Pastor had my wrist in a fierce grip. His bulging eyes were just inches from mine. All this in the short interval between me looking through at him, then bending to retrieve the plate. His breath roared. The skin of his face blotched with a dark passion.

'Please,' I begged. 'Don't hurt me. I'll open the door. Just don't hurt me!'

'You promised they weren't here! Now you've let them into the room!'

'Sir, I don't know what you mean . . . oh . . .'

'When you bolted me in here. Those damn women! They got past you when you opened the door. Stupid girl! You let them in!'

I thought he'd twist my wrist until he broke it.

'Sir! There aren't any women in there with you.'

'Call them out of here!'

'I can't – you're alone!'

He's going to drag me close so he can reach my throat. The knowledge he was going to kill me roared through my soul with all the fury of a runaway train.

'Pastor, I'll open the door.'

'*No!*'

'But I can't—'

'Get the women out. Not me.' He moaned with fear. 'For the love of God, just get them out.'

'I can't see anyone, sir.'

'There – look through the gap. See the chair? See them standing by it? One's all covered with blood, the other's carrying that *thing* on her back.'

'I don't see them.'

'Then stand up . . . look through the hole in the door.'

He released me all of a sudden. Gasping for breath, I dragged my arm back, grazing it against the hinged flap, then I rolled away from the aperture, so he couldn't reach me. A second later I raced back down the hallway. Following me, his pitiful cry. 'Nidabi! Can't you see them? Oh my God, get them away from me!'

It was two hours later before I could bring myself to check on him through the spy-hole. Though the angle was tight I could just make out he lay curled on the bed with his face to the wall, his hands over his head as if trying to hide. I endeavoured to see as much of the grim cell as I could. The chair. The bare boards. No women. Yet they were all too real to him. Mitre Rose in her white nightdress stained with the oozings of the grave. He must see her ghost carrying her coffin on its back, a macabre beetle-like shell. Dead Rose would be joined by Agnes Cutler – a phantom that displayed its gaping neck wound to him with its never-ending cataracts of blood. What menacing suggestions would those spirits whisper into his ear? *Make us three. Send Nidabi to her grave so she can join us here* . . . Not for the first time I ask myself how I will know if Pastor Hux is cured. Do I summon a doctor? Or do I wait for as long as I can? After all, if this ends badly then it's either the gallows for me, or working London's streets.

3rd September. I found Grace Tarant and Dolly West in the kitchen, boiling a kettle for tea.

Grace looked at me in surprise. 'My girl, what have you done to yourself?'

'Nothing.'

'You look as if you 'aven't slept in a week. What do you say, Dolly?'

'It's probably a cold. There's a lot of it about. The weather's been awfuller than winter.'

'Well, we brought you treacle cake.' Grace's thin face tightened into a smile. 'The baker gave me a whole big slab on account of my charms.' She unwrapped the greased paper from the cake, which was the size of a house brick. Then she set the sticky brown confection on to a plate. 'Oh, get me a knife, would you, Dolly? Best make it a carving knife – this piece is a proper beauty.'

When Dolly pulled the large knife from the drawer she turned with a look of horror as she remembered something. 'Did you hear, Nidabi? Another one of us has been done in Limehouse?'

'Oh, good Lord, yes.' Grace put her hand over her throat. 'Agnes Cutler, poor woman. It isn't a week since that I took beer with her at the White Hart. She'd been cock-a-hoop 'cos she'd made peace with her family. Then this! Killed in the street. A good woman like that.'

Dolly's blue eyes were wide. 'The murderer nearly cut off her head. They say it was hanging by a thread.'

Keeping my composure was hard. I wanted nothing more than to flee through the door.

'What's more, the police haven't caught the devil that did it, neither. Say!' Dolly turned her head so quickly her blonde hair flew out. 'Grace, why don't me, you and Nidabi catch the penny steamer back? We can show her the place in Viaduct Row.' Her face flushed with excitement. 'You know, no matter how many times they wash away the blood it keeps coming back. It just bubbles up from the ground like red tar. That's what happens when someone's met a savage end, doesn't it?'

'I don't want to hear about it.' Sickness rose in my throat. I remembered the gap in the dead woman's front teeth. The hog sound that came from her severed windpipe.

'Course, what got everyone talking last night is that Lizzie Wragg saw Agnes's ghost standing outside the Grapes tavern. Agnes was pointing in through the saloon window as if to tell everyone, "Whoever killed me came from in there."'

'Dolly! Shut up!' I pounded the table. 'That's stupid talk. There's no such thing as ghosts!'

'But that's what happened. Tell her, Grace. The ghost stood

holding her bleedin' throat with one hand while pointing the other at a sailor man through the window glass.'

'If you say that again, I'll knock you down!'

'Sweetheart, I only said—'

Grace shot Dolly a stern look. 'Leave it be, Dolly. Not everyone takes to murder stories.'

'But that's what everyone's saying—'

Grace snapped. 'Any more and I'll box your ears. Now pour the tea.'

A sulky pout set Dolly's lips.

'Now, this is lovely cake. Let's all sit down to enjoy it. Ooh, look at how moist it is.' Grace began to slice the delicacy. However, I realized that despite the small talk she awarded me appraising glances, as if sensing something wasn't right. 'Nidabi?'

'Yes.' I adopted a formal tone.

'Pastor Hux said anything about you moving on?'

'No.'

'It's been a while now, hasn't it?'

I nodded.

'He will soon, then,' Dolly added with a dash of venom. She still smarted from my scolding.

'You've been down our way,' said Grace, 'distributing to the poor.'

'And there'd been trouble,' Dolly added, 'I saw it. There was a right barney. I had to push Nidabi back into their trap, otherwise folk'd have beaten the bloody lights out of her.'

'We took food for the women. Some men stole it. The basket, too.'

'They'll bite the hand that feeds them,' Grace told me with feeling. 'If you do the same again, arm yourselves with muskets. That's the only way to stop those rogues. Now, eat your cake, you look as if you need some goodness inside you.'

'Here.' Dolly took my cup. 'Have a nip of this.' She uncorked a medicine bottle so she could dribble in a brown liquid. 'It's been so cold this summer I've taken to carrying whisky with me. That'll do your blood good.'

Her kindness touched me. 'Thank you, Dolly. I apologize for being short with you. I don't like tales of murder.'

'Say no more, my sweetheart.' Dolly leaned forward to squeeze my hand. 'Drink up and I'll freshen your cup.'

Grace pretended sternness. 'And Dolly? No more talk of ghosts, either.'

'Oh, that came from Lizzie Wragg.' She waved her hand as if shooing a fly. 'You know, she smokes hemp in her pipe? I don't know why I swallowed her gabble about seeing phantoms.'

'Come to that,' Grace said, munching her cake, 'there's nothing she hasn't seen.'

'That's right.' Dolly nodded. 'You know that slaughterhouse on Dock Road? Well, Lizzie swears blind that's a special place where they butcher hogs like you've never seen before. Pigs with men's faces, she says. See? Human features instead of snouts. She says that the Queen's doctor breeds them in secret at Windsor Castle. If you drink their blood while it's warm you never get old.'

The two women collapsed into fits of laughter. For the first time in days I found myself smiling.

'Give us your cup, Nidabi. This's going to warm you a treat.' Dolly trickled more liquor into the tea. 'Oh, dear. Down to the last drop, I'm afraid.'

'I know where there's more,' I told them. A moment later I was back with a decanter from the broken Tantalus.

'Oh, you shouldn't be doing that.' Grace's mouth hung open. 'That's his best whisky.'

'If he finds you've nicked it –' Dolly laughed – 'he'll skin you alive!'

'He'll have to catch me first.' They appreciated my joke, though when they appeared hesitant about accepting the liquor I added blithely, 'Oh, it's all right. Pastor Hux told me it's the best cure for a cold. He insisted I use it whenever I want.' That said, the women eagerly welcomed the generous tot of gold in each cup. Grace beamed with such good cheer I couldn't help smiling along with her.

'Now, there's not another man on earth, God bless him.' Grace raised her cup. 'Here's a lovin' toast to Pastor Hux, saviour of fallen women.'

While I sat in the kitchen with Grace and Dolly the events of last week became dream-like. We made such a merry little band that, for a while, I half-believed that the madness hadn't happened at all. When at last they declared they had to catch the ferry back to the docks I was tempted to accompany them. I recalled the taverns full of friendly people singing together

Simon Clark

in that warm, snug room. That had looked lovely. I didn't
doubt the two would have a grand time, and that beautiful
Dolly West, with her dancing blue eyes would draw the gaze
of every man in the bar.

What wouldn't be so lovely is after the tavern closed. That's
when these two women would have to earn their doss money
in the alleyways. Images of their rough treatment at the hands
of lusty brutes triggered darker thoughts. A picture came of
Agnes Cutler, dancing slowly round the yard with her skirts
pulled up. Then the blood, all that blood . . .

Later. At midnight I ventured into the north wing with a lighted
candle. Shadows slid along the walls, my dark companions,
yet even they deserted me, as if afraid to enter these forbidding quarters, where even the very walls breathed of past
terrors, and hinted at worse horrors to come. When I
approached the room where I'd locked Pastor Hux I saw that
he'd opened the flap at the bottom of the door. Now he lay
down on the other side of it with his arm pushed through the
narrow aperture. From this side that's all I saw of him: his
bare arm extended through the opening, a long, pale snake of
a limb. His hand 'walked' across the boards so he could explore
that area of floor with his fingertips. What he hoped those
roving fingertips would find I don't know. Maybe he thought
they'd alight on something – an Epiphany that would put an
end to all his troubles. Without doubt, he took pains to search
the floorboards repeatedly, the bare arm gleaming palely in
my candlelight. The search was as soundless as it appeared
endless. When the clock struck the half hour I retired to bed.
I hoped that the two phantoms that haunted the Pastor in his
cell wouldn't visit me in my dreams.

4th September. Detectives arrived at Lamplands. One of the
maids called upstairs to me as the men had presented themselves at the back door. Rather than admit them into the main
body of the house, I spoke to them in the kitchen. I thought
the domestic staff might remain there for whatever entertainment unfolded, but the old woman took them all down to the
laundry room to fold bed sheets. I invited the detectives to sit
at the table and take tea with me, but they said they preferred
to stand.

There were two of them – both robust looking gentlemen aged between forty and fifty. The afternoon was a warm one. Their faces pinked above starched collars.

So! You're here, I told myself. My heart sank and the world became faint around me. You've come like I feared you would. Now you'll take the Pastor and me away. Now, do I speak first? Is this a test of nerve? Do these gentlemen simply stare at me in the expectation my spirit will snap and I confess? Clearly, I was the focus of their attention. What do they find so interesting? Is it my appearance? My dark skin? Something seen aplenty in the slums but not in an elegant, if neglected mansion.

At last, the senior of the pair spoke to me. 'Good afternoon. We are policemen. This is Detective Constable Witham. I'm Inspector Leach. I'd very much like to speak to your master.'

I pressed my hands hard against my skirts, trying to muster calm. 'I'm afraid Pastor Hux isn't at home.'

Leach consulted his notepad. 'I have the owner of this house ... Lamplands, as Mister Posthumous Hux, a gentleman. He's a cleric?'

'You will have to speak to Pastor Hux about that, sir.'

'Of course. I take it you are in service here? Not his ... ahm?'

'I'm his housekeeper, sir.'

The other one spoke in a more forthright way, 'What's your name?'

'I am Nidabi.'

'Nidd-arbi? Spelling?'

'N-I-D-A-B-I. Nidabi.'

Detective Constable Witham noted it in his book. 'Nidabi. First name?'

'That's all.'

'What the devil do you mean, that's all?'

Inspector Leach wasn't as gruff as his colleague. 'We require your full name. Is Nidabi your surname?'

'I'm sorry, sir. It's the only name I have.'

'I see. Age?'

'I believe I am in the region of twenty-one years.'

'Place of birth?'

'Dover, England.'

'Really?' The gruff one's tone suggested he didn't believe me. 'Now, when you say that Mister Hux isn't at home, do you mean he's indisposed or he's absent from the premises?'

'He's gone to town on business, sir.' A wild lie.

'Hmm, unfortunate.' Inspector Leach rubbed his jaw. 'This place is out of the way.'

'I can ask the Pastor to telegram you with an appointment, if that will be convenient to you, gentlemen?'

The wasted journey irritated the gruff one. 'We need to interview Mr Hux at his earliest convenience. You see we have a description of a gentleman accompanied by a dark-skinned girl in Whitechapel. They were riding in a carriage, drawn by a black gallower.'

'Sir?'

'Your master owns a two-wheeler and such a beast?'

'Yes, sir.'

'Were you riding with your master in Old Conduit Street recently?'

'I'm not sure if I recollect, sir.'

'Come on, you know whether or not you rode through that street in the last four weeks.'

'I'm not familiar with London.'

'Not Whitechapel? Why, there's no mistaking the slum's odour, girl.'

'Sir, I believe the Pastor has missionary work in that quarter.'

'Detective Constable Witham.' Leach smiled as if he'd found the answer to a question that had plagued him. 'If Mister Hux isn't home then we shouldn't delay his staff any longer. Besides, it's not the done thing to interview the girl without her master's consent.' Leach handed me a card. 'This has my name, police rank and address. Do you know when your master will be home?'

'It might be several days, sir.'

'A pity. Ask him to write to me with a time when we can find him at home. It's important we speak to him as soon as possible. You understand?'

'Yes, sir.'

'Right, we'll see ourselves out. Good day.'

As they stepped out into the sunlit yard they replaced their hats. At that moment the horse whinnied in its stable and they exchanged knowing glances. I clenched my fist; they're going to come back and search the house now. What will they say when they find the man they want to interview locked in a room with that infernal asylum chair bolted to the floor? The damn horse whinnied again. However, they walked directly to a waiting carriage. A constable opened the door for them before taking the driver's seat. In moments they'd vanished back in the direction of the smoky, blue haze of London. My lie about the Pastor's absence would give me a day or two's grace. But I harboured no doubt that they'd soon hasten back. Lamplands wouldn't be my safe haven for much longer.

5th September. Midnight. If you can't sleep, what then? Do you count sheep? Do you imagine yourself gently swinging in a hammock? On coming to bed I slept for an hour then found myself wide awake. Although I no longer had power over events in my life it can, on occasion, comfort me to record what happens to me. So, tonight I sit here and write. Outside, a breeze stirs the trees into a hissing sound that rises and falls like surf rolling toward a beach. On the table in front of me are a pair of candles. Two are better at keeping the shadows at bay than one. Moreover, lately I've become anxious about burning just one candle in case a draught snuffs it out. Since the death of Mitre Rose the darkness in the house has become so much blacker. It becomes a palpable substance. A darkness to be felt. It threatens to suffocate me if I linger in its presence too long. There are times I fear the blackest of shadows will engulf the room; in those shadows will be awful demons that will carry me, screaming, into the abyss. Shadows, shadows, how they swarm in this tomb of a house. The candles reveal my reflection in the dressing-table mirror. *Oh, what haunted eyes you have, Nidabi. What grim countenance.* And as I sit here, so it starts again. The voice, calling. A mournful, plaintive sound that seems to emanate from the belly of the grave rather than from the depths of the house. 'Nid . . . ahh . . . beee. Nid . . . ahh . . . beeeeee.' *Shut up . . . damned ghost, damned canker of the spirit.* 'Nidabi.' *No. You're no phantom.* It's the Pastor again. Often at night he will be seized by a fit of calling. His voice ghosts through locked doors and along the corridor to my bedroom. 'Nidabi . . . Let me out! They're in here with me again. You've got to let me out!'

I whisper my reply: 'No, I won't release you, Pastor. Because

I promised I wouldn't free you. I won't break my promise . . .
this is love.'

My mind's eye can fly from the bedroom to speed to the
north wing and pass through the locked door of the Pastor's
room. There it finds the great bleak chair – a dark structure
of titanic proportions bolted to the centre of the floor. Where
is Pastor Hux? Maybe under the bed again, eyes screwed tight
shut, so he can't see his two night visitors. The pair of rotting
death heads that haunt him. He's described them often enough.
Mitre Rose scurrying with the coffin on her back. Agnes
Cutler, her throat all cut. Head hanging sideward. She has
things for eyes, he tells me . . . *things* he can't bring himself
to describe. Do the ghosts dance for him? Do they just stare?
Do they accuse him of failing them? Maybe they invite the
Pastor to join them in their cold and loveless world.

The voice rolls through the house again with an eerie power.
'Nidabi, let me out. I won't hurt you. I promise.'

{Inspector Leach, London, 6th September, 1888}

*Sir, I have yet to interview Mr Posthumous Hux, regarding
the death of Mitre Rose. Given the current state of public
hysteria due to the recent slaying of Agnes Cutler, I appreciate it's untimely to allocate much in the way of resources
to the Rose case. However, the night watchman gave me a
description of the man and woman seen on Old Conduit Street
the evening Rose was deposited on the pavement. Through
careful questioning of witnesses I was able to ascertain that
a couple matching this description have been distributing food
to the poor. Local police constables knew of this activity.
Moreover, they were able to direct me to a chapel in
Blackheath, attended by Hux. There, I interviewed members
of the congregation. Although they distanced themselves from
Hux's charitable mission, they confirmed that this gentleman
is not an ordained minister, nor welcome at their chapel on
account of his 'excessive zeal' and 'unsanitary domestic
arrangements'. They gave me Hux's address as Lamplands,
off Park Road. There, I briefly interviewed a female of Indian
extraction by the name of Nidabi. However, the female claimed
her master was not home. Both DC Witham and I suspected
she lied. I appreciate that the force is under pressure from*

other fronts, nevertheless, I feel we are near to closing the case of Mitre Rose. Sir, I respectfully request your authority to obtain a magistrates' warrant in order to search the dwelling known as Lamplands at your earliest convenience.

Ty's Book

6th September. In the café Vincent van Gogh brandished the knife. 'I am striving to reveal the evil passions of man with eruptions of red and green . . . blood-red, alien-green. See?' He'd set up his easel near the bar. In this spot he'd worked for three consecutive nights, surviving on coffee by the pint. At this moment he worked the knife blade on a dash of lemon-yellow paint to transform the lamp he painted into an inferno that seared the room with witch-fire. The greens and the reds he used to paint the night café evoked its wastrel occupants. He told me, though he painted the outer forms of the absinthe drinkers, he wished to expose their secret obsessions that centred on envy, greed, hatred, or fears so powerful they drove men to obliterate their senses in alcohol.

As he added specks of yellow to a vagabond's eyes to suggest the glint of daemonic urges he murmured, 'Every man and woman has a secret. Yet they'd never confess it to their closest friend, because though that secret burns inside of them they fear it. To even reveal it makes them afraid that the ones they love would be so shocked they'd reject them for ever.' He awarded me a knowing glance. 'Shopkeepers crave to be bullfighters. A pathologist might long to dissect a living human specimen. A nanny dreams of locking children in a cellar. A good Samaritan might suddenly harbour a fondness for stamping on beggars. So, Ty, what's my secret?'

'You don't have to tell me.'

The artist smiled. 'I have many secrets. You are one of them. I've not told my family about you. Isn't that an insane constraint? Because some day I might make a decision and have to act in a way that involves you. I put it badly because like all secrets that we embed deeply inside ourselves, they become near impossible to express rationally. But in the end we always do let them slip because they are so powerful. Many reveal their inner dreams through jokes, or doodles. Mine are all in these paintings. If you unravelled the code, my pictures would tell you about not only secret fears but my hopes, too.' He glanced at me as he worked a luminous green around the head of a sinister figure. 'Only I hope you never learn the code. Because I know you would flee from me and never return.'

Nidabi's Journal

6th September. It's been a week since Pastor Hux killed Agnes Cutler. Since confining him the Pastor has either been as silent as death, or has been shouting and running around the locked cell. From my bedroom I can hear the rapid pounding of bare feet on the floorboards. Today I realized I must do more for him than push food through that hinged flap at the bottom of the door. So I collected his shaving mug, soap, a towel and his razor. Thus equipped I entered the north wing to peer through the spy-hole bored in the door panel at eye level. Naturally, that Bedlam chair with its cruel leather straps drew my attention first. It was empty. So was the bed, which was in disarray with the pillows cast on the floor. I listened. Silence. Utter silence. Of Pastor Hux? No sign. I couldn't tap on the door because I held the tray with the shaving things and kettle of hot water.

I cleared my throat. 'Pastor Hux?' *Silence.* 'It's Nidabi. You'll be ready to freshen yourself, won't you, sir?'

I put my face to the spy-hole. An eye looked back into mine. I started back so violently that I nearly tipped scalding water down myself. After taking deep breaths to recover my composure, I leaned toward the door so I could look through the hole from a distance. It occurred to me that in a fit of passion he might drive a pencil through it into my eye. Eventually I made out a bloodshot eye with a reddened eyelid. The eye was like the dead eye of a fish.

'Sir . . . Pastor? I've brought hot water and a razor. You might like to shave.' No reply, just an unblinking stare. 'I can bring a clean nightshirt later.'

A rasp of his breath, then: 'Yes, dear Nidabi. My Nidabi . . .' Exhaustion reduced his voice to a croak.

Despite the weakness of the voice he appeared to have regained his composure. 'I'll set down the tray, Pastor, then I'll open the door.'

'Wait, Nidabi. I'll go to the chair.'

'Please don't sit on that.' I dreaded any thought of him perched on that monstrosity. 'Sit at the end of the bed.'

'No, Nidabi.' The voice was calm. 'Listen to me. Don't open the door.'

'I have to.'

'Not yet.' He took a deep breath that rasped with a morbid power all of its own. 'Listen to me. You must obey.'

'If that's what you wish, sir.'

'Don't cry, Nidabi. I don't know how to describe it plainly. But I experience surges of emotion. It's a dark, dark passion. I see it in my mind's eye. It's way off in the distance. I think I'm safe.' His words quickened. 'That it can't reach me, but then I know it's coming. This passion flows like an incoming tide. I know I can't stop it, for it engulfs me. It's horrible. It rushes over me in a flood. Then I crave to do *insane* things. I can't stop these cravings.' He took more rasping breaths to calm himself. 'You'll see the effects. I've made rather a mess of the place.'

'I'll do whatever makes you happy, sir.'

'Then stay there with the door locked. I'll call you when it's time to enter. But check I'm secure first. There's a chance I might not speak the truth if it takes hold of me.'

'Sir, I don't understand what you're going to do.'

The voice came with a little of its former sureness. 'I'm going to sit in the chair. I'll secure the leather straps round my ankles.'

Nausea rolled through me. That damn awful chair. It was for a howling madman, not kind-hearted Pastor Hux.

He continued in a matter-of-fact way, 'I can't fasten my own arm restraints, of course, but I've strung a chain about the chair. There's a padlock. I'll lock the chain around my chest to hold me there – if I need to be prevented from rising.'

A tear rolled down my face as I listened to the grim words.

'Nidabi. When I call out for you to look, ensure I'm in the chair with the chain around my chest. I'll take the key from the padlock and throw it across the room where I can't reach it. Then, when you're satisfied I'm restrained, unlock the door. Come directly to me. Fasten the straps around my wrists. You'll be safe then.'

'But I feel safe with you, Pastor!'

Gently, he tried to soothe me, 'Nidabi, hush.'

'I want to come in as you are. If you choose to kill me then so be it. I've lived like a human being since you rescued me. You do what you want with me!'

'What I need to know is that you're safe from harm. Just like those women are safe from harm while I'm in here. If you care about me, you'll allow me to tether myself to the chair. Nidabi, do we have an understanding?'

'Yes, sir. Because you wish it to be like this.'

'I do, Nidabi. Now, wait a moment.' Footsteps sounding, then, 'Come to the door now. Always check I'm away from it before you put your face to the aperture.'

In the muted daylight of the room I could see him in the chair. He still wore the dressing gown. His feet were bare, stubble darkened his jaw. Already he'd lost weight. His cheekbones pushed against the skin. I saw that he'd fastened the straps that would hold his feet to the chair legs. Then he drew the chain across his chest where he pushed the padlock hasp into the mechanism. I heard the click of the lock. As if this procedure sapped his energy he wearily pitched the key toward the door.

'I've done, Nidabi. If you're satisfied I can't harm you, enter the room.'

Quickly, I shot back the bolts and opened the door.

He gave a tired wave of the hand to beckon me. 'Come fasten the wrist straps. No, don't bother with the tray yet. Do these first.'

'There's no need for those. The chain will be—'

'*Do it*, Nidabi.'

'Sir—'

'I'm the devil now! Don't you understand that?'

'You're not the devil, sir, you're—'

'Fasten the straps, or get out.'

I had to bite my lip as tears formed in my eyes. But I did as he asked. In a moment, I had buckled the broad leather straps around his wrists. The cowhide was blackened with grime. How many other poor souls had been consigned to that Bedlam monstrosity's embrace?

'Nidabi. Make sure they're tight enough. Hurry.'

When I checked the restraints he sighed with relief, even though the belts dug into his skin.

'I'm sorry, sir.'

'Now, don't start that again,' he breathed. 'I regret I had to raise my voice, but this thing – *this devil* – inside of me . . . I'm frightened I'll hurt you. Not my dear Nidabi. Never, never.'

I stared. He'd lost so much weight. His eyes had sunk deep into his head. Fissures ran through his dry lips. He noticed my grief and forced the ghost of a smile. 'Weren't you going to shave me?'

'Yes, sir.'

'Then you be careful with that razor. It's sharp, don't you go cutting yourself.'

Lights are burning. I even lit the huge Byzantine lamp that hangs in the hall; the very device that inspired a previous owner of the house to name their home Lamplands. It's dark now. The sky is clear. With the Pastor free of the wretched chair again he is resting though his hands are fretful, as if they live independently of him.

In between writing my journal I've been working on maps of the moon. It may seem a frivolous occupation, yet it allows me to escape this world of worry for a while. I have inked the moon's craters, as well as its mountains and dark, mysterious oceans. When I find myself dwelling morbidly on the Pastor's condition I imagine myself soaring to that shining Lunar globe that hangs in our night sky. There, I can indulge my fantasy of standing on a headland that overlooks the Sea of Tranquillity. Soon I'll add a pale yellow wash to the maps.

That will have to be in what little time I can spare. There's a great deal of work to do around the property. As well as caring for the Pastor I have to feed the horse, clear the stable, lay fresh straw. This evening I cut back shrubs that encroach on the driveway. I also attempted to scythe the tangle of vines that threaten to choke the paths. What all this means, of course, is that by ten o'clock I am dog tired. Even brushing my hair before bed becomes an effort.

But I shan't complain. I can bear these labours. This is home.

{Inspector Leach, London, 7th September, 1888}

Sir, referring to my letter of the 6th inst, I am in receipt of the magistrates' warrant in order to make a search of Lamplands. As the house is of considerable size I request that you authorize the release of eight constables from the Cutler murder case. Since I wrote to you last I have gathered further information on the activities of Mister Hux and his female companion. Hux has never been ordained. His title of pastor appears to be something of a pose. He dresses in black though eschews ecclesiastical garments. One of the congregation at the Chapel of St Jude recalls that Hux first attended services there twelve years ago with a red-haired man of Dutch origin, who was of an excitable disposition, and somewhat given to eccentric opinions – opinions that Hux appeared to share. Hux is a gentleman of private, if diminished, means. Earlier this year Hux and the Nidabi woman perpetrated a violent assault on one Colonel J. Warrington. At the moment, this is hearsay, as I have yet to interview the Colonel. However, the incident lends weight to my suspicion that Hux was involved in the slaying of the vagrant known as Mitre Rose. I propose to revisit Hux's dwelling with a view to conducting a search thereof tomorrow.

Nidabi's Journal

7th September. He's gone. Pastor Hux left Lamplands during the night. How did he leave the room? Certainly not through the stout door as it was bolted from the outside. What he had done, I suspect, is the near reverse of what I'd accomplished some time ago, when I'd crept along the ledge to peer inside at that ugly chair with its leather straps. As I slept, Pastor Hux must have climbed out of the sanatorium window, then inched along the ledge three storeys above the ground. When he reached the landing window, which was ajar, he simply climbed inside, went to his room, dressed, packed clothes into a bag, and then he'd walked away from me. Now, this morning, I'm left alone with a sense of abandonment. No farewell note, no way of knowing where he's gone. The only souls I have seen are the domestic staff, so I'll maintain a pretence that everything is normal, that the Pastor is home but indisposed.

Later. Like a fool I couldn't be patient. This evening I hitched the gallower to the carriage before riding into town. I drove through the slums in the hope I'd see Pastor Hux. Naturally, I did not. But then did I realistically expect to see him standing there, resplendent in shiny top hat? In town the gallower became more difficult to control. Snorting violently, the animal bit other horses. The beast lives under a cloud of foul temper. When I at last coaxed it back into the stable tonight it kicked at the stalls so hard it sounded like cannon fire.

8th September. The gravestone of Keats bears the words: 'Here lies one whose name was writ in water'. My plans that appeared to be carved in rock were only writ in that same liquid after all. First thing this morning the domestics arrived. They are paid their wages on a Saturday, so in order to make everything appear commonplace at Lamplands I collected money from the drawer in the Pastor's study, put the correct amounts in envelopes, on which I'd written their names, then took them to the kitchen. The domestics were bustling around in an excited way as they lit the oven.

The eldest one declaimed, 'There were eight of them. All big types in police uniforms. They were sitting in a carriage. From what I heard they were going to arrest someone.'

One servant shovelled coal on to the fire. 'And it's so quiet roundabouts. I wonder who they're after?'

I did not wait. I'm not stupid. I've survived by my wits. If there's danger I smell it on the air. As quick as I could I flew upstairs. Without owning much it didn't take more than five minutes to stuff my clothes and journal into a bag. Didn't I say it would only be a matter of time before the police returned? For surely the ones that the servant spied are on their way to Lamplands. Those gentlemen would give me short shrift. The colour of my skin will ensure that I'm behind bars. They'll blame me for the killing of Rose, and that'll be it.

Back on the ground floor I rushed to a window. I expected to see constables running toward the house. Rabbits, however, sat nibbling green shoots alongside the driveway. They smell danger, too. If anyone got close they'd dart into the bushes. There wasn't much money left in the drawer now I'd paid the wages, a few shillings in small coin. Nevertheless I scraped it willy-nilly into the bag. That done, I exited the back of the house in the direction of the stable. If I could coax the recalcitrant beast into the forks of the carriage I could be smartly away. Where? I hadn't meditated on that particular question just yet. Nor would I have time now. The horse was as unruly as ever. It kicked against the stall, while it snorted furiously at me, its eyes rolling. It hadn't been resting in the stable. The devil had fretted until it had raised a sweat. Its black flanks glistened, steam rose from its body.

'Be still, please be still,' I coaxed, patting its neck as I did so.

Then my day became utter nightmare. As I struggled to calm the animal it bared its huge yellow teeth, more like a mad dog than a horse. After that, it turned round in the stable, spinning on its own axis, until I was dizzy. This pantomime went on and on. I even forgot my purpose for being there because every ounce of my attention had to be fixed on not being bitten or kicked. It was only when I heard the sound of human voices breaching the gallower's commotion that I thought to look through the stable door. And there they were. Three men in blue. They were joined by a man in everyday clothes: Detective Constable Witham, the gruff officer who'd questioned me a few days ago. He pointed at the outbuildings.

So, this is it. They'll find me here, then carry me away in chains. Even the nameless brute I held by the mane seemed to anticipate this course of events. With a snort of pleasure it swung its head sideways to butt me. The force of it knocked me against the wall. By the time I'd regained my breath the two constables were perhaps thirty paces from the stable door, the top half of which was open, the bottom half still bolted shut.

No, you won't catch me so easily. Keeping my head low so they wouldn't glimpse me, I slipped back the bolt, eased open the door, then I dashed at the gallower to strike its backside. With flaring nostrils, rolling eyes, it roared, aimed a bite at my head, which took a hank of hair, then it erupted from the stable. I ducked back to avoid the back kick of its rear hooves as it tore into the sunlight. The two policemen put their hands up to grab the horse and bring it under control. Of course, they hadn't made the acquaintance of that particular brute. It wasn't content with escaping into the grounds. Instead, it took a malicious delight in charging the men like a bull. They scattered. Still running, it bore down on the detective. He escaped by ducking back into the house. The gallower, its mouth chomping, ran straight at the glazed door, smashing every single pane of glass with the force of the collision.

Now, I must flee any way I could. I grabbed the bag then left the stable via a rear window. With luck, the building's mass would hide me from sight. Picking up my skirts, so they were free of my feet, I ran into the bushes. Soon the sound of the rampaging horse, together with the men's shouts, receded.

At last I reached the road. Then there was nothing for it but to walk. In this prosperous suburb of modern redbrick villas my face would mark me out a stranger. I must head for the more populous quarters of London. From my travels with the Pastor I knew a steamer ran from the pier at this part of the

Thames to Limehouse docks. Though I remembered correctly
the whereabouts of the pier, I found that there would be a wait
of three hours until its departure at noon. All I could do was
find a tea room to pass the time. When I did find one the lady
refused to serve me the meal I'd asked for on account of my
skin colour. When I showed her I had money, however, she
consented to me sitting out of sight in the back garden. So,
here I am. I've drunk the tea and eaten. Now, there is time to
write in my journal as the sun plays down through the branches.
It's a pleasant summer's day, yet the happy season doesn't care
one jot about human misery. I have nowhere to live. Once
again I'm alone.

Later. So, like I feared he would, he's struck. Limehouse is
in a fever of horror. Women gather in knots. They either shout
gruesome details at one another or they fall into a silence with
ashen faces. Everyone asks each other who could have slaughtered the woman in the early hours. The sailor in his cups?
The madman known as Leather Apron? The opiate-sodden
Chinaman? No, none of those make-believe villains. Pastor
Hux. He returned to these slums after he escaped Lamplands.
Now he has cut female flesh as that dark passion engulfed
his soul again. Pastor Hux is the culprit. All I have to do is
open my mouth. Frame his name with my lips. Then it will
be over. At least that's what I tell myself. But then a stronger
passion comes to the fore. Pastor Hux is sick. I still owe him
my love and my loyalty. This violence is but a symptom of
his malady. It will pass. Then he'll be restored to the gentle,
softly spoken individual who has sacrificed his life to help
others.

But I run ahead of myself. I arrived by ferry in the afternoon to find a borough gone mad. Men, women and children
swarmed through the tangled streets. Dogs barked. Fights
broke out. An organ grinder cranked the handle in a frenzy
to match the air of panic, his music a salvo of discord.
Costermongers rushed into this grim neighbourhood, antici-
pating an influx of gawpers, who'd pay inflated prices for
fruit, sugar pastries and illicit nips of gin. The tumultuous
scene reminded me of an ant's nest jabbed with a stick. A
nightmare vision of too many people robbed of their humanity
by a commingling of bloodthirsty excitement and terror.

Enough of chaos! I had the address of the lodging house Grace Tarant frequented. Now I didn't have a home I'd have to ask her advice about lodgings and work – *and what work!* In Dock Road, however, I heard a cry, 'Nidabi! Nidabi! What the dickens are you doing here?' From a throng of women a face set with sparkling blue eyes appeared.

'Dolly?' For obvious reasons I pretended to be ignorant of events. 'What on earth is happening? Is it a riot?'

She pulled me aside as a carriage thundered by with a dozen police constables, hanging on to their helmets. 'What a day you've chosen to call. The man's done another of us!'

'A murder?'

'More than murder.' Dolly's eyes bulged from her pretty face in horror. 'The poor wretch got all her innards turned out. They're saying he made a feast of her belly. Then the killer set fire to the house. The gas mains caught and the whole lot went up like a proper Vesuvius.' She shuddered. 'I tell you. At every corner I expect to see a fiend with blood dripping from his mouth.'

A boy ran by with an armful of newspapers. Headlines screamed MURDER! I knew the truth, just as surely as if the victim's ghost shouted in my ear. *Pastor Hux! He's slaughtered another.*

Dolly stood back as if noticing me properly for the first time. 'But look at you in your new jacket . . . and what's with the bag? Oh!' She put her hand to her mouth. 'He's said your time with him's done?'

Another untruth seemed the wisest course. 'Pastor Hux believes I'm ready to make my own way in the world.'

'But why come here, sweetheart? You should take respectable work while your face is still fresh.'

'I've nowhere to stay.'

'You could gladly sleep with me but they'll charge you fourpence to go shares at the lodging house.'

'I have some money.'

'Then why not you and me find Grace? She's got a friend who has a spare room. This way, Nidabi. Here, let me take your arm. God crikey! You're trem'lin like a leaf.'

'It's all this commotion. I'm not used to it.'

'Course, Lamplands is paradise compared to this sty, isn't it?'

'The killing . . . it shook me.'

'Of course, you're nervy about murder, aren't you? Don't blame you, of course. Now, what can I do for you, sir?'

A smiling man, dressed in a grey suit, tipped his bowler hat to her. 'Afternoon, ladies. You've heard about this brutal carry on, then?'

Detective. I wonder if my face paled beneath my dark skin.

'Course we have,' trilled Dolly. 'You'd be sleeping in the bone yard not to.'

'My name is Goodly. Did either of you ladies know the dead woman?'

Dolly answered for both of us, 'We don't even know her name ourselves yet, Mr Goodly. Are you police?'

'Far from it, miss. I'm a newspaper reporter. I rather hoped you could furnish me with some details about the woman in question.'

'You should ask a detective. They'll know more than us.'

'Ah, the police? They give the press only the barest facts. It's down to us to put meat on the victim's bones, so to speak.'

'They say it was the same murderer that did Agnes Cutler.'

'I hear that the devil eviscerated her. Have you heard likewise?'

Dolly shook her head. 'Eviss-rate? I don't know what that means, sir.'

The man grinned. 'Eviscerate? It means—'

I interrupted, 'Eviscerate. To remove the entrails. To disembowel.'

Dolly patted my arm. 'My friend knows everything. She even told me that there are mountains on the moon.'

'Really?' He looked at me with renewed interest. 'A fine intellect as well as beauty. I'd like to interview you, but somewhere more private.'

'Dolly, we should be going.' I became flustered.

'I'm sorry to disappoint, sir.' Dolly was genuinely regretful. 'Only I don't know nothing. Now, if you 'scuse us.'

'Of course, ladies.' He tipped his hat again, then vanished into the crowd.

Later. Write your name on a scrap of paper. Throw it into the breeze. Imagine that paper is your life. It blows away into unexpected quarters, skitters up blind alleys. Just weeks ago, my future appeared clear. I would continue to live at Lamplands

with the Pastor. We would conduct charitable work. I would
be happy. Now, blow fickle winds of fate. They've carried me
to a new life. Here I sit close to midnight. My home a narrow
room on the ground floor of a cottage that belongs to Mrs
Benyon, a friend of Grace Tarant's. It's situated in a back
street, just yards from a canal that's for ever shrouded in mist.
I've paid Mrs Benyon a week's rent in advance. For my six
shillings there's a chamber, seven foot by five. A bed, a chair,
a shelf that serves as my dressing table, a tea chest to store
whatever I own. Mrs Benyon provides a kettle of boiling water
in the morning so I can brew tea. My room shares a party
wall with a warehouse. That building looms above the cottage;
it's a monstrous goliath; as menacing as a raised fist. Through
the bottom of my bedroom wall bleeds a dark fluid; it smells
like rotting cabbage, so I leave a burning candle against the
wall in the hope it dispels the odour. Yet, though the room is
grimly dungeon-like, one of the upper panes of the window
has been marvellously painted by a previous tenant. To gaze
on it makes my spine tingle. An artist has depicted the moon
there in golden paint – it floats in a sea of shining stars. In
my imagination this lunar sphere becomes a celestial eye that
keeps watch over me.

Now – the scrap of paper that is my life has alighted here.
I have perhaps seven shillings left from the money I took from
the Pastor's study. Outside, the September night is cold. There
are people returning home from the taverns. My room backs
on to the communal yard. From the sounds reaching me I
know women sometimes take men there. There are scuffing
noises, boots on stones, soused questions, bodies pressed
against fences. Meanwhile, my mind is a river of thought.
Where is Pastor Hux? The murdered woman was called Edith
Soller – why had he killed her? What drove him to cut her
to pieces? Then burn her body.

Tonight, Dolly West bustled into the kitchen to tell me what
she'd heard about the victim. Although Edith had not been to
Lamplands, Pastor Hux had paid her doctor's bills last year.
I pictured her jotting a card to the Pastor: *Just a note of thanks*,
she'd write, then, like the others, she'd spin her bit of fiction.
*I've had it with working the streets. I'm now a kitchen maid
in a respectable household.* The Pastor would proudly add the
missive to his scrapbook. Now I saw Pastor Hux in my mind's

eye. He prowls these byways. His heart is broken by his sense of failure. He's hunting the whores. He's finding those that wrote him those 'harmless' little tales of a respectable life. Then when he finds such a female tramping the alleyways, with the musk of sin on them, that dark passion will rise. So it goes on. This morning he found Edith Soller. He coaxed her into a derelict house. There, he hacked open her flesh. When she was dead he broke a kitchen gas pipe then scattered matches on the floor. When the constables found the body their heavy tread upon the matches ignited them, in turn they triggered a gas explosion. The house burnt for hours.

We have entered the kingdom of nightmare. The only action I can take to end this horror is by finding Pastor Hux. Then again, the question I've asked a hundred times is this: when I find him – what then?

15th September. Newspapers are rich in fantasy, poor on facts. The police yield little hard evidence to the press, so reporters feed the public's insatiable appetite for murder stories with wild rumour. All the broadsheet hot air can be distilled into a few bare essentials. That Agnes Cutler and Edith Soller were slain by the same individual. And the police have not one whit of intelligence about the killer, never mind being close to making an arrest. Meanwhile, fear pervades London's slums with the same tenacity as its habitual rich stench. Meanwhile, new rhythms of life establish themselves.

I still occupy this room in Mrs Benyon's house. For a time I feared I'd have to resort to the streets like many a woman in this wretched place. If I can be described as being fortunate I've found employment with Hewitt's, a supplier of cooked eels to the neighbourhood's shops and taverns. Most of the street women would be denied this work because they don't have the requisite abilities. Mr Hewitt tested me when I applied for a position at his factory. He ordered me to carry a hopper of live eels to the massive cooking ranges that line the wall, then, when done, to remove the fish to a cooling room where the boiled flesh and its gravy congeal into a viscous mass. He also had me prove I had a fair hand for writing pot labels. The temperature in the boiling shed is withering. Not to mention the pungent odour. With the heat and the stench it is like labouring in the lung of a whale. There! It is respectable employment, if physically strenuous, and I don't fear getting my hands dirty. Working ten hours a day, six days a week earns enough for my rent together with a few extra shillings. And, yes, I still search the night-time streets. Pastor Hux is close. I can sense his presence. One day soon our paths will cross.

20th September. Poor Dolly West. Because you don't hurt anyone else in this life, it's no guarantee they won't hurt you. This evening I walked along the alley that led to Shambles Yard where Dolly now rents a furnished room. A thickset woman came bundling along this gloomy egress toward me as she headed for the street. Aged around fifty, crimson-faced, her white hair had pulled free to dance around her head like snakes in the Medusa fable.

Before she passed me, she bellowed back the way she came: 'Half is half! Ya won't cheat anyone again, ya slut!' Then she elbowed by with a, 'Out ma way, blast ya!'

Such violent hollering isn't rare on these streets, so I didn't think anything of it until I arrived in the yard. Rain fell into this enclosure bounded by houses that seemed to be sinking into the ground under the weight of their sagging roofs.

'Dolly?'

I saw Dolly West in her bodice and underskirt. She bent over a trough, her long hair hanging in the water, while she tried to work the pump handle. A dozen women watched from their cottages as Dolly washed her hair in the rain storm.

'Dolly, what's wrong?' I ran forward to see a pink stain spreading down her long blonde hair. 'Oh, sweetheart, what's been done to you?' Her face was a mask of blood.

'Dark lass? Yes, you! You Dolly's friend?' The woman who spoke held a shawl over her head to protect her from the falling rain.

'What happened to her?'

'She's had a falling out over some soap with Ganny Reardon. The old bitch gave the poor lass a right thumping. Sickened me to watch, it did.'

'Was that the woman that's just left?' Blood raced in my veins. 'Damn the bitch. I'll rip her eyes out!'

'Don't bother chasing after her. You'll only get a dosing of the same. She's like a mad bull. But this poor little scrap never hurt anyone. Not that it stopped Ganny knocking her against the wall like she was cracking a nut.'

Though Dolly had precious little life in her, she struggled to wash blood from her hair.

'Here, let me,' I told her gently.

'Nn-darb-ah.' She could barely frame the words with that ruined mouth. 'I . . . didn't cheat her . . . gave her young 'un half. I swear I did . . .'

'Don't bother about that now. I'm going to get you inside.'

'Don't want blood on me best stuff.'

'Damn your best stuff. I'll buy you new.'

'Ganny took my new shoes – 'cos of soap.'

'Come on, Dolly, sweetheart, put your weight on me . . . that's it. I can hold you. I won't let you fall.'

By inches I got Dolly out of the pouring rain and into her room. She'd made the place cosy enough. Along one wall there was a double bed solidly built from timber with a table beside it for her mirror and hairbrush. A groan burst from Dolly's lips with every movement. That Ganny woman had beaten her bodily as well. Bruises, grazes, scratches – every inch of her skin marked in some way.

'My bed . . . can't muck that up,' she protested as I set her down on it.

'Can you stay sitting up yourself?'

Though her head hung down, she managed a nod.

I said, 'I'll put towels down for you to lie on.'

'Can't mucky it with blood . . . got to earn rent money 'fore he collects.'

'Dolly, you can't work in that state.'

'Can.'

'No.'

'Gotta get my rent in hand.'

'You must stay in bed for a few days.'

'Them'll be the last days in this bed I have, then.' She flinched as she lay back on the towels. 'If I don't have the rent by Friday he'll put me out on the street. S'pity. This is best place I've had . . . cosy.'

'This Ganny woman is an animal. She had no right to do this to you.'

'She got mad over soap.' Dolly opened her swollen eyes a fraction. 'Said I'd given her less 'n half.'

'You stay clear of that woman.'

'Between us we'd been buying a full block of good carbolic. I cut it in half then dropped it off at hers. This time her youngest was there. Said she'd give it her ma . . . I reckon she cut a piece off for herself, then told her ma I'd cheated her.'

As dusk fell I lit the lamp then set to work, trying to undo what Ganny Reardon had done. I cleaned the wounds, changed Dolly into a nightdress, then got her under the bedclothes, where she cuddled herself like a hurt child. After that, I ran to buy ointment and rum. When I got back I fed Dolly sweet tea laced with the spirit. Her skin was clammy. The shock of the beating now affected her as badly as the physical blows. I sat at the end of the bed worrying about this as I watched Dolly lying there in a fretful state.

'Nidabi?'

'Yes?'

'There's sixpence in the tin . . . there on the shelf. Buy me face powder.'

'You can't work tonight, Dolly.'

'I need my rent money.'

'No.'

'Please, Nidabi. I don't want to go back to the doss house.'

'Don't think about that. Now, where's your landlord's house?'

'Why?'

'I'll worry about the why, you just give me his address.'

So I was back in half an hour with the deal struck. It was more than Dolly's usual rent but the ten shillings I paid covered the next seven days, and he'd send round a good broth for Dolly's supper. And while she was off her feet I'd leave bread and cheese every morning before I started work. On opening the door I found Dolly sitting up in bed with a petticoat in her hands that she'd been trying to put on.

'It's arranged,' I told her. 'I've talked to your landlord. Your rent's paid until the end of next week. A girl's going to come every day with your supper.'

Dolly wept. 'You're a good soul, Nidabi. I was frightened out of my wits that I'd lose my home. You're the kindest person I've ever met. You're an angel – a living angel.'

'All that's expected of you, Dolly, is to get well. Here's the rum. Keep taking sips.'

'Pastor Hux lost a good one when you left.'

His name caught me by surprise. Tonight, for the first time in weeks, the Pastor hadn't been the uppermost thought in my mind. What had been important was the well-being of Dolly West. There was another matter of course. I'd spent my own rent money on Dolly's room. Now I'd have to beg extra hours at the factory to earn back that ten shillings as quickly as possible.

1st October. Just when Pastor Hux began to seem like any other figure that had passed through my life to be despatched to the past, it happens again. A month ago Agnes Cutler and Edith Soller fell to the blade. Then nothing. London stopped talking about the murders. If mentioned at all, people would just shrug. 'Oh, well. He's got away with it.' Then they'd changed the topic of conversation. Gone? No. Just two days ago the murderer struck again. This time six streetwalkers were despatched in the space of twenty-four hours. The method of slaying is always the same. He carves open their throat. Followed by a frenzied stabbing of the torso. Afterwards, there appears to be some recapture of calm, if not sanity. The killer attempts to cover his tracks, but his disposal of the corpse is too hasty to be effective. Victim one: dropped into a canal. Two: dumped in a cellar. Three: placed in a burning hansom cab; the panic-stricken horse injured children playing in the street as the beast tried to outrun the fiery vehicle attached to its harness. Four: left in sewer. Five: concealed amongst animals' parts in a slaughterhouse. Six: the most grossly mutilated body roughly buried in a cemetery. The remains were excavated by hungry dogs.

Pastor Hux, where are you? Why are you driven to do this to the women you loved? The poorest of the poor. Why punish them for the frailty of their nature? They don't revel in whoredom. They don't enjoy this way of life. Why execute these unfortunates for a crime that civilization has inflicted on them?

Ty's Book

22nd October. Tonight I felt such power – the power of Vincent van Gogh's hand. At midnight I walked by the artist's yellow house. Because his home lay in darkness amid the silent houses I didn't think to call. Yet the moment I passed the door it swung open with a crash. Vincent seized my arm, then he bundled me into the room. His eyes were fire – a searing emerald fire.

'You! Look at this!' Vincent dragged me deeper into the room.

'What's the matter?' I asked in panic. 'Have you been hurt?'

'Pastor Hux. This evening I dreamt I walked with him.' Vincent appeared excited, yet he mastered it with an uncharacteristic calm. There was something so sure about him; an air of certainty, as if he'd uncovered the truth behind a great mystery. Moreover, there was such a power in his hands, and with that power came absolute control. He guided me to a chair that faced a canvas on which he'd been working.

'When I lived in London, Pastor Hux and I would walk for miles at night. In my dream I saw it all with such clarity. The River Thames is blackness, yet sparks dart across it – brilliant red rubies, fiery spots of dragon blood. Brick walls are deepest russet. Above a furnace an orange glow melts into the sky. In those streets a miracle happens – the wretched and the beautiful collide; they form a magical pact. A sight that revolts the eye can in the next moment become enchanting. When a squalid hovel is touched by moonlight it becomes a palace of gold. All the city would wait for us. We'd possess those secret alleyways, we'd haunt its squares. No part of it was concealed from us; nothing of those boulevards forbidden. During the hours of darkness we'd explore that great metropolis. How we'd talk. Two friends united by a single passion. Always we reflected on the plight of the poor. How we yearned to rescue humanity from poverty. Ty, the things we saw!' In the gloom his green eyes grew brighter. 'Children slept in doorways. Mothers ravaged by fever sang on street corners for pennies to buy milk for their babies. That beautiful lament touched heaven itself. The times Pastor Hux emptied his pocket of coin for those downtrodden souls. I tell you, he moved through the night as an angel glides through the woe-filled heart of Man. He saved dozens from starvation.' Excitedly he ran his fingers through his hair. 'I decided I must paint that living saint from memory or my heart would explode. So this is it.' He struck a match then held it to the painting. 'This is how I see my friend. The Midnight Man.' The flame revealed the painting in a fiery glow. 'You being here brings a symmetry. A new friend watching the illustration of an old friend in oils.' The moment he lit the lamp a thunder of hooves shook the house. 'Ah, listen, Ty. They are bull-running tonight. It is the Sator Diabolus.'

'But that's illegal.'

'Ha! Of course it is. There are laws forbidding it. Penalties of fines. Threats of prison. But see who hunts the bull? The man in the bull mask is the mayor's son. With him are the stationmaster, the chief of works and half the lawyers in Arles! Sator Diabolus, corrupt Latin for "devil maker".'

By lamplight in that small room of the yellow house Van Gogh resumed work on the painting. His knife made slashing strokes. Blue paint squeezed directly on to the canvas from the tube became streaks of nocturnal sky. Out in the square, the bull – a veritable nightmare beast – pounded across the earth. Its iron-tipped horns scraped along a wall in a blaze of sparks. Indeed, this was the rite of Sator Diabolus, the devil maker. Running the bull through town was an ancient custom when Rome conquered France. On this night most Arlesians stay home. No one will publicly admit to witnessing it. This is when the town's luminaries become as wild as the animal they pursue. See them! Their faces painted blood-red. The man in the bull mask has a quest: not merely to kill the bull, but to transfer its powerful, fighting spirit into his own body. Likewise, Vincent van Gogh: not so much painting as battling the canvas with the paint-bloodied knife.

The lamp's brightness meant I had to close my eyes until I

watched through only the narrowest of slits. Out in the night, the rhythm of hoof beats; a sound so deep I felt it in my belly. Add to that the heavy fumes of paint, and now the artist's measured dance of creation at the easel – all of this mesmerized me until I occupied a strange realm between wakefulness and sleep. Vincent's red hair gleamed in the lamplight; his skin shone; he swayed to harmonies only he could hear. His free hand he held above his head. Fingers made a slow beckoning motion as if he drew musical notes down from heaven. In turn these ran through his body to emerge through the other hand as strokes on canvas. In that drowsy, dreamlike state I watched him evoke the Midnight Man.

Knife blade, fingers, brush, he used all these to draw the figure from that cauldron of violet, black and searing yellow. Meanwhile, the bull roared. A concussion as the monster cannoned against a wall. A man cried out. Yet I could not take my hypnotized gaze from the portrait. In that drowsy state it seemed less that Vincent painted the figure, than it emerged from the turbulent vortex of purple – a mysterious guest who approached from down long corridors of time. And so, the alchemy of genius took place in front of me. A scatter of brilliant stars on purple formed the background. The star in the upper left-hand corner grew into a giant of its species as he worked the paint with the ball of his thumb into a swirl of yellow that resembled the heart of a sunflower. Foreground: in slabs of black the artist rendered a clutter of buildings that were morbid enough to chill the blood. A furnace produced a splash of crimson. And the man Vincent painted? He manifested himself as a central darkness to the picture; a phantom shape haloed by red light. What I saw, as the battle between the bull and its enemy outside neared the end, was the painting of a man in a black coat and top hat. The face beneath the rim was drenched in shadow. The only suggestion of features, a pair of yellow smudges that might have been the ghostly gleam of eyes. At the time I'd swear no face existed beneath the severe line of the hat brim, yet now there are times I fear there were disquieting features lurking in shadow. But heavy fumes from the spirit lamp stupefied me. I could barely keep my eyes open.

Outside – sounds of battle grew louder. Inside – Vincent waged war on the canvas. *Both are fighting to the death.*

The truth haunts me still. I realized that the artist had crossed the bridge of no return. He wouldn't retreat now from his quest to create perfect art. For him it was either victory or self-destruction. Transfixed, I watched him paint Pastor Hux, a man who had become somehow faceless in my friend's mind. Faceless, yet with the uncanny sensation that at any moment the night-borne figure would break free of the canvas like a monster breaking free of its chains.

'There . . . it's finished.' Exhausted, he slumped back to regard the painting with a mixture of disgust and elation. 'The Midnight Man'. Not so much painting as summoning a creature that should have remained distant, hidden, and most absolutely forbidden. For a moment I wished with all my heart I could shred the grim image to atoms.

Outside, with a shattering roar, a beast died. Whether it was bull or man I could not say.

Nidabi's Journal

29th October. Fog, cold, darkness. Winter has its teeth in London already. I've tramped the streets in the hope of finding Pastor Hux. Three times I've been back to Lamplands. The place is locked up tight. Deserted. Work at the eel factory is brutal. I'm not afraid of hard toil, but my stomach has become very weak. I'm supposed to be working extra hours today. However, try as I might I've not been able to get out of bed. I promised myself I would write five pages. I think this is all for now, my head feels fit to burst.

12th November. This morning is the first time I've been able to sit. On the 30th October, I fell in the street with stomach pains. Then nothing much. Just faces that asked questions I couldn't understand. I fancied one night I sat in that evil chair in Lamplands and could not move even a finger; thick straps held me tight, and all the shadows became demons. Each demon wore the face of Pastor Hux; they slid into my eyes to blind my sight, and into my mouth to choke me. Into my ears they gurgled. '*Deeds, Not Words, Nidabi. Deeds, Not Words . . .*' This morning I woke to find Dolly West standing by the bed. She smiled that angelic smile. 'I brought you the orange you asked for.'

I slept again, only to open my eyes when Grace Tarant entered the room.

'You awake, dear?' She eased back the curtain. 'I'll fetch you some bread and milk.'

I shook my head. 'I'd like to eat my orange first.'

'Your orange?'

'Yes, please.'

'I'm sorry, dear. But you don't have an orange.'

'Dolly West brought me one this morning.'

'Oh, child.' Grace's eyes filled with tears. 'I told you yesterday. Didn't you understand?'

I shook my head.

'My poor lamb, you've been so ill your wits were all scattered. How were you to know what terrible things that monster's been doing?' Grace sat down on the bed so she could hold my hand. 'Nidabi, sweetheart . . . Dolly's been taken from us.'

Ty's Book

15th November. The artist stood outside the railway station. With him, a man in a black coat and the shiniest top hat I've ever seen.

Vincent said, 'Ty. This is my friend, Pastor Hux.'

The man lifted the shiny hat to me. Whereas Vincent van Gogh had at least an air of solidity with large hands this Englishman lacked physical substance. Narrow shoulders, a height little more than mine, his white hands were small with tapering fingers. He must have been in poor health because his grey face was gaunt, while exhaustion had cut dark rings under his eyes.

'Ty? I'm so delighted to meet you.' His voice was gentle. 'My friend here . . .' He smiled. 'My beloved old friend has told me so much about you that I feel as if I know you well. Indeed, there are times that I can almost believe the Hindu faith in . . . what's the word? *Reincarnation*. Ah, you'll have to forgive my French. It's very . . . tarnished? No . . . rusty. But, yes, I sometimes fancy that we knew each other in a former life.'

'Perhaps in the olive groves of Arcadia,' Vincent said with a smile; he was delighted to see this grey-faced man.

'Or the palaces of Samarkand.' Despite apologizing for difficulty with my mother tongue Pastor Hux was fluent. His sentences had none of the flatness that marred the speech of other English visitors. He turned to me again. 'You have a singular beauty, mademoiselle. Then I could appreciate it before my arrival, as Vincent here, an artist of formidable power, included your sketch in a letter.'

'Welcome to Arles, Pastor.' Vincent nodded along the street. 'You have plenty to explore. Our amphitheatre should be one of the wonders of the world.'

'I'm sure the town will do me good. London is permanently shrouded in fog these days. My health began to suffer.'

'Pastor, how long do you plan to stay?' I asked.

'I plan to winter in St Tropez. Of course, I did beseech my friend here to join me in England.' The man's brown eyes roved over the buildings. 'But I can see now why he'd prefer this bright, sunlit place to cold, wet London.'

As Vincent beckoned a porter to take the Pastor's luggage he said, 'After not seeing you for all these years don't rush off too soon. Promise me that?'

'Oh, I shall make the most of this place first.' His lips tightened. 'I want you to share Arles' mysteries with me. All its secret places.'

'Ah, we have a porter. He will take your trunk to the hotel. I have reserved a nice room for you there. I know the owner, too. She'll feed you good meals. Plenty of bouillabaisse. Then I will come and take you for long midnight walks.'

'I'll count on it. We'll discuss Tolstoy, Eliot, Delacroix.'

'Dickens, Zola, Shakespeare. The town will tremble.'

'It will echo for a thousand years.'

'You'll see my paintings. You will even sit for me!'

Red patches burned on the Pastor's cheeks. 'And don't forget, Vincent. We shall do as we did in the old days. We will read the Bible aloud for a whole evening. You recite one verse, than I shall *declaim* the other. Two voices, one true faith.'

They'd been talking like two old friends reunited but this caught Vincent's flow of words. 'Ah,' he began with a note of hesitation. 'Over the last few years I've reconsidered my attitude to the Bible.'

'And to God?' The Pastor's good humour vanished completely.

'No relationship is fixed. They're all in flux.'

'I see.'

For a moment the Englishman changed. I know it is strange to describe this, but the impression I had was that his eyes turned in on themselves; they became reversed in some way. Not physically, of course. But just for an instant, the Pastor appeared to gaze on another landscape inside his head. The muscles of his face became very tense. Then the moment passed. A smile crept on to his lips. 'We've plenty to discuss. Come on, Vincent, we'd best follow the porter. Does he know the address of my lodgings?'

They followed the porter with his handcart toward the centre of Arles. They made an unusual pairing. One man very straight backed, severely dressed in black with the top hat perched on his crown. The other was a shambling figure in the blue work clothes of a peasant, a straw hat plonked on his head in a haphazard fashion. Once more they talked to one another as I imagine they talked in the past. Now the Pastor lapsed into English when a French expression failed him. It's a language I don't understand. Not that I participated in their conversation now, so whether I understood him or not didn't matter. Lost in their own private world, they walked faster as they became engrossed in the conversation. Presently, the market day crowds obscured the pair from me, and I realized to even try and keep up with them would be futile.

*   *   *

Later at the night café.

'Didn't you find him odd?'

'Who?' Vincent drank brandy to keep out the cold.

'Pastor Hux. He's very pale and—'

'That's because he is from England. A cold northern land like my Holland.'

'No, not just his complexion. His manner.'

'You think him strange? I am the strange one, Ty. Now! My strangeness towers over his like a ziggurat.'

'He believed you'd remain exactly like you were in the old days in London.'

'When I loved temperance.' He savoured the amber liquor. 'And spent hours copying verses from the Bible. I love painting – that's the great force . . .' The last drop from the glass vanished into his mouth. 'The great force that holds sway over this old bear . . . this old Dutch bear . . . who creates thoughts instead of children. Where is that old devil, Gauguin? We sick artists should support one another . . . even if it's only to help each other stand after guzzling brandy.' He peered round the café. It was packed with farmers who'd come to drink their market day profits. 'Ty? Is Gauguin here? I don't see the brute.'

'He's been in the house all evening.'

Vincent frowned. 'The house? My house?' He'd drunk liquor on an empty stomach. Now he found it difficult to speak. 'Ah! No! *The* house where you and the beautiful ladies do their work. Essential work.' He tapped his nose. 'I see. The Dutchman understands.' He ordered more brandy.

'Why don't we have some food? I'm sure you're hungry by now.'

Suddenly, he awarded me a stare that held so much power. 'Tell me. Has Gauguin asked for you at the brothel?' His eyes melted from green and blue. 'Has he wanted you?'

I stared back. Even the hubbub of the café seemed to still for a moment.

'Damn me!' He brought his fist down on the table. 'I shouldn't ask you that question. Hush! Don't answer . . . *don't answer!*' With that he lurched away into the night.

17th November. I'd been walking back to the tenement by the river with my little sister, when Pastor Hux joined us.

'Vincent van Gogh. He's a good man.'

'I know he is, Pastor Hux.'

'He has helped you?'

'Yes.'

'Money?'

Even though Pastor Hux didn't wear the formal clothes of a man of God there was something priestly about his black garb at its most forbidding. He walked alongside, pretending to be conversational, but I sensed he was interrogating me. Would it be bad mannered of me to tell him such questioning is rude? But he is Vincent's friend, I told myself. He is strange, but I know Vincent is perceived by most as eccentric. It's probably just the Pastor's manner.

'Yes,' I said, answering his question. 'Vincent kept it secret from me, but he managed to save enough money for a week's rent. Without that I wouldn't have a home.'

'He's not a rich man. Nobody has bought any of his pictures yet.'

'I know. He set aside money from the allowance his brother sent him.'

'The money he needs for paints and canvas.'

'Pastor Hux.' I stopped walking so I could look him in the eye. 'Vincent lost two weeks' painting so he could pay my landlord. I tried to be angry with him. He shouldn't sacrifice his art for me, but it's his nature to be kind.'

'I've not known a kinder man.'

'Now, I shall have to get ready for work.'

'Work?'

'Yes, monsieur.'

'I was under the impression that Vincent supported you?'

'Not at all, monsieur. I am my own woman.'

'Surely not domestic service?'

'Pastor Hux. If you are accusing me of sponging off Vincent I can tell you I am not. I'm saving hard to repay the money he loaned me. It's no secret what I do for work. At least not from adults.' I leaned forward to whisper the next words so Brionne wouldn't hear. 'I earn money to give Brionne food and a bed. She's five years old. I won't have her slaving in the fields. You understand?'

After turning to watch Brionne skipping along the street,

he touched the brim of his hat, then said curtly, 'I'll bid you good day.'

{PC Morrow's filed letter, London, 18th November, 1888}

Sir, I have a matter of great importance to convey to you. This year I suffered some weeks of incapacity as a result of a violent explosion at the house where Edith Soller's body had been deposited. The murderer had cunningly severed a gas pipe then scattered the kitchen floor with matches. Constable Gordon trod on a match, resulting in a considerable detonation that took his life and cost me many broken bones. During my convalescence I had ample time to consider the details of this case, plus subsequent attacks on many innocent women in the region of Limehouse and Stepney. The last recorded case, where I believe the same killer was responsible, was the death of one Dolly West. After being stabbed her body had been flung into a tailor's workshop. My arrival on the scene was timely because I could point out to Detective Constable Witham that matches had been cast on to the floor. I then turned off the gas supply in the street, rendering it safe to enter once the fumes had dispersed. Dolly West's wounds, the cut throat, the frenzied stabbing of the trunk, were largely the same as those of the other victims. However, Detective Constable Witham maintains that lunatics have taken to copying the techniques of the killer of West and some twenty other unfortunates. However, despite my lower rank I must write in the strongest terms that I disagree with Detective Constable Witham. In the early stages of the investigation I identified a male suspect. There are rumours that individual has fled the country. Since the suspect departed these shores, cases that matched those earlier crimes have ceased. Therefore, I would urge you to publicly identify the one responsible for the death of Soller, West and others as the gentleman known as Pastor Hux. Moreover, to stress that he is still at large and extremely dangerous.

Ty's Book

18th November. Night time. A thick frost covered the grass. The man Arlesians call 'The Dutch Glow Worm' worked at his canvas on open land beside the railway line. He'd hung four lamps from the long branch of an olive tree just above his head so their amber light bathed the picture he painted. He didn't know I was there. I'd crept into the cemetery to leave a slice of honey cake beside my little brother's gravestone. It was from there I could see the solitary red-haired figure beneath the tree. His hand worked round and round in big circles as he formed a yellow halo about the painted stars. In the distance a dog barked. Houses were marked out by light spilling through open shutters. Faint scents of wood smoke reached me from the charcoal burner's yard. The night was still. Its icy sharpness pricked through my clothes to find skin. I shivered. To visit the cemetery at night was safer. Sometimes its visitors would shout at me to leave. Though it is secular land owned by the municipal authority they tell me a pagan shouldn't be there, that I'm unclean.

To visit George at night I can crouch with one arm resting on the gravestone as if I have my arm round the shoulders of a little boy. When I speak to my brother does his ghost catch the words? Is there a spirit that survives the body to care about what I say? I tell George that Brionne and I love our new lodgings in the tenement. That we are well fed – to say these things makes me feel happier. I add that Vincent's health is a little better, though he is still in a continual fever of work. Also, Vincent has invited his friend Gauguin to share the yellow house. For a while it raised his spirits; now, however, they argue so ferociously that I'm afraid to call on Vincent there. Gauguin is in the throes of a great love affair – a love affair with himself and his imagined talent. I haven't taken to him at all. So far, I have managed to avoid his attentions when he uses the brothel, though I probably won't be able to escape him for long. What troubles me most at the moment is the English visitor, Pastor Hux. There are thoughts swimming behind his eyes that terrify him. I'm sure of it. I've seen the gentle expression of his slip, then his eyes turn inward on to sights that appear to instil in him absolute horror. It is the same expression worn by old soldiers who come to me who have experienced dreadful wars. Sometimes they'll point out a battle scar on their naked bodies to impress me; but then their faces change as the cruel memory comes rushing back to wreck their peace of mind. So tell me, what secret does Pastor Hux hold close to his heart?

As is my habit, I unburdened my mind to George as he sleeps in the earth two metres beneath my feet. Under the olive tree the artist still captured the night sky. The stars were very bright. Even from there I could see that Vincent ably transferred the beauty of the haloed points of light on to his canvas. Normally, to watch this gifted man at work would, for a while, take away my fears, yet why can't I get Pastor Hux out of my mind? Why am I filled with such a grim sense of foreboding?

Nidabi's Journal

18th November. Stars showed through the smoke haze trailing from houses. The brandy in my stomach carried a warmth that would last most of the night.

I said to him, 'There are mountains on the moon.'

'What the dickens are you talking about?'

'There are mountains on the moon. I've seen oceans, too.'

'You don't say.' The soldier gripped my arm as we turned into a yard. 'Here'll do. Now, put yourself up against the wall.'

His breath came in great gusts of billowing white vapour. Someone had been boiling onions in a communal cookhouse. I could smell them distinctly. At least now I had time to marvel at the silver moon reflected in a pail of water. An orb as bright and as round as a new sixpence. The sight of it made me dreamy. 'There are mountains on the moon. I've seen them. What's more, I know the world offers me more than this.'

'You've got brains, lass, but it's not your brains I'm interested in.'

I clenched my fists. 'I'm not going back to the life of a whore. I'm not!' With that, I broke free then raced back to my home by the canal.

Tonight, for the first time I nearly fell back into my old ways. It was seeing the moon watch over me, that old celestial friend, that reminded me there are other realities beyond this one; indeed, there are more opportunities than those we see at this very moment. But how long can I resist streetwalking when poverty becomes too much to endure?

Ty's Book

19th November. Pandemonium. That word isn't powerful enough to describe the chaotic scene in the early hours of this morning. Nor the panic, nor the excitement, nor the outpouring of fury; nor the way people rushed into the streets.

I was close to finishing work for the night. I'd heard the church clock strike two in the morning. Soon after that came a clattering from downstairs as if a mob were running through the house. That was followed by a woman's scream. More women contributed to the shouting. Soon after came the deeper male voice of the brothel-keeper trying to restore order. A fight? That's what occurred to me. It wasn't unusual for a scuffle to break out in the doorway if a man had been causing trouble, or an enraged wife had discovered her husband's whereabouts. Yet, the sounds weren't consistent with a brawl. Even as I listened different voices rose up through the cacophony to call out the same name.

'Ty!'

'It can't be.'

'I tell you, it's Ty! She's out there in the yard!'

'Oh my God! Did you see the state she was in? If I live to a hundred I'll still see that every time I close my eyes.'

'It can't be Ty.'

'I tell you it is! I've known Ty for years. I'd recognize her anywhere.'

The brothel-keeper boomed, 'Fetch a lamp. Hurry!'

'No, it can't be Ty. She's here. Someone fetch her.'

'Ty? Ty!'

The urgency of the call brought me scrambling out of bed. Something awful had happened. My heart beat so hard it knocked against my ribs. It's Brionne, I thought in a panic, she's hurt. I tugged the sheet from the bed, wrapped it round me, then raced barefoot down the stairs. In the hallway a crowd of women had gathered, some dressed; many were in their nightdresses or underclothes. The brothel-keeper carried a lamp. He trimmed the wick so its light filled the stairwell. My friend Chloe sat on a stool but she was being supported by another of the women because her head drooped as if she were ill.

'Chloe!' I shouted. 'Has someone attacked her?'

'No, she's fainted,' said the woman. 'She rushed in here to tell us that she saw you lying dead in the yard.'

'Me?' I shuddered despite the impossibility of the words.

Chloe raised her head. Her lips had turned blue with fright. When she saw me her eyes widened, 'Oh my God! Oh, sweet heaven . . . It was you, Ty. I was sure of it. Your hair's the same as . . . oh, God . . . then who's out there in the yard?'

'I'll go see,' the brothel-keeper told us. 'Keep that front door locked. Don't let anyone else in.' The occupants of the house surged after the brothel-keeper as he walked down the passageway to the back door. He held the lamp high in front of him. 'Easy now,' he called. However, the pressure of women from behind forced him into the yard. 'Oh my dear Lord,' he gasped, then cried in a loud voice, 'Get back inside. Whatever you do, don't look!'

Only it was too late. The women poured out into the yard. Those at the front had seen what lay there on the stones. Screaming, they tried to turn back into the house with their hands over their mouths, but the out-rush of spectators forced them deeper into the yard – and toward the object of their horror. I was carried there, too, the sheet still wrapped around me. Because I'm much smaller than the other women I couldn't see what they'd witnessed. All that was clear to me in the lamplight was this shocking fact: they were so frightened that they jammed their hands over their faces, yet I could see their staring eyes glittering through the gaps between their fingers.

The brothel-keeper called out to his wife to summon a gendarme. In the midst of all those bodies I had to endure the jostling as they desperately tried to return to the house. One moment I saw only nightdresses and colourful bodices, the next the group divided into two. Suddenly, I no longer noticed the commotion, or heard the shouts. I looked from the edge of the panicking swarm, looked as night forced its hand of darkness upon the world, looked as my mind became engulfed by torrents of dread and terror. All too clearly I saw the object of horror. At that instant there was only myself and the girl. No one else existed. I had all of time itself for my eyes to travel over the figure lying there in the lamplight. *Yes, it could be me.* The words seemed oddly out of place, yet true. We shared the same slightly built frame. Her skin? As dark as mine, while her black hair fell in thick waves that were identical. Her dark eyes were wide open. Oh, perfidious world: if she had one cut upon her body she had a hundred. Jagged fissures had been opened on her face by a blade. Her once brightly embroidered skirt had been spattered in gore. Blood ran in a crimson tide across the stones to pool around my bare feet. Moving was impossible. Looking away from that fallen human being was impossible. Shouts of 'Keep away! Don't look!' Women sobbed. By this time, men from the upper rooms had rushed into the yard to see what had happened; only now they staggered as if they'd fall when they saw the mutilated corpse.

'Look at her eyes!' cried one of the men. 'Look at her eyes! She's seen the devil himself!'

Oh, yes, those eyes . . . Before the light of her life had gone out, those eyes had beheld the personification of Death.

Later. Despite Gauguin's perpetual claims of ill health he climbed a tree that afternoon in the square. There he stood on a branch, as robust as a young buck ape. Lately, I'd discovered

Gauguin's claims often contradict the evidence. He states he is a poor artist yet he dresses like a dandy in striped trousers and a green velvet jacket. Forty years of age, he is older than Vincent van Gogh and never lets my friend forget this, nor his greater experience as a painter. Gauguin's hooded eyes for ever peer secretively out from above his aristocratic nose. When I first saw his face it made me think of the word 'assassin'. And in my mind he remains 'the Assassin'. An aura of heartlessness surrounds him. At that moment, as he stood in the tree, his cruel eyes consumed the shocking spectacle.

'What a day,' he shouted down to us as the crowd surged forward. The howls of the Arlesians were so loud they shook the bones in my skull. 'You should see this . . . hey, the pair of you! Vincent! Ty! Give me your hands, I'll pull you up!'

Vincent shook his head as he pushed back against the flow of people. 'It's not right,' he told me, 'they shouldn't do this.'

Now on the upward slope of the street I could see above the heads of the excited throng. Two Italian sailors still kicked out their legs as they dangled from ropes that were strung from the hotel balcony.

I tried to stop Vincent's headlong charge through the mob. 'Vincent. They had blood on their jackets.'

'There is no evidence they killed the girl. There was blood on their clothes because they'd been fighting in the bars.'

'Vincent—'

'Now, these –' he pushed aside men rushing forward to enjoy the sight of the sailors being strangled – 'idiots have lost their minds. The bloodlust is on them. Whenever there's murder here, Arles always does the same thing. The entire town goes berserk!' Breaking away from the mob, he loped back in the direction of his house. As he went he ran his hands so wildly through his red hair I feared he'd suffer one of his collapses. At last he made it to his door; there he tumbled through it, then slammed the timbers shut on the world.

'Leave him to his grief.' Pastor Hux stepped from the gloom of an alley. A black raven of a man. His brown eyes fixed on me as he added, 'There was so much blood.'

I nodded. He must have been one of the thousands that had filed through the brothel yard earlier that morning to ogle stones that were still scarlet – a vivid, glistening scarlet – where the killer had spilt the woman's blood. *Say something to the man, Ty. Don't just stare at him.* Only there was some-thing about his way of eyeing me. The words froze inside my throat.

'Ty?'

'Pastor?'

'They say the girl looked just like you?'

'Yes, Pastor.'

'Same age, same height. Hair and skin colour all alike.'

'I heard that, too.'

'And in the yard of the house where you're employed?'

'I know, Pastor. She'd been hacked to pieces.'

'What was she doing there?'

'I heard that she was a gypsy girl. She'd gone out to search for a dog that had left its kennel. People are saying that Italian sailors dragged the girl into the yard where they murdered her.'

'It shouldn't have happened to her. It really shouldn't.' His eyes glistened.

'No, Pastor. No one should suffer like that.'

'Were the wounds . . . ahm, excessive?'

'The work of a madman, Pastor. Whoever did it cut off her ears.'

He blanched. 'Her ears?'

'Yes, Pastor. Sliced off her ears. Now they can't be found.'

'So, this is the outcome?' His eyes fixed on the two figures hanging from the balcony. Though they were strung high enough for their feet to be above the heads of the crowd their corpses were battered by stones. Some of the raging mob struck the men in their bellies with brooms. All through this savagery the people of Arles cheered. He nodded. 'Justice has been done.'

'Pastor Hux, I disagree. The gendarmes haven't finished their investigation. A mob dragged the pair out of a bar, then set on them. Your friend Vincent tried to stop it, but his neigh-bours held him down while the men were lynched.'

His eyes bored into me. 'You're right, Ty. I stand corrected. That isn't justice. It's revenge. Even so . . .' The muscles in his face became tense. 'You remind me of a dear friend I left behind in London. She was called Nidabi.'

'Was, monsieur?'

He grimaced. '*Is* called Nidabi. She's very much alive.'

'Vincent mentioned that you'd written to him about Nidabi. And that we resemble one another?'

'Remarkably so. Nidabi loved astronomy.'

Loved? Again, past tense.

'Once she found a telescope in the house. Afterward, she rushed to tell me how she'd seen mountains on the moon. Now . . .' A smile tightened his grey lips. 'It would mean a great deal to me if we could walk together. What do you say, Ty?'

'Where, Pastor? The streets are dangerous today. Wouldn't it be safer for you to return to your lodgings?'

'I thought the two of us might visit that beautiful church that overlooks the river. We could both pray for the murdered woman.'

'My sister will be waiting for me.'

'Ah, Brionne? How old is she?'

'Just five years of age.'

'Five? Then best hurry along.'

'Thank you, Pastor Hux.'

I felt the man's eyes burn into my back every step of the way.

Nidabi's Journal

21st November. Two days ago Dolly West was buried at St Patrick's. Everyone in London, it seemed, wanted to touch the coffin that contained a victim of Pastor Hux (not that anybody knew the killer's name but me). Word had it that if women pressed their fingers against that coffin wood they would be safe from murder. Thousands were there. Roads were blocked with sightseers. The closest I could get to the funeral were the cemetery gates where a mass of people jostled to enter, even though constables shouted that they wouldn't be allowed into the service.

This morning I went to pay my respects. Earth around the

grave ran with mud. Pieces of turf had been cut to be carried away as trophies by the spectators. Even now, there were a dozen people staring at the oblong of broken dirt that marked the grave pit. Around it lay bunches of flowers. Six feet down the friendly girl with bonny blue eyes lay where the woes of this world could reach her no more.

'Dolly, I know who killed you. It was the same man who fed you and kept you safe in the past.' I had murmured the words so the gawpers couldn't hear. 'The man is Pastor Hux. I don't believe he wanted to hurt you. He couldn't bear the notion that he'd failed in his life's work. He believed he saved women who couldn't help themselves. He was so proud of the letters he received that told him that we now lived respectable lives. The disappointment was too much for him.'

A boy pulled at a woman's skirt. 'Ma, what's the foreign bint sayin'?'

The mother gave him a glare that was meant to silence him.

'Ma? Can them sort talk to dead folk?'

The mother pulled the boy away to hurry him back along the path to the gates. A cold rain began to fall that darkened the headstones. Low cloud loomed over this grim burial ground like the roof of a tomb.

'Dolly, forgive Pastor Hux. He's a sick man now. You might think I should tell the police who murdered you. But you don't punish people for being ill.' Pulling off my glove, I crouched down so I could rest my hand on the earth beside the flowers that had been laid there.

'Here! Don't take the bloody lot. Leave some for proper folk.'

A hand crossed in front of my face. It gripped one of the paper roses and snapped it from the wire. A plump man with blotched cheeks threaded the bloom into his buttonhole. A green hat that looked a size too small rested on his head.

He grunted, 'Go on, girl. Help yourself now. Just don't take 'em all. Do you understand our tongue? Don't – take – all – the – flowers.'

The man was in the company of a colourless wisp of a woman in a black bonnet.

I stood upright. 'I don't want to steal the flowers. I was paying my respects to my friend.'

'Oh, you're one of her sort? One of the alley cats?'

'We're not alley cats.'

'Best watch your step, m' girl. The Man o' Death's going to be carving you up one of these dark nights.'

'You shouldn't take flowers from the grave. They're Dolly's.'

'I'll do what I bloody well like, y' devil.'

The wisp spoke to him – more of a hiss than a full voice. 'Don't have anything to do with her, Albert.'

'I'll do what I bloody well like, woman.' The other sight-seers turned to us at the sound of his angry growl. 'A wife shan't order a man about. An' I'm not taking orders from no foreign devil, either.'

'Please, Albert.' The woman was frightened. 'Don't make a fuss.'

He grabbed her arm to shake her like she was a bag of straw. 'I'll fuss it up as much as I like. You mind y' quarters, d'ya hear?'

The woman was too intimidated to protest. All she could do was consent to the bully shaking her.

I looked down at the grave. For a moment the wet clay wasn't there. At the bottom of the dark pit was a coffin and a surge of emotion swept through me. The oak lid whitened until it became as clear as glass.

There's Dolly West lying in her winding sheet with the great knife slashes in her face. Her blonde hair is flecked with green moss. Her purple eyelids have shrunk back. The blue eyes gaze up, only they're dull now. They won't see the stars. They won't flash with laugher when I tell her we'll go out together and I'll show her the mountains on the moon.

That vision flowed into my head like molten brass. A searing heat filled me through. *There she is: a kind-hearted woman lying dead in her grave, while spectators gawp and tittle-tattle about the way she earned her money to keep herself from starving.* Now the man who stole Dolly's rose shook his fright-ened wife as if she was a bag of nothing at all.

'Ah! What the hell ya do that for?' The man touched the corner of his mouth.

I didn't even realize I'd struck him until he'd cried out those words.

I snarled, 'Let go of her! You're frightening her!'

'And I'll do more than frighten you, y' little bitch. C'm here!'

I'm not running away. You can count on that. I leapt forward again. Not scratching, not slapping. I'd learnt from my masters well. Fist! That's what breaks the skin. Fist! Fist! I punched him in the soft cushion of his face. His green hat flicked clear of his blotchy head to land in the mud. He punched back but I felt no pain.

Now the wife was released from the bully's grip she fought, too. Only she struck at me while crying in a shrill voice, 'You leave my husband alone. Stop hitting him!'

I kicked his shins. By now his face had become purple. Blood smeared his mouth. He cursed between gasps of breath.

The other ghouls had moved back. One woman shouted, 'Help! Over here! There's a mad woman!'

A couple of men who'd been digging a grave at the far side of the cemetery ran over. They grabbed my arms to pull me back. This gave the bully his chance.

'Hold her still,' he gasped. 'That's it. Pin her arms back.'

When I was helpless he punched at my head. The trees that were now stripped of their leaves appeared to turn far below me. Black slabs of gravestones. A stone angel with a face rotted by frost . . . wooden crosses – they all flew from me. At that moment I crossed over some gulf from this mortal realm into shuddering darkness.

From a vale of shadow Dolly West emerged, dancing, laughing. Moonlight shone on a spectral river. I found myself in a forest with trees that bore leaves made of glass. They chimed an unearthly music. A slow nocturne that haunted the night air.

'You're right, Nidabi.' Dolly spun toward me, her arms held out, her face shining with delight. 'I've been to the moon.' Then she hugged me so tight that my back ached. 'There really are mountains. I've walked on them. You told me the truth!'

Happiness filled me. I was so pleased to hug Dolly that I closed my eyes. She smelt of lavender. Her excited breath sounded loud in my ear. When I opened my eyes I flinched with shock. For, there in the moonlight, a dark figure stepped out from the shadows. Beneath the rim of the top hat was a hollow void where two eyes hung suspended. Like two balls of white glass they burned so cruelly. The man slowly approached us. In his raised hand he gripped a dagger. The chimes from the trees became disordered, chaotic – a jangling dissonance that made my skin crawl.

'Dolly. It's Pastor Hux.' As I spoke the words I felt her body stiffen in my arms. 'Don't worry, sweetheart. I can protect you this time. He won't hurt you if I'm here. You hold me tight. I'll keep you safe.' Even as Dolly pressed her face against my shoulder her body hardened as if becoming wooden. Instead of the warmth I felt a moment ago, a cold damp seeped through my clothes to touch my skin. Her head sagged limply against my shoulder. I smelt something animal that had gone rotten. Her face gradually altered its composition.

Dolly's voice came as a hiss. 'Nidabi, sweetheart. I've got to leave you now. Will you kiss me goodbye?'

Fissures of white and grey and brown bulged up toward my eyes. A red stain marred the spongy mass. Quickly, I jerked my head back. The groan I heard was my own. My neck ached. The red stain was my own blood spilt on the soil. I pushed myself on to one elbow. Still I found myself looking down at the grave just a foot from my face, as if an uncanny gravity held me there. When at last I lifted my head I saw the man and his wisp of a wife were gone. A dozen women with colourless faces stared down at me. They didn't move. They didn't say anything.

I asked, 'Are you real? Or have you risen from your graves, too?'

One whispered to her companion, 'Is she drunk?'

Hah. Real as this dirt they were. Eventually, I climbed to my feet, my skirt and jacket streaked with clay. I took ten swaying steps along the path toward the cemetery gate. Then stopped dead. Abruptly, I turned round and walked back to Dolly's grave.

This time when I talked to my friend I didn't mutter. My voice rang out as clear as a cathedral bell: 'Dolly West. I promise I'm going to find the man who did this to you. And when I do he's going to beg God that he doesn't live one moment longer!'

I marched from the graveyard with the people staring. They thought I was mad. Maybe I am. But that was the time of transition. The pivot. For me, one world existed before I was knocked down on to the grave. That world died the second I made my promise to Dolly. *In this new world I exist with one purpose. And that is vengeance.* I sit here writing in a blaze of fury. Inside me burns the vision of the man I will one day find. The man known as Pastor Hux. Then, when I do, heaven help him.

Ty's Book

22nd November. The mistral blew hard. It rushed Arles like a barbarian attack. Jets of cold air pummelled men and women walking home from work that evening. Mistral is a Provençal word for 'master'; indeed, that cold north-westerly soon mastered the town. Children fled indoors from it. Shutters slammed as if the houses themselves had woken in panic and were now sending out an alarm that danger was imminent. Along the promenade, where old Roman tombs line the way, crimson leaves flew from the trees: a blizzard of vibrant colours. By the time I reached the artist's house it was dark. The wild tempest made its own bleak music in the narrow streets. By turns, it cried so much like a human voice that shivers crawled through my bones. Then it would rise into an angry shriek before subsiding into soft sobbing. If heartbroken souls should ever wander alone, lost in everlasting darkness, this would be the night for such a legend.

The door of the yellow house lay open when I arrived. The light fluttered as a draught played on the wick. I found Vincent van Gogh sitting at the table in the downstairs room. Unblinking, he stared at the wall, as if his focus was on some distant place beyond it. Dried leaves spiralled in a maelstrom across the floor tiles. Fragments of them stuck to a new canvas that wasn't yet dry. The painting depicted tiny figures walking through a grove of trees beneath a sky of angry, turbulent cloud that seemed as if it could shatter the walkers any moment it wished. I hurried inside, then forced the door shut against the brutal thrusts of the mistral. He didn't appear to be aware of anything – not the leaves; not the storm; not me.

'Vincent? Has anything happened?'

He didn't answer. Now the door was at last properly shut the leaves stopped their mad rush and died to the floor. Shards of a red bowl lay scattered at one end of the room.

'Monsieur Van Gogh, are you all right?' I squeezed his hand in mine as it lay on the table. The muscles were tense as if he anticipated a living nightmare to burst through the door. Outside, gales cried across the rooftops. They emoted suffering and anger. I asked again, 'Vincent? What's wrong?'

'Art is all wrong.' He spoke in whispers. 'My art is all wrong.'

'It's Gauguin again, isn't it?'

Vincent became suddenly animated. 'It's the arguments. When I discuss the paintings I love my words shock him, they burn, like voltage sears his body!'

'Gauguin tells stories about you at the brothel, Vincent. They are exaggerations. He uses them to make himself look good.'

Vincent ran his fingers through his hair. 'He paints like an angel. But as a man he is impossible.'

'It won't be good for you, Vincent, if you fight all the time.'

'Perhaps if I could earn money – if it's at all possible – then Gauguin might be more content. But whatever happens . . . Oh, God.' Vincent turned so he could seize both my hands. 'But promise me this, Ty. Make an oath on your sister's life!'

'What oath? What do you want me to do?' I was frightened by his intensity.

'Promise me. If he comes to the brothel and asks for you, swear that you will refuse him.'

'I don't know if I'd be allowed to say—'

He shook me. 'Promise that.'

'I'll try, but—'

'Swear that you'll have nothing to do with him. Don't you realize I'm terrified? I'm afraid that he'll hurt you to get back at me.' He clamped his hands over his face, his fingers splayed out like the bars of a cage across his eyes. 'It's this mistral. It drives everyone mad. But if Gauguin ever hurt you I'd commit murder!'

He's going to lose possession of himself, I thought. At any moment he's going to run out into the street to scream his rage at the world. I decided if his fury did erupt I would throw myself on his body to calm him. If there were trouble the gendarmes would surely put him in jail. For months the Arlesians had complained to the mayor that the man was insane. An outburst from Vincent would be the excuse they needed. When he did move it was to scoop a newspaper from the floor.

He took a deep breath. 'Ty, we also argued about this. No, not art this time. Gauguin came home this afternoon to find me brooding over this.' A trembling finger indicated an article headed THE LONDON DISEASE. 'In London a madman has killed innocent women – poverty's victims that are forced into prostitution by circumstance. I thought Gauguin would care. You know what he said to me, Ty? He laughed, then he said, "Pah, Brigadier" – that's the name he uses to mock me as you know – "Pah, Brigadier! Whores are like thistles. Cut one down and three grow in its place." That led to old arguments.' He sighed. 'So the crockery is smashed again. Gauguin leaves for the bar.'

'You're not in the wrong, Vincent. He is.'

'I never thought of him as callous. This account of women butchered in the streets? It troubled me. I detest it is happening. Yet he just laughed it away with "Pah! Come with me, Brigadier. When we're soused we'll find a big strong woman. We'll make violent love to her, then throw her back into the street!" And I'd just read this to him. About murder.' He crumpled the newspaper.

'I'll put everything right.' No sooner had I started ordering the room than he joined me. Soon we were crouched beside one another as we picked up splinters of pot.

'So this is how we met?' He gave a tired smile. 'This is our sacred rite for just you and me. We kneel down on the ground. We rescue the fallen.'

We then talked about everyday things. He asked after Brionne. Tut-tutted over the storm that prevented him from working outdoors. While I brewed a fresh jug of coffee I encouraged him to eat, but he insisted he wasn't hungry. At least he was calm again. For a time he picked fragments of leaf away from a new painting of blue-tinted hills. Outside, gales rushed through the street with a huge hissing that rose to a full-blooded scream. The noise made the house vibrate around us.

'Ty,' he breathed, 'before I began this painting I asked myself, should I use a brush to paint blocks of colour? Or instead of blocks should there be passionate streaks of purple that make the cloud boil with rage?' He fixed his eyes on the brushwork with absolute concentration. Air currents sighed beneath the door. 'Those kinds of questions I can answer. But who do you ask when it is a bigger question? If I said to myself, "Vincent, look here – this ambition of yours to become an artist – is it time to admit that you've failed?"' The coldness of that air penetrating the room was no match for the cold deluge that gushed through my body. 'Ty? To whom could I address the question of whether I have failed in my life's work? Who would give me a truthful answer I could rely on?'

'Vincent, you shouldn't ask these things.'

'I wish I didn't have to ask. But I must. Canvas that costs two francs per metre? I daub it with expensive paint. Forty francs a week feeds me and keeps this roof over my head. How much do I contribute to my upkeep? Not one franc. Not so much as a sou. My brother, Theo, despatches my allowance every week.' His voice was soft, understated, an absence of passion that alarmed me more than rage would have done. 'Theo's sent me money for years. I have been a bottomless pit into which Theo pours his salary. You work hard for your money, Ty. Then, when you should be resting, you take care of the little girl. Often you end up looking after me. And all the time I am covering canvas with paint that could be liquid gold for what it costs my brother. For what? My paintings don't sell.' There was an anxious, searching quality to his eyes. 'So: there's my question. Who will give me a truthful answer? Have I failed?'

'Vincent. Whatever you do, don't ask Gauguin that question. He'll use it against you.'

'No, I won't trouble Gauguin.' He shook his head. 'Who then?'

'It seems to me,' I began hesitantly, 'that our minds house more than one individual. I haven't put this in words before, so it's hard for me to explain.'

'Go on.' Many would have mocked me but Vincent was interested.

'I haven't read this in a book, or been told it, but I have

come to believe that we are born with a mind that is complete and fully formed in itself. You might have seen a newborn baby that has understanding in its expression. The midwife will cry, "Oh? Just look at his eyes. He's been here before." Then within a few hours of birth this awareness will sink back down. The baby will become just like we expect a baby to be. You think this is ridiculous, don't you?'

'Far from it. Once I rescued a kitten from being drowned in a sack. It was a tiny thing. Its eyes hadn't opened yet. I had to squeeze milk into its mouth from a little bit of sponge. What astonished me was the fact that even though the kitten grew up isolated from other cats, it knew how to catch mice. How could it know how?' Vincent touched his red hair at his temple. 'They call it instinct. But all those skills arrived intact inside its head when it was born. God given.'

'So it's my belief, Vincent – and tell me to be quiet if it offends your religion – that we are born with an old mind that is profound and wise. As we grow into adulthood it sinks down in our brains as the personality we identify as our *self* gains strength and learning. But the old mind isn't destroyed, even though we are inclined to neglect it. The old mind continues to speak to us. Its language is dreams. In my heart of hearts I believe that it cares deeply for us, and does all in its power to guide us.'

'Like a guardian angel?'

'You do think I'm stupid!'

'No, Ty. What you are explaining has roots in just about every faith in the world. Some would call this wise old mind the soul.'

'It takes time to understand dreams. Every night you must ask the question you need answering before you sleep. It might not happen straightaway but eventually you'll notice your dreams become different. They are like a foreign language that you learn to translate. The answer you are looking for will be contained in a dream.'

'And you practise this?'

'It isn't witchcraft.' *Does he think I'm mad?* I continued in a defiant tone as the mistral sent fluting notes through the town. 'I've practised this for years. Problems I face at work, or how to find a home, I ask whatever this thing is we're born with. It's not magic, it's nature. Try it. You'll discover this blessing for yourself, and then you will never accuse me of madness.'

'Ty, I would never do that.' He held out his hands to placate me. 'Sit. I want to talk about this. Now, don't they—?' Before he could finish the sentence there came a sharp rap on the glass.

Vincent sighed. 'If it's those boys again.' He opened the door. 'Ah? My dear fellow. What a night! Quick – come out of the storm.' He stepped back to reveal Pastor Hux. The man stood there in his black coat, gripping the top hat in one hand.

'Sit down, Pastor. We have hot coffee. There's bread, too.'

He nodded a greeting to me, then turned to Vincent. 'Thank you, I've just eaten, but please go ahead.'

'We've just been having a wonderful conversation about the human psyche. Ty has developed a remarkable practice where she—'

'Oh, the Pastor won't be interested.' To discuss my private belief with this dark-swathed Englishman would be like revealing an intimacy.

'Don't be afraid of ridicule, Ty.' Vincent poured the coffee. 'The Pastor and I would walk through night-time London talking for hours about the lives of saints, and all things holy. Isn't that right, Pastor?'

'We did.' He carefully arranged the coat tails before sitting. 'And after all those hours of conversation we agreed on one maxim: deeds, not words.'

'Ty has a mind that's untainted with indoctrination. From her observations on life itself, she has made deductions about the human psyche.'

'Vincent – monsieur – my ideas might appear heathen to a man of God.'

'I see.' The Englishman's voice chimed with the bitterly cold mistral. 'So you have never had religious tuition?'

'No, sir.'

'Then perhaps you shouldn't dismiss God without reading the Bible first.'

That was the moment that Vincent realized the Pastor and I didn't see eye to eye. 'Pastor,' he said, 'we shouldn't be fixated on scripture. Shouldn't people first seek God in their own hearts?'

The Pastor growled, 'Those who desert God are capable of

anything. Any bestiality. Any depraved act. To kill without guilt. Is that what you want?' It seemed then that the Pastor's eyes gazed inward not outward.

'I haven't abandoned God. You misunderstand me.'

'I wonder if I have. You see, Vincent, I came here to Arles because I hoped we could work together.'

'Then we shall.'

'I gathered from your letter that you saved this girl from whoredom, yet she still works in the brothel.' Even though he turned toward Vincent he didn't appear to see him. The man's focus was held by some inner image that wouldn't release him from its grip. 'You knew that, didn't you?'

'Of course. She has a sister to feed. Her brother died this year . . . she's determined to—'

'Friend, we could have worked together to ensure women like Ty – the poorest wretches on God's earth – needn't sell their bodies.' Gales shook the door. A screaming note rose outside. 'We could have put an end to their sin.'

Vincent rose. 'Pastor! I have no money. My nerves are in shreds. Most days it's all I can do to hold a paintbrush in my hand. To change people's lives by even an infinitesimal fraction is beyond my power.'

'I promised myself that together we'd save women like this.' He stabbed his finger at me. 'Clearly, I'm mistaken. Here my mission has failed before it's even begun.'

For a while no one moved in the room. Then Vincent rushed to where a framed canvas leant with its picture to the wall. 'If I have a mission,' he said, 'it's to communicate emotion and ideas through my work. I was saving this to show you later.'

'What is it?'

'I painted you from memory.' For a moment Vincent van Gogh appeared as a nervous schoolboy, eager to present his work to a much-respected teacher, yet anxious lest it prove a disappointment. Too many times in the past people have scorned his art; they dismiss it as primitive and strange. Vincent paints in such a wonderful way that those observing his master-pieces discover their own inner nature reflected there. Because of his anxieties he kept the painted side of the canvas hidden. 'One night I dreamt that we were walking through London again. In this study I strove to evoke your spirit, rather than any forensic accuracy of features. Here is an impression, a manifestation . . . yes? Look . . . see for yourself.' With that, he turned the frame so the Englishman could inspect the composition. 'I call it "The Midnight Man".'

The subject of the portrait gazed at it with those cold eyes. He didn't speak, his expression revealed nothing. For a long time he absorbed the detail – the swirl of stars on a purple background. Then the figure itself: a man in black; a face obscured by shadow; the eyes pools of yellow.

Eventually, the Pastor spoke. 'Monsieur Van Gogh. In your picture, I see a demon presiding over hell on earth. Is that how you see me?' His eyes burned with a baleful light. I sensed his growing rage.

Abruptly, the door crashed open, admitting a hurricane. Leaves, scraps of paper, clouds of dust blasted into the room to swirl around our heads.

'What lies are you fishwives telling about me?'

Gauguin roared into the room. Taking his cap off, he flung it away like it had just bitten him. Then he smashed the door shut. The man was so drunk he could barely stand.

Vincent spoke in a friendly way. 'Gauguin, sit down. We've made fresh coffee.'

'Damn your coffee!' He dragged off his coat, snarling like an angry bear as he did so. 'Arles! What a town. Have you ever seen weather like it? This place is the dirtiest hole in the south. The waiter cheated me out of ten francs. The absinthe tastes like ditchwater. Ah? It's you!' He lurched round to focus his eyes on us. 'The Unholy Three. Now there's a portrait for you. The Algerian vampire; she's bled many a man dry. The mad Dutchman – he weeps over every dead sparrow he finds. He squeezes a whole tube of yellow paint out on to a canvas then cries out: "Gauguin! Gauguin! Look at this. I've painted a lemon!" Ha! And the final subject of our oh-so noble painting.' He shook his finger at the Pastor. 'The English Conger Eel. Cold and slippery. What eyes you've got, sir. God help us, he really has got the eyes of a fish. Cold as charity!'

'Gauguin, please drink some coffee.'

'Blast your coffee, Vincent. I'm getting out, I tell you. Have your damn brother wire me the fare out of this cesspit.'

I snapped at the drunk. 'You should thank Vincent for

putting a roof over your head. But oh, no, you burst in here and insult him.'

'I'm Gauguin, the generous. I haven't insulted *merely* him alone. I've insulted the three of you! The little artist, the English Conger Eel and the Algerian Vampire.'

Hux rose to his feet. Even more stiffly formal than usual he intoned, 'It's time I returned to my hotel. I trust your friend will be in improved spirits tomorrow.'

'Improved spirits? Improved spirits?' Gauguin used his hand to pantomime a quacking mouth. 'Improved spirits? No, I'll be far worse! I'll be bloody sober. Sober in this dirty hole is worse than a posting in hell!'

'Then it'll be a valuable rehearsal for you, monsieur, seeing as hell's your destination anyway.'

'Come here, *Mister* Conger Eel. We'll stroll down to Hades together.' Gauguin lunged at Pastor Hux. Vincent jumped to put himself between them. The winds rose in a howl. A shutter slammed against the wall.

I shouted a warning. Gauguin turned his drink-sodden face to me, thinking I was begging them not to fight, but I pointed at the windows. There, every square centimetre of glass in both the door and window was crammed tight with faces. They were grinning at us, their eyes bright with a cruel glee. Vincent van Gogh's neighbours had poured out of their homes to make a feast of the drama unfolding in the little yellow house. With a shout Vincent wrenched open the door, then rushed into the street to shove the rabble from his home. Some even stood on the window ledges to make sure they had a perfect view of the fight inside the house.

Vincent cried out as they scurried away laughing. 'How many times do I have to tell you?' Even the storm seemed to howl with malicious laughter. 'Why won't you leave me alone?'

The Arlesians disappeared to leave Vincent standing alone in the road with leaves streaming by him. He ran his hands through his hair in utter misery. He called out again. The mistral, however, snatched the words from him to scatter them unheard into the night sky. By the time he returned to the house Hux had gone. Gauguin had passed out in a chair.

Nidabi's Journal

15th December. I vowed to put an end to Pastor Hux. As vengeance for what he did to Dolly West and the others? Or to prevent him killing again? Ultimately, the result is the same. Now, for the first time in my life, I'm riding in a carriage pulled by a locomotive. The sense of speed isn't as dizzying as I imagined it would be, though the engine is a fearsome beast with its bellyful of steam. For a time I believed I would never make this journey. It seemed as if Pastor Hux had become invisible. Weeks passed with me existing in timeless limbo. I ate, I slept, I worked. Newspapers I devoured in search of reports of the killer. All the detectives' work has led to nothing. But I'm ahead of myself. To return to last week: after all that wandering about London in the hope I would see the Pastor by chance, it occurred to me to return to Lamplands. If I harboured any hope I'd find him there working in his study, it was dispelled the moment I opened the entrance gates. Branches had fallen on to the driveway and not been cleared away. A sense of abandonment haunted the place. The stable lay empty of the gallower. However, I did find one of its iron shoes, which I used to break a glass pane, so I could unlatch a window to the kitchen. Regardless of the state of a house, the postman continues to deliver letters. I found dozens on the mat. There I stood under the massive lamp in the hall as I opened envelope after envelope. Some were from the Pastor's solicitor warning him his finances were in disarray. Many letters were from women who told their stories of new-found respectability, though I'd met several of the correspondents plying their trade in the back streets. Then an undated letter provided the answer I'd been searching for.

2 Place Lamartine,
Arles

My dear Pastor Hux,
    I should have warned you in my earlier letter that
Arles at this time of year can be extremely cold. Bring
clothes that would be suitable for a London winter. I
know you are interested in Roman architecture, so here
is a sketched detail of our amphitheatre in Arles. It shows
a round arch on the first floor of the external travertine
shell. In Northern climes ruins become dark, moss-
covered skeletons. Here, in the blaze of intense light, the
stonework shines like mother of pearl. I think you will
be greatly pleased. Here's to a pleasant journey.

Vincent

So this is my destination: Number 2 Place Lamartine, Arles,
a faraway city in France. That's where I will find the man
who destroyed the lives of those he at first protected. Soon
the train will arrive in Dover; after that, I take a ship across
the English Channel. Already it's dusk. The symbolism of a
night-time sea journey isn't lost on me. This is a voyage into
the unknown where the destination must be death – has to
be death! But that death? Will it be Pastor Hux? Or will it
be me? Now an irresistible power is rushing me toward that
final reckoning.

Ty's Book

20th December. Vincent and Gauguin were exhausted. Both
men's faces were streaked with paint – red, blue, green, and
a most vivacious orange. They sat at the table in the café,
which had become an oasis of golden light in the dark.
    Gauguin gestured me to sit. 'Join us, Ty.'

I hesitated.

'I might scratch but I don't bite. Sit down.' His voice was gruff but he smiled.

'Don't you dare insult her, Gauguin. She's my friend.'

'I won't say a word out of place, Vincent. Besides, Ty would give me back double. She's intelligent, she's a tigress. Ty only keeps her claws from my face because I'm your friend. Now, drink up.'

Still dazed by the intensity of the day's work, Vincent grimaced. 'Ah, that portrait, Gauguin. Why did you paint me as if I look insane?'

'I painted what I saw.'

'That I'm mad?'

'Of course you're mad. We're all mad. We have to be crazy to paint.' Gauguin beckoned a waiter, who'd appeared from behind the counter with a bowl. 'Boy, over here.' He rapped the table top in front of Vincent. 'This is the one.'

'I didn't order food.'

'No, old comrade, I ordered it for you.' Gauguin patted him on the back; this time his smile was genuinely friendly. 'You've got to eat, Vincent. Put some flesh on those Dutch bones of yours.'

'Then you should be eating, too.'

Gauguin nodded toward a woman with long red hair at the counter. 'I've seen what I'll have on my plate today.' He winked. 'Uh-ho, here's the Conger Eel. I'll bid you good-night, good sir, good lady. Now eat your soup, brother. Then tomorrow we'll paint the entire universe a better place.' With a stone-faced nod at Pastor Hux he moved away from the table to whisper something into the redhead's ear, who awarded him a welcoming smile. Pastor Hux joined us. He placed his top hat on the table. Many in the bar glanced across at this strange black-dressed figure; a raven amongst the Arlesian brightly coloured peacocks. As he and Vincent chatted about their day he ordered a glass of cordial. Then the subject turned to dreams.

'I don't dream,' Hux declared.

Vincent raised his eyebrows. 'Never?'

The way Hux shook his head with his lips crimped severely together was more suggestive of someone suffering from too tight a collar. This is a man who has put a greater part of his self behind a wall. When we dream we yield our self-control. Dreams are uninhibited; they are wild animals. This man, Hux, despises any notion of losing self-possession. To admit to dreaming would be to admit feral thoughts. Perhaps dangerous thoughts.

Vincent stirred the rich brown soup with his spoon. 'Dreams are natural. They open doors to other worlds; perhaps ones that are only normally accessible after death. Why, even dogs dream.'

'Precisely.' Hux sipped his drink. 'Modern man must remain vigilant, otherwise the ways of the beast will steal upon him, then civilization, a fragile thing at best, will be lost for ever.'

'Come now, Ty believes dreams are the language of our *inner* self.'

Hux glared at me. Gauguin is infuriating, but his comparison of this Englishman to a conger eel is unnervingly accurate. Hux has the cold stare of a predatory fish.

'If you listen to dreams,' Hux began, 'how does one know that dream voice isn't Satan's?'

Vincent rubbed his jaw. 'Then couldn't it be the voice of God? Doesn't the Gospel of Matthew repeatedly state that an angel appeared to Joseph in *his* dreams to give commands?'

'That account is enshrined in the Bible. Another matter entirely.'

Vincent became animated as passion returned to his voice: 'Ty says it is possible to receive communication from our other inner self, an inherited mind, through dreams. Can you test whether that hypothesis is real in a laboratory? No! But you can practise it yourself, then listen to what your own heart tells you is true.'

'A dream can propagate all kinds of blasphemy.'

'I've used Ty's device myself. I was gripped by this over-whelming conviction that I'd failed in my life's work to become an artist. I asked myself, have I failed? Or am I producing paintings of merit? I didn't know. So, I lay down at night with this question running through my head – is it time I stopped painting for ever?'

Hux radiated disapproval. 'So how did this inner self reply?'

'Not words. It showed me the most vivid imagery. I saw myself in a cornfield, and I was painting from the brightest palette you've ever seen.' The light flashing in Vincent's eyes was electric. 'Sometimes I stood to paint, sometimes I sat, then there was a time when I lay on the earth to draw.'

'Pray, what did all this cornucopia of visions convey to you?'

'That I am meant to continue with my work. Don't you see? My heart is telling me to paint and keep painting, whether it's on my feet, on my knees or flat out in the dirt.'

'That's not commitment, it's insanity.'

Vincent smiled. 'So long as it doesn't prevent me from painting then I will continue.'

Pastor Hux found Vincent's words repellent. 'I'll say it again: I really did believe that we could work together to save women like this.' He favoured me with a curt nod. 'Now you indulge yourself in ravings about dreams, and sacrificing your soul.'

'Hardly raving. But Ty here showed me how to ask one of the most important questions of my life – whether or not I should turn my back on art. Now I have my answer. My life is my work. I'll risk my health and my sanity for it. That risk no longer worries me.'

He stood up. 'My faith in you, Vincent, has failed.'

'You came here expecting to find Vincent van Gogh as he was at twenty. I've changed. So have you.'

'I'll bid you goodbye. I'm leaving first thing in the morning.'

Vincent rose. The two men regarded one another across the café table. The black crow of a man, and the artist in his blue workman's clothes, paint marks on his face, red hair glinting like copper in the lamplight. For a moment I believed Pastor Hux expected Vincent to beg him to stay. Vincent, however, held out his hand. Even Hux's stone face registered a flicker of surprise.

'So? There's nothing more to be said?' Hux gave the briefest of handshakes.

'You can revisit a town you love and find it's not the same as you remember it. That's true of friendships.'

'Then I must confess to you, Monsieur Van Gogh, I am alone in the world. I have no family and no friends.'

These words struck Vincent hard. He began to speak but Pastor Hux turned away, then swept out of the café as if an invisible force drove him out.

'Are you going to speak with him?' I asked.

'He resented your presence here, Ty. I prefer your company to his.' He shook his head. 'I'd prefer not to meet the man again. Now, for the good of our nerves, a glass of something.' He caught the boy's eye. 'Waiter? Brandy for two.'

Just as a stumble fells you quickly, or a horse bolting into a crowded market wreaks carnage in a moment, so, this happened. After leaving Vincent in the café I returned home. There, pinned to my door was a small brown paper parcel, which I pulled from the tack. Perhaps because there was no weight to it, and I wondered what it could be, I smelt it. Its rotten sweetness made me flinch. Despite common sense telling me to throw it on the floor I found myself unfolding the paper in the light of the hallway lamp. Yes, of course, I knew its content would be terrible. Only a dreadful momentum carried me forward. I couldn't stop myself peeling back that final leaf of wrapping that had been stained by a dark fluid.

There, in the palm of my hand, on its bed of paper – black, and oozing, and stinking of rot – an ear . . . a human ear. A rounded one, as delicately perfect as a seashell: its curves, its hollows, its rounded lobe pierced for a ring. A freckle revealed itself against the dark skin as a grey star. For whole moments I don't think I even breathed. At last I noticed lettering that showed through the stain on the paper. For a while I couldn't decipher it, the pencil marks were so faint. Then it became so suddenly clear the words rushed at me: *This should belong to you.* The urge to throw the scrap of flesh from me was almost overwhelming. *You know who this ear belongs to?* The question stopped me. Because I knew the answer. *The gypsy girl murdered in the back yard of the brothel. The ear is hers.* Instantly, I knew this delicate structure wasn't to be tossed into the dirt. Carefully now, so I didn't drop it, I opened the door of my apartment. Once inside, I emptied a little basket that contained my hairpins, arranged a clean cotton handkerchief in the bottom, then set the ear, still cupped in its brown paper, on to that. This fragment of humanity might not lead the gendarmes to her killer, yet this was the respectful thing to do. After that, I put another cloth over the basket, then hurried to the gendarmerie in the centre of town. The officer at the desk turned very pale when he saw what the little container guarded.

'Where did you find this?' he asked at last.

When I explained he brought a detective who questioned me for the best part of half an hour. The answers I gave him he wrote down in a pocket book. I heard him tell the gendarme that he, too, believed the ear had been carved from the murder victim, and that from the odour there had been an attempt to preserve it in cognac. Despite the alcohol I'd consumed earlier in the night with Vincent my nerves chimed like bells. I wouldn't be able to sleep if I went straight home, and as Brionne stayed at a friend's house, I made my way to the yellow house. Despite it being after midnight the artist hadn't retired. With luck Gauguin wouldn't be home to mock this story. At my knock Vincent opened the door.

'Ty?' He beckoned me in. 'This is a night for visitors. There's someone I'd like you to meet. Another traveller from England.' He stepped back to reveal a woman who rose from a chair. 'Ty, this is Nidabi.'

Nidabi's Journal

21st December. Another country. Even the air smells different. Everywhere I catch the scent of exotic spices and the odour of this foreign earth.

Because I had Vincent van Gogh's address in Arles it was a simple matter to find his house – it's a tiny yellow cottage on the corner of a street. The smell of its interior is heady: there are rich fumes of coffee mingled with those of paint and turpentine. It seemed to me that the whole building was crammed with landscapes and portraits of the most brilliant colours imaginable. From the beginning of my adult life I have survived by both my body and my wits, so I knew being always truthful isn't always wise. I introduced myself to the red-haired man who answered the door as Nidabi, a close friend of Pastor Hux. He knew about me and I him, the Dutch artist who'd befriended the Pastor in London many years ago.

I fully expected Pastor Hux to be there. I could have taken the pistol from my bag and shot Dolly's murderer in the heart, and everything would be done. But, though my plan had hitherto worked so smoothly, it now unravelled at that very moment.

'Pastor Hux?' the artist echoed in lightly accented English. 'Yes, he was here, miss, but he told me the night before last he was leaving Arles.'

'Could you tell me where he's gone? Please, it's most important.'

'Miss, I wish I could, but I've had word that he's already left. You see, we didn't part as amicably as I'd have wished . . . but that doesn't matter now. For your sake we should find him.'

'Thank you, Mr Van Gogh.'

'Please sit down . . . no, here, closer to the fire. It's freezing out. The mistral is cold enough to cut you in two.' As the artist used his large freckled hands to heap coal on to the fire he said, 'You've had a long journey. I hope you're not here with bad news for my old friend?'

This is where the lies begin. 'No, on the contrary.'

'Oh?'

'It's a delicate matter of the heart, Mr Van Gogh. You understand?'

'But of course.' From the surge of emotion that crossed the man's face he'd immediately concluded that the Pastor and I were lovers. Now what? He wonders if there've been arguments and separation. And now I've journeyed thousands of miles to confess my undying love for the Pastor? To accept his proposal of marriage? If that's what the artist believes, all well and good. He nodded as he reached a decision. 'Trust me. I'll do whatever's in my power to find Pastor Hux.'

'Thank you.' The bag rested on my lap. I squeezed the material to feel the solid presence of the hidden pistol. 'You don't know what that means to me.'

'It'll be my pleasure.' He was genuinely delighted to help me. I told myself that this man, Vincent van Gogh, possessed a good and loyal heart.

'Sir?'

'Yes, miss?'

'I'd ask a favour.'

'Of course!'

'Would you please use my name – Nidabi. The Pastor has told me so much about you that I'm uncomfortable with the formality of titles.'

'I'd be delighted. Nidabi. Then, please call me Vincent. Otherwise I feel someone is addressing my father.'

We talked for a while about my life at Lamplands. I explained how Pastor Hux had saved me from the Colonel. Vincent listened with such a force of concentration it seemed as if his green eyes burned right through me to see each individual atom of my soul. At one point, after eleven o'clock that night, a robust man kicked open the front door. Though he'd been drinking he had an air of cool poise. I don't understand French; nevertheless, I soon realized the man demanded money. Even though Vincent appeared reluctant, he nevertheless fished coins from a little box. The loud stranger appeared contemptuous of the amount. Then he noticed me. He grinned, then asked what I took to be a question. Vincent answered in French. I heard both the names 'Hux' and 'Nidabi' in the answer.

'Pah!' The stranger's disdain was blatant. In a second he'd wrenched open the door, then staggered out into the night.

'That was Gauguin,' Vincent explained. 'He's, ahm . . . celebrating.'

We continued to discuss how best to find Pastor Hux. A spirit of romance fired Vincent's blood. Hux and I would soon be reunited, he seemed confident of that.

'Several years ago, I lived with Sien,' he confessed. 'She bore a child, a grand little boy. I'd have dearly loved to have married her, but my family intervened; they threatened me with the lunatic asylum. Sien was a poor woman, she had to earn her money any way she could, but she was as kind as an angel.' I didn't have chance to respond before an urgent knock sounded on the door. 'Oh, Gauguin again. If he wants more money for drink, he'll have to go pawn his boots.'

This time he opened the door to a small, doll-like woman of around twenty. She was dressed in brilliant orange skirts, and a little black jacket. Swathes of dark hair rippled in the breeze. Straight away, her onyx eyes darted at me. Vincent spoke words of French to her then turned to me.

'Nidabi. This is Ty.'

'Pastor Hux mentioned her to me. You sent him a sketch.'

'Ty has no English. If I have your permission I'll explain why you're here.'

For several minutes they spoke to one another. Unlike my countrymen they moved their hands in an extremely expressive way as they talked. At the end of the conversation Vincent introduced the two of us. I shook her hand – *how small it is!* I noticed that our skin's of a similar hue. The way she studied my face, I surmised she was trying to divine some of my personal history. That I was once a whore? Yes, she must see that worldly glint in my eye. But then that's no secret. Pastor Hux had written to Vincent about me and vice versa.

Vincent said, 'Now, you'll be exhausted by your journey. Have you taken a room at a hotel?'

'I came straight here from the station.' By rights, the body of Hux should be lying cold on the floor by now, but no, that wasn't to be.

'Good.' Vincent clapped his hands together. 'The hospitality of a real home is best. Ty insists that you stay with her. In the morning we will find Pastor Hux.'

So that's how it went. Within moments I walked beside the slightly built woman to a building that stood by the river. It was quite new with welcoming gas lamps in the hallway. One odd thing happened though. Ty had been smiling as we walked. However, when we reached her door she paused as if something shocked her. The focus of her shock appeared to be a thumbtack in the panel at about head height. Attached to that a scrap of brown paper fluttered in the draught. Sight of this frightened her, so she quickly unlocked the door, then gestured me inside. Once we were indoors she was happier. Repeating words of French to me, she pointed at various items – furniture, a hand pump in the kitchen, a bathroom. Then a separate room with a bed.

'Nidabi?' She used both hands to pat the air. A sit-down gesture. I chose a chair. Thinking hard, she held up one finger. 'Moment.'

I think she was asking me to stay sitting. I nodded. After flashing me a bright smile, she opened the door of the apartment and left.

Ty works as a whore. Has she gone to fetch a client? What were the French customs relating to whoredom? Does she intend to find a man for me? Would it cause offence if I refused? A moment later I heard voices outside the door; a latch clicked, the door swung open and Ty walked in. She guided a girl of around five years old in front of her. Clearly she'd collected the child from a neighbouring home. Relief swam through me so strongly that I relaxed into the chair with a sigh.

Ty rested her hand on the girl's head. 'Brionne.'

The girl, who closely resembled Ty, regarded me with bright eyes.

Then Ty said, 'Brionne? Nidabi.'

The little girl bowed to me as Ty smiled fondly at her. Then there followed a domestic pattern. Ty got the girl, whether daughter or sister, ready for bed. Although I couldn't understand the language I heard Brionne use the name Ty several times, so I concluded that Ty was indeed an elder sister. Moreover, the two appeared to live here alone. Ty, helped by Brionne, cut cake and poured milk into glasses. This was our post-midnight meal. After that, Ty put Brionne to bed on the sofa. Then she laid out blankets on the floor. When I protested that I should sleep on the floor instead, she spoke words to me that, although unintelligible, were clearly scolding. At last I relented. Soon I lay in the warm double bed with the sound of the river lapping outside my window. The pillow was a curious roll of cotton fabric stuffed with feathers, deliciously comfortable. In seconds I was fast asleep.

21st December. Ty explained through gestures that she had to take Brionne somewhere. School? A friend's house? I'm not sure. So, here I sit at a table that overlooks a glittering river. A brisk wind whips shreds of black cloud across an otherwise blue sky. The air is very clean, a freshness that is sharp in one's nostrils. The pale houses all have bright red roofs. There is something so strange about Arles. As if I've entered a fairy tale world – a fabulous realm where the extraordinary not only *might* happen, but *must* happen! But the *why* of being here? My purpose – my quest – that shines like a single star. Pastor Hux killed women in cold blood. He butchered my friend Dolly. Without doubt the man will kill again. If a dog that you love becomes rabid you have no choice but to destroy it. Through no fault of his own the man's sanity has foundered. The instant I see him I will take the pistol and shoot him dead. I have decided. Mark my words: *it will happen.*

Ty's Book

21st December. When I returned home from the Night Woman's house, where I'd left Brionne, I found Nidabi sitting at the window that overlooks the river. She had been writing in a leather-bound book. She smiled when she saw me.

'Nidabi. Uhm . . .' I moved my fingers to depict walking. 'Vincent?'

Nidabi slipped her book into the bag that she clutched tight to her always. Then she spoke some English words; we both nodded as we smiled, understanding each other through gesture, rather than speech. We'd go to the yellow house. Perhaps Vincent had found out where Hux had gone. But why Nidabi was so eager to be reunited with that cold eel of a man was a mystery to me. We walked side by side through windswept streets. They were busy with it being the last market day before Christmas. Drovers arrived from the Camargue, marching their flocks of geese into Arles for the feast-day tables. Nidabi linked arms with me. She appeared anxious. That could be credited to at least two things: her desire to be reunited with her lover, and the alien quality of this town. It probably wasn't like her London at all. To hear so many speaking a foreign tongue might try the nerves. Nidabi's apprehension made me recall my discovery again. That dreadful parcel fixed to my door. So much had happened that I had precious little time to think of it. I hadn't even had the opportunity to tell Vincent. The words on the bloodstained paper still made me tremble. *This should belong to you.* A deluge of shivers cascaded down my spine. There hadn't been time to consider that sentence logically. It was open to different interpretations. A gift by a lunatic? A random act of madness? Or, far more shockingly, did that statement have the specific meaning: *this should be* your *ear, Ty. You escaped by chance due to me mistaking the gypsy girl for you; next time you won't be so lucky* . . .

I decided to return to the gendarmerie so I could tell them that a threat of murder has been directed at me. Yet, as so often happens, intentions are easily wrecked.

Chaos seized the yellow house. After arguing with Vincent, Gauguin had stomped away to telegraph Theo van Gogh, demanding the rail fare to escape Arles. In the heat of words, a bottle had been smashed in the doorway. Vincent's spirits were shaken; although he told me what happened in French, he salted his conversation with Dutch phrases I didn't understand. This time he was sure that Gauguin would leave. That's when the absolute terror of impending loneliness flooded those melancholy green eyes. He has troubles enough of his own; if I told him about that scrap of flesh pinned to my door it might be too much for his nerves, so for the time being I must keep it from him. Nidabi can't have known what was happening as she can't make sense of our tongue. Nonetheless, she immediately helped me sweep up the broken glass. After that we made coffee for Vincent. I bought sugared bread from the bakery then had my work cut out persuading him to eat. Constantly, he returned to dab spots of sulphurous yellow on to a painted landscape. He ran one hand through his hair in an agitated way as he tried to master the brush in the other hand. The artist appeared so gaunt that morning I couldn't help but worry. If Nidabi felt any impatience at not being able to ask Vincent about Pastor Hux she didn't show it. It was only after another ten minutes that the artist blinked as if he'd woken from a deep sleep. He looked round in surprise.

'Bonjour, Ty. Nidabi—' The word after 'Nidabi' I didn't understand. A greeting in English perhaps. 'Sit down. It's so cold outside. I'm afraid I haven't any fresh coffee yet, I've been busy with the blessed sky here . . . oh? There is coffee! I must have made it earlier. I'm becoming so forgetful. Tut! And I argued with Gauguin . . .' An expression of shock struck his face. 'Oh my Lord . . . You've been here a while, haven't you? And didn't I tell you this already? About the bottle . . .' Not only his hands but his entire body was shaking now.

Nidabi spoke soothingly to him while pouring more coffee into his cup. He nodded. For a moment he spoke in English to her. His voice was calm now. She listened, while nodding every now and again, then he turned to me. 'Ty. I've told Nidabi what I know. While I slept Pastor Hux came here this morning. Gauguin answered the door, but he had a terrible hangover, which makes him more foul tempered than you can imagine. Pastor Hux asked if he could see me. Then Gauguin took pleasure in telling him, I'm sorry to say, that Nidabi had been here last night – and you had gone to find work in a brothel. Why did he lie? As I say, a hangover turns him into the devil. Gauguin told the Pastor he'd find Nidabi in the whorehouse, then shut the door in his face. That's all I know.' Vincent sat brooding by the fire. Every so often, he'd use both hands to bring the cup to his lips. A moment later he stood up. 'You know, I think I'll get some air.' Suddenly, his spine arched backward. Grunting, he clamped his hands to his head as a bolt of pain shot through his skull, then he toppled backward on to the stone floor. Nidabi was possessed of a passionate strength. She flew to him and held his thrashing head as convulsions took hold of him.

'Thank God, you were so quick,' I told her as his convulsions subsided. 'When he thrashes like this it can injure him. See? There's not a mark on him.'

She answered as if she understood. Then we paused, realizing that although we didn't speak the same language, we understood the fundamental meaning. I crouched there beside the unconscious man with tears on my face. Nidabi gazed at me with such sympathy it only made me weep harder. Quickly, she hugged me with a fierce compassion. *Well, here we are.* This kind of seizure had felled the artist many times before. All we could do was carry him to bed between us. He grunted as if he wanted something but I couldn't make out the words. For a time, I left Vincent in Nidabi's care while I went to the Night Woman's house as I was due to collect Brionne at noon. When I reached the woman's house it was mid-afternoon. Bless her, as always she understands. I explained I had to care for a sick friend and asked if Brionne could stay an extra night, promising an extra five francs that week. After she'd agreed I found Brionne playing with her friends in the yard. I spoke to my sister, then kissed her with a promise I'd collect her first thing in the morning. The winter night was already drawing in when I reached the yellow house. Nidabi stood on the doorstep, her dark eyes anxiously searching the street. She reacted with a pleased smile when she saw me. When I stepped into the kitchen I noticed she'd tidied the place. The fire blazed. There was fresh coal in the scuttle. Whether she'd bought it or she'd simply helped herself to fuel from a neighbour's yard I had no way of asking. Nevertheless, at least the room was bright with a welcome heat after the chill of the afternoon.

I nodded my approval. 'Vincent?' I asked.

Nidabi mimed sleeping. I looked in on Vincent. A noble and serene figure at rest: he was nothing like the agitated man when awake. He's exhausted, I told myself. He'll have been kept awake all night by Gauguin who'd argue furiously about everything from art to his hatred of this provincial town. For a moment, I watched Vincent to reassure myself his respiration was even. He did seem at peace so I returned to the kitchen. Seeing as I'd brought my book with me, I pulled it from the bag. Writing is a panacea. The greater the number of words that flow on to the paper, the more my nerves are soothed. I'm sitting here in the yellow house writing this now. Nidabi laughs, then draws out the leather journal I'd seen earlier. Smiling, as if we share a joke, we face each other across the table and fill pages with words. I wish I could hold a conversation with the English woman. More than our work, our age, and the colour of our skin, I'm sure we have so much in common.

Late: ten o'clock. Just now Gauguin burst into the house. The man has spilt red wine down his shirt. *That temper!*

'Ah!' Gauguin exclaimed as he saw the books in front of us. 'Greetings, my pair of scribblers.' He belched. 'Ack, Ty, where's my little Brigadier?'

I replied, 'Vincent's upstairs – sleeping.'

'Pah! Any word from his brother?'

'None.'

'Typical! What are the women like at your brothel?'

'How can I answer that?'

'Tall? Short? Fat? Ugly? Sweat like mules, squeal like hogs?'

'I can't imagine what you find beautiful, monsieur.'

'If a telegram comes from Paris, have it sent to your brothel.' He winked as he steadied himself. 'If you're working later I'll make sure I find you there.'

I indicated my book. 'I look forward to recording your performance.'

'Ha! Then buy new pens and a whole flagon of ink!'

'I will also record your arrogance, Gauguin, and that you only came to Arles so you could belittle Vincent, sneer at his work – and delude yourself that your daubs are better than his masterpieces!' I stood up, fists clenched. 'So, the sooner you get out, the better!'

After shooting me a wary look, as if he'd previously under-estimated me, he stumbled out into the night. The door swayed in the breeze. Nidabi caught my eye and we both laughed at the same time. She tilted her head as if to ask what this was all about. I mimed a hopeless inebriate drinking from a glass. She knows exactly what I mean.

The clock struck midnight when we heard the shouts. On market days fights aren't uncommon when drovers have had a skinful. Then came a distinct shout that was taken by a dozen different voices: 'Murder . . . Murder!' Clearly suspecting a disturbance, Nidabi snatched up the bag she always carries. Into it she slipped the book then sat there with an air of expectancy. It's strange. But all the time she kept her hand *inside* the bag. Now came running footsteps. Through the windows we could see people dashing in one direction. 'Murder!' Voices rose in a fury of shouting. At that moment the vision of the severed ear hurtled back to me with such force that I ran to the door and threw it open. The mob, racing pell-mell, exerted its own gravity. Before I knew it, I was drawn into the mass and hurrying with them. Beside me was Nidabi. She couldn't have understood the shouts, yet some-thing of the crowd's shock and excitement communicated at a level that was pure animal. In a lane not far from the amphitheatre a crowd jostled in the gateway of a stable yard. Boys climbed on to the walls to peer inside. They'd been laughing at the drama of it all; when they looked down inside, however, they recoiled. Some scrambled back, weeping. That sea of humanity produced a current, which carried everyone by the gateway as people behind shoved hard to view the crime's grim aftermath. Gendarmes had given up struggling to hold back the hordes. Instead, they stationed themselves so they could shine their lanterns into the yard. Now the crowd's shouts had been transformed into pitiful wailing as much as calls of excitement.

In the press of bodies I glanced to my left. Nidabi was there. She hung on to my arm with such a fierce grip I didn't know if I'd faint from the crush of Arlesians against me or her grip. At least, however, we weren't parted. Then with the abruptness of an explosion I found myself at the edge of the throng. A courtyard lay bathed in light. Here, the people close by were as quiet as stones. Nidabi hung on to my arm still. The moment she saw into the yard she whispered something with desperate urgency. What stretched out on the earth must have been human once. I can understand that. But at that moment all I saw were scattered shreds of raw meat. Then, as my eyes followed the bloody pieces of flesh that had been arranged in lines that radiated from the centre like rays of light from the sun, I saw slashed remnants of clothes on which a figure lay. A figure? No . . . that describes the body of a man or woman. These were bones . . . all bones. A scarlet ribcage that dripped on to the cobbles. A red spine. A skull where once a face had been. A halo of pale gut around the head.

Nearby, a man hissed, 'Lord, it's a woman. Look at the hair.'

The pressure of the human tide behind us was relentless. We were carried away from the scene. Nidabi and I hung on to each other as we somehow made it back to the yellow house. While I was sick to my stomach, she raged in fury. I didn't understand any of the words. At last, it gave way to silent weeping. She sat in the chair with her hands crossed over her stomach as convulsions shook her. At one point she talked to me in a sob. There was such a sense of urgency; her voice was electric; I couldn't take my eyes from her face. I made out the name Pastor Hux repeated a dozen times. I understood that to mean she was either concerned for his safety or she needed him to consol her. I put my arms round her, but she pushed me away.

'Vincent,' she begged. 'Vincent!' Clearly, she needed him to translate her words.

I followed as she rushed upstairs. Almost immediately she burst back out of his room with a look of dread on her face. Fearing the worst, I pushed by to look inside. His bed was empty. By the time I had reached the kitchen again she was sat at the table. Dragging her book from her bag, some iron object came with it. When I saw what it was I started back. A pistol. Quite a small one, with a short barrel of bluish metal. Thrusting the gun back into the bag, she fumbled the book open to tear out a page. That done, she picked up a pencil and began to write at a furious pace, the point scratching at the paper like the claw of a beast. She filled the page with an explosive script. After folding it, she wrote a name, then underscored it twice.

'Ty!' She gripped my hand. 'Ty? Vincent!' She pressed the paper against my palm. A second later she snatched up her bag before running out of the door to vanish into the night. In the stillness after her departure, images of the slaughtered woman in the yard overlay the kitchen. The images were a product of my shocked mind, yet they seemed as real as the canvases on the wall. A mass of bones that oozed red gore. A scarlet, dripping ribcage. A ribbon of pale gut swam through the air as sinuous as a snake. The skull denuded of its human face glided toward me. And burning through all that came the words I'd read yesterday: *this should belong to you.* Would the latest murder victim turn out to resemble me? Surely it would. Because it's me, Ty, the killer wants. He yearns to stab that dagger into my heart. For a moment I was sure I'd faint dead away. The room spun, the skull loomed ever closer, empty eye sockets glistening. *Hold on to yourself, Ty.*

I forced myself to examine the folded paper Nidabi had given me. Written there, a single name: *Vincent.* I studied the note, but couldn't make head nor tail of its language. However, the furious rush of script screamed its importance to be read – and read now! For a while I froze, simply not knowing what to do, but knowing there were many things I *should* be doing. For one, I was supposed to be at work. Only that was impossible with events unfolding outside the door. The gypsy girl's ear? I should speak to the gendarmes about that, and the killer's message written on the paper. However, not only would officers be too busy to bother with me because of the murder, I could see that the gendarmerie just across the way had closed its doors as a precaution now that a mob had taken to the streets. If anything, all I craved was to collect Brionne from the Night Woman then hurry us both home where we could lock the door on the outside world.

Still in a quandary, I didn't hear him enter. The voice startled me. 'Ty?'

I spun round to see Vincent there. His face was ashen. 'Have you seen what the butcher did to her?'

'You shouldn't have gone there, Vincent.'

'I didn't intend to. It was like sleepwalking. I found myself in the stable yard. I thought I was in a nightmare. All that blood . . .'

'Here. Sit down. Drink this.' I poured brandy into a cup as he reached the chair before his legs failed him.

'Ty? What's gone wrong with the world?'

'Try not to think about what you saw.' Even as I spoke I trembled as images of crimson skulls raced through the walls.

He shuddered. 'You saw it, too, didn't you?'

'We didn't intend to. The crowd carried us along.'

'We?'

'Nidabi was with me.'

'Where is she now?'

'I don't know. A few moments ago she ran from the house.'

'Nidabi should be indoors. It's not safe. And it's not just the murderer, they have started to riot.'

'Vincent, she—'

'When they're in this state they can do anything. Everyone's losing their minds . . .'

I thrust the paper at him. 'Nidabi wrote this before she left. She asked me to give it to you.'

He tried to focus on the folded page. His eyes were red-rimmed and sore. One appeared strangely blank, as if tonight part of him had died inside. *How much more of this nervous pressure can he take?*

'Nidabi wrote it the moment she knew you weren't home. She tried to tell me something important, only she couldn't make me understand.'

His fingers trembled as he smoothed the page and began to read. The way his hand went to his mouth revealed it filled him with dread. 'I don't know how—' he began, then faltered. 'All this feels like a nightmare to me. Ty, I'm frightened I'm imagining this. The blood. The bones in the stable yard. After I fell today . . . those thoughts inside my head are bad enough . . . now this.'

'Does she say where she's gone?'

'Give me a moment. I'll try to give you the sense of it, but my God . . . it's hard to concentrate.' He reread the letter. 'Nidabi writes: *Vincent. I don't know what your reaction to this will be. On my life I swear it's all true. I know Pastor Hux is your friend. However, I must tell you that in London this year Pastor Hux cruelly murdered innocent women. I witnessed him slay one by the name of Cutler. He butchered more, including my friend Dolly West. I believe he struck again tonight. The cruel destruction of the body is identical to some of his London victims. In the name of humanity, sir, I beg you to report this to the police – have them arrest Pastor Hux before he murders again.*'

Now, so much is clear. I realize why the gypsy girl's ear had been left at my door. It was Pastor Hux who had written on the bloodstained paper: *this should belong to you.* If Hux gets his way, I will be the next to die.

22nd December. Arles is transfigured. The nature of the town is changed by the men and women that swarm through its maze of streets. Seemingly, the entire population have decanted from their beds. At two o'clock this morning Vincent and I hurried through the cold night air. People shouted. They hammered on doors to rouse neighbours. Men fired rifles into the air. Bullets glowed red as they flew upward into the night sky to become lost amongst the stars. Dogs joined the river of people. Yells, cries, the baying of hounds, it all grew so loud I had to press my hands over my ears. Even the smell of the place was different. Instead of the aromas of coal smoke there was the pungent sharpness of spent gunpowder. This was like the midst of war. I glanced at Vincent as we ran. His hair gleamed bright in the streetlight, while his eyes strained forward to find a safe path through. In one street a group of men had set upon a youth I knew to be a thug, but not a killer.

Vincent put himself between me and the vigilantes as we passed by. 'When the mob are in this mood anyone will do.' His eyes scoured faces as he moved. 'We'll go to the gendarmerie headquarters first. But if you see Nidabi tell me.'

Then he added grimly, 'Pastor Hux, too.' In his fist he gripped Nidabi's letter so tightly his knuckles had blanched white.

We'd barely gone a dozen paces when we came across Arlesians trying to batter their way into a bakery. Tellingly, a Spanish name was blazed across its hoarding.

'As I said, for a lynch mob anyone will do. Especially foreigners.' He took another step before shaking his head in frustration. 'It's no good this way. They're blocking the alley; we must go back.'

The urgency to report what we knew to the gendarmes made us run faster. Yet the streets were clogged with people. Shock at the killing turned to anger. Their blood was up now. They were determined to catch the assassin. Once they had their man they'd tear him apart with their bare hands. As we crossed a square the townsfolk constantly grabbed hold of our arms to stop us.

'Have you heard about the murder?' they'd ask. We'd reply that we had and that we were in a hurry, but they'd still hold on to us. 'It was a schoolteacher. She was only twenty-five years old.' And this: 'The monster cut away her stomach. He took it away with him.' Then another: 'See this rope? When we find him, we're going to hang the swine!' This blood-thirsty pack! A lust for violence raged in their hearts.

It became a never-ending struggle to disentangle our arms from clutching hands. At every street corner there were bands of men in a fever of excitement: each convinced they knew the identity of the killer.

'They're convinced they know the guilty man,' Vincent grimly pointed out, 'but everyone's giving a different name.'

Once again these man-hunters fired their muskets into the air. Shouts rose into cries, dogs howled. At the point of exhaustion we reached the central gendarmerie.

'Closed – how on earth can it be closed?' Vincent shook his head in bewilderment. 'Look, the doors are chained shut. But see? There are lights upstairs. Hey! Hey, gendarme! We need to speak to you!'

Instead of a reply from inside, an old woman shrilled, 'All the gendarmes are at the town hall. They've caught the murderer.' Her eyes burned with excitement. 'Hurry up, or they'll have him hanged before you get there.'

'Vincent,' I began, 'they know it's Pastor Hux.'

'The man must have been soaked with blood,' he said. 'It's possible they caught him as he tried to flee the town.'

Now we ran with the mob; we were truly part of it. Its wild fury energized us. Both of us moved faster than we'd done before. The expression on those faces? They blazed with a passion – a bloodlust – it reworked their features into something not human. It was as if we'd fallen into a city of demons. Normal laws didn't apply. *This is a place where the unimaginable is possible – even a certainty!* By now, word had got round. The mobs abandoned trying to break into the houses of men they suspected. Everyone converged on the town hall. Soon we reached the screaming horde. They shook their fists at the brightly lit windows. The mayor stood at one window where he bellowed down at the crowd. No one heard a word. In front of the main doors at least twenty Zouave soldiers in their blue and orange uniforms endeavoured to prevent the mob from breaking into the building.

A silver-haired woman howled, 'They've got the bastard. But they won't let us have him!'

Vincent called out to the woman against the baying of a thousand men, 'Do they have his name?'

She shook her head. 'His name? Does it matter? He's the killer.'

'An Englishman?'

'No! The devil's Italian!'

Her shouting the word 'Italian' ignited the crowd. It howled, 'Bring out the Italian! He's ours! Bring him out, or we'll burn the place down!' When the mayor tried to placate the mob they pelted him with dirt for his troubles.

Vincent's face crumpled with dismay. 'Ty, they have got the wrong man. It's like last time. When they lynched the Italian sailors.' He waved his arms to try to attract the crowd's attention. 'Listen to me! The Italian didn't kill the woman. Let me through. Please, let me through. I've got to tell the mayor!' Vincent tried to push into this swarm of humanity. 'Let me through. I know who the killer is.'

'We all do, mate,' a youth shouted back. 'But they won't let us have him.'

'It's not the Italian!'

They recognized Vincent now. 'Oh, it's the mad Dutchman.'

'He says he knows who killed the schoolteacher.'

'Him? He'll be telling us the goblins under his bed killed her.'

Some laughed. Most, however, turned nasty.

'Go home, you lunatic!'

'Take care, or you'll wind up on the rope, too!'

Vincent persisted. 'Let me through. I need to speak to the mayor!'

The pack turned on Vincent. They cursed him as they pushed him back.

'And take the little whore with you.' A woman grabbed me by the hair.

Many shouted encouragement. 'Give her a good hiding, Marie. Go on, beat her dirty little brains out.'

Vincent dragged me free of the howling women. Moments later we ran across the square, away from the town hall.

I panted, 'We need to tell the gendarmes that Pastor Hux is the killer.'

'The mob will tear us apart if we try again.'

'What now?'

'Wait. It's all we can do. When the mob are calm I'll take Nidabi's letter to the gendarmes.' He reached the yellow house. 'As soon as they read it they'll arrest Pastor Hux.'

'Pray that they will.' Yet I couldn't help myself adding, 'If he hasn't fled by then.'

Ty's Book

Undated. Didn't we know it was inevitable? Could there have been another outcome? Now. Don't delay this another moment – it happened! You can't turn back the clock and replay it all in a different way. At last there's ample time to write down everything that happened on that dark, terrible day.

On the night of the schoolteacher's death we couldn't reach the gendarmes to show them the letter Nidabi had written. We could only wait. Perhaps by morning the mob would have cooled enough to go home. Gunshots, however, continued throughout the night. Clatters of feet running by the house. For a long time I couldn't even think of sleep, so I wrote in my book to take my mind off the madness, especially the image of the mutilated woman lying at the centre of the spoke-like pattern of bloody flesh. Vincent van Gogh sat in the chair by the fire. My lasting impression is of him staring at the wall with red-rimmed eyes. He brooded on this killing just like the slaying of the gypsy girl. Just when I didn't think I'd sleep at all I found myself waking on the sofa to an urgent knocking at the door. It was morning. Even before I was fully awake Vincent had opened the door to admit the postman, Monsieur Roulin. He bustled in, breathless, the skin above his beard flushed bright red. 'A damned thing,' he was saying. 'It's a damned thing.' *The killing of the teacher? Everyone's obsessed by the crime.* But Monsieur Roulin held up a letter as he repeated, 'A damned thing, Vincent. I've left my round to bring it straight away.'

'What's wrong, Joseph?'

'The world's gone wrong, that's the truth, my friend. Poor Madame Tournier, the schoolteacher, last night. Then this!' He shook the envelope. 'I pray it's not a practical joke, but I thought you should see it at once.'

Monsieur Roulin handed the letter to Vincent, who took it to the table to read. 'The envelope's edged in black. It's news of a death.' He paused, a frown deepening the lines in his forehead. 'I know this handwriting. It belongs to Pastor Hux.'

'I saw the black border,' Roulin said. 'I knew you should have it at once.'

'It hasn't been franked.'

'No, it never reached the sorting office. One of the postmen had collected it from the box at the station. He saw it was addressed to you, and with it being a notice of bereavement he thought I should bring it to you as soon as possible.' He nodded at the envelope. 'See the brown fingerprint mark on the envelope? Blood! That's why I suspect it might be one of the idiots playing tricks again.'

Vincent grimaced. 'I know the man who wrote this.'

'Then I'm sorry that you have bad news. I'll leave you in peace.'

As soon as Roulin had gone Vincent read the letter. Then he turned to me. 'Sit here, Ty. Hold my hand.'

'What's the matter?'

'This letter is as much for you as it is for me. Here. Sit down. Grip my hand as tightly as you can. I won't pull away, keep holding tight.'

'Is it from Pastor Hux?'

Vincent nodded as I sat down beside him, then he spoke in a gentle voice, 'It's dated today, the twenty-second. He must have posted it within the last few hours. This is bad news, Ty. We must keep our nerve.' He began to read. '*My dear Vincent. I write to confess this to you: I have failed in my life's work. It's as brutal a truth as I can express. For the past ten years I've struggled to rescue women who are so poor that they are forced into the worst degradation imaginable. They accepted my hospitality; often they stole my possessions, but that didn't matter to me. No, this was the final blow: I believed I'd helped them find respectable work but I eventually learned that they were lying to me. They had returned to their life of moral depravity. So be it. I've failed. I must accept God's will. This summer, however, I suffered an illness of the spirit. I did terrible things to the women I strived to help. When I am lucid I am appalled by my crimes. Yet I find there is no way of stopping myself. Until now, that is. I further confess that I killed a gypsy girl in the mistaken belief it was your friend, Ty. Last night I killed again; yet it's the nature of this sickness that I don't yet recall who I destroyed, or how, or where. It was only when my senses returned that I found my hands soaked with blood. The heart I took I have preserved in honey. I don't know why. My mind is lost to fog and darkness.*'

Then Vincent read out the lines that shattered my senses. When I opened my eyes I realized he'd gripped me by the shoulders so I wouldn't fall. He asked, 'Did you hear that part of the letter?'

'Would you read it to me again?'

He did so: '*What I am about to do now, my old friend, seems so right. Good fortune has reunited me with Nidabi, the only woman I can trust in this world. With me here is the little girl, Brionne. Once she was destined for the brothel like Ty, her sister. I have saved this child. It's just three days until*

Christmas. When that sacred day at last dawns we will have left this earthly vale of tears for paradise; our suffering done. The three of us will be at peace. Yours, in fond memory, Pastor Hux.'

What then? A dazed flurry of memories. Running beside Vincent through the streets of Arles. More than once, I asked: 'He's going to kill her, isn't he? He's going to murder my sister!' Blood-red images of mutilated women seared my mind. Time and again I stumbled, and Vincent helped me to rise. The gendarmerie. Again, locked. To the town hall. Shutters torn from houses burned in heaps. Dogs barked. A hundred riflemen guarded the building to hold back the screaming mob. Violence boiled the very air. Vincent struggled to reason with the soldiers. They shook their heads before ordering us away. I told myself: I can't imagine there will be any more tomorrows. The sun's burning out. This is the end of time. As we returned to the house it seemed as if the ghost of my brother George became my shadow. How soon until Brionne joined him?

Much later, Nidabi's journal came into my possession. It took several months before I could translate it, and so read the events that befell her and my sister on that fateful day.

Nidabi's Journal

22nd December. It's three o'clock in the afternoon. My journey started from London seven days ago. Now this farmhouse is my final destination. Just a few hours ago I left Ty in the home of Vincent van Gogh to search the streets of Arles. The stars were brilliant in the night sky. Frost left its glittering touch upon the pavement. I sped through the passageway to the river, to the amphitheatre, through a maze of alleys, then back along the Aliscamps, where Romans lie in their necropolis. Pastor Hux had killed the woman we

had seen lying eviscerated on the ground. I was certain of
that. Certain enough to leave a note with Ty for Van Gogh.
I told him about the murders in London. That Hux is the
culprit and must be arrested. Now, I'll never know if Vincent
read it. As I ran along the avenue of tombs I hunted Pastor
Hux, the pistol in my bag. When I found him I knew what
I must do. Yet, as happens so often in life, fate will twist
your expectations. Yes, I searched for Hux. I didn't find him.
No, as I entered a quiet street I heard that voice.

'Nidabi.'

There, in the cold starlight, I could just discern a seated
man. A black top hat glinted as if a spectral fire burned across
its surface.

'Pastor?'

'Nidabi. Did I have any doubt that you'd come? Not the
slightest.'

I took a step closer. Pastor Hux sat in a two-wheeled carriage.
He held the reins of a black mare, its eyes ringed with silver
hairs, an unearthly impression of a phantom horse.

'Nidabi, do you remember when we rode together to feed
the poor?'

'Yes, sir.' At that moment I felt as if I'd shrunk inside of
myself somehow. I'd become a tiny figure before this gigantic
presence. It's strange but that tortured saint of a man, who'd
turned into a monster, appeared to draw darkness into him;
he fed on shadow, grew larger, more menacing; a distillation
of pure evil. *Stay firm. Remember what you must do.* Slowly,
so as not to draw attention to my actions, I moved the bag to
allow me to reach into it for the pistol.

'Why don't you come up here and sit beside me?' he asked.

'Thank you, sir.' *So much the better, Nidabi. You can put
the muzzle to his head before you pull the trigger.*

'Sir? You know I prefer Pastor to sir.'

'I'm sorry, Pastor.'

'Don't apologize, Nidabi. I heard from a vulgar painter by
the name of Gauguin that you'd arrived in Arles. We're
reunited. That's all that matters.'

I hesitated.

'You're still concerned about my illness, aren't you, Nidabi?'

'Oh, no, Pastor.'

'You've every reason to be. I must have frightened you back

at Lamplands. But I'm calm now. Come join me. I know now that God Himself intends us to ride together.'

I climbed up to sit beside him in the open carriage. Lit by starlight, his face appeared as if it were carved in blue marble. I couldn't make out a single human feature there, only a cold, fixed mass. Set deep in the bluish-white were twin shadows that no longer seemed like eyes, but pits of darkness.

'Nidabi.'

'Yes, Pastor?'

'You recall I saved you from the Colonel?'

'Of course, Pastor.'

'Are you grateful?'

'You must know I am.'

'Then will you trust me, and comply with what I'm going to ask of you?'

'I owe you my life. I will do anything you say.' I had no hesitation in promising anything he wished, because soon, when the opportunity presented itself, I'd reach into my bag for the pistol. Justice would be done. The nightmare ended.

Gently, he urged the horse forward. He took the road out of town toward undulating countryside that rose in pale mounds. Even better. I'd kill him some distance from the town. No one would hear the shot. My actions had the certainty of destiny now. With an extreme slowness so he wouldn't notice, I slipped my hand into the bag. I feigned calmness as he talked.

'Our futures are not set in stone, Nidabi.' He spoke with a hypnotic softness: the syllables pulsed to the same rhythm as the hoof beats. 'We should constantly adapt our lives to reflect changing circumstance. A while ago someone said that our dreams are a pictorial code sent to us by an inner self, which is wiser than we are. That inner self acts as our guardian angel. At the time, this notion struck me as a blasphemy. But since that illness struck me down I repeatedly dream that I am riding on a train through darkness. It leaves the track, yet still continues to run ever faster through a landscape riven with chasms. In the carriages are all the women I've ever helped. Some are dead. But they still continue to act as if they are alive. I know the train no longer has a destination. Nevertheless, its driver frantically tries to find a way through

the treacherous landscape. Because there is no track the wheels
rip into the earth. Sliding . . . sliding . . .'

Slowly, I began to draw out the weapon as I listened to the
flow of words.

'Isn't that a singular dream, Nidabi? If I apply the theory
that the dream was sent to me by that wise inner self of
mine, can I interpret it as a warning? Was it saying, "Listen,
Pastor Hux: This steam train is your life's work. See how it
has gone off the rails. Notice, sir, how the vehicle that holds
all your hopes and ambitions has lost its way. Witness how
it labours through a lethal landscape – pitfalls and chasms
await. Where it might plunge to oblivion at any moment."
Isn't that what the dream means, Nidabi? This lost, direc-
tionless engine, which holds me captive – is it a metaphor
for my failure?'

'I can't say, Pastor.' *It's dark. He'll not see the revolver. It
is time . . .*

'Nidabi. Remember my maxim?'

'Deeds, not words.'

'Precisely. I've longed to tell you this. Tonight, I saved a
young orphan girl.'

The words made me freeze.

He continued. 'Brionne, the young sister of a brothel whore.
Without doubt, if I hadn't rescued her she'd have been lost
to a living hell.'

'Pastor? Is Brionne in good health?'

'You know her?'

'I've met her sister, Ty.'

'Ty, that's her. Then you'll be aware that the woman is
riddled by moral depravity.'

I made sure I spoke calmly. 'Where is Brionne now?'

'I have her safe, thank God. In a secluded house miles from
that Sodom.'

'Oh.'

'Are you not pleased?'

'I give thanks, too, Pastor. This world should wake up to
what you've done for the poor.' Without him noticing I returned
the gun to the bag. I couldn't kill him now. What if the house
couldn't be found and Brionne starved?

'You don't know how much I'm gratified to hear that,
Nidabi. We'll go to the child straightaway.' He urged the horse

faster through the night-time countryside. 'And once we're there, I'll tell you what I have planned.'

When Pastor Hux unlocked the bedroom door Brionne was pleased to see me. The little girl rushed to throw her arms about my waist, talking quickly in the sing-song voice as she did so.

I looked at the Pastor. 'I don't understand. What's she saying?'

'She's asking for Ty.'

The little girl's beseeching eyes were identical to her sister's. '*Ty? Ty?*'

'Pastor, don't you consider it cruel to separate her from her sister?'

'It would be the height of cruelty to leave the child in the care of a whore.'

I sensed his anger, so I appeased him. 'Of course. I just wanted to avoid Brionne becoming anxious.'

'It'll soon be dawn. You rest here in the bedroom with the child until noon. Then I want both of you to put on the new clothes I've bought for you.'

'You bought us clothes?'

'Of course. Gauguin told me you were here, remember? I realized you might not have brought much in the way of dresses. I took the liberty of buying for you. Are you displeased?' Again a note of barely suppressed anger. Brionne sensed it, too. She stood with her arm tight around my waist and her head against my stomach.

'I'm delighted, Pastor. It's so thoughtful of you.'

He nodded. 'Later, when you've put on your new dresses, we will eat lunch. I have prepared something special to celebrate our being reunited.'

'That would be wonderful, thank you.' I realized what I must do. After I'd retired to the bedroom I'd wait a while then tiptoe back downstairs with the pistol. With luck, I'd find the Pastor asleep; he must have been awake all night.

'I'll take your bag for you, Nidabi.'

'My bag?'

'Yes, we must put away material possessions, so we can concentrate on less worldly matters.'

'But I have my things—'

'I'll keep them safe.' With that, he took the bag from me before I could even think of drawing the pistol.

I couldn't let it pass into his keeping so easily. 'My journal's in there, Pastor. It soothes my nerves if I write.'

'Of course.' Instead of returning the bag, he opened the clasp, then pulled out the book. *Praise be!* In the gloom at the top of the stairs he didn't notice the pistol in there. After handing me the journal, he spoke to Brionne who nodded. He added in profound tones, 'A sleep will do you both good.'

My only option was to enter the bedroom. Alas, my plan went even further awry. As soon as Brionne and I were inside he closed the door and turned the key in the lock. Seconds later, I heard the creak of the stair as Pastor Hux returned to the kitchen. Now there was nothing I could do but put Brionne to bed, then lie down myself.

Rain swept down on the farmhouse to beat the kitchen window. This is an ancient building with dark beams that appear only with supreme effort to hold aloft low ceilings that press down like the lid of a coffin. The gloom reinforced the notion that we had been consigned to a mausoleum. A fireplace yawned wide, a huge cavern of a structure built from rust-coloured stone. Every so often, raindrops would fall down the chimney to hiss on smouldering logs. Outside, a field of dark vines writhed beneath angry torrents of air, until the hillside resembled a monstrous, bristling creature. There were no other farms, just a slippery mud track that wound up from the road to end here at our door. *We're alone. It's as if we've been transported to an alien landscape beyond the reach of other mortals.* A shiver went down to the roots of my bones. Inside, picture the scene. The clock on the mantel chimed two o'clock in the afternoon. The Pastor sat at the head of the table. Brionne sat at one side, I at the other. At the Pastor's bidding we had bathed, then donned the clothes he'd bought. Brionne and I now wore long white cotton dresses that were belted with red velvet cord at the waist. The Pastor had attired himself formally in black; the only exception to this forbidding thrall of raven garments, a shirt of dazzling white. We ate the meal he'd prepared: a spiced casserole followed by almond cake. The cake wasn't to my taste, being even more heavily spiced than the meat dish.

However, he'd poured honey over the confection, which he bade us eat with a spoon. Brionne appeared not to care for dessert either, but the Pastor spoke in French to her, gently urging her to finish it. When we'd done he gave Brionne a doll and told her to play. The aftertaste of the cake, almost like tin, stayed unpleasantly on my tongue.

'Nidabi.' He sat with both hands resting together on the table. 'You know that the authorities in Arles will search for us?'

'This house is very secluded.'

'It'll only be a matter of time before they find the man who I rented it from, then they'll come here. Brionne will be returned to her sister. In ten years she'll be a whore.'

'Then we should move on.'

'That's what I intend.'

I rose. 'We should start as soon—'

'No! Please sit down, Nidabi. Listen to what I've got to say.'

His voice held a gentle, mesmerizing quality. 'I have found a solution to our problem. Only it doesn't lie with us for ever fleeing across Europe, expecting to wake with the police pounding on our door.' His grey lips tightened. 'Wouldn't it be a mercy to leave this world behind?'

'And so we will . . . when we're old.'

'Wouldn't it be preferable to go now? Brionne will be safe with us in paradise.'

Now! This is the moment to seize the child. We run from the house. We hide amongst vines. The madman would never find us there. My muscles tensed. I'd have to grab Brionne and flee. I wouldn't have time to find the pistol.

Pastor Hux continued in that hypnotic voice. 'For us, suicide would be glorious. Remember, Nidabi. Deeds, not words.'

'It would be wrong to hurt the child, Pastor.'

'There are plenty of ways to leave without suffering pain.' From his jacket he drew the army dagger – the same one he'd taken on our journeys to Limehouse. Its blade tapered to an evil point. 'Nidabi, I recall Vincent van Gogh writing to me some years ago. He told me about a woman by the name of Margot Begemann. She loved him so much that death was preferable to being parted from him. They were out walking in the fields when she said, "I wish I could die now." Then she fell to the ground.'

In advance of any words something deep inside cried a warning. My eyes locked on the dish that was streaked with honey. 'Pastor. You put something in the cake.'

'It will make us sleep,' he said. 'Soon we'll wake to a better world.'

The bitter taste on my tongue was stronger than ever. 'You've poisoned us.'

'Don't become agitated, please. Yield to it, Nidabi.'

'What have you used?'

'It acts quickly . . . without pain. Trust me.'

What now? Grab the dagger? But he keeps it close to him. And I know what carnage he can wreak with it.

'Pastor. You should have taken me into your confidence.'

'You're a good woman, Nidabi. Only it takes courage to swallow poison. If you'd known your nerve might have failed you.'

'Pastor, how long?'

'We fall asleep within the hour.'

We sat there for whole minutes. I didn't know whether it was the blazing fire, or the effects of the poison, but my skin grew hot all over. From time to time the Pastor would speak soothingly to Brionne or myself. I sensed he experienced a quiet elation. His plan had worked. *We die together.* The breeze blew hard against the house. The up-draught in the chimney turned into a beast-like roar that carried with it a rush of sparks. At that moment Brionne put the doll aside and groaned. Then, suddenly, in a sobbing voice she called out. I recognized the pleading note, even though I couldn't understand the words. Pushing back the chair, I ran to Brionne who now grimaced as the agony tore through her.

'Oh, dear God,' Hux breathed, 'it wasn't supposed to hurt.'

'Pastor, she's in agony. Do something!'

The madman gripped the dagger. For a moment I saw him falling on us to hack at our bodies until we were dead. Although I'd got hold of Brionne to stop her thrashing about on the stone floor, I looked round for a weapon. But there weren't even any fire irons by the grate. Instead of approaching us, he stepped back to the wall. *He's going to stand guard. He'll stay there until we die.*

'Pastor, she's in agony! Let me help her.'

'Whatever you do, don't let her retch. It's got to stay in her stomach. We're leaving this ugly, disgusting world behind. If it hurts – so be it.'

Brionne called out the name, 'Ty,' as she squirmed in agony.

'Pastor, you must let me find something for the pain. Can't you see how the child suffers?'

Stone-faced, he shook his head.

I clenched my fists. 'Pastor, you must!'

'No.'

'I demand that you allow me to help her. Or do you want to hear the child's agony? Do you want to see her convulsing on the floor?' I surged on, blood roaring through my veins. 'Listen to me! Can you bear to look into Brionne's eyes as the poison takes hold? Look at her, then tell me you don't care.'

'I . . . uh . . .' He pressed his lips together. *He's weakening.*

'Pastor, you are like Icarus who flew too near the sun. You tried so hard to help the poor your mind has become ill. But I know there is a good man inside of you still. So, I'm appealing to that kind, gentle soul that saved lives. I am addressing the man who rescued poor wretches like me. Remember how proud you were when I told you that I took such pleasure in studying the stars? Pastor, there are mountains on the moon. One day people will walk on them – and on that future day perhaps human beings will have listened to their hearts, just as you did, and they will have ended poverty and famine. They will share your compassion. I appeal to you to be strong, to conquer the evil in your heart. I demand that the gentle man who I knew, and loved, permit me to ease this child's suffering. *Now.*'

Conflicting forces within the Pastor waged war on one another. He shuddered as good vied with evil. Then, at last, 'That door in the corner is the larder. Look in there . . . but don't try and leave the house.'

'I promise.' The moment I stood a pain tore through my stomach. I gasped, 'If I can give her wine . . . to dull the pain . . . ease her passing . . .' Behind the larder door was a stone counter full of jars and bottles of wine. Tucked amongst those, a flask labelled laudanum. Brionne's scream rose to a piercing shriek.

'Nidabi! Hurry up, for pity's sake.' His voice revealed distress rather than anger.

I glanced back over my shoulder. At that moment two souls vied for control of Hux. Briefly, the stone-like expression would melt, then I'd see the man as I'd first known him all those months ago, when he was a warm, humane individual, who loved to hear me talk with such naïve delight about the moon. However, another personality was hell-bent on brutally crushing the gentle soul. A second later, the face of unfeeling stone asserted itself. His grip tightened on the dagger. This, the lunatic creature that butchered defenceless women. A monster that gloried in terror and blood.

With my back to him, and blocking the entrance to the larder, he couldn't see what I did next. After placing a pint tankard on the shelf in front of me, I filled it halfway with laudanum, then added water from a jug.

When I turned with the tankard he snapped, 'What have you got there?'

'It's a mixture of water and wine, Pastor.'

Brionne muttered, 'Ty, Ty, Ty,' as she lay there in her white dress, a paralysis creeping over her.

Pastor Hux barked, 'What are you waiting for?'

Before I could reply the door swung open with a crash. Storm winds carried in a swirl of leaves. Pans hanging from a rack clattered as the cold air struck them. The Pastor stared at the open door, then his eyes followed something I could not see.

'What is it?' I asked, but he remained fixed as if he beheld something that shocked him to the core. 'Ah, now I understand,' I told him. 'You're frightened, aren't you? Something has entered the house – and it terrifies you.' The tempest swirled leaves around the floor in a wild vortex. 'You see the ghosts of those you killed. Edith Soller, Dolly West, all of them. Worst of all is Mitre Rose. Is she following you, Pastor? Does she carry the coffin on her back? Is it your terror of being haunted by these women that has driven you to suicide?'

After slamming the door shut he screamed, 'Make her drink it!'

The Pastor used the dagger to point at the girl. Pains burned in my stomach. Gales surged around the house with menacing intent. They drew from the eaves a wild fluting sound, the notes were discordant, yet there was an urgency in their rhythm that made me walk swiftly. I knelt beside the girl, and cradling her head in my lap, poured the liquid into her mouth. Though she coughed much of it back, I persisted – even fiercely holding her jaw open so I could tip the laudanum down her throat. The Pastor clamped a hand against his stomach. I offered him the tankard.

He screamed back, 'Why do I need that? Why should I fear pain? This is the price of my journey! From this world to paradise!' He leaned back against the wall as his legs weakened. 'If you need it, then drink! I'll not touch a drop.' He clenched his jaw. 'Dear God in heaven . . . I'd die now.' He gasped for breath. 'But I'll wait until you've gone first. Then I'll follow! Understood?'

I nodded.

'If you want it . . . blasted well drink.'

I didn't need telling again. I drank half the tankard's contents. The mixture of laudanum and water dampened the tremors in my muscles. The poison still burned in my stomach. However, the opiate in the laudanum made all the pain dissolve into a golden mist. I poured more of the liquid into Brionne's mouth, then held her face upward so she was forced to swallow it. Soon, she, too, became still.

Now. Here, in that golden mist. All is calm . . . all is calm. The once tortured notes, the dissonance, the madcap melody of the storm has, to my drugged mind, become a gentle lullaby. A song to soothe the nerve. I've shared the tankard with Ty's little sister. There is no pain. We're limp as dolls. No pain. Four o'clock chimes come singing from the timepiece on the mantel; the fire burns bright in its cavern. The phantom on the roof still plays his flute. A lilting game of melody versus discord. It is hard to guide the pencil now. I daresay this hand of mine will be hard to decipher. But I force myself to write. There is a reason. It keeps me awake. Senses held in focus. It stops the sleep that so desperately, so hungrily, demands to steal my mind away.

Pastor Hux leans back against the wall. His eyes are still on me. He grips the dagger – the silver, shining dagger that cut those women to pieces. Does he see the ghost of Mitre Rose prowl with the coffin on her back?

It's a battle of endurance now. A fight to the death. Pastor Hux versus Nidabi. *Who will fall asleep first?*

Ty's Book

An account of 22nd December. When I announced I couldn't wait in the house a moment longer Vincent agreed. 'If we can't talk to the gendarmes,' he told me, 'we'll have to search for Hux ourselves.'

A cold rain began to fall as we hurried to the train station.

I protested. 'In the letter Hux said he plans to kill Brionne and Nidabi. Why would he catch a train?'

'He might be lying.' Vincent helped me through crowds that still bayed for blood. 'And he still might have to travel to where he plans to . . .' He finished the sentence with a shrug. 'We know he's left his lodgings.'

At the station it was unusually quiet. One of the railway porters sat under a canopy as he brooded at the rain.

'Monsieur,' Vincent panted, 'have you seen a foreigner dressed in black? He would have been with a woman – and a little girl, so high.' He held out his hand to indicate Brionne's height.

The porter shrugged.

Vincent pressed on. 'We think he might have caught a train out of Arles.'

'No, he didn't.'

'You've seen him?'

'Haven't you *seen* the riots? Oh, you're the foreign artist, aren't you? Monsieur Van Gogh.' That explained everything to the porter, who now only paid attention to lighting tobacco in his pipe. I darted forward to kick the side of his foot. 'Hey?'

'Listen to me,' I snarled. 'Did you see a stranger all in black today?'

He gave a sullen shrug. 'The stationmaster cancelled the trains on account of the riots. There's no point anyone being here – least of all me.'

We left the station. 'How can we search every house in Arles?' I begged.

'I don't believe he's in the town.'

'The trains aren't running.'

'Nor do I believe he'd have left on foot if Brionne was with him. A five year old couldn't walk far enough for Hux's liking.'

'We can ask at the carriage stations.'

'But an Englishman with a French child that might be calling out to the driver that she's being kidnapped?' His eyes were crimson from lack of sleep. I didn't know how much longer his nerves would hold out. 'No, no! He must have driven a carriage.'

'But he didn't own one.'

'So he'll have bought a carriage in the last twenty-four hours. Where would you buy one in Arles?'

That morning we ran from stable to stable to enquire. I still see all those shaking heads. 'An Englishman? No, not here.' Noon came and went. We were exhausted. Vincent's face became a near death mask behind his red beard. More than once his legs failed him, and he stumbled. Each time I helped him to his feet. Meanwhile, angry townsfolk still rushed through the streets. They shouted that they'd hang the mayor as well as the Italian barricaded in the town hall. Whenever there was a crime, Arlesians always suspected foreigners first. If only we could have calmed the mob and made them understand. Men fired muskets into the air. I led Vincent to a dilapidated stable where an old man sat cleaning a bridle.

'Monsieur,' Vincent began, 'we're desperate for information.'

'Desperate?' The old man sang a typical Arlesian *aye-aye* of recognition. 'You're the artist.' This usually meant a cold shoulder, however: 'Good afternoon, monsieur. My friend, Roulin, enjoys your painting.'

'Did an Englishman call here asking to buy a carriage?'

'Indeed so, I sold him one yesterday. A little two-wheeled cart. But I didn't have a horse he could afford.'

'What did he do?'

'He came back an hour later with an old nag that won't last a week.'

'Did the Englishman tell you where he was going in the cart?'

'Frankly, monsieur, he spoke barely a dozen words to me.

It's possible he talked more to the field monger. The old crook sold him the nag.'

'The field monger?' Vincent frowned.

'I know him.' I raced down the street. 'His yard is in the next square!'

When we arrived the field monger had begun to unload his cart. It was piled high with dead pigs and sheep that he'd collected from the farms that morning. He'd boil them in vats that already spewed their stink into the winter air.

'Monsieur?' Vincent panted.

'Go to hell, the pair of you.' The thickset man pulled a piglet from the heap.

'You sold a horse to an Englishman.'

'What if I did? It's none of your business.' The field monger fixed me with a look. He was recalling the day he made use of me in the field.

Vincent pleaded, 'We're desperate to know where the Englishman is. He's with a woman and a little girl, she's—'

'Get out of my yard.'

'Monsieur, please.'

'I'll put the dog on you.'

Vincent moved closer to the burly man, who stood with the mouldering carcass on his shoulder as if he hadn't a care in the world. Vincent's eyes blazed. 'You sold the Englishman a horse. Do you know where he went?'

'Clear off. Take the whore with you.'

Vincent drew a cut-throat razor from his pocket. Now his hands were sure, there wasn't a sign of a tremor as he opened the blade.

'If you want a shave do it in your own house.' The field monger laughed. 'Get out, before I lose my temper.'

With surprising ferocity Vincent pushed the man back against the cart. The carcass fell from his shoulder as the artist lifted the razor level with the man's eyes.

'Go away, Dutchman. You daren't use that thing on me.'

'Monsieur. You know I am Vincent van Gogh. The question I ask now is this: if you believe I am mad, why don't you believe I'll cut out your eye?'

This time the brute sagged back against the cart, his strength draining from his limbs. He couldn't take his eyes off the blade. Raindrops beaded on its keen edge.

'Monsieur, do you believe I'll cut you with this?'

Now, with a look of fear, the field monger nodded sharply.

'If I'm mad, then a madman is capable of anything. Isn't that so?'

'Monsieur, don't do anything you'll regret.'

'I'm crazy, remember. How can I regret anything?'

'The Englishman . . . he bought the horse from me. He also asked directions to a farmhouse. Please, Monsieur Van Gogh, take the razor away.'

'Which farmhouse?'

'It's known as the Old Vinery . . . out on the road to Saint Marie.' The man never took his eyes from the blade. 'A near ruin. It stands right at the end of a track.'

'I know the place,' I cried, 'but it's miles away!'

With a sudden burst of strength Vincent seized the man by his shirt front and hurled him across the yard. 'Monsieur, we need your cart. Ty, get up on to the seat.'

Shaking with terror, the felled bully cowered on the wet ground. Vincent leapt up on to the bench beside me to grab the reins. In seconds he urged the horse into a gallop through the streets. I hung on tight as the cart jolted between the houses. People stared at us as we raced by – the dark-skinned girl from the brothel and the flame-haired artist! Their expressions were of amazement.

Vincent turned to me. 'We can go faster,' he called over the pounding hooves, 'if you push out the animals.'

As the cart bucked wildly, I scrambled into the back. Fired by the same passion that drove Vincent, I rolled corpses of sheep and pigs out of the cart where they bounced down on to the road that would take us to the madman's house. The last, a huge old boar, fell with a terrific thump. As it rolled into the gutter I noticed we were leaving Arles behind.

It was past four o'clock on that December afternoon. A cold, cold rain fell. Black cloud oppressed the land with a power that was nothing less than menacing. Already darkness closed in. A deep gloom engulfed the fields where the storm made the vines writhe like serpents. *This is the night for terrors*. For the first time in hours I had chance to picture Brionne's face. I tried hard not to imagine what terrible things Hux might have done. Even so, her fear was cruelly easy to picture. *God help her, she's only five years old.*

Death. In a *dead* world, in the *dead* house on its grim mound. That was the impression that overwhelmed me the moment Vincent forced the farmhouse door. He had to catch me as I reeled backward; a dark mist seemed to rush through my head. But he wouldn't let me fall on to that rain-sodden yard. Instead, I found my senses return as he, despite his own state of near collapse, helped me into the kitchen. Only I wished at that moment my senses had never come back. For this is what I saw.

Three people. A fire roared in its grate. The storm drew jarring notes from the chimney – a symphony for the damned. *Three people.* They weren't moving. My muscles seized. All I could do was turn from one dead face to another. Nidabi sat to the table with her head on her arm, which in turn rested on the open journal. Pastor Hux sat against the kitchen wall with his legs straight out in front of him. Face grey. Eyes closed. And Brionne?

Clad in a white dress, Brionne lay in front of the fire. Her dark hair had been brushed so carefully it shone in the firelight. *Three people.* All still. All with their eyes closed.

At last I spoke as if in a dream. 'There isn't a mark on them.'

Vincent darted to the table. He picked up glasses, smelled those, and did the same with a plate smeared in a dark sauce. He discarded it with a shake of his head, then picked up a bowl that bore cake crumbs. The moment he sniffed it he flinched.

'He's fed them poison.'

Once more a dark mist flooded my senses. The kitchen seemed to whirl away from me until I stood in a lightless void. Shapes moved around me, dream-like, tenuous, yet suggestive of dead loved ones – my mother, my father, poor George . . . Then reality slammed back. Table. Pans. Fire burning in the grate. *Three people* – Nidabi, Brionne, the monster called Hux. All poisoned. When I lifted my head the first thing I saw was the kitchen window. For a second I believed my brother's dead face looked in at me. His eyes bulged – shocking white mounds that rose from their sockets. His mouth yawned open. He was struggling to draw breath. Then a faint cough. I flinched, expecting to see George coughing from the diphtheria that claimed him.

'Ty!' Vincent shouted. 'Ty! Come here!' He pulled Nidabi back so she sat upright on the chair. Nidabi coughed again.

I stared, not believing what I saw was any more real than George's ghost at the window. 'She's still alive?'

'Just pray we're not too late.' Then he spoke to the woman. *'Nidabi. Nidabi!'* He asked her a question in her tongue. The muttered reply I couldn't understand. Quickly, he said to me, 'She's doesn't know which poison . . . but she managed to get Brionne to drink laudanum after they'd eaten. Nidabi's had some, too.'

'Laudanum?'

'Laudanum's an antidote to certain poisons.'

'She's going to be all right?'

'I don't know. We've got to make them sick it up. Check Brionne.'

I flew to my sister. As I lifted her she stirred. Her eyes opened. They were so dead looking . . .

Vincent called, 'Make her vomit. You know how?'

'Yes.'

'When she's vomited have her drink water, then make her bring that up.'

We did what we had to do. Within ten minutes Brionne was fully conscious. Nidabi sat on the chair with her head in her hands as convulsions wracked her body. Even so, Vincent had managed to speak to her. He called across to me.

'After Hux gave them poison Brionne began to suffer stomach pains. Nidabi said she only intended to give her alcohol to kill the pain, but she found laudanum. She knew that's an antidote to strychnine. That's the poison Hux would be most likely to use. I expect—'

I'd been busy with Brionne and had stopped looking at Vincent as he talked. When he fell silent all of a sudden I glanced across the kitchen. Hux stood behind the artist. The madman's face was a dreadful blue. Blood trickled from the corner of his mouth. Some vestige of life remained, however. He had his hands about Vincent's throat, strangling him from behind. Vincent's knees sagged as he struggled in vain to pry the hands from around his neck.

With a yell I dashed to drag Hux away, but he only shrugged me off. He was more dead than alive now. Yet that dark passion would drive him on until he'd finished what he'd started in this farmhouse. On that hateful face, an expression of pride; a righteous aura of the crusader reaching his Jerusalem. Now he'd take two more souls. The first thing I saw when I searched for a weapon was a dagger; it lay on the floor by the wall. The movement seemed all one. I seized the dagger then rammed it with all my strength into the back of the maniac's neck. The effect was electric. Releasing Vincent, he jerked both hands up. Then, as if they crawled like a pair of giant white spiders, they crept around the back of his neck to find the jutting handle. *He'll pull it out. Once he does, he will use it on us.*

'Ty . . .' From the shadows stepped Nidabi. She swayed as if she'd lose her balance at any moment. Taking a deep breath, she gestured to me to stay back. Then this slender woman put herself between us and the murderer. He said something in his own tongue, and gestured to her to help him. All the time blood streamed along the blade that was embedded in his neck. It fell in huge, red splotches on the floor.

Nidabi stared right back into his eye; her force of will held him. Then she pushed him in his chest. Another thrust; he staggered backwards. He tried to stop her next push, only he was weak from the poison and loss of blood. Another hard shove made him grunt. Again it forced him back. Another push. Another step. Now he stood with the kitchen fire blazing behind him. He'd become the silhouette of a ruined statue, a corroded Satan. Nidabi approached him again. These shoves weren't random. I knew what she was going to do. This time Nidabi yelled as she surged forward with both arms straight out in front of her.

Such was the force of that final thrust that an '*Uph!*' escaped the Pastor's lips. For a moment he fought to regain his balance. He even turned his head to look back at the inferno that awaited him. On seeing the destination, he screamed with all his might. Then he reached the point of no return. Pastor Hux toppled backward. His head, together with the top half of his body, slammed down into the huge cave of a fireplace. Flames burst outward. Sparks, embers, burning logs cascaded from the hearth to tumble across the floor. Pastor Hux rolled from side to side, shouting. Thankfully, I couldn't see his face, the flames were too bright – much too bright. Nidabi stumbled toward the blazing jaws of the fireplace. I grabbed her, held her tight.

Vincent had recovered enough to call, 'I'll bring Brionne. You get Nidabi out of the house!'

Burning logs rolled against wooden furniture so dry and wearing so many coats of varnish that it exploded into flame. All I could see of the Pastor were his kicking legs as we ran from the searing heat of the farmhouse into cooling rain.

The man's howls of agony could be plainly heard as Vincent drove the cart down into the night-time valley. I sat on the boards in the back with my arm round Brionne. Nidabi sat alongside me. We didn't utter so much as a word as we watched the flames of the burning farmhouse grow and grow in the darkness, until it seemed as if the summer sun in all its searing brilliance blossomed from the winter soil. A whirlwind roared through the vineyard. Its soaring notes merged with the screams of the man, took possession of them. And then, as if the violent flow of air tore the soul from his mortal body, the sound rose with an unearthly cry over the hillside to take leave of this earth for some other realm. With that last surge of the tempest our world fell silent. The storm and the man's cries had gone.

Postscript

{Asylum, Saint-Remy de Provence, 1889}

Patient Name: Vincent van Gogh
Age: 36
Profession: Artist
Next of Kin: Theo van Gogh, brother.
Nature of Illness: profound psychological disturbance rooted in epilepsy with episodes of hallucinatory psychosis.
Treatment: hydropathic baths; iodide of potassium; laudanum.
General observations: passionately committed to painting, Van Gogh was resident in Arles where he suffered a mental crisis on the 24th December, 1888. During this seizure he cut away the lower portion of his ear with a razor. He delivered the severed flesh to a woman with an entreaty to keep it safe. There followed mental seizures, which led to hospitalization. The patient is reluctant to discuss his self-mutilation. Nevertheless, he admits to frightening hallucinations. During these seizures he imagines that he is being poisoned and, moreover, that he sees poisoners and victims of poison everywhere. In the main, he is outwardly serene, courteous, and continues to produce paintings of a uniquely vivid nature.

Brionne's Diary, 1910

It is twenty years since Vincent van Gogh chose to end his own suffering. Today, my sister and I walked through the warmth of an Arles spring to the yellow house. The last time I saw it I was five years old. The artist's former dwelling is much smaller than I recall. It stands on a street corner near our hotel and has recently been converted into a shop that sells tobacco. Ty rested her hand on its yellow wall. She may have murmured some words, but I stayed back so she could find peace there. I was moved by the way she gazed up at the windows as if expecting to see a familiar face appear. A moment later I saw a figure standing some way along the street. The woman was tall and beautiful, and she was just as I remembered from all those years ago.

'Nidabi received your letter, after all,' I said, then I noticed my sister's expression. 'What's wrong?'

'I'm nervous about meeting Nidabi again. It's been twenty years.'

'She's going to be as anxious as you are. Don't worry.'

Ty took a step forward. 'Brionne? Aren't you coming with me?'

'Not yet. I'm going to leave you alone together to become reacquainted.'

I crossed the street to the shade of the trees. From there, I watched the two women walk to meet one another. Within moments they strolled along the boulevard arm-in-arm in the warm sunlight. I can see them in my mind's eye now. Both are oblivious to the bustle of the street. They're re-visiting a time when to glance in through the doorway of the yellow house would reveal a red-haired man, applying paint to canvas with such passionate intensity. Since then much has changed. Ty owns one of the most successful perfumeries in La Rochelle. My sister's hard work ensured

I received a first-rate education, allowing me to qualify as a schoolteacher. Nidabi never did return to England; instead, she works as a translator in Paris. The portrait of the murderer is still in her possession – *The Midnight Man*. For her to guard it brings her a degree of satisfaction and inner peace. Justice has been done.

Even though the world at large doesn't know *The Midnight Man* they do know the name of its artist. Ignored by the art galleries in life, his work now enchants critics and the public alike. Vincent van Gogh's paintings are not only a shining triumph, they are also his immortal flame.